Elle James, a *New York Times* bestselling author, started writing when her sister challenged her to write a romance novel. She has managed a full-time job and raised three wonderful children, and she and her husband even tried ranching exotic birds (ostriches, emus and rheas). Ask her, and she'll tell you what it's like to go toe-to-toe with an angry three-hundred-and-fifty-pound bird! Elle loves to hear from fans at ellejames@earthlink.net or www.ellejames.com.

USA TODAY bestselling author **Barb Han** lives in north Texas with her very own hero-worthy husband, three beautiful children, a spunky golden retriever/ standard poodle mix and too many books in her to-read pile. In her downtime, she plays video games and spends much of her time on or around a basketball court. She loves interacting with readers and is grateful for their support. You can reach her at www.barbhan.com.

Also by Elle James

One Intrepid SEAL
Two Dauntless Hearts
Hot Combat
Hot Target
Hot Zone
Hot Velocity
Navy SEAL Survival
Navy SEAL Captive
Navy SEAL to Die For
Navy SEAL Six Pack

Also by Barb Han

Sudden Setup
Endangered Heiress
Texas Grit
Stockyard Snatching
Delivering Justice
One Tough Texan
Texas-Sized Trouble
Texas Witness
Texas Showdown

Discover more at millsandboon.co.uk

TWO DAUNTLESS HEARTS

ELLE JAMES

TEXAS GRIT

BARB HAN

MILLS & BOON

First Published in Great Britain 2018
by Mills & Boon, an imprint of HarperCollins*Publishers*
1 London Bridge Street, London, SE1 9GF

Two Dauntless Hearts © 2018 Mary Jernigan
Texas Grit © 2018 Barb Han

ISBN: 978-0-263-26578-1

39-0618

MIX
Paper from
responsible sources
FSC™ C007454

This book is produced from independently certified FSC™
paper to ensure responsible forest management.

For more information visit: www.harpercollins.co.uk/green

Printed and bound in Spain
by CPI, Barcelona

TWO DAUNTLESS HEARTS

ELLE JAMES

This book is dedicated to all the wild animals in Africa that make it such an interesting and beautiful place to visit. Also, to the people who strive to keep those animals safe from poachers. They deserve a chance to live and roam free of harm.

Chapter One

"Nope. I'm not going." One look at the plane they'd already flown in twice and he was out. Done. Finished. He put himself in harm's way too often to risk it on vacation.

Percy "Pitbull" Taylor spun on his heels. He started back toward the van and the driver who'd brought six members of his SEAL team to the small landing strip outside of Camp Lemonnier on the Horn of Africa. "Twice was enough. I thought you'd snared a ride with the 160th Night Stalkers. I prefer helicopters. You know how I feel about crop dusters."

Buck clapped a hand to his shoulder and turned him back around. "Now, don't go getting your boxers in a twist."

"I don't wear boxers," Pitbull grumbled.

"You've flown with Marly twice. She's a good pilot and she knows her plane. And it's not a crop duster. Besides, nothing bad happened on the previous two flights. What makes you think anything will happen this time?"

Pitbull frowned as he let Buck guide him toward

the small bush plane they'd used in their last operation to rescue the US Secretary of Defense's son and his hot, tough-as-nails assistant. "Yeah, but three's a charm." He tipped his head toward the offending aircraft. "Look at it. I swear it's only held together by spit and duct tape."

With a low chuckle, Buck leaned closer. "Don't let Marly hear you badmouth her bird. She might decide to leave us behind."

"That would be just fine with me." Pitbull sighed. "I can't believe you talked me into doing this." He shook his head. "I'd have been perfectly happy waiting for our next assignment back at camp."

"Seriously?" Diesel shot a glance over his shoulder as he walked ahead. "You have the chance of a lifetime to go on a safari in Africa, and you'd rather stay at Camp-Hot-As-Hell-in-the-Friggin'-Desert eating MREs?"

"I can't believe the CO granted us leave here in Africa." Harm came up from behind Pitbull, sliding his backpack over his left shoulder. "Somebody slip something into his drink last night?"

"I think he got a little pressure from the Sec Def," Big Jake said.

"One week." T-Mac grinned back at Pitbull and Harm from where he walked next to Diesel. "One whole week to get a real feel for the majesty of the savanna and experience all the animals we only see in zoos." The man practically skipped toward the plane, his step quickening as if he feared the CO would show up and pull their leave request. T-Mac had a knack with animals. He planned to own a ranch when his gig with the navy was up. He talked nonstop about the horses, cattle, llamas and other exotics he planned to populate the ranch with when he got out.

That was T-Mac.

Pitbull couldn't think past the plane standing in front of him. He much preferred helicopters. Oh, he knew they were more dangerous than planes, but he'd grown accustomed to them. The whopping sound of rotors soothed his anxieties about heights and leaving the ground. The single-engine prop job of an airplane didn't give him the warm fuzzies. Far from it.

As they neared the plane, Pitbull's nerves stretched. He focused on the pilot walking around the exterior, performing preflight checks.

They'd met Marly Simpson a couple weeks ago, when she'd helped them on a mission. They'd needed air transport in a hurry and had been forced to skip the call to their usual helicopter support team. She'd come through in the pinch.

But hell, they weren't in a pinch now. Why the hell did they have to fly in that tin can?

Marly wore a khaki-colored flight suit, the outfit hugging her slender body like a glove, accentuating every curve. The woman was a no-holds-barred, tough gal who could hold her own in any conversation or situation. She flew all over the African continent in that rust bucket, transporting people and cargo to the most inaccessible, dangerous and god-awful places without batting a single pretty eyelash.

Yeah, Pitbull had noticed Marly and the fact she

had a sexy, slender neck, ripe for kissing. Her long sandy-blond hair hung down to her waist when she pulled it out of the perpetual ponytail she wore, but that didn't make the fact they were flying in a single-engine prop job to their vacation destination any more appealing to Pitbull. It helped, but not enough.

Marly completed her inspection before they reached her and turned in their direction. "Hi," she said in her unassuming, warm voice, a smile spreading across her face. "Great to see you guys."

Harm reached her first.

Marly held out her hand. "Harm, you're looking well."

"You, too." Harm shook her hand and stood back as she greeted the rest of the team.

Diesel took her outstretched hand and pulled her into a bear hug. "Can't tell you how glad we were when you said you could take us to Kenya."

"My pleasure." She smiled up at Diesel. "How's Reese?"

He gave half a smile. "She's in the States. She promised me a date when I got back."

Marly's lips pressed together. "Long-distance relationships. They can suck."

"Yeah." Diesel shrugged. "But what can you do? If you love someone enough, you can work it out. And I'm not ashamed to admit I'm completely smitten with Reese."

"Never thought I'd hear those words coming out of your mouth." Buck bumped Diesel's shoulder with one of his own. "What changed your mind?"

Diesel laughed. "You have to ask?"

"Reese." Big Jake pushed his way through the rest of the team and hugged Marly. "Guess Diesel found his soul mate, or some other drivel."

Diesel balled his hands into a fist, a fierce frown pulling his brows low. "I take offense to your calling Reese drivel. And since when do you use words like *drivel*?"

"You know I don't mean anything by it," Big Jake said. "I'm just jealous." He hooked his arm over Marly's shoulder. "Will you be my soul mate, Marly? I like an independent badass of a woman."

Pitbull's fists clenched at Big Jake's casual claim on the pretty pilot. Why he should tense when another man made a move on Marly was beyond him. It wasn't as if he had a stake in the game or wanted her for himself. A navy SEAL's life was no place for relationships. Besides, Marly lived and worked in Africa. Other than the occasional mission, they never saw each other. Again…not that he was interested in seeing Marly.

Although he had to admit, she wasn't bad looking. Maybe a little less womanly than Pitbull's usual feminine fare.

She chortled and threw a light punch into Big Jake's belly. "Is that how you see me? As a badass?"

"Damn right," he replied, rubbing his gut. "Any woman who'd risk flying in and out of some of the most hostile territories in Africa—that alone is downright kickass in my books. And you have a helluva right hook."

She nodded. "I'll take that as a compliment." Tipping her head to the side, she stared up at his six-foot-four-inch frame and narrowed her eyes. "As for being your soul mate, I'll have to think about it." She unhooked Big Jake's arm from around her shoulders and turned to the others. "You can stow your bags in the luggage compartment or behind the back seat inside the plane."

While Diesel, Big Jake, Harm, Buck and T-Mac stowed their gear, Marly turned to Pitbull. "What about you?"

Pitbull's pulse quickened and his brain scrambled at her direct stare. *Shit.* What was it about this woman that tied him in knots? He squared his shoulders and lifted his chin. "What *about* me?"

"Are you looking for a soul mate?" Marly's brows rose.

"Oh, hell no," he answered. "What would I do with a soul mate when I'm never in one place long enough to grow roots?"

"Exactly." Marly nodded toward the plane. "Besides, I have my soul mate." She patted the plane's fuselage. "He doesn't argue with me much, sweeps me off my feet and carries me anywhere I want to go."

Pitbull frowned. "Your plane?"

Marly shrugged. "I don't have to worry about him cheating on me."

"Until another pilot comes along," Pitbull pointed out.

"I don't have to cook for him," Marly continued.

"You have to feed it aviation fuel, which can't be cheap," Pitbull countered.

"He doesn't care what I wear or whether I put on makeup."

"You got me there." Pitbull's lips twitched for a second. He stared at Marly's fresh, clean face and sparkling blue-gray eyes. "But seriously, you don't need makeup."

Marly's cheeks filled with a soft pink color, giving her a more feminine look. "Thanks. And for that, you win the prize."

Pitbull's lips curled into a wry grin. "What prize?"

Marly smiled. "Copilot's seat." Before Pitbull could protest, she clapped her hands sharply and faced the men standing around the plane. "If you're ready, we can get this show on the road."

"But—" Pitbull started.

Buck pounded Pitbull's back. "Congratulations, you lucky dog. You'll have the best seat on the bus."

"If you like it so much, *you* take it." Pitbull waved a hand toward the plane.

"I wouldn't dream of depriving you of such a prime location." Buck winked at Marly. "I'm sure the pilot will take very good care of you."

"You know damn good and well how I feel about this plane," Pitbull grumbled low enough for Buck to hear without clueing Marly in on their earlier discussion.

Buck cupped the back of his ear. "What's that you say?" His brows rose high, his lips curling into a devilish grin. "You were going to tell Marly how you felt about her pride and joy?" He whacked Pitbull in the back hard enough to send him staggering forward. "Go ahead. Tell her how much you love flying in fixed-wing aircraft." The bastard crossed his arms over his chest and waited.

Marly stared at Pitbull, another smile tugging at her lips.

Caught between Buck's taunts and Marly's expectant stare, he did the only thing he could. He lied. "I can't wait to ride shotgun."

Marly's eyes narrowed briefly. If he hadn't been watching so closely, he would have missed it. But then her face cleared and she grinned. "Great. I'll brief you on how to land this baby in case something happens to me."

Pitbull shot a horrified glance her direction. He ran his gaze from the tip of her toes to the top of her head. "Holy shit, Marly. You aren't expecting to croak while flying, are you?"

She laughed, a throaty, surprisingly sexy sound that caught and held Pitbull's attention, despite her random threat of dying while in flight. His heartbeat ratcheted up and his groin tightened. What the hell? Marly wasn't the kind of woman he usually found attractive. He went for dark-haired, curvy women who knew how to flirt and didn't expect anything past a one-night stand.

Marly's face lit and her eyes shone. "Don't worry," she said. "I'm as healthy as a horse."

His heart hammering against his ribs, Pitbull forgot to be angry or disconcerted about having to ride in the cockpit of the aircraft. For that moment, he was lost in Marly's laughter and smile.

Damn. This couldn't be good.

He tore his gaze from her fresh face and happy smile to watch, without really "seeing," as his teammates climbed aboard the aircraft and settled into their seats.

"If you're ready," Marly said beside him and touched his arm. "I'll close the door behind us. Really, I'm fine. I won't pass out and die during our flight." She held up her hand. "Scout's honor."

He frowned. "I'm holding you to that promise. And I doubt seriously you were ever a Scout." Then he ascended the steps into the tiny plane. Hunkering low to keep from bumping his head, he passed down the aisle and settled into the copilot's place on the right.

Taking full responsibility for the aircraft, Marly secured the door behind her and joined him, resting a hand on his shoulder as she lowered herself into her seat.

Where her hand had been remained warm long after she removed it. If he were honest with himself, he'd own up to the tingling sensation sizzling through his body at her touch. Obviously he'd been too long without a woman in his bed. But now was not the time to be thinking of such a thing.

Marly was the pilot, nothing more.

"Buckle up, buttercup," Marly said, fastening her safety straps. Over her shoulder, she told the others, "As you all well know, this isn't your usual jetliner flight. I'll be your pilot, or rather, copilot—with Pitbull's assistance—and flight attendant. Please fasten your seat belts and keep them fastened until we land. There will be no beverages served on this flight, and there is no lavatory." She gave the guys in the back a wicked grin. "If you should need to relieve yourself…hold it until we make our refueling stop halfway there."

"Well, damn," Buck complained. "I wanted a beer."

T-Mac followed with, "And I was really looking forward to the peanuts."

Big Jake waved a dismissive hand. "Ignore the whiners. We're all set. Let 'er rip."

"And by 'let 'er rip,' he means make a smooth takeoff and an even smoother landing," Pitbull mumbled.

"I heard that." Marly's pretty pink lips twisted. She slapped a headset against his chest. "Wear these so you know what's going on."

He slipped the headset over his ears and plugged the wires into the communications ports. "Do I want to know what's going on?"

She leaned back and gave him an assessing stare. "Pitbull, are you telling me you're afraid of a little ol' plane ride?" Her brows rose into the hair swooping down over her brow.

Buck leaned forward. "Bingo! Give the lady a prize."

Marly shook her head. "You have nothing to worry about. I have over three thousand hours flying this plane alone, and more in other types of aircraft. I started flying at thirteen, over fifteen years ago. I think I can handle it." She checked the instrument panel, flicked several switches and started the engine.

As the propeller spun into action, Pitbull's gut clenched.

"Relax. We'll be there before you know it," Marly said into the mic.

Her voice filled the earphones of his headset, reassuring Pitbull when he needed it most.

Marly spoke to the nearby air traffic controller, got her instructions and started the plane taxiing toward the runway. "With all you go through as a navy SEAL, I can't believe you're afraid of flying."

"I'm not afraid of flying," Pitbull said through clenched teeth, his fingers digging into the armrest at his side. "I'm afraid of crashing."

"But you fly in helicopters all the time," Marly reasoned, pushing the throttle forward. The aircraft gained speed as it barreled down the runway.

"I do it as part of the job." Pitbull tensed, praying the runway was long enough. "And helicopters don't eat up thousands of feet of runway to take off."

Still grinning, Marly kept her gaze on the runway ahead. "Yeah, but when the propeller stops, helicopters drop like a rock to the earth. Airplanes, on the other hand, can glide for miles." Just as they neared the end of the runway, the plane left the ground, the wings seesawing slightly as they lifted the craft into the air.

Pitbull leaned back, willing the plane to continue its climb. "Planes can glide for miles, but they still need thousands of feet of runway to land. Helicopters don't. Besides, I'm used to flying in helicopters, not planes."

Her hands steady on the yoke, Marly handled the aircraft like the expert she was. "Stick with me and I'll have you singing a different tune."

Pitbull shot a glance her way, his groin tightening despite the knot in his gut. He'd like to stick with Marly long enough to get to know her lithe body and the taste of her pink lips. The woman was sexy when she was all into her element of flying.

Pitbull wished he could enjoy the view more. And he might if he could relax, like she said, and enjoy the ride. But this wasn't Pitbull's preferred method of transport. It would take a whole lot more time in the craft for him to get even remotely comfortable. In the meantime, he'd suffer through, for the sake of the team.

MARLY ALMOST FELT sorry for Pitbull. Once she was over five hundred feet in the air, she shot a glance his way.

The man was as tense as a drawn bowstring. His knuckles were white where they curled around the armrest, and he stared through the front windshield unblinkingly.

She couldn't talk him down from his panic. She'd already tried. The best she could do was to land the plane safely and smoothly.

Marly had to admit Pitbull had been the one to catch her eye among the navy SEAL team members. His hard-packed body, square jaw and intense expression made her heart flutter, an occurrence she hadn't experienced in her twenty-nine years. Until she'd met the SEAL team and Pitbull.

Knowing he had a deep fear of fixed-wing aircraft didn't diminish his attraction in the least. It actually increased it in Marly's eyes. It proved he wasn't perfect, like she'd originally thought. After her first encounter with the team, she'd read up on the elite units of navy SEALs and what it took to become one. And wow! This man sitting beside her had braved some of the worst conditions and treatment, muscled through and had become one of America's best.

From what she'd learned from others among the team, they'd deployed multiple times to the Middle East, Africa and other places around the world on deadly missions. Pitbull couldn't be afraid of much, if he strode headlong into danger.

Marly had waded into dangerous situations on more than one occasion and been scared she wouldn't emerge alive. But somehow, she had. Many times she'd considered moving back to the States and setting up a charter service there, but her mother still worked in the small villages of Africa, helping serve the poor and sick. Until her mother left Africa, she figured she might as well stay. Marly didn't have friends or family in Virginia, where she was born. Why go back?

She glanced over at the man in the seat beside her. Perhaps if she had someone to go home to…

Not that Pitbull was that someone. Marly had grown up independent, running wild in the villages where her mother and father had worked. She wasn't sure she'd be able to handle a full-time relationship. Freedom was everything to her.

And sometimes, with that freedom came loneliness.

Time passed. Marly made the scheduled stop to refuel at a small airfield halfway to their destination in northern Kenya. Her landing was so soft, she could have been kissing the ground. It didn't matter—Pitbull had a death grip on the armrest anyway.

The men clambered out, made their visit to the latrine and hurried back as the attendant completed the refueling. Pitbull offered to let someone else sit in the copilot's seat, but there were no takers.

Marly hid a smile. She didn't want someone else riding shotgun. She liked the view inside the cockpit.

Her takeoff was a little less graceful as she hit a couple pockets of air that tipped the wings slightly, making the plane wobble on the ascent. Marly sighed. She couldn't win every time.

Over the next hour, the color slowly returned to Pitbull's knuckles as he loosened his grip on the armrest.

Marly glanced at the savanna ahead and spotted some of Africa's finest wildlife. She turned her head toward the rear of the plane. "If you look out to the southwest, you'll see herds of water buffalo and zebras."

The men in the seats behind her leaned forward and peered through the cabin windows.

Pitbull sat forward and craned his neck, scanning the land below.

"If you look carefully, I'll bet you can see a pride of lions lurking nearby." Marly tipped the nose of the plane downward.

Pitbull sat back, his grip tightening again on the armrest. "What are you doing?" he said, his voice clipped, his lips pulled back into a tight line.

"It's okay," Marly said. "I'm getting a little lower so you can see the animals."

"Isn't that what the safari is for?" Pitbull asked.

"Yes, but you can't see the vastness of the herd from the ground like you can from the air."

Buck laid a hand on Pitbull's shoulder. "Stop worrying and start drinking in this amazing view."

Pitbull closed his eyes briefly, sucked in a deep breath and let it out before nodding and reopening his eyes. "You're right. I need to stop worrying. This plane will get us there."

"And the excellent pilot," Buck added.

Marly shot a grateful smile over her shoulder. "Thanks for the vote of confidence."

And then, without warning, the engine sputtered, coughed and died.

Marly set the plane altitude for the best glide speed and turned her focus to the control panel. Her experience and training kicked in.

"What's happening?" Pitbull's voice said into her ear.

She didn't respond, needing every second of her attention on safely landing the disabled plane. Because they were so low already, Marly mentally went through an abbreviated emergency checklist and low-

ered the landing gear, all while scanning the surroundings for a suitable place to land.

Marly keyed her mic. "Mayday, mayday, mayday."

"Holy hell," Pitbull whispered beside her.

She'd promised to keep him safe on this flight,
probably jinxing them all in the process. "Bravo-
bravo-niner-eight-niner, experiencing engine fail-
ure. Bearing down on the savanna twenty miles north
of the All Things Wild Safari & Resort, seven souls
on board."

The air traffic controller acknowledged her distress call and offered to send a rescue crew to the location of their transponder.

Marly eased back on the yoke, trading airspeed for
altitude, aiming the plane in the direction of the longest, flattest spot on the huge field. Unfortunately, it
was occupied by a herd of zebras and water buffalos.

She couldn't take her gaze off the ground ahead,
so she raised her voice loud enough that the men in
the rear could hear. "Gentlemen, brace yourselves for
a rough landing."

Chapter Two

When the engine cut out, Pitbull's heart slammed against his ribs and pulsed through his veins until Marly gave the warning to brace for landing. Then, as with all dangerous assignments, he drew into himself and focused on the mission.

In this case, it was to survive and get everyone out of what would surely be burning wreckage, if they were lucky enough to be alive upon landing.

"Move, damn you," Marly muttered into the mic, her concentration on the zebras trotting across the field in front of the descending plane. "Move."

The closer the plane grew to the herd, the faster they ran.

Pitbull leaned forward, his breath lodged in his throat, counting the seconds until they ran over the black-and-white-striped creatures. Just when he thought they'd hit one of the animals with the landing gear, the herd split, shooting out to each side of the aircraft and far enough away that the wings didn't touch them.

The plane floated toward the earth, slowing, slowing, slowing…

A horn sounded.

"What's that?" Pitbull demanded, searching the interior and exterior of the plane.

"Stall warning. Relax," Marly said through gritted teeth. "I've got this." She set the plane down on the savanna, the wheels kissing the earth. Once the nose wheel was down, they bounced across the uneven terrain.

By the time the plane came to a halt, Pitbull was convinced he'd rattled away every tooth in his mouth. But they were alive, the plane was intact and no fire ensued. He let go of the breath he'd been holding and leaned back in his seat.

"Wow, Marly," Buck said from the rear. "That was amazing."

Marly sat for a moment, staring at the departing herds, her lips pressed tightly together. Then she nodded, as if pulling herself back to the present, and peeled her fingers from the yoke. She turned with a tight smile and faced the men in the back. "Well, you wanted a safari. I didn't see any reason to wait." She held up her hand. "Don't worry. I won't charge you extra for the exciting landing."

Harm shook his head. "What happened?"

"I don't know, but I'm going to find out." She pushed out of her seat and waded through the team to the door. Once she'd lowered the steps, she hurried to the ground and around to the engine compartment.

The team piled out, leaving Pitbull to exit the aircraft last.

He fought the urge to drop to his knees and kiss the ground. If his legs were a little wobbly, he couldn't help it. Though Marly had done an excellent job landing the plane among a herd of zebras, she could just as easily have crashed and killed every last one of them.

The water buffalo and zebras stopped running and went back to grazing, as though it were an everyday occurrence to be disturbed by landing airplanes.

Pitbull trailed behind the others as they followed Marly.

"Need a hand?" T-Mac asked.

Marly lifted the lid to the engine compartment. "Know anything about airplanes?"

T-Mac shrugged. "No, but I'm handy with a variety of engines and computer issues."

"You're welcome to look over my shoulder." Marly opened the luggage compartment and started tossing backpacks and duffel bags to the ground. "I have a ladder in here somewhere." Once she'd dumped everything else out of the way, she said, "There it is." She yanked a small ladder out and stood it beside the plane. "Unlike all of you, I'm not six feet tall." She climbed up and leaned over the engine.

"I've had engines quit in my car before due to fuel pump issues," T-Mac offered.

"The fuel pump was replaced during the last annual maintenance on this plane," Marly said. "But that doesn't mean it didn't go bad since then." She looked down at Pitbull. "There's a tool bag behind the back seat inside the plane. Could you get it for me?"

Pitbull nodded and hurried to comply. When he returned, Marly and T-Mac had their heads together, staring into the engine.

A flush of heat washed over Pitbull. He fought the urge to insinuate himself between the two. Hell, they were within kissing distance. Instead, Pitbull cleared his throat and shoved the tool kit between Marly and T-Mac. "Perhaps this will help."

T-Mac leaned back.

Marly didn't take the bag. Instead, she stared into the engine. "Could you hand me a crescent wrench, please?"

Pitbull bit back a retort, unzipped the bag and gave her what she asked for.

She reached into the engine with the wrench and jerked back her hand. "Damn. You'd think it would have cooled down by now."

"Here, let me see." T-Mac took her arm and inspected the inside of her wrist.

"I'll be all right." Marly tugged her hand free and bent over the engine again. A few minutes later, she pulled out a part, shaking her head. "Like you said, it's the fuel pump. Looks like it burned up." She handed him the part and leaned over the engine. "Thankfully, it's the only thing burned up. A new part and this plane will be in the air again." She straightened and grimaced. "It'll be a rough takeoff, but I've been in worse places."

"Speaking of being in worse places." Harm stepped up beside Pitbull. "How are we getting out of here?"

"I put in a call to the ATC. He said he'd send out a rescue crew." Marly closed the engine compartment and started to step down from the ladder.

Pitbull reached out and took her hand to steady her. When she laid hers in his, he felt the tingle of electricity race up his arm and spread across his chest. He didn't have time to analyze the feeling before she slipped on the last rung of the latter and pitched forward, slamming into his chest.

Pitbull went down, landing hard on his back, but cushioning Marly's fall. She landed on his chest, her hands on the ground on either side of his arms.

"Sorry," she said and scrambled to get off him. In the process, she kneed him in the groin.

Pain shot through him, wiping out the heat of the electricity her touch had generated. Pitbull doubled up, swallowing hard on the groan rising up his throat.

"I'm sorry," Marly repeated. As she straightened and brushed the dirt off her hands, her cheeks flamed red. She held out her hand to Pitbull.

"I'm all right," he said through clenched teeth, waving away her efforts. For a long moment, he lay still, willing the pain to go away.

"Well, damn." Marly knelt beside him and started to reach for the parts still pulsing with pain. "Is there anything I can do to help?"

He let go of his package and grabbed her wrist to keep her from touching him down there. Hell, if she didn't leave his parts alone, it wouldn't be long before he embarrassed himself in an entirely different way, pain be damned.

Buck laughed out loud. "Can't believe you let a girl clock your nads, dude." He nodded to Big Jake. "You get one side, I'll get the other."

"I'll get up when I'm ready," Pitbull insisted.

"You're ready," Big Jake announced. With one of his buddies on either side of him, Pitbull was brought to his feet. Not that he was quite ready. He did his best to stand up straight, thankful the pain faded with each breath.

Marly stared across the grassy plains, the color still high in her cheeks. "Shouldn't be too long. The ATC would have called someone close to our location. We never know what we're going to get." She entered the plane and walked from front to rear.

"Well, we might as well enjoy being this up close and personal with the African natives." Diesel walked past the tip of a wing and stared out over the savanna. "I don't think I've actually seen a water buffalo or zebra from this close."

"You're not as close as you'll be on the safari." Marly pulled a rag out of her back pocket and wiped the grease off her fingers.

"May I?" Pitbull held out his hand for the rag.

Marly's brows drew together, and she ran her gaze over him as she handed him the towel.

His lips quirked upward. "Don't be so suspicious." He leaned toward her and wiped a smudge of grease from her jaw. "You missed a spot."

Her cheeks blossomed with color. "Thank you."

She swiped the rag from his hands and stuffed it back into her pocket before turning to the others. "We're not too far from the resort. If we're lucky, we won't have to wait more than an hour before someone shows up to take us there."

"An hour?" Buck asked.

Marly shrugged. "You never know who or how they will arrive. I'm assuming in a ground vehicle."

"I'd give my left nut for a whirly bird," Pitbull muttered. "We wouldn't be in this situation if we'd started out in a helicopter."

Marly rounded on Pitbull, eyes blazing, and jabbed her finger into Pitbull's chest. "If we'd been in a helicopter and the fuel pump went out, those vultures would be picking our bones clean." She redirected her pointer finger to a flock of vultures riding the air currents several hundred yards away.

Pitbull held up his hands. "Okay, okay. You made your point."

"Damn right I did. I'd like to see your helicopter pilots land as smoothly without an engine."

Buck draped an arm over Marly's shoulders. "You were awesome." He shot a glare at Pitbull. "We're alive, aren't we?"

Pitbull returned his buddy's glare and then nodded, letting the tension seep out of his body. "You're right." He held out his hand to Marly. "You did great landing the plane."

She stared at it for a moment, but didn't take it.

Pitbull dropped his arm, somewhat relieved. The last time she'd touched him with her hand, electricity had ricocheted throughout his body. He'd be better off enforcing a hands-off policy with Marly.

"I thought we were going to have zebra stew for dinner, as close as we came to landing on them," Harm said. "How did you know they'd get out of the way in time?"

Marly ducked from beneath Buck's arm. "I didn't. That was pure luck. Landing without damaging the plane..." She straightened her shoulders and flung back her ponytail. "That was all me."

It was true—Pitbull had been in the copilot's seat the whole way down. Marly had done a hell of a job piloting the craft to the ground among a herd of zebras and on bumpy terrain. "I guess I should thank you. But all I can think about is the fact you broke your promise."

She shook her head. "No I didn't."

"You said you wouldn't crash the plane," he told her.

"No, I said I wouldn't pass out while flying." She winked. "Those are two completely different things. And I didn't crash the plane."

Pitbull waved his hand toward the aircraft. "It's not flying."

She crossed her arms over her chest. "But it will, once I get the replacement part."

"How soon will that be?" Pitbull panned the surrounding savanna. "There aren't any aviation superstores anywhere nearby. And you can't seriously think you can take off on this field."

"I'm sure I can get a replacement part within a

couple of days. And when I can find a smooth enough stretch, long enough to build up some speed, I can get this bird off the ground." She shook her head, a disgusted look on her face. "What do you know about avionics, anyway?"

Marly walked several yards away and stood staring at the animals in the distance, her back to the men. The band holding her ponytail had slipped loose. Strands of silky, sandy-blond hair caught in the breeze.

Pitbull couldn't tear his gaze off her slim, athletic figure encased in the form-hugging flight suit.

Buck leaned close to his friend and whispered, "You're a knucklehead."

"What's your point?" Pitbull snapped back, too engaged in his view of Marly to care what Buck had to say.

"She landed the plane," Buck said.

T-Mac added, "That's right. We're alive. You should be down on your knees, groveling at her feet."

His teammates were right. What was it about Marly that got Pitbull all fired up? She was smart and sexy and knew her way around her airplane. Why couldn't he leave her alone?

She turned, a smile on her face.

That smile hit him square in the chest like a round from a .55-caliber machine gun. He almost staggered back a few steps with the impact.

"Here comes our rescue team." Marly pointed to a cloud of dust rising from the grass, heading straight for them.

The men gathered around Marly, like cowboys circling their wagons.

"Are you sure that's our rescue team?" Pitbull asked.

"Who else would be out in the middle of nowhere?" Marly's brows dipped. "Seriously, the ATC had our coordinates from the transponder. They had to have passed them on to whoever they called."

"We've seen some of the welcoming committees here in Africa," Harm said, squinting at the oncoming vehicle.

"If you're worried, wait behind me." Marly unzipped her flight suit to reveal a pink bra beneath and a shoulder holster. She pulled out a nine-millimeter handgun.

The team all backed up several steps, every man raising his hands.

"Whoa there, Marly," Buck said. "Do you know how to use that thing?"

She glared at him. "Do you think I'd carry it if I didn't?"

Buck shrugged. "Some women do."

"I'd be a fool to fly around this country unarmed, now, wouldn't I?" She nodded toward the vehicle now visible through the cloud of dust. "Looks like a safari wagon."

"And it's not empty." Pitbull dove for his backpack, unearthed the M4A1 he'd stashed inside and quickly assembled the main parts.

"Hold your fire, Zippy," Marly said. "They wouldn't come out without a contingent of armed men. The animals can cause enough damage, but the poachers and warring rebels are even more dangerous. Wait and see."

"If we wait too long, we could all be dead." Pitbull took up a position in the shadow of the airplane and lined up his sights with the driver of the oncoming truck.

"I'm with Pitbull." Harm reached for his backpack and pulled out a .45-caliber handgun.

The other four men did the same. Soon, everyone waiting at the plane was armed and ready for whatever was headed their way.

The big truck pulled to a lumbering stop several yards away from the plane.

A woman appeared out of the cloud of dust, wearing tall leather riding boots, khaki slacks tucked into the top of the boots and a matching khaki shirt, unbuttoned to reveal an ample amount of cleavage. She swept a wide-brimmed safari hat from her head and shook out auburn curls. "We're here to help."

Buck let out a long, low whistle. "Wow."

She was followed by three dark-skinned men dressed in khaki uniforms and carrying machine guns.

Pitbull aimed for the first one, keeping all three in his peripheral vision. If any one of them made a move, he'd take them down.

"Hey, don't shoot!" a sultry voice called out. "We're really here to help."

Chapter Three

Marly shoved her pistol back into the holster beneath her flight suit and stepped forward, holding out her hand to the woman who came to a halt in front of her. "Marly Simpson. I'm the pilot. You got here fast."

The other woman was shorter, curvier and stunningly beautiful. Next to her, Marly felt like the ugly stepsister to Cinderella. She shoved aside the thought and shook the woman's hand.

"Talia Montclair. Nice to meet you." She shook Marly's hand with a firm grip and turned to the others. "I'm from All Things Wild Safari & Resort. We got a call from the local police to come pick up the passengers and crew from an aircraft since it went down closest to our operations." She stared around at the others. "Anyone badly hurt? I'm also a trained paramedic."

Buck lifted his hand.

Talia's brows rose. "What's the nature of your injury?"

He pressed the hand to his chest. "You just stole my heart."

Talia planted her hands on her hips, her lips quirking on the corners. "Seriously, was anyone injured in the landing?"

"No." Pitbull stepped out from the shadows and lowered his rifle. "Thanks to our pilot." He glanced at Marly with a slight nod and then held out his hand to Talia. "Percy Taylor."

Marly chuckled softly. Finally, the man acknowledged her skill in landing the plane. But did he have to hold Talia's grip for so long?

"That's his real name, but we call him Pitbull." Buck bumped Pitbull out of the way and held out his hand to the safari representative. "Graham Buckner. But you can call me Buck."

Talia grinned. "Percy, Graham, nice to meet you." She faced the other four men. "I'm assuming the rest of you are Dalton, Harmon, Trace and Jake?" Her smile spread wider.

They nodded as one.

"Good." She clapped her hands together. "My safari adventurers. And I see you couldn't wait to get started and decided to land in the middle of our first stop for tomorrow." She waved her hand toward the herd. "Welcome to Kenya. Like what you see so far?"

Marly's lips thinned. For the most part, the men weren't looking at the herds of wild animals. Instead, they were drooling over their safari guide, Talia.

Heat built in Marly's gut. And not the good lusty kind. More the jealous, burning, I-can't-compete-with-that kind. She glanced down at her flight suit that did little to disguise her lack of a voluptuous figure. She was too tall and lanky to be considered feminine. Not that it had bothered her. Until now.

She dared a glance at Pitbull. She was pleased to see he wasn't looking at Talia.

Instead, his gaze was on Talia's guards.

Talia must have noticed their regard. "Don't let my men scare you. We have to come armed." She nodded toward the SEALs' weapons. "And I'm glad to see you brought your own firepower. We run into all kinds of four-and two-legged aggressors out here. It pays to be prepared." Talia glanced toward the plane, her eyes narrowing. "Speaking of which, we might want to push the plane into the tree line."

Marly glanced around the open field, searching for a stand of trees large enough to park the plane beneath. "The engine isn't working."

Talia smiled. "I'm sure you can get some old-fashioned brawn to help get it where you want it to go. I wouldn't leave it out in the open. You never know what might happen if it's left alone."

Familiar with the nature of the inhabitants of the savannas and jungles of Africa, Marly agreed. Gangs of miscreants, poachers and rebels would have the plane stripped of anything salvageable in no time.

She located a copse of trees three hundred yards to her south. "If we could get it to that stand of trees, I'd feel better about leaving it."

Pitbull stepped forward. "Let us handle it."

The six SEALs and the three guards positioned themselves around the aircraft at Marly's direction and began pushing the plane across the bumpy terrain and toward the trees.

Talia followed in the truck.

Once they had the plane positioned between the trees, Talia hauled out a large bundle from the back of the truck and dropped it on the ground. "You can use this camouflage netting to conceal the plane. Trust me, I wouldn't want anyone to find it. We've had some near misses with a local rebel group. The cowards try to get our people alone. Then they attack and steal whatever they might sell on the black market. They'd steal this plane piece by piece if they found it."

"Should I stay with the plane until the part comes?" Marly asked.

"I think it will be okay as long as you conceal it well enough."

"Great," Marly said, grabbing a corner of the netting.

The others took up the other ends and dragged the net over the nose and wings, and finally over the tail.

When they had secured the ends to the ground using sticks and rocks, Marly stood back and examined the effect. From a distance, it would blend into the shadows of the trees.

Talia waved toward the truck. "We can fit two inside—me and one other—and the rest in the back. I'll let you figure out who goes where."

Pitbull hurried to the front of the vehicle and opened the passenger seat. "Marly," he barked like a command.

Marly, unused to having men open doors for her,

glanced toward the rear of the truck. "I can ride in the back. You guys are the clients."

"Don't be ridiculous." Buck hooked her arm, marched her to the passenger side and handed her off to Pitbull. "You'll ride up front. We're used to eating dust."

"So am I," Marly argued.

Pitbull leaned close and whispered in her ear, "Are you always this disagreeable?"

She frowned at him. "Sometimes I'm even more so."

Pitbull gripped her around the waist and lifted her up to the seat, ending the argument.

Marly sat down hard, shocked that he'd manhandled her so easily. She'd always considered herself to be too big to be girly. But Pitbull had just proven he was strong enough to sweep this independent, no-nonsense woman off her feet.

Her heart fluttered and her cheeks heated. Where his hands had clenched around her waist still tingled with awareness. She clamped her mouth shut and stared forward, refusing to look back at the man who'd set her blood speeding through her veins and pooling low in her belly.

What was wrong with her? This man was a US Navy SEAL. He probably had a woman in every port. Even if he didn't, his job had him traveling the world at the drop of a hat. Nothing could ever come of a relationship with such a man.

Nothing.

PITBULL DIDN'T REGRET ending the argument with Marly by lifting her into the truck. He did regret the lingering electrical current running up his arms and down to his groin. *Focus, man. Focus.*

They were in Kenya for only a week. *Let's go on a safari*, his teammates had said. *It'll be fun*, they'd assured him. Nothing was fun about the raging lust spinning through his body for the woman he'd just touched, not when he knew it wouldn't go anywhere. He wouldn't be able to act on it. Thankfully, Marly would be gone as soon as she had her fuel pump. Hopefully that would be by the end of the day. Then he could concentrate on having a good time seeing all the animals and enjoying the resort. And maybe they could convince the 160th to send a helicopter out to retrieve them. They could call it a training mission to extricate military personnel from a hostile environment.

He climbed into the back of the truck with the other members of his team and held on tight. The trip to the resort was across the savanna and into a forest. An hour later, they pulled up to a large, rambling house made of wood and stone. The house was surrounded by smaller huts with a similar wood-and-stone design—individual cottages Pitbull guessed were options for their guests.

Talia parked the truck in front of the main house and climbed down.

"I have each of you in your own bungalow, but meals will be in the main house dining room," Talia said. "Breakfast and lunch are casual. Dinner is formal. Please dress accordingly. Follow me, if you will."

She entered the house, leaving the door open behind her for them to follow.

The main house had a grand entrance with staircases on each side curving up to the second floor. Shiny mahogany handrails and furniture gave the rooms elegance in a rugged land of wild animals and dangerous people.

"The dining room is to your left. Normally I rent out the guest rooms, but they are unoccupied at the present time. I thought you would prefer your own bungalows while you are with us at All Things Wild Resort. You're welcome to take advantage of the living areas and the sitting room on the main floor. At the back of the house is a game room with a pool table and a bar. I'll leave you to explore for yourself while I get Miss Simpson situated and gather the keys to your bungalows."

"I'm up for a round of pool." T-Mac started for the rear of the house. "Anyone else?"

Buck pushed past the others and followed T-Mac. "Count me in."

"I could go for a beer," Harm said.

"Me, too," Diesel agreed. "Maybe two."

"You're welcome to the beer, wine and the liquor cabinet. It's all included in the price of the week," Talia informed them.

Big Jake laughed. "You might regret telling them that."

"No worries. We have a well-equipped bar, and the wines are from local vineyards." Talia motioned for Marly to follow her. "I have a satellite phone in the study, if you'd like to call someone about fixing your plane."

"Thank you." Marly followed Talia into a beautifully appointed study. The walls were lined with built-in bookshelves. A massive mahogany desk graced one end of the room. The room had a masculine scent of books and wood.

Talia crossed to the desk and lifted a portable satellite phone. She handed the device to Marly and then turned to a computer monitor, bringing up a browser. "Help yourself to the internet. We do most of our communications via satellite. Unfortunately, we're too remote for most cable or electric companies to keep up with those pesky lines."

Marly thanked Talia, sat down at the computer and pulled up an internet browser to locate a replacement for the fuel pump. An hour later, she had a man on the phone with her answer. Not the one she wanted to hear, however.

"Five days?" Marly shook her head, despite that the guy on the other end of the communication couldn't actually see her face as she spoke. "You can't get it to me any sooner?"

The man answered, "It's the best I can do. Take it or leave it."

Marly drew in a deep breath and let it go. "I'll take it. Thank you."

She stood and stretched. What now? She hadn't come prepared to be here for almost a week.

Talia poked her head through the open door of the study. "Find your part?"

Marly nodded and grimaced.

"Let me guess." Talia tipped her head to the side. "It'll be a week before they can get it to you."

Marly laughed. "You know how things work in these parts, I take it."

"Yes, indeed." Talia crossed her arms over her ample chest and leaned against the door frame. "The kitchen stove quit working once when I had the resort booked solid. It took over a month to get a replacement. My chef and I had to cook everything on the outdoor grill, rain or shine. We were not amused."

"Thankfully, it'll only take five days, not a month. But I didn't come prepared to stay overnight, much less five days."

"No worries. I can loan you clothes to last you, and we have extra toiletries for guests who've forgotten items." Talia touched her arm. "I can even cut you a deal on a room for the five days, since we're not full at this time."

"Thank you for the room offer." Marly bit her bottom lip. "Though I'm not sure your clothes will fit."

Talia ran her glance from Marly's head to her toes. "You're taller, so the full-length pants won't fit, but I have some formal dresses that will be ankle-length on you and shorts and capris you might fit into. We'll make it work."

"Dresses?" Marly cringed inwardly. "I haven't worn a dress since I was in grade school."

Talia's brows rose. "Darling, you'll have to around here, if you want dinner." She spun toward the door. "And I'll bet you have some great legs hiding under that flight suit. Follow me. You'll be staying in one of the upstairs suites inside the house. And I'll get you fixed up with clothes. If not from my wardrobe, well, people have left articles of clothing over the years. They've come in handy when luggage doesn't arrive with the guests."

Marly swallowed her groan. She liked her *own* clothes. They fit her and she felt like herself in them. *Beggars can't be choosers*, she reminded herself. She just hoped the tops Talia offered didn't hang on her chest, making her appear to be an underdeveloped teenager.

Again. Beggars can't be choosers.

TALIA HAD SHOWN Pitbull and the other members of his team to their individual bungalows while Marly made her calls to locate the spare part she needed to get her plane back up in the air.

Pitbull welcomed the time away from Marly. Since they'd left that morning, he couldn't get his mind off the feisty pilot. After their last mission, he hadn't expected to see her ever again. Even then, he'd felt that spark of something, if not between them, then at least on his side. He didn't much care for women who wore a lot of makeup or ratted their hair to achieve bigger, brassier hairstyles. He liked that Marly was natural and that she didn't apologize for it.

He tossed his backpack on the bed, tugged his T-shirt off and headed for the shower. After riding in the back of the old truck, he felt as if he had an inch of dust coating his body and filling all the crevices.

Nothing a little soap and water won't cure.

If only soap and water could wash Marly out of his head.

He turned the shower to a cool setting and stepped beneath the spray. As he lathered his body, running his hands over his skin, his thoughts drifted back to Marly and that damned flight suit. He wondered what it would be like to undress her body from that all-enveloping garment, starting at the zipper and working his way down. The glimpse of her hot-pink bra had only left him wanting to know more. Such as, did she have matching hot-pink panties?

His groin tightened and his shaft swelled at the image in his mind. She'd be appalled at his lusty thoughts, but he couldn't seem to stop them. At that moment, he wondered how her long legs would feel wrapped around his waist as he drove into her.

Pitbull reached behind him, turning the water to an even cooler temperature. He didn't need to show up at dinner and embarrass himself. The guys would rib him endlessly.

After rinsing the soap from his hair, face and body, he turned off the shower, stepped out of the tub and toweled dry with one of the huge luxury towels provided.

As a navy SEAL, he wasn't used to lavishness. Three squares and a bunk were all he'd come to hope for, and sometimes he went without. Having a shower at all was always a blessing. He pressed the towel to his nose and sniffed the light floral fragrance. Again, he thought of Marly and how that towel would wrap around her slender body twice.

He flung the towel over the curtain rod, pulled his razor out of his shaving kit and scraped three days' worth of beard from his chin. With a clean body and a smooth chin, he strode into the bedroom naked. Talia had said dinner was formal. He dug inside his back-pack for his best white long-sleeved, button-down shirt and his only pair of dark trousers. He didn't have a suit jacket, but he could at least dress nicely for dinner.

The men had been warned that they needed at least one dressier outfit for dinners during their stay at the resort. Pitbull would have preferred to show up in his jeans and a T-shirt, but he had to respect the proprietress's rules. He shook his trousers and shirt, hoping to knock the wrinkles out. When that didn't work, he searched the small bungalow and found an ironing board. Great. Just what he wanted to do on vacation at a safari resort.

Pride forced him to pull the board and iron out. In less than ten minutes, he had the wrinkles smoothed. While the garments were still warm, Pitbull slipped into them and pulled on socks and shoes. He found the necktie he'd picked up at the Post Exchange on Camp Lemonnier, looped it over his neck and knotted it expertly. He might not have grown up in the best neighborhood, but his mother had taught him how to knot a tie for church.

He smiled at her memory. The woman had worked hard all her life, only to die of breast cancer when Pitbull had been in BUD/S training. She'd insisted he not come home for her funeral, knowing how difficult the training was and how much harder it would be to have to start over.

He still regretted not being with his mother at her bedside until her last breath. His parents had always been there for him and believed in him. They always told him that he could accomplish anything he set his mind to.

Except save his mother.

As an only child, he'd felt the burden of guilt for not being there for her when she'd needed him most.

His father had been there, comforting her as she left life and, as he'd said, joined the angels.

Pitbull had never been sure of angels and religion, but he'd experienced days in battle when nothing but a miracle could have saved them, and then it had. He liked to think his mother had been watching over him.

His father was still alive, living in Virginia, still a little lost without his wife. He'd been heartbroken by the loss and hadn't dated or dared to love another woman since. Pitbull visited him as much as possible when he was Stateside in Little Creek, Virginia.

Having witnessed his father's heartache, Pitbull had been hesitant to get that involved with any woman for more than a date or two. He didn't want love someone he might lose, and suffer the way his father had.

This thing he was feeling about Marly was nothing more than insta-lust. It would fade and she'd be out of his life when they left Africa.

He ran a comb through his hair, smoothing it into

place. The longer he took to get ready, the more jittery he became. Dressed thirty minutes early, he had nothing else to do but wait. Hell, he might as well wait outside.

He found himself anxious to see Marly again. How could that be? He barely knew the woman.

Chapter Four

Pitbull stepped out of his bungalow and noted Buck standing outside his. He gave the other man a slight lift of his chin and sauntered over to join him.

Buck wore a black button-down shirt and black trousers with a red necktie. He tugged at the tie. "Damned things are like a noose. Whoever invented them was either masochistic or sadistic."

Pitbull nodded. "I don't understand dressing in formal clothing for dinner. What's wrong with jeans?"

"Women." Buck shrugged and tipped his head toward the darkening shadows in the nearby trees. "Did you hear the hyenas laughing?"

His lips quivering in laughter, Pitbull shot back, "They think we look funny, too?"

With a snort, Buck started toward the main house. "I guess early is better than late to a formal dinner."

Pitbull glanced around. "Wonder if the others are ready."

"They were the last ones at the pool table and are running late. They'll find us soon enough," Buck responded.

As they neared the front entrance to the house, the sun was setting in a radiant wash of orange, red, mauve and finally blues and purples. The gap between the trees gave them just enough of the spectacle to make them stop and stare for a long moment.

The front door opened behind them.

"Gentlemen, won't you come into the study for a drink before dinner?" Talia stood in the doorway, dressed in a long gown that hugged every curve of her body like a second skin. The neckline was low, dipping past her breasts, but not quite down to her belly button. The woman was well endowed, and gravity hadn't yet made its claim there.

"Now I can see why formal dinners can be a draw," Buck said beneath his breath as he followed Talia inside. Louder he said, "Talia, you look amazing."

"Why, thank you." Talia stopped in the foyer and turned a smile toward Buck, her lips spreading across her expertly made-up face. "Wait until you see Marly. I got to experiment with clothes and makeup. I barely recognized her."

Pitbull's brows drew together. He hoped Talia hadn't painted Marly's smooth, natural complexion with a ton of makeup. He liked Marly's fresh face and naturally pink lips.

"Where is she?" Buck asked, craning his neck to see around Talia.

"She was combing her hair when I left her. Hopefully she won't be much longer." Her glance shifted from the men in the entryway to the sweeping staircases.

A figure moved toward the landing and paused at the top.

Pitbull's breath caught in his chest. He stared up at the woman standing there. She had on a sapphire-blue dress that hugged her body like she was born in it. The top crisscrossed her breasts and rounded the back of her neck in soft, iridescent folds. The skirt clung to her waist, hips and thighs, falling to the tops of her ankles, shimmering with every move and exposing a hint of her tight calves. Rhinestone-studded, low-heeled sandals completed her outfit, emphasizing her delicate feet.

With one hand on the rail, she descended the stairs, her head held high, sandy-blond tresses pulled up in a stylishly messy bun with strands falling down around her cheeks. Her gaze caught his, holding it all the way down.

Without realizing he'd moved, Pitbull found himself at the base of the stairs, his hand resting on the rail, his foot on the first riser.

A low whistle sounded next to him. "Is that our Marly?" Buck asked in a hushed tone.

Marly gave a lopsided grin. "It's me," she said and laughed.

When Buck held out his hand to her, Pitbull brushed it aside and reached out to take hers for himself.

Marly laid her fingers in his palm and shook her head. "You act as if you're staring at a unicorn." She wiggled her fingers in front of his face. "For that matter, you might as well be staring at a unicorn. When I leave here, you'll never see me in a dress again."

"Oh, Marly, darling, you look fabulous." Talia joined them and gave Marly a hug. "I knew that color would suit you perfectly." Talia stood back, admiring Marly's transformation. "Don't you boys agree?"

"You look nice," Pitbull said. "I almost didn't recognize you."

"Beautiful, sweetheart." Buck leaned in and bussed Marly's cheek.

Her face flamed with color. "It's just a dress. A borrowed one at that."

"But you wear it so well," Talia insisted. "I have another dress that will be just as spectacular on you for tomorrow night."

"No." Marly held up her hand. "I can wear this one every night. You don't have to dress me in something different every evening."

"I insist," Talia said. "I don't often have lovely ladies visiting. It would be my pleasure. And you wouldn't want to deprive me of the fun, would you?"

Marly bit on her bottom lip and studied the other woman.

Pitbull could tell she was debating what she wanted to say to her hostess.

Finally Marly sighed. "I don't mind at all. If you want to dress me like a doll, I won't stop you. But I draw the line at corsets. I don't do corsets."

Talia laughed. "I'll remember that."

The front door opened, and the other four members of Pitbull's team entered. They gathered around

Marly, congratulating her on her amazing transformation.

"You look like an entirely different woman," Harm commented.

She laughed out loud and then frowned. "No matter what I'm wearing, I'm still the same old Marly. And, for the record, I'd rather wear my flight suit and hiking boots than a dress and heels any day."

Talia raised her arms, urging the crowd of people toward another door. "If Miss Simpson and you men are ready, we can go into the dining room to be served."

Pitbull offered Marly his arm. As they entered the formal dining room, he leaned close to Marly and said, "You look amazing."

She ducked her head. "Thank you."

"But seriously," Pitbull added, "I prefer you in the flight suit and boots."

She shot a glance his way. "You don't like the dress?"

"Don't get me wrong, the dress suits you. But I like the pilot, Marly—the woman who likes to putter in airplane engines and get grease on her cheek."

She ducked her head again, color blooming in her face. "You do?" Glancing up, she caught his gaze. "Why?"

Before Pitbull could think of a response, Talia interrupted his thoughts.

"There are no assigned seats. You may sit wherever your heart desires." She pinned Marly and Pitbull with a stare and a half smile.

Was it a challenge? Pitbull didn't know, nor did he care. He was still working through how he would answer Marly's question without revealing too many of his internal thoughts.

He held out a chair for her and waited while she got situated. When he went to sit in the space beside her, he was outmaneuvered by Buck.

"Hey." He laid a hand on Buck's shoulder.

"You snooze, you lose, buddy." Buck grinned up at him. "Besides, I want to get to know this new, sexy Marly. She's *hot*."

By the time Pitbull turned to the seat on the other side of Marly, Big Jake had settled in.

When Pitbull glared at him, he frowned. "What? Do you want me to move or something?"

He wanted to say *Get the hell out of my seat*, but why? Marly wasn't his property. He had no more of a valid reason to sit beside her than any one of his teammates. They all wanted to be close to the beauty she'd transformed into. The only difference between him and them was they wanted her for what she'd become. Pitbull wanted Marly for the woman in the flight suit, not the one in the fancy blue dress.

He took the seat across the table from her and contented himself with staring at her as often as he liked.

The meal was excellent, served in seven courses. By the time dinner was over, Pitbull could swear he'd ground his back teeth into nubs. Who ate dinner over the space of two hours? The longest meal he'd ever had lasted maybe fifteen minutes, tops. In the mili-

tary, you ate fast, not knowing when you'd be interrupted by enemy fire.

He wanted out of the suffocating pretentiousness
of the house, out in the night where he could stretch
his arms and legs, and remember what it meant to
be free. At least there, the animals wouldn't give a
damn which fork he used with the salad and which
he used with dessert.

When the dessert was served, he jammed it down
his throat, pushed back from the table and half stood,
ready to make a run for the exit.

"Mr. Taylor, are you up on the dangers of the African safari?" Talia asked.

He sat back down in the chair. For a long time, he
didn't say anything. Finally, he nodded. "I know not
to move around alone in the night and to make sure
my weapon of choice will bring down a man or an
elephant, whichever attacks me first."

Talia nodded. "You're right. The four-legged animals can get testy when you invade their space. They
usually don't attack in this area, but we've had a rogue
lion sneak in the past few nights and steal away a
farm animal or, in the worst-case scenario, a child."

Marly's soft gasp could be heard around the table.
"Did they find the child?"

Talia shook her head, her mouth turning downward at the corners. "Sadly, no."

Marly glanced down at her half-eaten cheesecake.
"I'm sorry to hear that."

Talia forced a smile to her lips. "My goal wasn't to
make for depressing dinner conversation. I just want

you to be aware of the dangers lurking in the dark. Don't go out alone, and don't assume you're safe. The animals have learned humans can be easy targets." She placed her palms on the table and stood. "That said, please don't hesitate to enjoy the walled gardens behind the house. We've never had any big cats attempt to scale the walls."

When Talia had risen from the table, all of the men rose with her.

Pitbull pushed his chair up to the table. "On that note, I could use some fresh air."

"Please, make yourself at home," Talia said. "And you're welcome to play pool as late as you like, or have drinks at the bar. The house is well insulated, so the noise won't bother other guests."

Harm nodded toward T-Mac. "You and I have a game to win. We can't let Big Jake and Diesel claim the title."

Big Jake shook his head. "I'm out. I'd rather have a beer and watch." He tipped his head toward Buck. "Let Buck and Diesel clean your clocks."

Buck cracked his knuckles. "You won't have a chance against me and Diesel."

T-Mac laughed. "I've seen you play. You're all talk."

"Put your money where your mouth is," Buck said. "I've got a twenty saying we'll win."

"Make it thirty. I could use the extra cash in my pocket," T-Mac shot back.

"You ladies care to join us?" Harm asked Marly and Talia.

Talia smiled. "I'd love to."

Marly shook her head. "I'll pass. Sounds too intense for me. I've had my share of intensity for the day."

"Right." Harm nodded. "Landing a plane in the middle of a herd of water buffalos and zebras has to be a bit extreme." He shrugged. "If you get bored or lonely, join us anytime."

"Yeah." Buck winked. "We'll be up late wiping the floor with these guys."

The five men and Talia left the room, heading for the back of the house.

Pitbull rounded the table and stopped in front of Marly. "I could use some peace and quiet. How about you?"

"The garden sounds like the place to be. I don't know about you, but the guys can be overwhelming in large doses."

Pitbull nodded. "Yeah. I get that." He held out his arm.

Marly frowned but slipped her hand in the crook of his elbow. "This is all so foreign to me. I grew up for the most part in small villages, running barefoot, wearing jeans and shorts." She plucked at the dress. "I'm not used to this kind of finery. I feel like a big fake."

Pitbull led her toward the exit and they emerged from the house into the garden, where exotic flowers and bushes and their softness surrounded them, along with the familiar fragrance of roses. They reminded him of his mother's rose garden.

"You wear that dress beautifully. But I get what you're saying. The only times I wear suits are for funerals and the odd covert operation. These danged ties are killer." He reached up and loosened the knot at his neck.

Marly chuckled beside him. "Here, let me." She turned to face him, reached up and pulled the knot free on the tie. "Better?" Her eyes sparkled with the reflection of the moonlight glinting in her irises. Her lips curled in a pretty smile, and it was beyond Pitbull's ability to resist her.

"Much." He pulled her against him.

Marly raised her hands to his chest, but didn't push back.

Pitbull lifted one hand to cup the back of her head. The other circled to the small of her back, pressing her hips against his. "I don't know if it's the moonlight, this garden or that dress, but right now all I want to do is kiss you."

Her fingers curled into his shirt and she stared up into his gaze. "You do?" Her voice wasn't much more than a whisper, her breath warm on his chin.

"Tell me to let go, and I will."

"PLEASE, DON'T." MARLY clung to the man, her knees more like wet noodles, incapable of holding her up.

He chuckled, his breath stirring the loose hairs around her face. "Don't what? Don't hold you like this?" He tightened his hand at the base of her back, pressing her body to his more firmly. "Or don't let go?"

She swept her tongue across her lips, afraid to

voice what she wanted, but more afraid he'd take her silence as a rejection. "Don't let go." Marly leaned into him, reveling in the feel of his hard muscles beneath the crisp white shirt. She wanted to run her hands over his bare skin and inhale his masculine scent. He was intoxicating. If she didn't watch out, she'd be drunk with her lust. And then what?

Marly stilled her hands' roving. "You should know something about me." She had to say it. He might as well know.

Pitbull stared down into her eyes. "What's that?" He kissed her forehead, the tip of her nose and each cheek.

Marly closed her eyes, loving the feel of his lips against her skin. "I've been around men all my life, but I'm not well versed in the art of seduction. I've been too busy to have a love life. I don't know how to be feminine and girly. I've only been on a couple dates, and they were disasters." She opened her eyes and grimaced. "What I'm trying to say is, I hope you're not disappointed."

Pitbull lowered his head, taking her lips in a kiss that changed her world. Her insides exploded with sensations like she'd never felt before, sending electrical charges zipping through her veins and nerves. She couldn't recall a time she'd had so little control of her reactions to another human being.

Marly curled her hands around his neck, afraid that if she didn't hold on, she'd melt to the floor, every bone in her body liquefying at his touch.

When he traced the seam of her lips with his tongue, she opened to him on a soft gasp.

His tongue swept past her teeth to tangle with hers, caressing, sliding in and out, warm, wet and tasting of the strawberry cheesecake from their dessert.

Tentatively at first, she dared to meet his tongue with hers.

His arms tightened around her and he stepped closer, their bodies now touching from shoulders to thighs. The heat generated between them eclipsed that of the lingering savanna warmth.

Marly wanted to be even closer, but that could be accomplished only by being naked. She slipped her hands beneath the collar of his shirt, loving the feel of his skin and the sinewy muscles of his neck and shoulders.

Pitbull's hand at her back slipped beneath the edge of the low-back gown, sliding toward the rounded curve of her bottom.

She tensed, unused to a man caressing her naked skin. He slowed his descent and held true, his fingers massaging, tempting, relaxing her until she sighed and once again leaned into him.

When he finally lifted his head, he pressed his forehead to hers and removed his hand from beneath her dress. "You tempt me like no other."

Marly gave a shaky laugh, not quite sure how to respond. "Ditto," she said, wishing she could dream up something hot and sexy to say in return. Hell, she wasn't cut out for the mating rituals others were so much better at. Pitbull had to have been with a dozen women, all of whom likely had more experience in their little fingers than Marly had in her entire twenty-nine years of living.

"Hey." Pitbull tipped her chin up, forcing her to look into his eyes. The light from the moon shone down on his face, illuminating a concerned dent in his brow. "What's wrong?"

"I'm not like other women," she said tentatively.

He laughed. "How so?"

"I told you. I'm not experienced. I don't know how to make you…" She shrugged, her cheeks burning with embarrassment.

"How to make me want you? How to make me long for another kiss? How to make me want to toss you over my shoulder and take you to my cabin for the night?" he offered.

"Yes. That." She stared up at him, wishing she knew any of the skills required in flirting.

"Would it help to know I appreciate that you aren't like other women? That I'm so turned on right now, it's all I can do not to rip off your clothes and have you right here?" He set her away from him and ran a hand through his hair.

Her insides hummed with the lingering effects of his kiss and the words he'd just said. "You want me?"

He chuckled and pulled her close to him again. "You tell me."

This time she could feel the hard ridge beneath his trousers. Marly's eyes widened. If she had the courage, she'd reach out and touch it. Alas, she didn't know what was expected or considered acceptable on a first date. Yes, she'd dated. But not often enough to know all the rules and etiquette.

Not that this had been their first date. But it had been their first kiss. This romance thing was confusing. She drew in a deep breath to steady herself and let it go, glancing up at Pitbull. "Where do we go from here?" With all her heart, she wanted him to say *Back to my cabin*.

He cupped her cheeks and pressed a kiss to her forehead, then took a step backward, dropping his arms to his sides. "You'll go to your room, and I'll go to my cabin."

Marly frowned, disappointment like a knife in her gut. "Are you sure that's where you want to go?"

He shook his head. "Oh, hell no. But for now, it'll have to do." Pitbull jabbed a thumb to his chest and then pointed at her. "You and I are in two very different places in our lives. Not to mention, we're usually separated by an ocean. Whatever this is…nothing will come of it."

"So?" Marly took a step forward. He wanted her. He'd said so in no uncertain terms. "What's stopping us from being together now?"

Again he shoved his hand through his hair. "Marly, you're not the type of girl a man can make love to and leave. You deserve someone who will stick around and be there for you."

"What if I don't want that?" Okay, so she didn't know how to flirt. But she did know what she wanted.
Him.

"You said you don't know what you want," he pointed out.

"That's not what I said. I said I didn't have any experience in the lovemaking department." She stopped when she got so close, she could feel the heat of his body without touching him. "What if I want you to teach me what I need to know?"

Pitbull held up his hands. "If I were any other man, I'd take you up on it. But I can't do that."

"Why?" She laid her hand on his chest and flicked a button open on his shirt. She wanted him so badly, she threw caution to the wind, took a deep breath and dove in. "No strings attached. I won't expect you to fall in love with me or be there after you leave Africa." She forced a saucy smile, cocked her brow and challenged him with a direct stare. All the while she quaked inside.

"What do you have to lose?"

Chapter Five

Marly couldn't believe the words coming out of her own mouth. Was this the same woman who'd just admitted she didn't have experience in making love? She'd just handed him the proverbial key to her bedroom, giving him carte blanche, no strings attached. Holy hell! What was he waiting for?

He raised his hands to grip her arms. "You don't really want this."

Oh yes, she did. "No? In the short time since you met me, have you known me to say something I don't mean?" She flicked another button on his shirt.

His chest rose and fell on a deeply inhaled breath, and then he caught her wrist in his hand. "No. Not like this."

The wind left her sails and she stepped back, pulling free of his grasp, her entire body flushed with the warmth of embarrassment. "I'm sorry. I told you I wasn't good at this." She turned and walked several steps away. "You're right. We should go our separate ways and forget what just happened."

Most likely, Pitbull wouldn't even think about the

fiery kiss ever again, unless he was telling the story about the bush pilot who'd given a pathetic woman's imitation of seduction. His teammates would get a great laugh out of that one.

"Marly." Pitbull's deep voice sounded directly behind her, and he reached out to touch her shoulder.

She shook it off and took another step away from him. "Really, you should go play pool with your friends, or go back to your cabin. Alone."

"I'm not leaving until you're safely inside the house."

"Talia said they never had wild animals in the walled garden." She waved toward the ten-foot-high brick-and-stucco wall. "I'll be fine."

Pitbull made no move to leave.

Marly spun on the high-heeled sandals Talia had loaned her and nearly fell. Gathering as much dignity as she could after wobbling on her feet, she lifted her chin and said, "Please, just go." She turned away and started for the rose arbor.

A low, throaty growl rumbled in the shadows, bringing her to a grinding stop.

Marly froze, her heart skipping several beats before racing ahead, pounding against her rib cage. Had she imagined the sound?

"Marly," Pitbull said in a low, ultracalm tone. "Don't turn around. Back up one step at a time, slowly."

"You heard it, too?" she whispered.

"Yes."

With fear tempting her to spin and run, she let Pitbull's voice fill her senses, his calm, reassuring tone wrapping around her like a shield. She took a step backward, then another.

The shadows in front of her shifted, and a pair of eyes appeared and blinked. Another throaty growl made Marly freeze again.

"I'm coming to you," Pitbull said. "Don't stop."

"If I move, he might jump on me," Marly said, her voice low and scared. She could barely breathe for the fear seizing her chest.

A hand slipped around her waist and pulled her backward, behind Pitbull's large, brawny body.

As the animal separated from the shadows, Marly gasped. "It's a leopard."

"Shh. He's coming toward us." Pitbull stood in the cat's path, shielding Marly.

"What are you going to do?" she asked.

"I don't know. This is my first time in a face-off with a wild animal."

"Well, you can't sacrifice yourself. Let's move toward the house." She hooked her hand into the back of his trousers' waistband and tugged him backward toward the house.

The faster they moved the quicker the leopard followed, emitting another low growl.

Pitbull planted his feet in the gravel path. "He might think we're running away. Running will only make him chase us. You get to the house and alert the guys. I'll block the leopard and keep him from coming after you."

"I'm not leaving you to die." Marly tried to step

around him. "Let me block him while *you* go for help. You're not wearing heels and can get there and back faster. And, if I need to, I'll shed these heels and run."

While they stood arguing about who should go, the leopard stalked toward them, closing the distance a step at a time.

When he was within leaping distance, Pitbull balled his fists and sank into a fighting stance.

"Seriously, Pitbull? What are you going to do? Punch it in the face?"

"I didn't bring my rifle. Do you have any other ideas?"

The leopard sank into a crouching position, its eyes narrowing.

Marly wanted to throw herself in front of Pitbull, but he had her pinned behind him with one arm while preparing to throw a punch with the other.

Bracing herself for the attack, Marly was surprised when the leopard rose to all fours and walked toward them, seemingly calm. As he approached Pitbull's legs, he leaned forward and sniffed.

Pitbull and Marly remained still, not moving or talking.

The big cat slinked closer and rubbed his cheek on the side of Pitbull's pants, making a rumbling sound like a muffled motor.

"Is that cat purring?" Marly asked.

"I sure hope so," Pitbull said.

"Mr. Wiggins!" a female voice said from behind Marly. "Oh, dear. There you are."

Marly glanced back over her shoulder to see Talia

standing in the open doorway of the house. "Is Mr. Wiggins bothering you two?" she called out. "He has a habit of hiding when new guests arrive. I've been looking all over for him."

"You mean he's not wild?" Marly asked, her voice shaking.

Talia laughed. "Yes and no. Yes, he's a wild animal, but no, we raised him from a cub. His mother was killed by poachers. He would have died had we not taken him in."

Mr. Wiggins rubbed against Pitbull's leg, then Marly's, and finally headed toward Talia.

She leaned down and scratched the big guy beneath the chin. "I'm sorry. I should have warned you. He's fairly harmless."

Marly laughed, the sound wobblier than she would have liked. "Fairly?"

"Oh, you know, he's big enough to knock someone down when he's playing."

No, Marly didn't know, but she'd take Talia's word for it.

Pitbull took her hand, pulled her against his side and faced Talia. "Thank you for clarifying."

Talia straightened, her eyebrows rising. "You didn't think... Oh, I really am sorry. How disconcerting to see a wild leopard coming out of the rosebushes when I'd said the garden was perfectly safe." She waved them toward the house. "Come in and let me get you a drink."

Pitbull shook his head. "No, thank you. We came

out to enjoy the stars and roses." He tightened his hold on Marly. "Unless you want to go in."

She shook her head. "No, I'd like to see those roses we came out to enjoy."

"Then don't let me and Mr. Wiggins keep you." Talia bent to the big cat. "You're so very naughty. Get in here." She held the door for Mr. Wiggins. Once his six-foot-long body passed through, she had to wait for the three feet of tail to clear before she could close the door.

Finally alone again, Marly glanced up at Pitbull and burst out laughing.

He chuckled slowly at first, then laughed louder along with her.

The sexually charged, tense mood of earlier had passed, along with the fear of being ripped apart by a wild beast.

Pitbull held out a hand. "Let's see those roses."

She placed her palm in his and they walked through the garden in companionable silence.

Marly found herself chuckling again.

"What's so funny?" Pitbull asked.

She shook her head. "I really thought Mr. Wiggins was going to have us for a snack."

"You and me both." Pitbull stopped in the archway of a rose-laden arbor. He pulled her into his arms, his hands resting at the small of her back. "I didn't want it to end that way between us."

"You and me both," she repeated and looked up into his eyes. "You were right, though." She cupped his cheek.

"I was?"

"Yes." She brushed a thumb across his lips. "Anything between us would never last."

"It really is too bad." He captured her hand in his and brought it to his lips. "I like the way you laugh."

Her breath caught as he pressed his lips to her fingertips. "And I like the way you kiss." She sighed. No use dragging it out any longer than they already had. "Well, I guess it's time to call it a night." She leaned up on her toes and pressed a kiss to his cheek. "Thank you for the walk in the garden."

Before he could stop her, she pulled free of his grip and hurried back to the house. In the back of her mind, Marly pictured her exit another way. She imagined Pitbull running after her, telling her that he couldn't let their passion end so abruptly and he wanted her to be a permanent part of his life.

But he didn't. She entered the house, wishing for something she knew would never happen. Her best course of action would be to steer clear of the SEAL, get her plane fixed and get on with her life.

Her cold, lonely life.

Alone.

Wow. She'd never thought of it that way before she met Pitbull. Now she couldn't think of it any other way.

PITBULL REMAINED IN the garden for a short time after Marly left. He'd been tempted to rush after her and beg her not to go to her room, but to come with him to his bungalow, where they could spend the night making passionate, meaningless love into the wee hours of the morning.

He had no doubt that despite her claim to be inexperienced, she'd be an ardent lover, eager to learn and try new things. Pitbull knew making love to Marly would only make him fall in love with the woman and possibly make her fall for him. And what would that get either of them? Heartache, loneliness and depression.

He had a job to do with the US Navy. He never knew where he'd be deployed next or when. Not only that, he was based out of Virginia, across a wide ocean from Africa. He couldn't ask Marly to give up her life on a different continent to be a navy wife, waiting in Virginia for her man to return. She wasn't the type of person who could sit around a house or apartment waiting. It would drive her crazy in the first week, much less the months he could be gone.

Add to the absences the likelihood of returning home in a body bag. A navy SEAL's job was all about danger. They went into enemy-infested places on some of the most dangerous missions. Coming back alive was never a guarantee.

And, hell, the woman was a pilot. She could die just as easily in a plane crash.

An image of his father placing flowers on his mother's grave passed through Pitbull's memories. No, he couldn't put himself through that kind of heartache, either.

He tipped his head toward the moon shining down on him. Why was he even thinking long-term about

Marly? He'd known her two weeks, tops, and only on the few flights she'd taken him on. Today, he'd gotten to know her on a more personal basis, and he liked her even more afterward. Especially the way her body fit against his. She wasn't short like most of the women he'd dated. She was tall and slender and kissed like nobody's business. If her reaction to his kiss was an example of her inexperience, he'd take an inexperienced woman any day! His lips still burned with the need to kiss her again.

What he wanted was more time with Marly. But that would be foolish. After this week, they'd go their separate ways. She'd fly her plane in the African bush, and he'd return to Djibouti or some other mission the navy saw fit to assign him to.

Thank goodness he and his team were going on safari tomorrow. He'd have all day with the heat and dust to drive Marly out of his mind. By the time they returned, he'd have his head on straight again. And then, with the distance, he'd get over her soon enough.

With that plan in mind, he returned to the house, stepping through the back door. He could hear his teammates laughing and talking loudly in the game room. He thought about joining them, but changed his mind and headed for the front entrance. He'd gone only three steps when Buck emerged from the game room, smiling and throwing a comment over his shoulder. "Told you we were unstoppable." He caught sight of Pitbull and hurried over to sling an arm over his shoulder. Buck's breath smelled of liquor.

"Booze good?" Pitbull asked.

"Had to drink to give the other team a handicap." Buck chuckled. "We still won."

"Headed to your bungalow?" Pitbull asked.

"That I am, buddy. That I am." He walked toward the front entrance, leaning heavily on Pitbull. "Marly came in from the garden by herself. You two break it off?"

Pitbull stiffened as he reached for the knob and pulled the heavy wooden door open. "Who said we had anything to break off?"

Buck stepped through the door and slammed a hand to Pitbull's chest. "Seriously, man. The game room windows overlook the garden. You two were sucking face like a couple of teenagers. Kinda hard to miss."

Great. Pitbull helped Buck keep his balance as they descended the steps to the ground. He'd be the target of every joke the next day. Forcing a nonchalance he didn't feel, he shrugged. "So?"

"When Marly came in by herself, we figured you blew it."

His lips twisting, Pitbull fought the urge to hit something. Namely his friend. "Thanks for your vote of confidence."

"No worries, buddy. I tried to give you a second chance to fix whatever you broke with her."

"How's that?"

"I invited her to join us on the safari tomorrow." Buck grinned as they came to a stop in front of his bungalow. "This is my stop. Thanks for walking me home. Do you want a kiss good-night for your trouble?" Buck winked.

"Hell, no." Pitbull shoved the man toward his door. "Go to bed and sleep the booze off. We have a long day ahead of us."

And an even longer night. Not only was he assured of dreaming about the woman, he'd have her with him and his team throughout the next day. There would be no escape or distance to allow him to get over Marly.

Thanks, Buck. Remind me to return the favor someday.

"About Marly." Buck hesitated at his door.

Pitbull tensed. "What about Marly?"

Buck's brows knitted. "She turned us down. It seems Ms. Marly would prefer to tinker with her plane than vacation with a bunch of mangy SEALs. Night, dude."

With a mixture of relief and disappointment, Pitbull entered his cabin, stripped and climbed into the comfortable bed. He lay for a long time with his arms crossed behind his head, staring up at the ceiling.

Thankful he wouldn't have to be with Marly the next day, he couldn't understand why he suddenly had the urge to cancel his spot on the safari. Staying back at the resort would defeat the purpose of getting Marly out of his head. He rolled over and punched the pillow. He could have had Marly in his bed. Instead, he was sleeping alone tonight. That is, if he actually got any sleep.

The warmth of her body lingered in every place it had touched his. And the more he thought about her, the harder he got.

Well, hell. So much for sleep.

Chapter Six

Marly originally hadn't planned to go on the safari with the SEAL team. She wanted to check on her plane and make sure the local poachers hadn't discovered it and looted everything they could pull, yank or drag from the wings, engine and interior. When she'd gone to Talia before heading to bed, she'd asked if she could borrow a vehicle.

The resort owner shook her head. "I just sent one of my guys into the nearest town for supplies. He took a truck. I have the one we'll be using tomorrow for the safari, and our other truck isn't working right now. It's with a mechanic. So that leaves us with one truck until the other one gets back late this afternoon."

Marly tried not to show her disappointment. "I see."

Talia's face brightened. "On the safari, we'll be going through the area where you hid your plane. You can ride along with us, and we'll make sure we stop to check on it."

Marly didn't want to intrude on the SEALs' safari, but she was worried about her plane. If joining their safari was the only way to get to her plane, she'd have to go.

She'd planned on spending her day away from Pitbull, hoping having him out of sight would get him out of her mind. Apparently, that wasn't to be an option. She resigned herself to being in Pitbull's company all day, and headed for bed.

Though the air-conditioner kept the house cool, Marly tossed and turned, throwing off the covers and then freezing. Hot, sultry dreams plagued her throughout the night, reminding her of what she'd brazenly offered the man—and what he'd so callously declined.

Marly hoped Pitbull was as sleepless as she was. It would serve him right for rejecting her offer.

Before dawn, she gave up on any pretense of sleep, crawled out of the comfort of the bed and dressed in her favorite pink bra, flight suit and boots. Thankfully, someone had laundered her only outfit, then returned it by before she'd gone to bed the previous evening. After performing her morning ablutions, she went in search of coffee.

Marly followed the scent of fresh bread and bacon to the kitchen on the first floor. She smiled as she passed Mr. Wiggins lounging like a regular house cat on the cool tile of the front foyer.

The kitchen was huge and equipped with everything a chef would want to add to a wish list. A man with a white chef's hat stood in the center manning two skillets, deftly scrambling eggs and frying bacon at the same time.

"Looking for coffee?" Talia entered the kitchen behind Marly. She wore her uniform-like khaki slacks tucked into leather riding boots and a khaki shirt with All Things Wild embroidered above the right breast pocket. She appeared well rested, her hair combed and her makeup minimal but evident.

Did she ever show up disheveled?

Marly swallowed her catty thoughts about the woman who'd welcomed her without question and offered to lend her clothing and toiletries for her stay. What little Marly owned was stashed in her one-bedroom apartment in Nairobi, Kenya. "I'd give my right arm for a cup."

Talia led her to the coffeemakers, poured a cup and handed it over. "I have some clothes you could borrow for the safari, if you like."

With her hands wrapped around the warm mug, Marly inhaled the fragrant brew and smiled. "Thanks, but I like my flight suit."

"Could get hot out there." Talia poured another cup and set the pot back on the burner.

"I'll manage. Thanks to one of your staff, the suit is clean."

Talia nodded. "It was the least I could do. The fact you landed that plane where you did was amazing."

Marly shrugged. "I've landed in worse spots. There's not always a landing strip where I go."

The other woman shook her head. "I don't know how you do it. I'm a nervous wreck when I fly."

"It's second nature to me. My father started me flying when I was barely tall enough to see out the windshield of his old plane. He flew people all over Africa when there weren't that many planes flying. I rode in the copilot's seat for many of his flights."

"Got more coffee where that came from?" Big Jake entered the kitchen, filling the space with his broad shoulders.

Soon the rest of the SEAL team were standing in the kitchen, waiting for Talia to pour enough coffee to give each one a mug.

Marly stood back, observing all of the men, but one in particular.

Pitbull. He had yet to make eye contact with her. But that was okay. She wasn't sure how she'd react when he did. She could quite possibly melt into the tile of the kitchen floor. Or she could keep herself together and pretend he meant nothing to her.

Talia waved her arm toward the door. "My chef has prepared a hearty breakfast for you. I'm sure he'd like to have his kitchen to himself to complete preparations. If you'd care to adjourn to the dining room, we can get this day underway."

The men shuffled into the dining room, joking and jostling as they went.

Marly was mildly disappointed and a little angry when it was Big Jake, not Pitbull, who held her chair for her. Pitbull had chosen a seat at the end of the table, opposite from her.

If that was the way he wanted it, so be it. Marly could easily have handled her own chair, but she smiled up at Big Jake and thanked him for helping her. He settled in the seat beside her and talked to her throughout the meal.

After the fluffy scrambled eggs and bacon were consumed, along with a hefty number of Danishes, Talia pushed back her chair and stood.

The men followed her lead and stood as one, coming to attention.

"The truck leaves in fifteen minutes," Talia said. "The earlier we get out there, the more we'll see."

"We'll be ready," Big Jake assured her.

She sent an inclusive smile toward Marly. "Oh, and Ms. Simpson will be joining us."

At Talia's announcement, Pitbull's gaze shot toward Marly. He didn't appear to be too pleased. Marly couldn't agree more. She really needed the distance from the man who turned her insides to mush. Still, his apparent shock disturbed her. She raised her brows and met his stare head-on. If he didn't want her to go, he could speak up.

After a long moment, he turned and walked away.

Marly considered that a win on her part. Not that she felt like she'd won anything of value, but she refused to back down from any challenge, real or perceived.

So he wasn't happy she was coming on the safari. Tough!

PITBULL HAD SPENT a rough night tossing and turning, his libido so jacked up he couldn't find relief from his urges or the heat of the savanna night. He'd finally fallen asleep in the wee hours of the morning, only for his alarm to go off a couple hours later. He'd looked forward to riding around, looking at the amazing animals Africa had to offer, free of the one person who had his insides knotted since that kiss the night before.

But no.

Marly was going with them.

Part of him was happy. The other part tightened like a rope in a tug-of-war contest between bulldozers. He'd be sure to ride in the back of the truck, away from Marly and temptation.

He'd hurried back to his bungalow for a hat and his weapon. When he returned, a guard had taken the driver's seat inside the crew cab of the two-ton truck and Talia sat in the passenger seat, holding a microphone in her hand. A canvas awning had been stretched over the wooden ribs, giving the people in the rear much-needed shade for when the sun beat relentlessly down on them later in the day.

Two guards, packing submachine guns, were seated in the back, near the tailgate. Marly sat forward near the cab.

"Wouldn't you be better off riding in the cab?" he asked her as he climbed up the tailgate, into the rear of the truck.

"I'm fine here," she responded.

T-Mac, Buck, Big Jake, Diesel and Harm climbed up behind Pitbull, forcing him closer, until his only choices were to sit across from Marly or beside her. Rather than touch her, he sat across, careful not to let their knees bump. As soon as the truck lumbered into gear, he knew he'd be fighting a losing battle.

Every pothole sent him sliding in his seat, his knees knocking into Marly's, sending all kinds of electrical currents racing across Pitbull's nerves. Good Lord, how was he going to survive the day without going stark-raving mad?

The first few times they connected, Marly's gaze shot up to his. Then just as quickly, she dropped her eyelids and hid her expression.

But he'd seen it. The recognition and response to their connection. Though she'd given him the cold shoulder this morning at breakfast, she couldn't hide the flare of fire in her eyes when they'd bumped knees. And based on her desire to further their relationship the night before, she had to be feeling something.

Talia's voice came over the intercom. "If you look to our left, you'll see a pride of lions lounging in the shade of that tree. We'll slow down to give you time to view."

The truck lumbered to a near standstill. Everyone in the back pivoted to stare at the trees. Pitbull's knees bumped Marly's once more, but she didn't seem to notice. Her attention remained focused on the shadows where a pride of tawny lions lay.

His teammates had their cell phones out and were snapping pictures. T-Mac had a high-resolution digital camera with a zoom lens, taking close-ups. Pitbull had decided, even before they left Djibouti, that he'd get copies of T-Mac's pictures. He'd take better quality images than anything Pitbull could. Since he wasn't trying to capture images of the lions, he was able to really see them and enjoy studying the antics of a couple of small cubs.

"You must be used to these glimpses of nature," Buck said to Marly.

"I'm familiar with them." She smiled. "I never get tired of seeing the variety of animals, and I never lose sight of the fact that they are wild."

"Oh, look ahead of us. There's a small herd of elephants," Talia said. The truck lurched forward and the people in the back held on to their seats.

Pitbull couldn't see what lay in front of the cab.

The truck rumbled across the terrain, hurrying to catch up with the pachyderms.

All of a sudden, the truck skidded to a stop.

"Everyone, please stay in the truck," Talia said, her voice tense over the speaker.

The two guards in the rear of the vehicle jumped down and ran to either side of the cab doors. Once they leaped up on the running boards, holding on with one hand and gripping their weapon in the other, the truck edged forward and stopped again. The engine grumbled and shut off.

For a moment, the silence was deafening after the loud rumble of the truck's diesel engine. But the silence didn't last long. The crack of gunfire sounded, followed by the desperate trumpeting of elephants.

All six of the SEALs leaned out of the sides of the truck, craning their necks to locate the source of the gunfire.

"We have poachers in the area," Talia said over the speaker. "Please remain seated. We'll get you back to the resort immediately."

"Wait!" T-Mac yelled. "We can't let them kill the elephants."

"Right. We have to do something," Big Jake agreed.

"I can't afford to have my guests die on my watch," Talia said, then directed the driver to turn the truck around.

As the vehicle slowed in the turn, the SEALs jumped out, two at a time.

The truck stopped and Talia dropped to the ground. "What are you doing? Get back in the truck."

"We can't let them kill those animals," Diesel said.

"You'll get yourselves killed trying to stop them." Talia shook her head. "Not only would that be bad for my business, but I kind of like you guys in one piece."

Big Jake pulled his handgun from beneath his loose shirt and checked the magazine. "We know how to take care of ourselves."

Talia stared from one man to the next. "Poachers play for keeps. If they get a chance, they'll kill you. And if they don't kill you, the elephants are stirred up. They might decide you're as much a threat as the poachers, and stampede. Please. Get back in the truck."

"No can do, ma'am," T-Mac said.

Big Jake held the passenger door for Talia. "Ma'am, you need to take the truck and Ms. Marly, and get far enough away that you don't get caught in the cross-fire." He nodded toward Pitbull. "Stay with them in case something happens and trouble heads your way. They need your protection. Get them to safety."

When Talia made no move to get back into the truck, Big Jake's hands circled her waist and he lifted her into the seat.

Talia glared. "I'm not going to talk you out of this, am I?"

"No, ma'am," Big Jake said. He tipped his chin toward Pitbull.

Pitbull wanted to be in on the action, and they needed to put a stop to the poaching, but he was just as concerned for the women.

"I want to go with you," Marly insisted. "I have a gun."

Her words settled it for Pitbull. "Yeah, but you're not going." As Big Jake had done with Talia, Pitbull lifted Marly into the back of the truck.

"At least take the guards with their machine guns," Talia offered.

Big Jake nodded. "If you promise to get the hell away from here."

Talia gave the two guards their orders and climbed into the truck. "Be careful. I don't want to have to explain to the US government why five of their finest were killed on a safari."

Pitbull glanced at Talia. "Do you need me to drive?"

"No, my driver is more familiar with the vehicle and terrain."

"Okay then. I've got your back." He climbed into the bed of the truck, his weapon drawn.

Marly tried to duck past him. "I want to help."

Blocking her exit, he refused to let her climb out.

She crossed her arms over her chest. "You're not the boss of me," she argued, trying to get around him. "I want to help the animals just as much as they do."

"You'd only slow them down. I'm betting you're much faster flying than running." His tone softened. "Look. I care about what happens to the elephants as much as you do, but think about it. You'd be a liability and take the team's focus off the goal."

The five SEALs and the two guards had already taken off through the grasslands, running toward the sounds of gunfire and elephants' screams.

Marly stared after them, her brow furrowed, her bottom lip caught between her teeth. "What about your team? They might get hurt."

"They can take care of themselves." At least, he hoped they could in the face of poachers and raging elephants. Pitbull wished he could be with them to make certain they all came out of it alive. Those men were his brothers.

Marly sat back on the bench and held on as the truck sped away from the scene. Her gaze shifted from the men running toward the problem and back to Pitbull. "You want to be out there, too."

He met her gaze. "You know it."

"But you're stuck babysitting me and Talia." She shook her head. "We're big girls. We can get back to the resort on our own."

"You don't know that. There's safety in numbers."

"Still, you would never forgive yourself if something happened to your teammates." Marly looked back toward the men as they disappeared over the horizon.

"We each have our job to do. Whatever happens out there happens." He nodded toward his team before turning back to her. "And what happens here, I'll take care of you."

The driver slammed on the brakes and the truck skidded to a stop, throwing Marly and Pitbull to their knees and sliding across the metal truck bed.

An elephant's trumpet sounded so close, it made Pitbull scramble to his feet.

Something hit the truck hard, rocking it on its wheels.

"Hold on!" Pitbull cried.

He dragged himself to his feet and peered through the slatted side panels at the same moment a huge gray behemoth rammed the side of the truck, knocking him backward. He hit the metal floor and slid toward Marly.

They were being attacked by a huge bull elephant. The truck lurched sideways, tipped up on the left wheels and slammed back on all six.

"We need to get out of here!" Pitbull yelled. Before the last word was out of his mouth, the elephant rammed the truck again, pushing so hard, the wheels left the ground, again. The entire vehicle teetered for a moment and then fell over on its side.

As if in slow motion, Pitbull tumbled, bounced off Marly and hit the wooden bench. Pain shot through his back and hip, and he cracked his head on something hard. Finally, he stopped, flat on his back, lying on the side rails of the truck bed with Marly sprawled across his chest, her face close to his. "Are you all right?" he asked.

She nodded, pressing her hands to his chest in an attempt to sit up.

The truck rocked again, but it wouldn't tip any more. This time when the elephant rammed it, the vehicle slid sideways across the ground.

Marly clung to Pitbull, and he held her tightly to him as the attack progressed.

After several more attempts to crush the truck, the elephant trumpeted and moved on toward the other elephants in the distance.

When the beast was gone, Pitbull looked up at Marly. Her lips were close enough, all he had to do was lean up and…

He claimed her mouth, thrusting his tongue between her teeth in a raw and savage kiss.

Marly's tongue met his in fierce response. For a brief moment they lay still, exploring each other's mouths until they were forced apart by the need to breathe.

Marly laughed. "I thought we were goners."

"You? I was staring the big guy in the eye when he hit the side of the truck."

Marly planted her hands on his chest. "We need to check on Talia and her driver."

As much as he'd rather kiss her again, Pitbull had to get out of the truck bed and make sure the others were okay.

Marly crawled out backward, inching beneath the collapsed side panels and awning. When she was clear of the debris, she held back the canvas and some broken slats for Pitbull's exit.

As soon as he could, Pitbull rose to his feet, shook off the pain and stiffness and ran for the cab. "Talia?"

"We're in the cab," she said. "I'm okay, but the driver is hurt."

Pitbull climbed up on the passenger side of the vehicle, braced his feet on the side panel and opened the door.

Talia stared up at him, her hair disheveled, a red-and-purple bruise appearing on her right cheekbone.

"Give me your hand," Pitbull commanded.

Talia reached up, clasped his hand and let him pull her out of the cab of the truck and lower her to the ground.

Marly was there to steady her as her feet touched down.

Talia turned to face the overturned truck. "What about Henry, the driver?" She stepped away from Marly's hold and rested her hand on the downed vehicle. "Can you get him out on your own?"

Pitbull glanced down at the man still lodged behind the steering wheel. "Henry?"

The driver blinked and moaned. He seemed to be coming out of unconsciousness. He looked up at Pitbull. "What happened?"

"An elephant tipped the truck," Pitbull answered. "Do you think you can come out with a little help?"

Henry glanced at his surroundings and tried to get up. "I can't move."

"Try unbuckling your seat belt," Pitbull urged.

The driver hit the buckle and released the belt, causing him to slip farther down. He grabbed the edge of his seat, dragging himself up and over the gearshift. Once he had his feet beneath himself, he reached out for Pitbull's hand. Between Pitbull pulling and Henry climbing onto the sides of the seat, they got him out of the truck and down to the ground.

Talia hugged the man, tears trickling from her eyes. "For a while there, I thought you were dead."

"I'm all right, ma'am. Just sore." He touched his fingers to the dark skin of his forehead and winced. A lump had started to form and was quickly growing to the size of a guinea egg. "The question is how we're going to get this truck back up on its wheels." He dropped his hands to his sides and studied the problem.

Marly stood near the end of the truck, her gaze following the direction the bull elephant had gone. "I hope that elephant doesn't decide to trample the men."

The trumpeting ceased and the savanna quieted.

"Hopefully, that's a good sign. Now all we have to do is wait for the guys to make it back to us."

Pitbull wanted to go and see what had happened to the elephants and his teammates. But to do so would leave Talia, Marly and Henry without any protection. Another elephant attack, and they'd all be dead.

Chapter Seven

Marly knew exactly how Pitbull felt. Every glance he shot in the direction his teammates had gone only made her regret tying him down even more. "I'd feel better if you went after your team."

"Yeah, me, too," Talia agreed.

Pitbull shook his head. "No, we have to figure out how to get back to the resort."

"We can walk. It's about eight miles," Talia said. "The radio inside the truck wasn't working. It could be as simple as a loose connection." She gave Pitbull a weak smile. "If I can get back inside the truck, I'll see what I can do."

"Let me," Marly said. "I'm pretty good with stuff like that. I'm always tinkering with my plane, the radio and electronics."

Again Pitbull glanced in the direction his friends had gone. "T-Mac's the technical guy. He'd have it working using bubblegum and a twist-tie."

Marly studied the overturned truck, searching for a way to climb up into it.

"You really think you can get it working?" Talia asked.

Marly shrugged. "I won't know until I get a look at it."

Talia cupped her hands. "Let me give you a boost."

"Please." Pitbull gripped Talia's arms and set her aside. "Let me." He cupped his hands and bent over.

Marly rested a hand on his shoulder, stepped into his palms and let him raise her up to where she could sit on the side of the truck. "Do you have any tools stashed somewhere inside?"

"Usually behind the passenger seat, but they could be anywhere in the truck now. I'm sure they got thrown around, as well."

"I'll find it." Marly pushed the passenger seat forward and peered down into the cab. "I think I see it."

She slipped over the edge, braced her feet on the back of the seat and then inched her way into the cab, wedging herself behind the passenger seat and the driver's seat until she could feel the tool bag with the tip of her foot. But she couldn't reach it with her hands. She didn't have room to turn or bend to pull it up.

Once she was sandwiched between the back wall and the seats, she couldn't get herself back out. Marly grabbed on to whatever she could, but she didn't have the arm strength to pull herself up and out. "Great." Looked like she'd have to do just what she didn't want to—ask for help from the man who made her crazy.

Again, she grabbed onto the passenger seat and strained her arms, moving her body mere inches. But if she continued moving inches, she would eventually get out.

A shadow blocked the light from the sun. Marly looked up.

"Need a hand?" Pitbull's voice was both welcome and annoying at the same time.

They couldn't stay out there all day waiting for her to figure out how to get out of a tight situation. She needed to fix the radio and make that call for help. What if the men going after the poachers needed medical attention?

Marly swallowed her pride and nodded. "Yes."

Pitbull reached a hand into the cab. Marly placed her fingers in his.

The warmth and strength reassured her she was doing the right thing. Awareness ricocheted through her body, making it hard for her to breathe normally. The man was sexy, he smelled good and he was oh, so strong.

He pulled her up to sit on the side of the cab.

"I found the bag, but I couldn't bend to reach it." She glanced back down in the vehicle. "I'll have to go in headfirst."

"Let me."

She shook her head. "No, your shoulders are too broad."

"Then let me hold on to you on your way down and back."

"That should work. I just don't want to get stuck standing on my head."

He chuckled and motioned for her to go back into the truck.

Marly more or less dove in. Slowly, of course, but headfirst, walking her way down the backs of the seats on her hands.

Pitbull gripped her hips as she went, and then moved his hands to her thighs and finally to her knees before she reached the opposite door of the cab.

Breathing had become a luxury with Pitbull's hands all over her legs and her blood rushing to her head. As she grabbed the handle of the tool bag, all she could think about was what those hands would feel like against her bare skin. "I'm ready," she croaked as more blood rushed to her head, scrambling what few brain cells hadn't been singed by her lusty thoughts.

Backing out the way she'd gone in was a little more difficult, with the weight of the tools and only one hand to work with.

Pitbull didn't seem affected by any of that. Before she knew it, he was doing all the work and had her out of the cab and sitting on the side before she could tell him she could do the rest herself.

Her cheeks heated and she reached out to steady herself, her hand coming into contact with Pitbull's muscular thigh. If she thought she was struggling to breathe before, she was bordering on hyperventilating now. "Uh, thanks." Marly ducked her head, afraid she'd give herself away if she looked into Pitbull's eyes.

She set the tool bag on the side of the truck and

shifted the passenger seat back into position. Then she dropped down inside the truck and stood on the opposite door. The radio dangled from its mount, the wires hanging loose. "I'll need a Phillips screwdriver and a pair of needle-nose pliers."

For the next few minutes, Marly worked on the radio, with Pitbull handing her the tools she requested.

Once she had the wires reconnected, she turned on the radio and tested the mic. The reassuring sound of static filled the interior of the cab.

Within minutes, they had notified the nearby park service, who had a truck and winch. They would be at their location within the next hour.

With Pitbull's help, Marly climbed out of the truck and dropped to the ground.

"Here they come!" Talia announced, her eyes narrowing. "One, two, three, four, five, six…seven!" She beamed. "They're all coming back, and from the look of them, in one piece." She sucked in a deep breath and let it out in a long, heartfelt sigh. "Thank God."

Minutes later, Marly, Pitbull, Talia and Henry were surrounded by the others, everyone talking at once. But before they could tell their stories, the park truck showed up and they all put their backs into getting the two-ton truck back on its wheels. Between the winch, the other truck and all of their efforts, they lifted the truck upright. Talia climbed into the cab and the engine started on the second try.

A cheer went up from all standing around. Harm and Big Jake bent a couple of fenders back into place to keep them from rubbing on the tires. Everyone else worked to strip away the canvas awning and the broken slats. Soon they were on their way back to the resort, the sun angling toward the horizon.

Marly sat beside Pitbull in the back of the truck. She couldn't think past the fact that their thighs were touching.

Every bump made her slam against him until he slipped his arm around her shoulders and they swayed together. After he did that, she didn't notice the heat of the day, the dust swirling around their heads, kicked up by the truck tires, or every bump seeming to chip away at her tailbone on the hard, wooden bench.

Though they all wanted to know what had happened, they agreed to go back to the ranch and get Henry cared for before they shared their stories. Shouting over the diesel engine would have made them hoarse by the time they rolled into the resort compound.

As it was, they searched the landscape for rogue elephants or poachers, on their guard for any other threat. By the time they stopped in front of the resort, they were hot, tired and covered in a layer of dust.

Marly almost wished they hadn't stopped. Having Pitbull's arm around her the entire way had been nice. She wondered if he'd want to hold her again, after they'd had a chance to clean up. Her pulse quickened in anticipation.

ANOTHER VEHICLE WAS parked in the parking area in front of the main house. Diesel and Big Jake helped Henry to the house.

As they neared the door, it opened and a young, handsome man stepped out.

Talia smiled. "Dr. Thompson. Thank you for coming. We had a run-in with a bull elephant and I'm afraid Henry took the brunt of it."

"That's why I'm here." He stepped to the side, allowing the men helping Henry to pass through the entrance. "Bring him into the living area."

"I am quite all right," Henry insisted.

"You might be," Talia said, "but let the doctor check that bump on your head and anywhere else you might be hurting." She turned to the others. "Anyone else injured? Dr. Thompson can take a look."

None of the men took her up on the offer.

"We'll just get cleaned up," Harm said.

"The chef will have dinner ready in—" Talia glanced at the clock on the wall "—oh, dear. In fifteen minutes. Just come when you're ready. No hurry."

Big Jake reappeared in the doorway and winked. "We're SEALs, ma'am. We're never late for chow."

Talia smiled. "Well then, I'll see you in fifteen minutes."

Big Jake left for his bungalow, followed by the others.

Pitbull slowed as he passed Marly. "You should let the doctor check you over."

Although it was nice that he was looking out for her, Marly didn't feel the need to see the doctor. "Other than a few scratches and bruises, I'm fine." She raised her eyebrows. "What about you?"

He pressed a hand to his ribs. "Like you, just a few bruises. I've had worse."

They stood for a moment in silence. The closeness they'd shared on the trip back to the resort seemed to be slipping away, and Marly didn't know what to do to hold on to it. "I'll see you in fifteen."

"I'm sure Talia wouldn't expect you to be ready that quickly."

Marly's lips thinned. "I can be ready in five."

Pitbull held up his hands. "Sorry. I didn't mean to imply that you were slow." He bent to press his lips to her cheek. "You're an amazing woman, Marly Simpson." Then he left her standing there and hurried toward his bungalow.

Marly touched a hand to her cheek and watched until Pitbull disappeared around the corner of the house. She couldn't make heads or tails of that man. One minute he was pushing her away, the next he was kissing her.

Hell. She didn't know where this was going or how it would end, but she did know she wanted more.

PITBULL FELT LIKE his entire body had been tossed around in a rock tumbler. Every muscle ached and he knew he'd be covered in bruises, but he didn't care. He wanted only to shower, change into his fancy clothes and get back to Marly. Damn. When had he become obsessed with the woman?

Oh, yeah. Somewhere between crash-landing her airplane and being rolled by an angry bull elephant.

After a quick shower and a once-over of his body,

he shrugged and dragged on his clothes. Bruises to his body he could live with. What about his heart, though? He'd never found a woman he'd even considered falling in love with. What if she got cancer and died, like his mother? Or was hit by a train, or crashed in an airplane?

And then there was his job. He'd be deployed, and she'd get lonely and leave him while he was gone. That's what happened to so many of the SEALs he'd known. Nothing like getting a Dear John letter, or worse, divorce papers served while away at war. Why risk his heart, only to have it broken?

Yeah, he'd be smart to keep this light. Just a fling. No commitment and no strings attached. As long as Marly understood that, why shouldn't they spend the rest of the week in each other's beds? Assuming her offer of the night before remained open.

He dressed in his shirt and trousers and pulled on his boots. After briefly finger-combing his hair, he slung his tie around his neck and left the bungalow. Ten minutes had passed when he found himself half walking, half jogging back to the main house.

"Where's the fire?" Buck called out from the doorway of his bungalow. "Hold up. I'll walk with you."

Pitbull stopped and waited for his friend, a little frustrated at how slowly the man was walking. But he told himself Marly couldn't have gotten through her shower as fast. Women had to blow-dry their hair and shave their legs or something. She wouldn't be ready as quickly as him. No way.

"I heard Talia say you guys had some trouble with a bull elephant," Buck said as he joined Pitbull.

"I'd rather tell the story once when we're all at the dinner table. Same with you. I want to know what happened with the poachers."

"Well then, what should we talk about while we're waiting for everyone else?"

"Who said we have to talk?" Pitbull's concentration centered on getting to the house—and Marly.

"What's with you and our Marly girl?" Buck shot him a sideways grin. "And don't play dumb with me. You had your arm around her the whole way back to the resort. Are you two a thing?"

Pitbull wasn't ready to talk about Marly or what he was feeling toward her. Not yet. He didn't even know where it was going. "We're not a thing."

Buck nodded, his lips twisting as he walked beside Pitbull. "I hear Talia is planning on having music after dinner. There might be dancing. I think I'll ask Marly to dance with me." He tipped his head toward Pitbull and raised his eyebrows. "Since you're not a thing, I figure she's fair game."

Pitbull's hands balled into fists. After the day he'd had, he was one breath short of slugging his friend. Instead he forced a shrug. "You can ask her." Hopefully, she'd spit in his face and turn him down flat.

"You know, she's not a beautiful woman, not in the classical sense. Not like Talia," Buck said. "But she's feisty and tall. Until she wore that dress last night, I didn't realize just how long her legs were."

Pitbull rounded on his friend and jabbed him in

the chest. "You hurt Marly and you'll have me to answer to. Do you understand?"

Buck held up his hands as if in surrender and chuckled. "Just poking the bear. I figured you had a thing going with Marly, but I wasn't sure you knew it yet." He nodded. "You know it now, don't you?"

His breathing came in ragged huffs, anger simmering so close to the surface, Pitbull could erupt at any moment. "Don't push me, Buck. Marly's a good woman. She deserves to be treated with respect."

"And you're just the man to do that, right?" Buck grinned.

Pitbull wanted to knock the man's teeth out, and danged if he knew why. This was his *friend*.

"Hey, what's going on out here?" Big Jake's voice carried to them from the front entrance to the house. "Do I need to break you two up and send you to separate corners?"

Buck waved at Big Jake. "No. We're good. Just getting a few things straight. Aren't we?"

Still caught up in his anger, Pitbull fought to calm the fire burning inside. He nodded and turned toward the house, falling in step beside Buck. "We're good."

"Oh, and Big Jake?" Buck said as they climbed the steps to the front door. "Just to set the record straight, our man Pitbull doesn't have a thing for our pilot, Marly, but he doesn't want anyone else to dance with her. Got it?" Buck tapped Big Jake's chest and ducked past him before Pitbull could take a swing.

Big Jake frowned. "Is that so? You and Marly?"

He grinned. "Doesn't surprise me in the least. I knew it all along." Big Jake held open the door.

"What do you mean, you knew it all along?" Pitbull passed through.

"Seriously?" Big Jake shook his head. "You two are all googly-eyed with each other. It would take a moron to miss it."

"Googly-eyed?" Pitbull stared at the big guy. "Since when do you say things like *googly-eyed*? What's happening to my teammates?"

"Yeah, and you're trying to change the subject." Big Jake chuckled. "I'll let it go. But you should know the rest of us aren't blind. We saw you two kissing in the garden last night."

Great. His entire team thought he and Marly had something going on. Well, at least that might keep them from making moves on the pretty pilot until they left the resort.

Why he cared…

Reason kicked in. So many of the SEALs he knew who'd dared to have a relationship with a woman ended up dumped after the first deployment. One guy he'd known had quit the team when his wife demanded that he be home more often. Then she'd dumped him for an accountant. He'd been heartbroken on top of giving up a job he'd loved.

As he entered the house, his gaze whipped to the top of the staircase Marly had descended the night before. She wasn't there. Good. That gave him time to get his act together so that he didn't make a complete idiot of himself.

One by one, the men assembled in the open living area. Talia stepped into the room wearing a black-and-white gown in a bold geometric pattern with black spike heels. She had smoothed back her hair and pulled it up into a modern design that exposed the long line of her neck and her high cheekbones. The petite woman was pretty enough to be in a fashion magazine. But she wasn't Marly.

Talia swept her arm to the side. "We can head for the dining room. Marly will be joining us momentarily."

The SEAL team followed Talia into the entryway and toward the dining room.

Pitbull lagged behind, his gaze going to the top of the stairs again. And there she was.

Marly's gaze connected with his and she lifted her chin.

Pitbull swallowed hard.

The gown she wore was a magnificent, vivid red. The neckline dipped low in a V between her breasts, and a slit ran all the way up, almost to the top of her thigh. Her long, slender leg peeked out from between the folds of the red fabric to showcase a silver high-heeled sandal.

"Holy hell, Marly," Pitbull said, his voice choked with desire.

Her cheeks flushed a pretty red that complimented the gown. "I know. It's too much, right?" She turned and started to walk back to her room.

"No, it's not." Pitbull found himself walking up the stairs. "You just look…" He fought for words that could accurately describe what he was seeing. "Stunning."

The red in her face deepened. "You think so?"

"I say what I mean." He walked the rest of the way to the top of the stairs and held out his arm. "May I escort you to the dining room?"

She smiled. "Thank you. I wasn't quite sure I'd make it down the stairs in these shoes." Marly chuckled softly. "I think Talia likes to dress me."

"She knows what suits you."

"I never was one to wear dresses." Marly gathered the skirt in her free hand and started down the wide staircase at Pitbull's side. "But I think I could get used to it. I've never felt more feminine."

They'd reached the bottom and stepped out across the foyer to the dining room.

Pitbull leaned close. "I still like you better in your flight suit," he said, and meant it.

The men stood around the table, waiting for the last members of their party to join them.

Buck was the first to see Marly. This time he didn't whistle. His mouth dropped open and he simply stared. "Wow."

"He said it." Harm shook his head. "Wow."

"Wow." Big Jake cupped the side of his cheek. "What happened to the badass pilot in the jumpsuit who landed a crippled plane in a field full of wild animals?"

Marly turned away. "I'm going to change."

"No, no. Marly, stay." Talia hurried forward and gripped her arm. "You look absolutely fabulous. I never made that dress look like that. For one, I tripped over the skirt. It was too long. And two, it needed a longer, leaner body to do it justice."

"Darling, you do it justice," Buck said.

Pitbull glared at the man.

Buck grinned. "All bets off tonight, dude. I'm dancing with the lady in red."

"Me, too," Harm said.

"Count me in," Big Jake added. "We can't let a dress like that go to waste."

"Watch out, guys," Buck warned. "Pitbull might take offense to everyone stealing his girl."

Marly shot a quick glance at Pitbull. "What are they talking about?"

Pitbull clenched his fists and held his temper, trying to appear calm when he wanted to land a fist in the face of every man in the room. "We should be seated before the chef decides we aren't interested in the meal he's prepared." He held the chair for Marly, while glaring around the room at any man who dared to sit to her left.

The others took the hint and left the seat beside Marly open. Pitbull took his seat next to her and counted the minutes until they could quit the dining room and go back to the garden to stare at the moon and make out.

"Now that we're all in the same room and we don't have a diesel engine roaring in our ears, could you tell us what happened with the poachers?" Marly said, starting the conversation.

Pitbull liked that she didn't wait long, but jumped in, demanding the story.

"Sure." Diesel popped his napkin out straight and settled it in his lap. "By the time we got to where the poachers were, the elephants had pretty much handled the situation. Apparently the poachers were trying to kill a female with long ivory tusks and snag her baby. They had a truck with a trailer."

Big Jake picked up the story. "They had shot the cow several times."

Marly gasped and reached for Pitbull's hand beneath the table.

"But they didn't use an elephant gun. The bullets were too small and hit the wrong areas to kill her."

"But they shot her?" Marly asked.

"Yes," Harm said. "Which only managed to make her mad. She was calling all of her buddies to come help."

"We circled wide, seeing as the herd had converged on the poachers and their vehicles. They were stomping the crap out of them."

"Like what the bull elephant tried to do to us," Pitbull muttered.

"Yeah." Buck grinned. "I'd like to hear that story."

"Next." Pitbull waved his hand. "Continue."

"The poachers were aiming out the windows of their vehicles and firing randomly, hoping to scare off the elephants," T-Mac picked up. "We couldn't let them hurt another animal, so we moved in as close as we could get without letting the elephants see us.

We figured they'd think we were with the poachers and attack us, too."

"Like T-Mac said, we moved closer," Big Jake said. "We fired at the poachers. They were so shocked by our presence they spun out and drove off."

Buck grinned. "We followed them a little way on foot to see which way they were going."

Talia set her fork on the table beside her plate. "Which way was that?"

"South. Due south," Diesel said. "As fast as they could go. When we turned around to come back, the herd of elephants were in the way, and they were twitchy."

"By then, the big bull had joined them and stirred the womenfolk up again," Buck said. "They didn't seem to want to settle down."

"Bottom line, we had to swing really wide to stay out of their sight and out of charging distance." Big Jake grinned. "I don't know what you did to that bull, but he was madder than hell."

"Yeah." Buck stared across the table at Pitbull and Marly. "What did you do to make him so mad?"

Marly laughed. "We crossed his path."

"No, really. Did you poke him?" Buck asked. "Or did you tweak his nose hairs? Because that dude came lumbering in, trumpeting as loud as a trombone player on steroids."

"Then we came back and found you had tipped the truck over," Buck said, laughing. "How?"

"Well, for one, *we* didn't tip it over," Pitbull said. "That bull elephant must have heard the distress calls of his female harem, because he came running, determined to shut down anything that might scare or harm his girls."

"To keep his women safe, he displayed his powerful alpha male side and tipped the truck over?" Buck pressed a hand to his chest. "A guy after my own heart."

Pitbull laughed. "Sadly, that's exactly how it happened."

"Holy hell, Pitbull," Diesel said. "An elephant did that?"

"Yes," Pitbull said.

Talia drummed her fingernails on the table. "Did you see the faces of the men who tried to kill the cow?"

"We did better than that," Harm said. "Show them, T-Mac."

T-Mac took his cell phone from his shirt pocket, opened the device and displayed an image of a lot of grass. He enlarged the image and pointed at the middle. "I got a pretty clear shot of two of the guys before they scrambled for their truck." T-Mac pulled his cell phone out of his pocket and zoomed in on the faces of the two men. They wore black clothing.

"They dress like the guys who kidnapped Diesel's girl and hid her in the jungle along the Congo."

"Let me see the picture." Diesel grabbed for the phone and frowned down at the men. "Hell, they could also be the guys I chased off from trying to kill the gorillas we ran into along the Congo. At least, I thought they were trying to kill the gorillas. I wonder if they were trying to steal the babies, killing the mamas in the process." He shook his head. "It all happened so fast and I was just trying to keep them from massacring the entire group."

"Whoever they are, they can't keep savaging the animals," Talia said. "Not only does the All Things Wild Safari & Resort rely on the safaris to keep it open, the animals need to have a safe place to be what they are—wild." She sat back in her chair. "I reported the attack to the game warden. Hopefully they can chase down the culprits and put an end to the killing and stealing." Talia pushed back from the table and stood. "In the meantime, we need something to cheer us up. We've all had a helluva day." She walked to the doorway. "If you'll follow me to the parlor, I've had the staff roll up the carpet so that we can dance."

Big Jake cleared his throat. "In case you haven't noticed, there are only two women and six men."

Talia smiled. "I know. We women will take turns dancing with anyone who wants to dance." She grinned broadly at Marly. "Right?"

Marly started to stand. "I'm not much of a dancer, but I'm game. Besides, I've already been told this dress needs to dance."

Pitbull leaped to his feet and held her chair as she rose.

When Marly stepped around the chair, Buck was there with his arm held out.

Pitbull puffed out his chest and gritted his teeth.

Buck only grinned, hooked Marly's hand in his elbow and marched out of the dining room.

"Jerk," Pitbull muttered.

Big Jake clapped a hand on Pitbull's back. "You're not giving up that easily, are you?"

Pitbull unbuttoned his sleeves, shoved them up his arms and then stalked after Buck and Marly. The man knew better, but had still stolen Pitbull's girl out from under his nose.

Harm, Big Jake, T-Mac and Diesel followed Pitbull, laughing behind him. He figured they would all torment him by dancing with Marly. Well, he'd show them.

Music wafted through the first story of the big house in a lilting country and western waltz Pitbull recognized.

Buck and Marly were already whirling around the floor, Buck holding Marly far closer than Pitbull could stand.

Clamping his lips tight, Pitbull marched across the bare wooden floor and straight to Talia.

She turned from the stereo system where she'd selected the music and smiled. "May I help you, Percy?"

"Yes, ma'am. You could honor me with a dance." He held out his hand.

"Why, thank you. I'd love to." Talia took his hand and walked to the center of the room.

Not only had Pitbull's mother taught him how to knot a tie, she'd insisted he learn how to dance, teaching him the waltz and the two-step. She figured if he could do those two dances, he would be a keeper for any woman. His mother had loved to dance. Though he tried to give the appearance of being one tough guy, Pitbull had to admit, he'd gotten his love of music and dancing from his mother. He was just careful to never let on about it to the members of his team.

He swept Talia into a spin and danced her over to where Buck and Marly were waltzing to the music. Deftly, he spun Talia out, took Marly's hand and pulled her away from Buck and into his arms, landing Talia in Buck's embrace.

"Hey, she was my partner." Buck frowned. Then he smiled down at his new dance partner. "Well, hello, beautiful."

Talia laughed and danced away with Buck.

Pitbull pulled Marly into his arms. She felt right there. He refused to think past that. He wasn't in the market for a relationship, but he sure as hell didn't want one of his buddies to stake a claim on this woman. He'd sort out his feelings and courses of action later. For now, he just wanted to hold her in his arms.

Chapter Eight

Marly relaxed and leaned into Pitbull, her body seeming to fit against his like it belonged. "That wasn't very chivalrous of you."

He growled. "Buck only danced with you to poke at me."

Marly laughed softly. "Well, thanks. You know how to make a girl feel desirable."

Pitbull's face burned. "Not that you aren't beautiful. Because you are. Hell, you're too beautiful to be dancing with a crusty old SEAL in the middle of nowhere."

"You? Old?" She laughed. "What are you, twenty-nine?"

"Thirty."

"Two whole years older than me." She shook her head. "You'll be getting dentures and a cane before you know it."

He spun her out and back against his chest. "You know what I mean."

"No, actually, I don't, nor do I want to." She leaned her cheek against his chest. "But you smell nice."

"Woman, you're killing me."

"Mmm?" She slipped her hand across his chest. "What a way to die."

He grabbed her wandering hand and held it pressed against his heart. "What am I going to do with you?"

"I told you last night, but you weren't paying attention." She squeezed his hand. "I promise, no commitment, no strings attached. Just you and me, all night long." What did it hurt to put it out there again? She refused to beg, but he wasn't indifferent to her. The ridge of his trousers, pressing into her belly, was proof.

She swayed her hips and pelvis, sliding across his arousal. Yeah, he was fully aware of her, and wanted what she wanted. Then what the hell was the holdup?

Her blood ran cold as a thought crossed her mind. She straightened and blinked up at him. "You're not married, are you?"

Pitbull laughed out loud. "Really? You're asking now?"

"That wasn't an answer." She stepped away from him, her heart sinking into the pit of her belly. "Oh, my God, you're married."

He shook his head. "No, I'm not."

Her eyebrows knit. "Then what's holding you back from taking me up on the offer?"

"Nothing." Pitbull pulled her back into his arms. "Something stupid like the desire to protect you from heartache."

"How noble." She traced a finger around one of

the buttons on his shirt. "Nobility can be very boring. I thought you were a risk-taker."

"I am," he said. "When it involves bad guys holding guns, I'll all over that. But please don't make me break a woman's heart."

"How do you know you'll break my heart?" She tipped her head upward and stared at him in challenge.

He kissed the tip of her nose. "Okay, maybe it's *my* heart I'm afraid I'll break."

She smiled, her eyes bright in the light from the chandeliers above. "Now you're pulling my leg. You SEALs are all over the world. How many women do you have waiting back home for you? One? Two? Maybe three?" She snorted. "Break your heart, my big toe."

"I don't have a woman waiting for me anywhere. Up until now, I've kept my distance, never dated anyone more than once or twice before I broke it off and made it perfectly clear I wasn't into commitment. I love my job, but the life of a SEAL isn't conducive to relationships." His hand tightened around her waist.

"You're thinking too hard on this." Again Marly laid her cheek against his chest. "Sometimes you just have to go with your gut."

He slowed, his feet barely moving to the music. The song ended and he continued to sway.

"The music stopped," Marla whispered.

"Did it?"

"Mmm." She pressed closer, not wanting the night to end.

The next song was a lively country and western two-step.

T-Mac stepped up to Marly and Pitbull.

Pitbull shook his head. "Sorry, her dance card is full." He hooked Marly's elbow and led her toward the exit. Instead of walking out to the garden as they'd done the night before, he guided her past Mr. Wiggins in the foyer to the front door and out into the moonlight.

Marly's heartbeat quickened. What did this mean? Holy hell, was he going to…? Were they going to…? Would he think less of her when he discovered she wasn't wearing underwear?

At the bottom of the stairs, he stopped and took her hands.

She curled her fingers around his, squeezing hard, a little afraid of what came next but more afraid he'd change his mind.

"Relax." He bent to kiss her forehead. "We won't do anything you don't want. Right now, I just want to walk with you in the moonlight, away from the crowd."

"The guys will be down to one female to dance with," she said, her voice shaking and breathy. God, she was a neophyte at seduction.

"Well, Talia seems to be right at home dancing the night away."

Marly nodded and swept her tongue across her suddenly dry lips. "What's next?"

He laughed and slipped an arm around her waist. "We walk."

She let him guide her down the path past the bungalows. Once they were out of range of the lights from the buildings, the moon lit up the sky, the stars spreading out like so many diamonds on a bed of black velvet.

"This is what I love about the wildest parts of Africa," Marly said.

"What's that?"

"You can see the stars. There's not as much light pollution like in the big cities. I could fly for miles and miles and see nothing but stars."

"Do you ever get disoriented?"

She laughed. "No. I have my instrument gauges to keep me straight."

"Unless the engine cuts off the power?"

"I'm trained for all the possible scenarios." She tilted her head and glanced up at him. "Still not convinced it's safer in a plane than a helicopter?"

He shrugged. "I imagine I could get used to it, given enough time in fixed-wing aircraft."

"You'll have to come up with me again."

"I will, on our trip back to Djibouti."

She sighed.

"Why the big sigh?"

"Just thinking about Djibouti." She leaned against him. "Our time together is limited to just a handful of days. Less, if I get my plane up in the air sooner."

"What are you trying to say?"

"When my part is in, I'll be gone."

"You'll be back for the return flight, though."

"Yes, but once you're back in Djibouti, you won't need my services anymore."

"That's sad." He took her hand and brought it to his lips. "You see, in the couple days we've been together, I've learned a lot about you. Most of which I like."

"You do?" She stared up into his eyes, lit by moonlight. "Like what?"

"I like the way the moonlight makes your hair turn silvery blue." He brushed a strand behind her ear. "I like the way you wet your lips when you're nervous." Pitbull bent to press his mouth to hers in a soft butterfly kiss. "And I like you best when you have a smudge of grease on your cheek." He touched a finger to her lips when she opened her mouth to protest. "Don't get me wrong. You took my breath away tonight in that red dress. I'm sure I had to pick up my jaw off the floor at the sight of your leg peeking out from that dangerous slit." He pulled her into his arms and crushed her to him, the evidence of his desire nudging her belly again.

"Dangerous?" She touched his chest, her fingers curling into his shirt, her heart racing at his words.

"Or the scandalously low cut of your neckline." He traced the fabric, brushing his finger all the way down the V. "Babe, you had me so hot and bothered, I could barely swallow that delicious dinner."

"Have you thought maybe…maybe we should just go with it and get each other out of our systems?" She darted a glance up at his face.

"More often than you can imagine." He cupped

her face and tilted her chin upward. "I can't get you off my mind."

She leaned up on her toes and pressed her lips to his. "What are we waiting for?"

He laughed out loud and hugged her close. Then he set her to arm's length. "Care to go to my cabin for a drink?"

"I thought you'd never ask."

He took her hand and started toward one of the bungalows, walking at first, then getting faster with each step. By the time they reached Pitbull's bungalow, they were running and laughing.

Pitbull pushed the door open, swept Marly up into his arms and carried her across the threshold.

She tried not to read too much into the gesture. He was caught up in the moment, trying to get her into his bed before she changed her mind.

Like that would happen.

Once inside, Pitbull kicked the door shut behind him. Instead of setting her on her feet, he carried her past the little sitting room into the bedroom.

A huge king-size bed took up the center of one wall with mosquito netting draped from the ceiling to all four corners. It made the bed even more intimate and inviting.

When Pitbull finally stopped at the foot of the massive bed, he lowered her legs and let her slide down his front, his arms tight around her waist.

Marly wrapped her arms around his neck and held on. Now that they were where she wanted him, all of her insecurities rose up to paralyze her. What did she do? Should she strip out of her clothes? Take his clothes off him? She knew she wanted to be naked as soon as possible. But would Pitbull think she was too forward and needy?

She stood back and lifted her chin. "Look. I can fly a plane and land it just about anywhere. But I could use a crash course in what I think we're about to do, before I can fly on my own."

Pitbull's brow wrinkled. "Crash course?" Then his frown cleared. "Sweetheart, go with your gut. There's no instruction booklet that comes with making love."

"No? What about the *Kama Sutra*?"

With a deep chuckle, he pulled her into his arms. "That's just to give you ideas on different positions. You know. To keep it fresh."

"Who takes off their clothes first? Or do we undress each other?"

"I think we need to find that drink first." He led her to the cabinet in the corner of the bedroom. "What would you like? Beer, wine?"

"Do you have whiskey?" she asked.

He looked at her with his eyebrows raised.

She shrugged. "My father taught me to fly and to drink whiskey. I like Scotch whiskey best."

"A woman after my own heart." He poured whiskey into two tumblers and handed her one.

She tossed it back, enjoying the burn in her throat and the immediate numbing effect. Before he'd finished his own glass, she handed him hers. "Hit me again."

"Do you know how sexy you are, standing there

in that dress, asking for a second shot of whiskey?" He put his glass and hers down on the minibar and dragged her into his arms. "I don't know what will happen between us after we leave here, but I can't hold back any longer. I have to have you in my arms." He crushed her mouth with his and thrust his tongue through to slide against hers.

He ran his hands over her shoulders and down her back, snagging her zipper as he moved lower. Then his fingers slipped inside her dress and caressed the small of her back, and moved lower to cup her bottom.

Marly's heart raced, her blood burning through her veins. She trailed her hands up Pitbull's chest, loosened his tie, pulled it free and tossed it over her shoulder. Without pausing a second, she went to work on the buttons on his shirt.

Go with your gut, he'd said. Well, her gut said get him naked. And he seemed to be of the same mind, getting her there. Her heart sang in anticipation of making love with this man. He was strong, built like a brick house and so darned sexy, he took her breath away.

Marly tugged his shirttails out of his trousers and pushed the shirt over his shoulders.

He shrugged free and reached for the straps of her dress, sliding them over her shoulders. The dress floated past her hips to pool in a sea of red at her ankles. She stood before him in nothing but the silver high heels she'd borrowed from Talia.

Pitbull took a step back, his gaze sweeping over every inch of her.

Her cheeks burned and she fought to keep from covering her small breasts. Next to Talia's curvy shape, Marly felt inadequate and boyish.

He shook his head. "Sweet Heaven, you're beautiful."

"No, I'm not." She did raise her hands to cover her chest. "I'm too small in some places and too tall to be feminine."

He took her hands in his and brought them to his lips. "You're perfect. More than a mouthful is too much, and I like that you aren't the size of a little girl. You're more my equal, someone who can hold your own in an argument and possibly kick butt in a fight."

"That's not very girly," she said, staring down at his hands holding hers.

"It's extremely sexy, and the kind of femininity I love about you." He raised her hand to his cheek. "And I kind of like the fact you're only wearing high heels."

"Well, don't get used to them," she said with a shaky laugh. "They're coming off." Marly stared at his broad, naked chest and let her gaze travel downward to the waistband of his trousers. "Seems to me you're a little overdressed."

"I can fix that." He let go of her long enough to strip out of his shoes, trousers and socks.

She grinned. "Nice to know I'm not the only one going commando tonight."

"Yet another thing to love about you. I can't believe you weren't wearing anything under that dress."

"Talia told me anything I wore would leave a line

beneath the fabric. And good grief, a woman can't show lines beneath her clothing." She gave him a twisted grin. "I really prefer my flight suit."

Pitbull tossed his socks to the corner and straightened. His body was a honed piece of machinery, all muscular with a six-pack across his abs. Not an ounce of fat graced the man's body.

Marly wet her lips and stared, drinking all of him in like a parched creature trapped in the desert. "Yeah, you really know how to intimidate a girl."

"Why should you feel intimidated?" He stalked toward her, his eyes narrowing, his lips slipping upward at the corners.

"Look at you, all hard as stone, with muscles from head to toe." She rested her hands on his chest, reveling in the steely hardness. "Are these real?"

"You bet they're real." To prove it, he scooped her up in his arms and tossed her onto the bed.

"Hey, you don't have to go all Neanderthal on me," Marly protested, though she kind of liked that he could lift her and toss her like she weighed nothing. She doubted many men could do that. At five-foot-eight, she wasn't light.

"You bring out the caveman in me, sweetheart." He grabbed her ankles and dragged her to the edge of the bed.

Marly squealed and sat up.

Pitbull parted her legs with a nudge of his knee and stepped between them. Then he cupped her chin and lifted her face. "Now's your chance to say no. I'll back off and respect your wishes. But if you choose to continue, I can't guarantee I'll be able to stop."

The deep tone of his voice raised gooseflesh on her arms. "Don't keep me waiting. I wouldn't have walked through that door if I didn't want this."

"I don't know what will happen tomorrow, and I don't care. Tonight, it's you and me." He bent and took her lips with his, kissing her slowly as he explored her mouth with his tongue. He tasted of whiskey, and was warm, wet and completely intoxicating.

Marly wrapped her arms around his neck, deepening the kiss. She pressed her breasts to his chest, wanting to feel her skin against his. This was where she'd wanted to be since the kiss in the garden the night before.

Without ending the kiss, he laid her back on the comforter and pressed his body to hers, his staff hard against her belly.

Desire coiled tightly at her core, sending waves of heat throughout her body. She could die in his arms that night, no regrets.

"I want to be inside you so badly," he whispered against her lips.

"I want it, too," she responded, her voice husky, heavy with lust.

"But first, I need to show you how good you can feel." He kissed a path along her jaw and down the length of her neck to the pulse beating wildly at the base of her throat.

"I'm feeling pretty good right now," she said, her

body writhing beneath his. "Any better and I might spontaneously combust."

Pitbull chuckled. "Darlin', you haven't felt anything yet."

"No? I could swear I am right now."

He sucked the nipple of her right breast between his teeth and pulled hard.

Marly arched her back, rising with every flick of his magical tongue on her nipple. "Oh my," she moaned. "I see what you mean." She couldn't breathe. Every time she tried, he touched another nerve and made it sing. In the process, Marly gasped and sucked in a deep breath, tension drawing her body tight, like a bowstring.

Just when she thought it couldn't get better, he switched to the neglected breast and treated it to the same enchantment.

By the time Pitbull abandoned both breasts and moved south along her rib cage, Marly was so aroused she thought she might come apart.

Pitbull never let up. He kissed, nipped and flicked his way over every rib and then lower, to the triangle of hair covering her sex. He kissed the curls, parted her folds and tongued that narrow strip of flesh.

Marly had only ever heard of a man touching a woman there with his tongue. She wasn't a virgin, having had sex with a missionary's son when she was in her early twenties, but she'd never had a man do what Pitbull was doing to her.

She drew up her knees and dug her heels into the mattress, lifting her hips, urging him to continue.

Her blood burned through her veins, her heart beating so fast, she could barely catch her breath. And she didn't care, as long as Pitbull didn't stop.

He slid a finger into her channel, and followed it with another, and yet another, stretching her entrance. At the same time, he sucked her nubbin between his lips and flicked it with his tongue.

"Oh, sweet heaven, what you're doing to me!" she cried.

One more flick and she came apart. Tingling started at her center and spread outward to the very tips of her fingers and toes. Finally, she knew. This was what all the fuss was about.

He continued tonguing, flicking and pumping his fingers until she'd dragged out every ounce of her release. When she came back to earth, she lay still, as emotionally and physically spent as if she'd been running a marathon.

Pitbull climbed up her body and leaned across the mattress to reach into the nightstand.

"Remind me to thank Talia for thinking of everything. She stashes condoms in the drawers." He reached in and held up an accordion of condoms.

"An excellent idea. It's not like you can walk around the block to the local drugstore to stock up." Marly took the strip of condoms, tore off one and opened the package.

He held out his hand. "I can do it."

Marly shook her head. "I want to."

"Let me guess…you've never applied one."

Her cheeks flushed red. "You know too much about me without me even saying anything."

"You aren't hard to read, darlin'." He touched her cheek with the backs of his knuckles.

She leaned her face into his hand. "I'll take that as a compliment."

"You should. Too many women hide who they are. I like that you don't. Marly, you're real." He kissed her and slid between her legs, his erection nudging her entrance.

Marly drew up her knees and lifted her hips, wanting him to consummate their lovemaking. Wanting him to fill that empty space that was more than physical.

He bent to kiss her again, easing into her as he thrust his tongue into her mouth. He moved slowly at first, then increased the speed, rocking in and out of her.

Marly raised her hips with each of Pitbull's thrusts, matching his rhythm, wanting him deeper and harder.

Soon he was pumping in and out, faster and faster, the sound of skin slapping against skin and their combined moans filling the air.

That same feeling she'd had when he'd been touching her and making her crazy welled inside. Her core tightened, and she dug her heels into the mattress and raised her hips one last time.

Pitbull's body tensed. He buried himself deep inside her, giving her his full length. His body and shaft pulsed with his release.

That she'd brought him to this culminating conclusion catapulted Marly over the edge, and she shuddered with her own reaction. She rode the wave all the way back to earth, where she collapsed against the sheets on a sigh.

Pitbull chuckled and rolled with her to lie on his side, facing her. "Like that?"

"Mmm," she said, not yet up to forming words. What they'd done had gone beyond good. "That could easily become addicting," she whispered, her eyes closed, sleep tugging at her senses.

"Agreed." He kissed her eyelids and the tip of her nose. "Sleep, sweetheart."

After making love like that, surely she could stay awake and figure things out with him. But no, she drifted to sleep, a voice at the back of her mind wondering...

How am I going to let him go?

Chapter Nine

Pitbull lay awake long after Marly fell asleep.

She'd said something softly as she drifted off.

He'd leaned close to hear, but the words were little more than a whisper. She might have said something like *let him go*. But Pitbull couldn't be certain. For all he knew, she'd been having a dream already.

Let him go.

Was Marly already thinking about their separation? The longer he lay there with Marly in his arms, the more Pitbull realized he didn't want to let her walk out of his life. But they didn't have a choice. Their situation was well past ridiculous.

He was a navy SEAL based out of Virginia. She was an African bush pilot. Unless things heated up in Africa, this was likely the last time they'd be together without making great sacrifices—as in complete career changes on one or both persons' parts.

He brushed a loose strand of her hair back behind her ear, the simple touch tugging at his gut. He wanted to do this again. Not just for the night. If he was lucky, the plane part wouldn't be in until the end of their vacation week. That would give him a few more days with Marly.

It wasn't enough, but he'd have to be satisfied with it. He'd make it special. Then when he had to say goodbye, he'd have no regrets.

Right. No regrets. He already regretted the day of their parting. Damn. He'd made the ultimate mistake. He'd fallen for the woman.

He must have drifted off in the early hours of the morning, while the sky was still dark and the crickets still chirped. The next thing he knew, sun was streaming around the edges of the blinds, filling the room with light.

He blinked his eyes and glanced at the green numbers on the digital clock beside him. Eight fifteen. He tried to remember where he was. When he did, he sat up straight in the bed and stared around the room. "Marly?" he called out.

When she didn't respond, he leaped out of the bed and searched the bungalow.

Marly was gone, along with her dress and the silver high heels.

Pitbull jammed his legs into a pair of jeans, pulled on a T-shirt and pushed his feet into socks and shoes. He was out the door without tying the laces. Something inside him told him to hurry or he'd miss her.

He ran along the path to the main house, up the stairs and into the foyer. Voices sounded in the dining room. He ran to the room, hoping to find Marly and allay his fear of losing the woman.

Pitbull paused in the doorway of the dining room, searching for Marly. She wasn't there.

"About time you dragged yourself out of bed." Buck lifted his mug of coffee in a mock toast.

Talia motioned toward the counter against the wall. "Coffee's fresh. Grab a cup and take a seat. The chef made Belgian waffles with strawberries and whipped cream."

"Dessert for breakfast." T-Mac rubbed his belly. "I'll have to do three hundred sit-ups to burn that off."

"For a week," Harm added, also rubbing his belly. "They were delicious."

His team was talking about food when all Pitbull could think about was where Marly was.

Talia smiled. "If you're looking for Marly, she left thirty minutes ago with Henry and the guards. Her part came in, and she wanted to get started install-ing it before it got too warm. That, and she wanted to make sure her plane was still where she'd parked it. You never know, with the poachers and scavengers who find their way into the protected sanctuaries."

"Is there a truck I can use to go check on them?" Pitbull asked.

Talia shook her head. "I'd like to loan you the truck, but I have only one available, and I have a safari to conduct today with the rest of your crew."

"Are we going anywhere near Marly's plane?" Big Jake asked.

Talia nodded. "We can."

"Then you can drop me off? She might need help,"

Pitbull suggested. "Besides, that would free up one of your guards for the safari."

Talia smiled. "You and your team have proven they don't need guards. They can take care of themselves." She glanced at her watch. "We leave in ten minutes. I suggest you grab a bite to eat in that time."

The others stood and pushed their chairs in to the table.

Buck leaned close as he passed Pitbull. "Not like you to sleep late, Percy."

Pitbull scooped fluffy yellow scrambled eggs onto his plate, ignoring his friend.

"Wouldn't be because you were up all night, now, would it?" Buck said.

Pitbull grabbed a biscuit and threw it at Buck.

The jerk grabbed it midair and took a big bite out of it.

"What Pitbull does at night is none of your business," Big Jake said.

"Thanks, Big Jake." Pitbull stuffed a forkful of eggs into his mouth.

"Although, what Ms. Marly was doing coming out of your bungalow at the crack of dawn left me wondering." Big Jake chuckled and ducked the second biscuit sailing through the air.

Harm caught it. "No use wasting good food." He palmed it and left the dining room with the others, all of them talking and laughing.

At Pitbull's expense.

Marly would be appalled they knew so much about

her comings and goings. He'd warn her to be ready for some ribbing when she got back to the resort.

For the moment, he could barely wait to get in the truck and on his way to where she was working on the plane. He hoped like hell the poachers hadn't returned and decided to take whatever they wanted of the plane and its parts. Two guards and one tough woman weren't much against a band of scavengers armed to kill.

He jammed more food down his throat, tossed back a glass of orange juice and ran out the door, headed for his bungalow. Inside, he settled a hat on his head and his weapon in the holster beneath his left arm. He slung his M4A1 assault rifle over his shoulder. He night need it. The rifle would take down an attacker from a lot farther away than his handgun.

The truck was waiting in the drive at the front of the main house, his teammates standing in the back.

Buck and Harm each reached down, grabbed one of his hands and pulled him up into the back of the truck.

Big Jake pounded on the top of the cab, signaling they were all aboard. The truck lurched forward. The men sat on the wooden benches and settled in for a long day of viewing some of the most beautiful animals in the world.

Pitbull counted the minutes until he could put his gaze on Marly. He didn't like that she was out on the savanna without him. Then he realized, once he was gone from Africa, he wouldn't know where she was at any given time. Her job took her all over. She could be facing poachers, angry villagers and rebel fighters in just about any country on the continent.

"Worried about Marly?" Diesel asked over the roar of the engine.

Hell yes, he was. But he didn't have to let on to his buddies. He forced a shrug.

Diesel's lips twisted into a wry grin. "I swore I'd never get involved with any one woman. Life as a navy SEAL was hard enough without having to worry about someone else. But then I met Reese."

Pitbull glanced over at Diesel. "Who said I was involved with anyone?"

Diesel chuckled. "You've obviously got it bad for our pilot."

"So? Doesn't mean I'm going to do anything about it."

"No?" Diesel's eyebrows rose. "You're going to end it when we leave?"

Pitbull nodded.

"And it's going to be that easy?"

Why wouldn't Diesel shut up? Pitbull didn't want to think that far ahead. He'd handle one day at a time. When Marly's time with them was up, he'd deal with it then. "Look, I don't want to talk about it."

Diesel held up his hands in surrender. "Okay then. We're not talking about Marly and how much you're starting to care for her. I get it. I fought my attraction to Reese when I first met her in the jungle. Over the next few days, I'd grown fond of the woman and admired her strength and intelligence. By the time our mission ended, I knew I couldn't just walk away."

"Why are you telling me this?" Pitbull didn't want to hear what Diesel had to say. He knew a relationship with a SEAL was doomed from the beginning.

"We decided to give us a chance. Granted, I'll be away a lot, but that doesn't seem to matter to her."

"At least she'll be on the same continent as you, when you're home," Pitbull grumbled.

"Yeah, there is that." Diesel stared out at the grasslands. "If two people are committed, they find a way to compromise."

"That's just it," Pitbull said. "We went into this with no strings attached, agreeing on no commitment."

The corners of Diesel's lips quirked upward. "Yeah. That's how it starts." He clapped his hands together. "I guess you two will figure it out. If she's still working on that plane of hers, maybe we should leave T-Mac to help."

"Marly knows what she's doing, and I can hand her tools as well as anyone else."

"In that case, the guards could hand her the tools and you could go with us on the safari." T-Mac leaned into the conversation. "Let's see what she's got going."

Half an hour later, the truck pulled to a stop in front of the stand of trees, and the men leaped out of the back. Talia and Henry dropped down from the front.

Marly stood on a ladder, her head bent over the engine compartment. She straightened and turned toward the arrivals. Her gaze sought Pitbull's and then shifted to Talia. "I thought you guys would be on safari today."

"We wanted to check on your status before we headed out," Big Jake said. "How's it going?"

"Fine. I almost have the fuel pump in. Just have to connect the hoses and fire it up to see if it works."

"Need any help?" T-Mac asked.

"No, I don't think so," she said. "I'd like to get it running and at least move it to the landing field near the resort."

"How about we stay long enough to see if you get it started?"

"Don't delay your event for me," she said. "I've got this."

"We don't mind. We have a vested interest in that plane starting," Harm said. "It's our ride back to Djibouti."

"Okay, give me another minute while I attach the hoses." Marly's gaze slipped over Pitbull, and then she turned back to her work.

Pitbull wished the others would leave and take the guards with them. He'd like to have Marly all to himself. They had some talking to do after last night. This no-strings-attached business wasn't feeling right to him. He wanted to know what she was thinking. Was she still on track for saying *goodbye, so long, have a good life*, at the end of the week? Because Pitbull wasn't so sure he was on board with that scenario.

With everyone standing around, he couldn't have that conversation. Hell, he'd have to wait. And Marly didn't appear to need anyone's help fixing the engine.

The woman was an amazing mechanic, and damned cute in her flight suit. Pitbull wanted to get her alone so that he could peel the flight suit off her and expose that hot pink bra and her silky, soft skin beneath. His groin tightened at the thought. He turned away before anyone could notice.

A few minutes later, Marly climbed down the ladder, moved it away from the plane and started to pull the camouflage netting away from the propeller and fuselage. Soon everyone was helping to untangle the netting from the plane and folding it up to be stowed behind the truck seat.

"Well, here goes nothing," Marly said and climbed into the plane.

Pitbull held his breath and waited for the reassuring sound of the engine starting up.

Inside the cockpit, Marly flipped through what appeared to be a checklist. Finally, she set it aside and stared out at the propeller. The engine turned over and caught, and the propeller spun.

A cheer went up from everyone standing on the ground.

Pitbull grinned when he saw the smile on Marly's face. She gave a thumbs-up signal through the windshield.

"We might want to step back while she pulls the plane out of the trees," Big Jake said.

Henry moved the truck, and everyone else shuffled to the side.

Marly taxied the plane out of the shadows and stopped. She applied the brake, left the engine running and lowered the cabin door. "I'm going to fly it over to the resort landing strip."

"I'll go with you," Pitbull called out.

"Why?" Buck said with a wink. "She's got it going. Besides, what do you know about planes? You don't even like them."

"A guy can change his mind," Pitbull said. "Besides, if she has any more problems, she'll need someone to provide protection." Pitbull didn't wait for his team's response. He loped to the steps, climbed aboard and closed the hatch behind him. That way no one else could offer to assist. He'd have Marly all to himself.

Marly chuckled as she secured the locks in place. "I thought you didn't like flying." She turned to him and smiled.

"I don't. But I wanted to see you." He pulled her into his arms and kissed her soundly, his tongue pushing past her teeth to claim hers.

Marly leaned into him and deepened the kiss.

Though it was short, the kiss was hot and made Pitbull want so much more.

"The guys can see us through the window," Marly whispered, nodding to the men on the ground pointing at them. Buck gave a fist pump. The others grinned and waved.

"I don't care." Pitbull kissed her again and then set her to arm's length. "Let's get this bird in the air. The sooner we're back at the resort, the sooner I get to hold you in my arms. Without an audience."

Marly settled into her seat and began checking gauges and flipping switches.

Pitbull climbed into the copilot's seat and watched what she was doing. The more he knew about flying the plane, the better he'd feel. At least that was what he told himself.

She clamped on the headset and motioned for him to put on his. When he had, she asked, "Ready?"

Hell, no, he wasn't ready. They would be taking off on a rough field of grass, not a paved or even graded landing strip. He nodded.

Marly released the brake and set the plane in motion. Giving a final wave, she set off across the savanna. "In order to take off, I have to go fast enough to get lift. So hold on, it's about to get bumpy."

It was more than bumpy; it was teeth-jarring and insane. Pitbull held on to the armrests, his fingers digging into the leather.

He prayed they didn't run into a termite mound or anything else sticking out of the ground. As fast as they were going, it would be certain death.

The plane took off, skimming over the tops of several trees as it climbed into the air. They went from wildly jarring to incredibly smooth as soon as the wheels left the ground.

"Better?" Marly smiled over at him.

Pitbull relaxed his death grip on the armrests. "Much better."

"See? You're already getting used to flying in a fixed-wing aircraft. Before long, you'll prefer them."

"If you say so."

Marly keyed the mic and communicated with the closest air traffic controller, giving her destination as the All Things Wild Resort. Within a few short minutes, she set the plane down on the dirt strip and brought it to a stop.

"Not only are you a skilled pilot, but you're also a mechanic? You're positively perfect." Pitbull let go of the breath he'd been holding. "Will you marry me?" He winked.

Marly's cheeks reddened and she gave an awkward laugh. "Don't be silly. People in the bush do whatever it takes to keep things moving."

"I'm betting back in the States they'd require a complete overhaul of the engine after crash landing in a remote area."

She frowned. "I didn't crash-land. I brought the plane down in a controlled landing." Marly pulled the headset off and placed it on a hook over her shoulder. "You should have stayed with the guys going on the safari. I'm just going to be hanging around the pool for the rest of the day."

"Mind if I join you?" Pitbull asked.

She smiled. "I'd love it."

Pitbull lowered the hatch and climbed down from the plane. He held out his hand to Marly as she followed. As soon as her feet touched the ground, he pulled her into his arms. "The pool, huh?"

She leaned up on her toes and pressed her lips to his. "Unless you can offer a better alternative."

"You, me, my bungalow."

"I'm in."

"Good, because I've been dying to peel you out of that flight suit."

She laughed. "I'm the same beneath the suit as I was beneath the dress last night. Nothing's changed."

"There's something about that long zipper and the hot-pink bra that fascinates me." He touched his finger to the metal tab and drew it down several inches, his pulse ratcheting up as he did. "Yeah, it's the zipper."

"Come on." She took his hand and led him across the field toward the resort compound. "We need to get to your bungalow before we flash the help."

"Now you're talking." Together, they ran toward the gate, entered and were halfway to Pitbull's bungalow when one of the cleaning staff waved them down. "Ms. Simpson!"

Marly slowed to a walk. "Yes?"

"There was a phone call while you were gone." She pointed toward the house. "The man left a message. It's on the table in the entryway."

"Thank you." Marly shot a glance toward Pitbull.

"I don't suppose you can ignore the message."

"I can't." Marly sighed. "I'll only be a minute. Probably just a flying gig for after I drop off you and your men. I left word I'd be here for a while."

"I'll go with you. We can eat lunch before we hole up in my bungalow."

She gave him a weak smile. "Thanks."

Inside the front entrance was a table against the right wall. On it was an envelope addressed to Marly Simpson.

Marly tore open the envelope and read the message, her brows drawing into a V.

"What is it?" Pitbull asked.

Marly sighed. "Can I get a rain check on our plans?"

"Why?"

She handed him the note. "I have to fly."

"Can't someone else?"

"There's a shortage of planes."

Pitbull read the note.

Sick child needs evacuation to nearest major medical facility. Please call to confirm.

A phone number was listed.

"When there's a sick child, I can't say no," Marly said. "It's one of the most important tasks I perform as a bush pilot."

Pitbull nodded. She wouldn't be the person he was falling for if she ignored a distress call. He took her hands in his and nodded. "When do we leave?"

Chapter Ten

Marly checked her gauges and ran through her landing checklist in her head.

Landing gear down.

Flaps extended.

Fuel rich.

"Seat belts fastened?" she called out into her mic.

"Fastened." Pitbull's voice filled her ears, making her feel warm and happy all over. Until now, she hadn't realized just how lonely her life had become. Sure, she transported people all the time, but she didn't have the opportunity to get to know them. And until now, she hadn't met a man she was compelled to get to know better. Pitbull drew her to him like no other.

She glanced in his direction.

Pitbull gripped the armrest on the side of the aircraft with a white-knuckled grasp. The man was one tough SEAL, had deployed to some of the worst places in the most dangerous situations in the world, been transported by helicopter, been shot at, had grenades and rockets lobbed in his direction—and he was terrified of flying in fixed-wing aircraft. Still, he'd insisted on flying with her today, not knowing where he was going or what to expect when he arrived.

Marly's heart swelled. Not only was he a fantastic lover, he was willing to follow her while she performed her job...on his vacation.

Lining up with the dirt landing strip, Marly began her descent into one of the poorest areas in Africa. This landing strip was a lifeline to the missionary family who dedicated their lives to helping others in need.

Reverend Eugene Thomas and his wife, Hilary, lived and worked in the little village, teaching the inhabitants about the Bible, sanitation and healthy habits. Not only were they bringing Christianity to the natives, they were helping teach the children how to read and write and the adults how to build better homes for their families and much more productive ways to farm.

Hilary had put her nursing skills to work providing basic health care to the people. She'd stitched cuts, pulled teeth and delivered babies when called to do so, never wavering in her dedication to making the villagers' lives better. Now her own son was in need of medical care. The sooner he made it to a hospital, the better.

As Marly slowed their speed, the plane seemed to hurtle toward the ground until just before the wheels touched down. It seemed to float the remaining few feet when the tires kissed the dirt.

Beside her, Pitbull released a long, slow breath. He clapped his hands together once and gave her a tight smile. "Well done."

Marly laughed. "Glad you think so." She taxied to the group of people waiting at the end of the runway.

Villagers gathered around a tall, white-haired man.

Marly stopped short of the crowd and shut down the engine.

Once the propeller stopped spinning, she climbed out of the cockpit.

Pitbull was a step ahead of her, lowering the stairs. He climbed down and held out his hand for Marly.

She smiled down at him and let him help her from the plane. Sure, she didn't need it and would have made it out fine on her own, but it was nice to be treated like someone special for a change.

They walked side by side to the welcoming committee.

Small naked children gathered around their legs, touching their clothing and hands.

The tall white man extended his hand. "Welcome to Bunanga. I'm Reverend Eugene Thomas."

Pitbull gripped the man's hand. "Percy Taylor."

"Reverend. I've heard good things about your work here." Marly shook his hand next. "Marly Simpson."

"Thank you for coming so quickly. Our son's health has been getting steadily worse since last night. He needs to be taken to the hospital in Kinshasa as soon as possible."

"Any idea what's wrong with him?" Marly asked.

The reverend shook his head. "We don't think it's

contagious. No one else is sick like he is. We think it might be a parasite. But he's dehydrated and weak. The sooner they get him a fluid IV the better."

"Where is he?" Marly asked.

"Come with me." The reverend spoke to the people standing around in what Marly had come to recognize as Swahili.

The villagers scattered, running ahead of Marly, Pitbull and the reverend.

They were led to a small hut with a grass roof and dirt floor.

Reverend Thomas lowered his voice to a whisper. "My wife has been up all night with my son. She's very worried." He held back the canvas flap that acted as a door and waited for Marly and Pitbull to enter the small structure.

Inside were three army cots, several trunks and a collapsible desk in army green. On one of the cots lay a teenager. He was long and lanky like his father, but with black shaggy hair. Beneath his tan, his face was pale, his lips dull and cracked.

A woman with salt-and-pepper hair and deep shadows beneath her eyes sat on the cot beside the boy. She glanced up, and relief melted across her face. "Thank the Lord." She bent her head and closed her eyes. When she looked up again, she smiled. "I'm glad you're here. Martin hasn't spoken since late last night. I've tried to give him water, but he's not taking anything."

The boy's situation was dire. A person could die quickly without advanced medical care. And advanced medical care meant taking the patient to one of the big cities with established hospitals and life-support facilities. "We need to get him to the plane," Marly said.

The reverend started forward. "I can carry him."

Pitbull laid a hand on the man's arm. "Sir, let me." He stepped in front of the older man, bent to the teen and slid his arms beneath his back and legs. When he lifted, he cast a worried glance at Marly. "He's very light."

"All the more reason to get him to Kinshasa. Fast." Marly hurried to the door and held open the flap.

Pitbull marched toward the plane, not slowing until he stood in front of the stairs. "Where do you want to put him?"

Marly entered the plane first and adjusted several of the seats. "I had the interior modified to be used to transport patients." Soon she had converted one side of the aircraft into what looked like a hospital bed, sheets and all.

Pitbull carried Martin up the steps, careful not to bump him into the door frame. Once inside, he laid the teen on the makeshift bed and pulled the sheet up over his thin body.

Mrs. Thomas climbed in and took one of the seats near Martin's head. The reverend stood on the steps, looking out at the people gathered at the edge of the field. He spoke to them in Swahili.

They nodded and the older man stepped inside the plane and sat behind his wife.

"Get the door," Marly commanded, stepping into the cockpit. "I'll perform preflight."

Pitbull gave her a mock salute and a grin. "Yes, ma'am."

"And Pitbull—" Marly glanced back at him "—thank you for coming with me."

"Glad you let me," he said.

PITBULL CLOSED AND secured the door to the plane and then took his position in the copilot's seat, slipping the headset over his ears. "Where to?"

"Kinshasa," Reverend Thomas said. "The General Hospital of Kinshasa is expecting us. I radioed a message to them."

Marly started the engine and taxied to the end of the runway. Moments later they were heading into the wind, picking up speed. Then they were in the air, flying over the tops of the village huts.

Pitbull glanced back at the passengers. They didn't seem concerned about flying in a small airplane. The reverend and his wife were more concerned about their son. Hopefully he'd receive the medical attention he needed in time to save his life.

The flight took just under two hours. They landed at N'djili International Airport in Kinshasa, the largest of the international airports in the Democratic Republic of Congo.

They'd come full circle from a couple weeks prior, when they'd worked on an operation to protect the secretary of defense's son and his bodyguard, Reese Brantly. Now they were on a different type of lifesaving mission. Pitbull hoped this time the city didn't blow up in their faces. Last time, they'd barely gotten out of the city alive after an attempted coup against the existing government.

With air travel seemingly in full swing, Pitbull assumed the coup attempts had been completely neutralized. At least for the time being.

He climbed out of his seat while Marly powered down the engine and performed her postflight checklist.

"There should be an ambulance waiting to transport my son," the reverend said, bending to lift the teen.

"Hold on. I'll carry him down the steps, but first, let me make sure the ambulance is waiting." Pitbull opened the hatch and lowered the steps. He dropped down to the tarmac and shielded his eyes from the glaring sun. Several hundred yards away sat an ambulance.

Pitbull waved and the vehicle began crossing the concrete toward the plane.

Marly exited the plane and raised a hand to her brow. "Good. The sooner they get Martin to the hospital, the better."

Mrs. Thomas climbed down the steps and stood staring at the ambulance. "I've never missed the trappings of so-called civilization more than last night. You don't know how good it is to see that ambulance heading our way."

While Marly slipped an arm around the woman's shoulders, Pitbull entered the plane, gathered the boy in his arms and eased his way down the steps to the ground.

The ambulance came to a halt seconds later. Emergency medical technicians unloaded a gurney and rolled it over to where Pitbull stood.

He lowered Martin to the clean white sheet.

The ambulance crew loaded the gurney into the back of the truck and went to work, quickly checking the boy's vitals and starting an IV.

Mrs. Thomas was helped into the back of the truck to be with her son. The reverend would ride up front.

Marly followed the reverend around to the passenger side of the ambulance. "Do you need us to wait around to fly you back to Bunanga?"

The older man shook his head. "No. I'm not certain how long we'll be in Kinshasa. But I know how to get in touch with you when we need you." He hugged Marly and Pitbull. "You two were sent by the angels. Thank you." Then he climbed into the ambulance and the vehicle took off, lights strobing as they headed for the hospital.

Marly stared after them. "I hope Martin will be okay."

"Me, too." Pitbull slipped an arm around Marly's waist. "Do you want to stay until we know for sure?"

She shook her head. "If I could do something positive, I'd stay and help out. But I think they will have enough to worry about without me making them feel like they need to entertain me or find something for me to do." Marly glanced up. "We can go back to the resort and enjoy the remainder of the day. Just you and me."

Pitbull's pulse quickened and he slowed. "Unfortunately, by the time we get back, the others will be heading back in from the field."

Marly frowned. "Why so pessimistic? Even if they do show up early, we can have dinner and enjoy the sunset and then call it an early night. They don't have to know we'll be spending it together."

"About that..." Pitbull scratched the side of his neck. "They already know."

"Know what?"

"That you and I slept together last night."

Her cheeks flamed, but she squared her shoulders. "Well, I guess it doesn't matter anymore whether they know or not. It's not like I'll see them again after you leave Africa." She forced a tight smile. "Let's make the most of the remaining days."

"I'm with you." Pitbull took her hand and headed for the plane.

Marly had the airport operator top off her fuel tanks. Once that was complete, they boarded the plane, closed the door and took off for Kenya and the All Things Wild Resort.

"How long is the flight?"

"Two hours, give or take."

He sat back, his mind off the aircraft operations and already thinking about what he'd do to her body when they got to his bungalow.

He couldn't get enough of Marly Simpson, and he planned on making the most of what little time they had left together. At the end of their week, he'd say his goodbyes. He didn't look forward to that part of this vacation. Well, he'd just have to cross that bridge when he came to it.

The two hours passed quickly. Marly made a radio call to the resort frequency, letting them know she was on her way in. When they arrived back at the resort, they were met by Talia's guards and Talia.

Marly powered down the plane while Pitbull unbuckled his seat belt and stepped past her to open the door.

Talia was first up the stairs. "I'm glad you two made it back safely. How was the flight?"

"Smooth," Marly answered. "No problems."

"I'm glad. I almost wish you had stayed a night or two in Kinshasa," Talia said, her mouth turning downward at the corners.

Pitbull frowned, sensing the tension behind Talia's words.

Talia led the way down the steps to the ground. "We had more trouble today."

His gut knotting, Pitbull followed. "Anyone hurt?"

"Buck got nicked on the temple. Our local doctor checked him out. Luckily it was only a flesh wound."

Flesh wound. Another inch in the wrong direction would have killed his friend and teammate.

Pitbull's hands balled into fists. Once again, he hadn't been with his teammates when they'd needed him. Lusting after a woman had sucked every last brain cell out of his head. He couldn't do it again. At the end of the week, he had to let go of Marly or his team would suffer. He had to remain focused on missions.

Marly descended the steps and closed the airplane door. "You couldn't have known it would happen again."

"Yeah, but I could have been with them," he said through gritted teeth.

"After chasing off the poachers yesterday, we thought for sure they wouldn't be brazen enough to come back for more." Talia laughed. "That's what we get for being cocky."

"But you had armed guards and SEALs," Marly pointed out. "Surely that scared them off."

"They were waiting for us in a dry creek bed near the road our safari tours travel on a regular basis. If not for your trained SEAL team, we'd be dead. The two guards wouldn't have stood a chance. And if we had been with regular safari guests, they would all be dead." Talia shoved a hand through her windblown hair. "The point is, don't wander off. They're out there. Waiting for God knows what. I'm putting my guards on a twenty-four-hour watch to protect your plane."

"Thank you." Marly was amazed at the lengths Talia would go to to protect her clients.

The resort owner turned toward the compound. "Come on, let's get out of the sun. It's too blazing hot to be out without a hat."

The path from the runway to the house wound through a stand of trees, providing cooling shade from the heat of the late afternoon.

"This isn't right," Marly mused. "What do they want?"

"I don't know." Talia glanced through the trees as though she could see out to the rolling plains of the savanna. "Maybe they're mad we got in the way of their plans."

"Revenge?" Marly shook her head. "You'd think poachers are always on the run."

"Retribution against a threat they weren't expecting?" Pitbull suggested. "You would have turned around and gone back to the resort to report their activities if you'd had your normal clients on the safari."

"But your team isn't anything like our normal clients." Talia shrugged. "They could have been after your team today."

"Then we could have put your operation at risk by attacking theirs," Pitbull concluded.

"Didn't Diesel say he'd run into poachers in the jungle along the Congo?" Marly asked.

"Yes, and he managed to run them off."

Talia's eyebrows met in a V. "You don't suppose they were the same poachers, do you?"

"What are the odds that the same group of poachers would be in the DRC and Kenya?"

"From what my guys said, the poachers were trying to take a baby elephant when my team stopped them. They had a truck with a trailer big enough for a baby, not a full-grown elephant."

"They could have been after baby gorillas in the jungle," Marly said.

"A ring of thieving baby snatchers?" Talia's lips

thinned into a straight line. "Bastards! These animals have enough of a hard time surviving their harsh environment without humans preying on them and their young."

"No kidding," Marly said.

Talia stopped before the gate to the resort compound. "The chef will have dinner ready in just a few minutes. You two look like you could use some time to freshen up. We won't do formal wear tonight. We're having a barbecue, so jeans are fine."

"Great. I'd like to check in with my team first." Pitbull took Marly's hand and followed Talia to the gate.

As they entered the walled compound, Marly pulled her hand free. "I left my logbook in the plane. I'm way behind on tracking and would like to catch up this evening. I'll only be a few minutes. Don't wait on me."

Talia frowned. "I need to get back to the kitchen. I promised to help set up the outdoor tables."

Pitbull stopped and turned. "Go on, Talia. I'll backtrack with Marly."

"Pitbull!" Buck rose from a chair on the back patio and started toward them, a white gauze bandage wrapped around his head. "You missed all the fun."

Marly touched Pitbull's arm. "I can get the logbook myself."

He grabbed her arm to keep her from going. "It's not safe for you to be wandering around on your own."

She shook loose of his grip and smiled. "I won't be alone. The guards are out there, and I have my gun."

She patted the bulge beneath her arm. "I'll be back in just a second."

Marly took off at a jog back toward the plane. Before Pitbull could take off after her, Buck reached him and slung an arm over his shoulders. Buck faced the direction Pitbull was staring. "Where's Marly going?"

"Back to her plane for her logbook." He glanced at his friend. "Took one for the team, did you?"

Buck shrugged. "Just a flesh wound. I've had worse."

"I hear it was an ambush."

"Yeah. We didn't see it coming. Being on vacation is making us lazy or something."

"We're not so much lazy as not expecting anything like that to happen," Pitbull commented.

"Yeah, but we *are* in Africa. And we've seen how it's not such a stable environment, given our run-in with the poachers yesterday. We should have been on our toes." Buck grinned. "But we were hurrying toward a herd of giraffes. We were all staring at the giraffes, not our surroundings."

Pitbull grinned. "A herd of giraffes?"

Buck's lips formed a wry grin. "Yeah. They were amazing. I wish we could have seen more of them."

"Maybe tomorrow?" Pitbull suggested. "Surely Talia can locate the herd again."

Buck shook his head. "The gang decided they want to see Victoria Falls. You don't suppose Marly would fly us down there? I mean, how often are we in Africa?" He paused and added, "On vacation."

"Some vacation." Pitbull laughed. "But it's true.

We don't usually have free time when we're on the African continent. I'm sure Marly would take us. All we have to do is ask—"

The crack of gunfire sounded nearby, cutting off Pitbull's last word.

"What the hell?" Pitbull spun toward the landing strip, just out of sight of the house, the trees and all their shade blocking his view. He didn't wait for another shot to be fired. He ran back out of the gate and cut through the trees in a more direct path to the landing strip and Marly.

The sound of an engine firing up made his blood run icy cold. When he burst out onto the dirt landing strip, the plane was halfway down the runway, building up speed as it drew away from him.

Lying on the ground where the plane had been parked were the two guards, unmoving, their arms and legs at odd angles.

Dead.

Chapter Eleven

Marly had run all the way back to the plane, anxious to grab the logbook and get back to Pitbull. With time running short, she had only a few days with the man. She wanted to spend every second of it with him.

The guards stood near the plane, their weapons pointing at the ground. They appeared bored and hot. The afternoon sun beat down on them, making them sweat. Marly would ask Talia for bottled water for them. But first, she wanted her logbook.

She lowered the steps and climbed up into the plane. The logbook was in the pouch attached to the wall on the pilot's side of the airplane. She settled into the cockpit and retrieved her logbook, checking over the instruments one more time just to be sure all was well.

Just when she leaned forward to stand, she heard the sharp report of gunfire.

She gasped and fell back into her seat, her heart racing so fast it made her dizzy. Marly forced herself to be calm and think. Two shots. She'd heard two shots. What did that mean?

Two guards stood outside.

She glanced through the windows toward the spot where the guards had been standing. They weren't there. When she craned her neck, she could see lumps of khaki-colored uniforms on the ground.

Holy hell! The guards had been shot. Marly leaped out of her seat and ran down the aisle toward the door. She had to either get out and run for help, or close and lock the aircraft door to protect herself until someone came to her rescue.

She made it into the plane and was just about to pull up the steps into the craft, when seven men rushed the plane, stopping her before she could lock herself in.

The first one ran up the steps.

Marly planted a foot in his chest and kicked hard.

The man fell backward into his cohorts. The one behind him toppled into the one behind him, but the rest of them steadied the lead men and pushed them up and into the plane.

Marly had nowhere to go. She couldn't duck past them and escape. She had a gun under her flight suit, but one gun against seven armed men would be setting herself up to be killed.

The man in the lead grabbed her arm and spun her around.

She fought against him, but he was much stronger. In the struggle, he discovered her weapon. While he held her arms behind her back, another man yanked down her zipper, removed the gun and pointed it at her head.

"Fly this plane," he demanded, his voice heavy with a native accent.

"No," she said.

"If you don't," the man with the gun said, "he will." He nodded to the man holding her. "And it will mean certain death for all of us."

"I'm not flying this plane," she insisted.

"If you refuse to fly, we will wait for your friends to come, and then we'll blow up this plane and all of them with this." The gunman pulled a grenade from his pocket and held it up.

She said the first thing that came into her head. "You're out of your mind."

"We are very serious. Fly now, or you and your friends will all die."

"As will you," she pointed out.

"Do it now, before they come." He poked her with her handgun. "We are not afraid to die."

The man holding her lifted her off her feet and carried her to the pilot's seat, where he shoved her down and braced his hands on her shoulders.

Marly didn't have a choice. If she refused to fly, they'd kill themselves, her and the team when they attempted to storm the plane. If she flew away before the team reached them, she would be the only one in danger.

Marly started the engine, eased off the brake and taxied onto the dirt landing strip.

"Go!" The man with her gun bumped her temple with the barrel of the weapon.

"Knock me out and we'll crash into the trees. Now

back off," she said, sounding a lot more confident and brazen than she felt. Inside, her stomach churned so badly she feared she'd throw up all over the instrument panel. Swallowing hard on the bile rising up her throat, she concentrated on getting the plane into the air and away from Pitbull and his friends. The farther away she got, the less chance of her captors detonating the grenade and killing the navy SEALs.

The plane picked up speed, racing toward the end of the runway. When she was going fast enough, she eased back on the yoke and the plane left the ground, soaring up into the air.

Marly dared to glance down at the ground in time to see Pitbull run out onto the landing strip.

He'd come after her. Marly's heart swelled.

Not that it had done any good. But it made Marly feel a little better that he would have come to her rescue if he'd been given a chance.

The man holding the gun said something in Swahili and laughed. The others laughed with him. Still holding her pistol, he tossed the grenade to a man behind him.

Marly flinched, waiting for the explosion.

The men laughed again.

"Won't that explode if you drop it?" she asked.

The man laughed again and held up his hand.

The grenade flew through the fuselage and landed in his grasp. He immediately dropped it into Marly's lap.

She yelped and tried to jump up from her seat. The grenade slipped out of her lap, dropped to the floor beside her and bounced like a ball. The damned thing was made of rubber. They'd tricked her into taking off by threatening her with the explosion of a rubber ball.

She glared, making the men laugh harder.

"Fine. I'll just land the plane." She gripped the yoke and sent the plane into a one-hundred-eighty-degree turn.

The barrel of her handgun tapped her temple. "You will fly this plane to these coordinates." He handed her a piece of torn paper.

She didn't even bother to look at it. "Why should I? You can only kill *me* now that we're away from the resort."

"We have more men ready to attack your boyfriend and his American SEAL team. They do not belong in Africa."

"How do I know you're not lying?" Marly asked. "You've lied before. And how do I know you won't do it anyway? If I crash the plane, I take out the seven of you. Sounds like a win-win situation to me." She pushed the yoke forward, sending the aircraft plummeting toward the ground.

While the men in the rear scrambled to hold on, Marly surreptitiously adjusted the transponder code to 7500, sending out a silent plea, indicating she'd been hijacked.

The man with the gun held on to the seat he stood behind and said something sharply in Swahili.

The big guy who'd originally lifted her off her feet and sat her in the pilot's seat staggered to an upright position, grabbed her beneath her armpits and yanked her out of her seat.

The plane wobbled, but continued to dive toward the ground. The gunman dove into her seat and brought the aircraft under control. Again, he spoke in angry Swahili.

Her captor took off his T-shirt, ripped it into strips and tied her wrists.

Marly tried hard to leave a gap, but the man pulled tightly, the fabric seeming to cut into her skin. "You don't know how to fly this plane," she said to the man in the pilot's seat. "You might keep it level in the sky, but it's a hell of a lot harder to land than it is to fly."

He spoke again in Swahili. The man who'd torn his shirt tied one of the strips around her head and over her mouth.

It tasted of stale sweat and body odor.

Marly gagged, but couldn't remove it. With her hands tied behind her back, she was limited in what she could do. But her feet were still free.

The big guy had shoved her into one of the seats behind the pilot's seat. She couldn't get away from these men, but she sure as hell could make sure they didn't kidnap anyone else or any other baby animals. After hijacking a plane, they wouldn't want to take the time to release her. Hell, they probably would have killed her already, but they had to get rid of the body. By keeping her alive, they were keeping her body fresh.

All these random thoughts raced through Marly's head while she worked to get the nasty T-shirt material out of her mouth. If she was destined to die anyway, she might as well take them out with her and go down in a fiery crash. Besides, once they did get to where they were going, their plans for her couldn't be good.

Scooting lower in the seat, she drew back her legs and threw a kick at the pilot's head.

Contact!

The man's head slammed forward, bounced against the yoke and back against the seat. The plane shimmied and dipped.

No sooner had she kicked the guy than the big man who'd tied her up with his smelly T-shirt backhanded her with a heavy fist. He hit her so hard, her head snapped back and her vision dimmed.

Still sitting in the chair, she tried to stay awake to keep track of what was going on with her plane.

The man hit her again. Pain shot through her right cheek and she fell back in the seat, slumped against the side of the plane and fought back the gray haze engulfing her.

But she couldn't win the battle, and she slipped into empty, pain-free silence.

PITBULL RAN AFTER the plane, praying it would stop before it reached the end of the runway. No matter how fast he ran, he couldn't catch up. Marly's plane lifted up into the sky.

"No! No! No!" Pitbull shook his fist in the air.

Buck caught up with him, breathing hard and

pressing a hand to his injured head. "What the hell were you trying to do?"

"I couldn't let her go." He spun and walked several steps back the way they'd come and then spun again and marched toward Buck. "What can I do? How will I find her? Damn it, Buck. They'll kill her." He gripped his friend's collar.

Buck grabbed his wrists. "Get a hold of yourself, dude. We'll find her."

"How?" Pitbull dropped his hands to his sides. "Africa is a big continent. They could be going anywhere."

Buck shook his head. "I don't know, but I know someone who might." He grinned. "T-Mac. If anyone can find Marly's plane, it would be our man T-Mac. He's an absolute genius when it comes to computers and communications."

"But it's a plane, not a computer."

"Planes have transponders. Transponders talk to computers somewhere. T-Mac just has to find the computer, hack into it and locate our girl."

"They lose airplanes all the time. What will make Marly's plane any different?"

"We can stand here and discuss the merits of hacking or actually try something." Buck straightened the swath of bandages around his head. "Come on."

Pitbull ran ahead of him to the main house, yelling at the top of his lungs, "T-Mac, Harm, Big Jake, Diesel!"

All four men ran out of the house, followed by Talia and the chef.

"What's going on?" Big Jake demanded.

"Marly and her plane were hijacked. They killed the guards and took her and the plane."

"Holy hell," Harm said.

Pitbull faced T-Mac. "You can track her, can't you? Please tell me you can track the plane."

"I'll need my laptop and a strong internet connection."

"I'll get your computer." Diesel ran for T-Mac's bungalow.

"Follow me into my office. We have satellite internet," Talia said. "It's fast and pretty reliable."

"What else do you need?" Pitbull hated being so helpless.

"I need to know we aren't going to come under attack anytime soon." T-Mac stared at Pitbull.

"He's right," Big Jake added. "We need to make sure there aren't any other Tangos running around the perimeter or inside the compound."

Pitbull gave T-Mac a narrow-eyed glare. "You're not trying to get rid of me, are you?"

"If I said yes, would it work?" T-Mac challenged him with raised eyebrows. "I need time to figure this out. I've tracked a lot of things, but I haven't tracked an airplane. We don't have a GPS device implanted on Marly or the airplane."

"Do you know anyone who has tracked an airplane using whatever the airplane has on board?" Pitbull asked.

"I have some contacts," T-Mac said.

Talia threw open a door to a spacious office. The

walls were lined with bookshelves. A massive mahogany desk stood in the middle of the room with two wingback chairs in front of it and a leather office chair behind.

T-Mac paced the length of the room. "I really need my laptop."

"You're welcome to use my computer." Talia keyed her user name and password and stood back. "Go for it, and find Marly."

T-Mac sank into the office chair and placed his hands on the keyboard. A moment later, Diesel arrived with his laptop. He set the laptop beside the desktop monitor and fired it up.

Before he started his search, he glanced up at Pitbull and the rest of the team. "Standing around staring at me isn't going to help me find Marly any faster. Please, go take care of the guards before the buzzards do the job."

Big Jake gripped Pitbull's elbow. "Come, we have a job to do, and T-Mac has his job. He'll let you know as soon as he learns something."

"I need to be here when he finds Marly. You don't understand."

Jake nodded. "I do understand, but you're not going to help T-Mac by getting in his way."

Pitbull knew Big Jake was right, but he didn't like leaving, especially if the one man who was conducting the search found something significant that could lead to bringing Marly back. He wanted to be there when that happened. The sooner he knew where she was, the sooner he'd go to her.

Trouble was, they didn't have the transportation to go anywhere.

Pitbull grabbed the telephone on the desk. "Does this thing work?"

Talia nodded. "Most of the time. It's a satellite phone. It can be sketchy during bad weather. But most of the time it's reliable."

"Who are you going to call?" Big Jake put his hand over the one Pitbull had on the phone.

"The team back in Djibouti. We'll need backup and support."

Big Jake nodded. "Let me. You're a little too close to the problem."

The need to be proactive made Pitbull reluctant to hand over the phone. In his gut, he knew Big Jake was right. He was too upset to be coherent and calm. He handed the phone to Big Jake and then hovered beside him for support until he'd completed the call.

"What did they say?" Pitbull asked.

"They're going to scramble the team and call for support from the 160th Night Stalkers." Big Jake laid a hand on Pitbull's shoulder. "They're coming." He turned toward T-Mac. "As soon as we know anything, we're to contact them."

"They need to pick us up first," Pitbull insisted. "We have to be there for Marly."

Big Jake shook his head. "If Marly ends up being closer to them, they'll go direct."

"You're right." Pitbull's fists knotted so tightly his fingernails dug into his palms. "God, I feel trapped."

"And we all will feel trapped until we locate Marly

and get a ride out of here to her." Harm clapped a hand to Pitbull's back. "Come on. We need to check the perimeter and take care of the guards."

Pitbull gave T-Mac one last glance. "Find her."

T-Mac saluted him without turning away from the desk. "Will do."

The five men checked their weapons and ammo and then left the office.

Talia followed them into the foyer, her brow dipping into a V. "I need help taking care of the guards. I can't leave them out there for the buzzards to feast on."

"We can take care of them," Big Jake assured her. "I'm not sure how it works here, but shouldn't the police investigate?"

The resort owner drew in a deep breath. "I put a call in to the local authorities. They should be here within the next fifteen minutes." Talia wrung her hands. "Those guards were good men. I have no idea what to tell their families."

"We're sorry for your loss," Big Jake said. "But you might have a bigger problem."

Her eyes widened. "What do you mean?"

"How many guards do you have working this resort?" he asked.

"I had five, but I'm down to three. One fills in for the others and two of them work the night shift."

"It might not be enough," Harm said.

Talia nodded. "I hope I can get additional guards. They might not want to come to work on a resort where two have already been attacked and killed."

"I'm heading out to check the perimeter." Pitbull didn't have the patience to stand around inside the house. As it was, the walls seemed to be closing in around him. The sooner he got outside, the better.

He needed to search the grounds and out around the landing strip. What if the plane hadn't been large enough to hold all of the attackers? There might be more thugs waiting for sundown to make a break for it. If they could capture one, they could coerce him into telling them where they'd taken Marly.

Pitbull grabbed the doorknob and yanked open the door. "Are you coming?"

"I'm coming," Harm said.

"Me, too," Diesel said.

Pitbull stared pointedly at Talia. "You'll let us know if you hear anything from T-Mac or Marly?"

Talia nodded. "You bet. Anything. As soon as I hear."

Pitbull shot a last glance toward the office. He couldn't hover behind T-Mac, and he had to do something to burn off frustrated energy. Until they knew where the hijackers had taken Marly, he couldn't do much to rescue her. He could only kick himself for not going with her to the plane. Guilt gnawed at his gut. He couldn't imagine what she might be going through. Some of the rebel factions in Africa were cruel—especially toward females.

He and his team spread out, taking different directions upon leaving the compound, weapons drawn. After the two guards had been killed, they knew the attackers weren't messing around.

All they had to go on was finding the plane. What if the hijackers separated Marly from her plane? In that case, they'd be shooting in the dark to find her.

Chapter Twelve

Marly surfaced from a very dark and foggy place. Pain throbbed in her cheek and temple. When she opened her eyes, the darkness abated only a little. She blinked to clear her vision, but the darkness remained as a hazy gray twilight.

She lay on a hard surface, not the soft cushy mattress she'd shared with Pitbull at the resort. Where was she? Confusion cleared as memories rushed in. Marly sat up straight, her vision slowly adjusting to her surroundings. The hard surface was a dirt floor. The walls around her weren't those of her plane. Instead they were made of mud and thatch. The only light making its way into her prison was from a gap near the roof, and it wasn't much. Night must be falling. She'd been unconscious for a while.

Marly staggered to her feet, bracing a hand on the rough wall to steady herself while the world spun in protest. When her legs stopped wobbling, she straightened and searched the interior of her cell for the exit. A wooden door at one end of the small space was the only way in or out, and apparently it was locked from the outside.

She fought the urge to yell and shake the door violently. If there was another way out, she didn't want to alert her captors to the fact she was awake. For a long moment, she listened, straining to hear sounds of movement, talking or anything that would tell her what was happening outside. Several times she heard vehicle engines. Once she heard a shout in what sounded like Swahili.

And then she heard a moan. Soon the moan turned to quiet sobs from the other side of one of her cell walls.

Marly's heartbeat quickened as she crossed to the wall and leaned her head close. From the sounds of the sobs, it had to be either a child or a woman.

"Hey, can you hear me?" Marly called out in just above a whisper.

The sobbing continued.

A little louder this time, Marly called out, "Hey, can you hear me?"

For a moment silence reigned. Then a soft voice sounded from the other side of the wall. *"Oui,"* said a woman with a French accent. French was the official language of the Democratic Republic of the Congo.

"My name is Marly. Do you speak English?" Marly asked, praying the other woman did. Otherwise, it would be next to useless for them to combine efforts.

"Oui," she responded. "A little."

Marly sagged with relief. "Where are we?"

The woman started crying again.

"Hey, it's going to be all right. But I need to know where we are and why we were brought here."

Through her sobs, the woman managed to say, "We are to be sold and taken away to other countries."

Marly swore softly. If these were the same people who'd been poaching on national preserves, not only were they after baby animals, they were involved in human trafficking.

"Oh, no, they won't," Marly promised. If it was the last thing she did, she'd get out of this mess and take the other woman with her. "Are there more women?" she asked.

"Oui," the woman answered. "I do not know how many."

"My name's Marly," she said.

"I am Celeste," the woman answered, though the sound was more of a sob.

"Well, Celeste, we're going to get out of here. You hear me?"

"S'il vous plaît."

Marly searched the room again, even more intent on escape than before. She refused to allow herself and other women to be sold like cattle to the highest bidder and then used as sex slaves in God knew where.

The walls were dried mud and straw, but hard-packed and dense. It would take a long time to scratch her way through with nothing but her fingernails. She eyed the gap near the roof that allowed air and a little light from the moon to filter through. From where she stood, the gap didn't appear large enough for a human to fit through. But she wouldn't know unless she climbed up there and found out.

She'd been over the room several times and found nothing but herself and the dirt floor. Without a ladder or a chair to stand on, she could use only her hands and feet to scale the wall. How hard could it be?

She jumped and made a grab for the top of the mud wall. No matter how high she jumped, it remained out of her reach. With no toe or finger holes, she couldn't climb the wall. Using her fingernails, she scratched and dug into the hard-packed mud walls. All she managed was to break her nails down to the quick. If only she had something hard and sharp.

Marly almost laughed out loud. Too often she'd been poked by the underwire in her bra when it found its way out of the fabric and dug into her skin.

Quickly she unzipped her flight suit, peeled it down her torso and removed her favorite pink bra. A few minutes later, she had the underwire out of the bra. She slipped the bra into her back pocket, sans the wire, and zipped herself back into her suit.

Using the sharp end of the metal, she dug at the dirt walls in the corner of the room, creating toe and hand holds she could grip as she climbed the wall. The work was slow and steady, but what else did she have to do? She wasn't content to wait for the thugs who'd put her here to come back, rough her up and knock her out again. She had to escape and get the others out before they sold them to the barbarians who traded in human flesh.

One by one, she dug holes deep enough and shaped

for her hands to grip. By the time the moon had risen high into the sky, she reached the top of the wall and could see out of the building. There was only a four-inch gap between the roof and the thatched roof. Not enough for her to shimmy through but…

She pushed at the thatch. It gave a little but was tied snugly to keep the rain out. Pushing again, she could feel it give a little more. Using the underwire, she slashed at the binding holding the thatch together. The dull edge of the wire did little to cut through. Marly was persistent and kept hacking away, praying her efforts would eventually pay off.

"Marly." Celeste's voice sounded through the wall. "Someone comes."

Marly left the wire hooked in the thatch and dropped down the wall to the floor. She moved quickly to the opposite side of the room, where she lay on the floor as if she were still unconscious.

The door to her cell opened and a flashlight shone in onto her face.

Though Marly peeked through her lashes, all she could see was the flashlight's beam glaring at her. She could hear two guards speaking in Swahili. One of them entered the cell and kicked her with his boot.

Marly fought hard not to cry out or flinch. He'd caught her in the rib and it hurt like the devil. She hoped they'd move on and leave her alone if they thought she was still out.

Her luck continued to be lousy.

The men each grabbed an arm, hauled her out of the cell and dragged her through what appeared to be a small village with a mix of thatch-roofed huts and tin and plywood shanties. Between the huts and shanties were stacks of cages. Some had animals trapped inside.

As they passed by, the creatures locked in the cages sounded off. Some screeched like apes. Others cried like kittens.

This was where they were bringing the baby animals. Marly's chest tightened. Those poor babies, snatched from their mothers, cried pitifully, breaking Marly's heart. Somehow she had to help them and the women who were also being held. It wasn't enough to escape. She couldn't leave them behind.

The guards carried her into the only structure that appeared to have had any thought put into its construction, with sturdy wooden walls and a tin roof.

Marly didn't make it easy on the men. She relaxed her body, still pretending to be unconscious. When they dumped her on the ground in front of a table and chair, she lay still, hoping whoever she'd been brought to see would have them take her back to her cell to recover. Surely they wouldn't sell an unconscious woman?

"Ms. Simpson, I know you are awake," a man said.

She refused to acknowledge him, lying as still as possible, her eyes opened only enough for her to see through her lashes. Not that she saw more than a pair of boots and legs beneath the desk.

The man spoke in rapid Swahili to the two guards who'd dumped her on the floor. They bent to lift her again and plunked her into a chair, and then moved it to sit in front of the table. The tied her to the chair and left her to face their boss.

A single light hung suspended from the ceiling over the table and chairs. The man on the other side wore a boonie hat. The light hitting the brim cast his face in a deep, dark shadow.

"Ms. Simpson, cooperate and I might let you live." He had an accent that didn't sound like any in Africa. He wasn't South African or British. Hell, he sounded American.

Marly sat tied to the chair, her head hanging, her body limp. She didn't know how long she could pretend to be unconscious, but she didn't have another plan.

The man again spoke to the guards. One left the building and returned a moment later carrying a bucket.

Before she could guess his intention, he tossed the contents of the bucket at her.

Water hit her full in the face. The shock made her gasp and she sucked some in, resulting in a fit of coughing that destroyed her ruse of being unconscious.

Marly shook the wet strands of hair out of her face and glared across the table at the man with the shadowed face. "What do you want?"

The edge of his mouth turned up in a smile, the corner of which escaped the shadow. "That's better. Now that I have your attention, tell me all you know about the American SEALs you brought to Kenya."

She spit at the man's face. The bastard wasn't getting anything from her.

A sharp command from the man behind the desk

yielded an explosive backhand that caught her chin and knocked her backward, chair and all.

Marly slammed against the floor, her head bouncing off the dirt. She lay still for only a moment, pain radiating from her chin and the back of her head.

Then she was jerked upright again before the table. Her head spun and she fought the bile roiling up her throat.

"You will tell me why you've transported these men from one country to another in Africa. What is their mission? Why are they here?"

Clamping her lips shut, she sat silent, refusing to respond.

Another command in Swahili, and this time Marly saw it coming. She cringed and shifted her head to the side as the big hand with the gnarly knuckles whacked her, this time catching her ear. She teetered in the chair but didn't topple over.

"We could do this all night. Perhaps you need a different kind of incentive." He spoke to the guard by the door, who then turned and left.

"We like to know who is muddying our operations on the continent and who is behind sending covert operatives. Whether you tell us or we find out another way, we will neutralize the problem and continue what we set out to do."

Marly's jaw tightened. "Oh, you mean human trafficking and stealing animals from preserves to sell for profit? You must feel all tough and powerful, preying on those weaker than you."

He chuckled. "It's business. A profitable business."

The man was the lowest of low.

Marly's anger spiked, pushing her to lash out. She lunged forward, tipping the chair enough that she could stand on her feet, albeit at an angle. Then she rushed forward, ramming the desk and hopefully the face of the man responsible for the people and animals trapped in cages.

He scrambled backward, knocking over the chair he'd been sitting on and falling over it to sprawl on the ground.

Marly's momentum carried her onto the table. The legs on one side collapsed and she slid to the ground, landing on her side.

The guard with the killer backhand yanked her up and set her and the chair back where she'd been. He held out his hand to his boss and pulled him to his feet.

Marly's hair hung in her face, obscuring her view of the man in the boonie hat. She wanted to see his face to be able to identify him when she made it back to the authorities. He had to be stopped.

He pulled the hat back in place, shadowing his face again, and set his chair back on its legs but didn't sit. Instead, he walked around the table and stood in front of Marly, wiping blood from his chin. "You will pay for that outburst," he said.

The second guard entered the building, pushing a woman in front of him. She was a beauty, with soulful brown eyes and skin the color of roasted coffee. She'd been crying, the salty traces of tears still evident on her cheeks. She wore a torn business suit incongruous with the rural village.

She spoke in French, appearing to beg the man in charge.

He ignored her pleas and addressed Marly in English. "Ms. Simpson, meet Celeste."

Marly fought to keep from showing any sign of recognition. So this was the woman she'd been talking to on the other side of her cell wall.

"Since you refuse to cooperate with us, Celeste will pay for your obstinacy."

Marly's eyes narrowed. What did he mean?

"Shall we start over?" he asked and continued without waiting for her response. "What are the SEALs doing in Africa?"

"I don't know," Marly said.

Her captor spoke in Swahili.

Celeste's eyes widened and she cried, "No!"

The guard who'd brought her into the building punched her in the gut.

Celeste doubled over and dropped to her knees.

"You dirty bastard!" Marly tried to get up again, but the guard behind her planted his hands on her shoulders and held her down.

"Celeste, darling," the sadistic barbarian said in a calm and coaxing tone. "Ms. Simpson is the one responsible for your pain. Because she won't answer a few simple questions, you will be punished."

Celeste shook her head, clutching her belly, tears streaming down her cheeks. *"S'il vous plaît. S'il vous plaît."*

Marly's eyes stung. The bile threatened to rise up her throat again. "Don't. She did nothing to deserve this."

"Then tell me what I want to know," the boss said.

Marly swallowed hard. "The SEALs went to Kenya on vacation."

The boss spoke in Swahili. The guard behind Celeste yanked her to her feet and cocked his arm to hit her again.

"No!" Marly yelled. "Don't hit her. Please, don't hurt her. She did nothing. I'm telling the truth. They came for vacation."

"You're lying."

The guard punched Celeste in the belly again. This time, she crumpled and landed on the floor hard, lying as still as death.

Guilt swelled in Marly's chest. "They came for a safari. That's all they came for," she said, tears welling in her eyes.

"Then why did they interfere with my men?" he asked, his voice harsh. "Why were they armed?"

"They didn't come to interfere with your men. But they couldn't stand by and let your men kill the animals and steal their babies. That's just who they are. As far as I know, they're not on a mission. They came to relax." Marly stared at Celeste lying so still on the floor, wondering if the guard had punctured her lung or ruptured her spleen. She prayed the woman was alive.

Even deeper in her heart, she prayed the SEALs would somehow find them and rescue them from this impossible situation.

Chapter Thirteen

Pitbull and his team searched inside and the outer perimeter of the resort compound and past the landing strip. They didn't find any Tangos lying in wait to kill them or take out more guards, but they did find tire tracks in the dust on the far side of the aircraft landing field. They led away and connected to a road leading to and from the resort.

Buck had volunteered to stand guard on the dead men to keep the buzzards from making a meal out of their bodies. Everyone converged on Buck when they'd completed their search.

"Let's go back to the house," Harm said. "Maybe Talia could send the other guard with one of us to the nearest town to ask questions."

Buck nodded toward the house. "Looks like the authorities are finally here." A couple of men in official-looking uniforms strode toward them, followed by four more men carrying two stretchers.

The Kenyan detectives asked questions and made notes, took pictures and then motioned for the collection crew to load the bodies onto the stretchers.

Relieved of their bodyguard duties, the SEALs returned to the house and the office where T-Mac was working. The sun was well on its way toward the horizon, and as far as Pitbull knew, they still didn't have a clue as to where Marly and her plane had been taken.

Talia paced the far end of the room, talking on the satellite phone. When the men entered, she nodded, acknowledging their presence. "Look. I need more guards to keep my clients safe. Do whatever it takes, but have at least two more out here before midnight."

Pitbull headed straight for T-Mac. "Anything?"

T-Mac held up his hand. "Hang on."

A kernel of hope sat in Pitbull's belly, waiting for whatever T-Mac had to say.

The team's computer guru's fingers flew across the keyboard as he messaged someone on the other end of cyberspace.

"Ha!" T-Mac said as he clicked on a link the other guy provided. A dark screen appeared with numbers, letters and a lot of stuff Pitbull didn't recognize.

"We found the plane," T-Mac said. He pointed to the screen, where sets of numbers and letters flashed. "Our Marly was smart enough to set the transponder code to the hijack frequency 7500."

"How did you know that's the hijack code?" Pitbull asked.

"I told you I had a buddy who knows about airplanes. He helped me download the software that can monitor flights in the area. It took a while, but between the two of us, we found the airplane."

The kernel of hope swelled, filling Pitbull's chest. "Great. Where is she?"

"Looks like she's headed into the Democratic Republic of the Congo."

"Then what are we waiting for?" Pitbull started for the door. "Let's go get her."

T-Mac laughed. "We can't get there on foot. We have to wait for the 160th Night Stalkers to arrive."

As much as Pitbull wanted to be there when they found Marly, he wanted Marly to be safe, first and foremost. "Would it be faster for them to go directly after her?"

"They're in the air now. It might be faster to divert them to her location than to come here first—if we knew where the plane would land."

The blip on the screen blinked, giving Pitbull a little bit of reassurance that the plane was still flying, and Marly could be the pilot, alive and well. Getting to her would be his next hurdle, but as long as she was alive and okay, he could take a moment to be a little relieved.

Except not really. Until she was back with him, safe and sound, he would continue to worry and wish he wasn't so hampered by time and space.

He stared at the monitor, the only lifeline he had between him and Marly.

Suddenly the blip disappeared.

Pitbull's heart leaped into his throat. "What happened?"

"I don't know." T-Mac leaned toward the screen and keyed a message to his friend. Why did it disappear?

The friend instantly sent a message back. Let me check.

T-Mac waited, tapping his fingers on the desktop.

Pitbull paced behind him, his gaze on the monitor, willing the blinking light to reappear.

T-Mac's friend messaged, Either someone turned off the transponder or the engine stopped running.

Pitbull leaned over T-Mac's shoulder, reading the message. "What does he mean, the engine stopped running?"

"They could have landed and shut down the engine." T-Mac glanced up at Pitbull. "The alternative is the plane crashed."

The blood rushed out of Pitbull's head, making him dizzy.

T-Mac touched his arm. "Look, I like Marly as much as you do. Okay, maybe not as much, but I choose to believe they landed."

"Damn—" Pitbull cleared his throat of the knot forming there and started again. "Damn right, they did." He strode toward Talia. "We need to find out where the 160th is and divert them to the plane's last coordinates."

Talia handed him the satellite phone.

"T-Mac, you got those coordinates?" Pitbull demanded.

"Got 'em." T-Mac jotted the numbers on a pad and leaped from the chair.

Pitbull started to place the call to the 160th and stared across the room at Big Jake. "Do it." He handed the phone to his teammate and waited while Big Jake made the call.

A moment later he was in touch with the 160th flight dispatch. "Where did you say they are?" Big Jake held the phone closer, his eyes narrowing. Then his face busted out in a big grin. "Great. Thanks. BJ out." He ended the call and handed the phone to Talia. "Come, on team, we have a flight to catch."

"Where are they?" Pitbull asked.

Big Jake pounded Pitbull on the back. "Landing as we speak."

"Landing where?" Buck asked, yanking the gauze bandage from his head.

"Just outside the compound. Let's go!" Big Jake took off running toward the back of the big house with Pitbull on his heels.

As soon as he exited the building, Pitbull could hear the reassuring thumping of rotor blades beating the air.

They ran through the stand of trees and emerged near the landing strip in a cloud of dust spun up by the two helicopters just touching their skids to the ground.

Pitbull had never been happier to see those helicopters with the gunners hanging out of the side doors, waving for them to climb aboard.

Other members of their team from back at Djibouti were on board, spread out between the two choppers. The men high-fived each other and helped them get settled and strapped in. Once they were all aboard, the helicopters took off.

"They know where we're going?" Pitbull yelled over the roar of the engine and rotor blades.

Big Jake nodded. "They have the coordinates."

As they flew toward Marly, their teammates pulled out weapons and handed them off to Big Jake, Buck and Pitbull. Diesel, Harm and T-Mac would be outfitted similarly on the other chopper. Their unit had been looking out for them. Of course, they'd give them hell about stirring up trouble on their vacation. But that would wait until they got back to Djibouti and they were all sitting around drinking beer.

Pitbull didn't care, as long as they got to Marly in time to save her from the killers who'd taken out two guards to steal her and the plane she flew.

The sun descended to the horizon, slipping lower until it melted into the savanna. Darkness settled in and the stars popped out one by one, filling the sky with a blanket of diamonds.

Marly would have liked watching the sunset from the helicopter, and then she would have told him how much she liked viewing the sky without all the light pollution of the big cities. If he got her back...

Pitbull shook his head. No. *When* he got her back, he'd still have to let her go. She'd want to stay in Africa, and he had a job based out of Virginia. Hell, that bridge he needed to cross was coming far too fast. First things first, though. He had to get Marly back.

He wished he could fly in the cockpit as he had with Marly. At least then he could see where they were going and get a feeling for how much farther they had left to travel. Marly's plane had flown for a few hours. To catch up to them, they'd have to fly for as long, maybe longer. He wasn't sure how fast Marly's plane flew, but it had to be faster than the Black Hawk helicopters.

Pitbull stared hard at the front of the aircraft, willing it to fly faster than it had ever flown before. The sooner they got to Marly, the better.

BECAUSE CELESTE HAD passed out, the boss decided to slap Marly around some more until she couldn't see straight and barely hung on to consciousness. Finally, she let her head droop and half feigned unconsciousness. One more hit and she'd be out, but really, she could care less if they hit her as long as they took her back to the holding cell she'd left. At least there she had a chance of escaping. And she'd get Celeste out, even if she had to carry her out herself.

When the boss got bored with slapping her around, he waved to the guards, spoke in their language and then got up to leave.

The guards tossed the women over their shoulders like sacks of potatoes and carried them back to their respective cells.

Thankfully, Marly ended up in the one she'd worked on so hard. She was glad she'd done the work before they'd beaten her. After the way they'd treated her, she wasn't sure she would have had the strength to dig all those holes in the wall. She wasn't even sure she'd be able to climb up the wall and push her way through the thatch with her vision blurring and pain shooting through her head.

Once the guards dropped her on the ground, she lay there for a few minutes, listening to the sound of their boots as they walked away. When she was sure they were gone, she dragged herself to her feet and leaned her head against the wall. "Celeste."

No response.

"Celeste, please wake up."

A moan sounded through the wall.

"That's it. Wake up. I'm going to try to get out of here. Be ready for when I come to get you."

"Non," she said softly in her lovely French accent. *"Je ne peux pas.* I cannot."

"Yes, you can. If I can get out, you can come with me. You have to help me get the others out. I can't do it alone."

Silence stretched for a few moments. Marly thought Celeste had slipped into unconsciousness again.

Then Celeste spoke. "I will be ready."

Strengthened by the knowledge Celeste wasn't dead or still out cold, Marly stood, fought back dizziness and climbed to the top of the wall. The underwire from her bra still hung in the thatch. She used it again to hack away at the thatch bindings, putting everything she had into the effort, finally breaking through.

Parting the thick grasses used to make the thatch proved to be harder. Dirt, dust and mildew had fused the strands together. She cut through it with the wire and despaired of ever seeing the stars again.

Suddenly the thatch parted and she could see clear

sky with a plethora of twinkling diamonds shining down at her. A rush of tears stung her eyes. She blinked them back and continued widening the hole until she could fit her shoulders into it. Then she pulled her torso through, braced her feet on the wall below and pushed the rest of her body out. With her calves and ankles still trapped, she swayed, drinking in fresh air and freedom.

Footsteps crunching on gravel made her hunker close to the roofline. Below, a guard walked by, carrying a semiautomatic rifle slung over his shoulder, the barrel pointed at the ground. He appeared bored, his feet shuffling pebbles as he moved past.

Marly waited until he was out of sight around the corner of another structure before she pulled her feet out of the thatch. No sooner had she gotten them out than she fell backward, landing on the slick grass and sliding toward the edge of the roof.

She twisted, rolling onto her stomach and reaching out to grab hold of something, anything. The blades of grass used to make the thatch slipped through her fingers. She couldn't find purchase and plummeted to the ground.

Her feet hit first, her knees buckled and she fell back on her buttocks with a hard thump. The jolt didn't feel good on her backside, but nothing was broken and she was still conscious. She'd consider that a success.

Resting on her laurels wasn't a luxury she could afford. The guard could come back through at any moment, and she still had to get Celeste and any other women who might be held captive out of their cells.

Marly jumped to her feet and ran around the hut to the other side. The building stretched fifty feet to her left. She'd been in the outer cell with Celeste next to her. The doors were made of rough planks with rudimentary boards dropped into place, effectively locking the door without a lock.

Marly nearly cried out with excitement. Her luck was just beginning to change. Quickly she shoved the board up on Celeste's cell and swung the door open.

Celeste fell through and hugged her hard. *"Merci beaucoup,"* she whispered, hugging her again.

Marly closed Celeste's door and shifted the board back into the locked position. The guards wouldn't think they'd escaped if the doors were still closed and locked. She turned to the other woman. "There are more?"

Celeste nodded and pointed to the other doors. "They were in there."

Each taking a different door, they worked their way along the front of the building. After they'd freed two others, Marly positioned Celeste at the corner of the building to watch for the return of the guard. Marly and the freed women continued to empty the cells. Once they had all the women out, they huddled in the shadows between the long building that had been their prison and another whose roof had caved in and appeared to be abandoned. Counting Marly, there were ten women.

"Do you know if there is an aircraft landing strip near here?" Marly asked Celeste.

Celeste shook her head. "I do not know. I woke up here." She turned to some of the others and spoke in Swahili.

One woman nodded and pointed.

"She says they brought her in tonight on a road in that direction. She saw an airplane out there."

Marly's heart skipped a few beats, excitement building. They might have a chance to escape yet.

The scuffle of footsteps on the gravel had all ten women freezing in place. Marly pressed a finger to her lips. Hiding one person wasn't as big a deal as hiding a gaggle of females.

The bored guard walked past the gap between buildings where the women hid. Marly's eyes narrowed. She recognized him as the one to punch Celeste in the belly so many times.

One of the younger women gasped.

Marly froze in a crouched position. If she had to, she'd attack. She prayed it didn't come to that.

The guard paused halfway past the gap. As if in slow motion, he turned toward the women.

He didn't have time to raise his weapon before Marly sprang forward and hit him in the gut like a linebacker going after the quarterback. The man fell to the ground, the air knocked from his lungs.

Marly straddled him, pinning his arms to the ground, his weapon trapped between them.

Celeste slapped her hand over his mouth and said something in Swahili. One of the women grabbed a knife from a scabbard on the man's belt and slammed it into the man's chest.

It all happened so fast, Marly didn't have time to process what had just occurred. They'd killed a guard.

Holy hell. When the boss found out, he'd kill all of them.

Marly decided then and there that the boss couldn't find out. Not until they were long gone from there and on their way to freedom.

"Grab an arm," she said to Celeste. Together, they dragged the man into the abandoned building and left him in the deepest shadows. He wouldn't be found until the next day, if that soon. He might rot before they discovered him from the smell. As far as Marly was concerned, he deserved to rot in hell. He'd nearly killed Celeste. The only man worse than him was the one who'd ordered him to hit defenseless Celeste.

Once the guard was stashed in the dark, Marly grabbed his rifle and peered out of the abandoned building, watching for any other movement. At the far end of the camp, close to the building she'd been interrogated in, lights came on and an engine fired up. It sounded like the diesel engine of a big truck. Men carried cages and crates to the trucks, loading them one at a time.

Nobody came in their direction. They appeared to be concentrating on loading the truck. Marly guessed they were loading the animals, ready to ship them off for sale. She wished she could help them, but first she had to get the women to safety. Then she'd come back with Pitbull and his team and kill every one of the murdering, stealing, human-trafficking bastards.

Now would be the time if they were going to make a run for it. The truck's engine noise would mask the sound of the airplane engine starting up, buying them time to get away.

Marly motioned for the women to stay put. She ran to the corner of the next building, keeping to the shadows. With the lights shining at the other end of camp, hopefully the men would be night-blind and miss the movements of ten women escaping.

Marly shot a glance left and right. So far, the area was free of guards. She waved for the women to follow. When they were on their way toward her, she ran to the corner of the next building and the next until she stood at the edge of the village near the road the truck would have to travel to get out.

Two hundred yards away, gleaming silvery blue in the moonlight, stood Marly's plane. Parked close beside it were two tanker trucks, presumably containing gasoline or diesel for the trucks. What were the chances they were filled with aviation fuel? Slim to none. She prayed there was enough fuel left to get the plane and ten women off the ground and to the nearest airport with available fuel.

She was about to make a run across the wide-open expanse when a four-wheel-drive vehicle pulled out of the village and parked near her plane.

"No, no, no," she whispered.

"What?" Celeste moved up beside her.

"Please don't take the plane," she whispered.

Celeste's breath caught on a gasp. "That is him." She pointed toward the man getting out of the vehicle.

The boonie hat gave him away.

Marly's blood boiled and she nearly shouted out to the man who'd orchestrated what was happening to them. He walked toward the plane and pulled the steps down.

"He can't get away," Marly said through gritted teeth. "Not in my plane. Not in anything."

"He cannot be allowed to continue," Celeste said.

Marly lifted the rifle to her shoulder. "I won't let this happen." She'd fired rifles before, but never something like the one she'd pilfered from the dead guard. At two hundred yards, she doubted she'd hit the man. But he couldn't be allowed to get away. Lives were at risk. The futures of other women were hanging in the balance.

Knowing she'd never hit such a small target as a man at two hundred yards' distance, she did the only other thing she could, fully understanding the ramifications if she succeeded.

Chapter Fourteen

The 160th Night Stalkers set down the helicopters on the other side of a hill, a couple miles from the exact coordinates they'd been given of the last known location of Marly's plane. Two miles was a lot of ground to cover, but they couldn't risk giving Marly's captors a heads-up that they were on their way in.

With communications headsets on and M4A1 rifles locked and loaded, they scrambled out of the aircraft and hurried toward their destination.

Pitbull led the way, holding the GPS device with the coordinates keyed in. He didn't slow for a moment, pushing harder and faster than he'd ever pushed in his life. Lights ahead made him slow to a stop.

"Harm, cover me should anyone enter from outside this point," he ordered.

Harm was the second-best shot on the team next to Pitbull. In reality, Pitbull should be covering for the rest of the team, but he had to go in and find Marly. He would be less than useless providing cover when his heart and soul were trapped somewhere inside the village in front of him.

Harm got in position and raised his rifle to his shoulder. "Got your six," he said in Pitbull's headset.

Pitbull waved to Buck and Big Jake. "Follow me."

Big Jake motioned to the others. "Everyone else spread out on the perimeter and take out guards and sentries."

The men fanned out, circling the compound while Pitbull headed in, Big Jake and Buck close behind. Once Pitbull reached the first building, he pushed open the door and entered, shining his penlight around an empty room. He exited and waved for Big Jake and Buck to make their move while Pitbull provided cover.

Big Jake and Buck hugged the shadows and moved to the next building, securing it before they gave Pitbull the thumbs-up.

Bright lights lit up the night outside a larger building ahead. A truck was positioned outside the structure, and men were hurriedly loaded boxes and crates into the back. The sounds of animals screaming and screeching added to a sense of chaos and desperation.

Big Jake squatted in the shadows, raised his rifle to his shoulder and waited.

Buck and Pitbull bounded forward, pushed past Big Jake's position and moved on to the next building, a long mud-and-stick building with a thatched roof and doors lining the front. One by one, Pitbull and Buck checked inside each door. Pitbull almost missed it when he glanced in the last one on the end, but something caught his eye as he flashed his penlight around the room. Hanging from the corner ceiling was a bra. A pretty pink one, exactly like the one Marly had been wearing beneath her flight suit the day she'd pulled out her handgun.

"Buck," Pitbull whispered into his headset. "Come see this."

Buck entered the room behind him and shone his light at the pink bra stuck in the ceiling.

"See that hole in the thatch?" Pitbull chuckled and pointed his light at the corner where grooves had been scraped into the wall. He climbed halfway up the wall, snagged the bra and stuffed it into the cargo pocket in his pants. "She escaped."

"That's our Marly." Buck backed out of the building. "But where to?"

"Knowing her, she's going for her airplane. Anyone see a plane yet?"

"T-Mac here. We haven't made it completely around the west perimeter yet. No sign of an airplane on my side."

One of the other men reported in, "I'm only halfway around the east side. No sign of a plane yet."

"We came in from the south," Big Jake said. "Maybe it's on the north."

"Right," Pitbull said. "We're working our way around the interior." He exited the hut and provided cover while Big Jake and Buck advanced this time. They were getting closer to the men loading crates and cages onto the trucks.

"We found the stolen animals," Buck said. "They're all babies and they're loading them into the trucks."

"Any sign of Marly?" Pitbull asked.

"No," Big Jake said. "Covering."

Pitbull hurried forward, hiding in the shadows a little ahead of where Big Jake and Buck were positioned. He was worried about Marly. If she'd escaped and been recaptured, they might have been harder on her. Maybe they put her in one of the cages being loaded onto the truck. Until they checked all the outer buildings, he couldn't go there.

Though it frustrated him to no end, Pitbull continued the search. They cleared all the buildings except those nearest the trucks and the hive of activity. A smaller vehicle pulled away, heading to the north, away from the light and the truck.

By that time, they'd made a complete circle inside the village and were on the southeastern side, close to the trucks.

"Found your plane," T-Mac said in Pitbull's ear.

Pitbull was so elated, he nearly stepped out of the shadows. "Where?" he said past the knot in his chest.

"North end, a couple hundred yards from the village. There's a road out here. That's probably what they landed on."

"How close are you?"

"Three hundred yards. It's sitting out in the open."

"Any lights on the inside? Anyone moving around it?"

"No lights, no movement. Wait. A vehicle just came out of the village. It's stopping in front of the plane."

Pitbull was already moving north.

"Pitbull, maintain situational awareness," Big Jake warned him.

Pitbull slowed, realizing he was out in the open. Any person who was a decent shot could take him out with one bullet. Then they'd know they'd been infiltrated. His team would be at risk.

Pitbull pulled himself together and ducked back into the shadows, raised his weapon and waited for Big Jake and Buck to move.

Buck let Big Jake go ahead. "You all right?" Buck asked.

Pitbull gave Buck a thumbs-up. "Ready?"

Big Jake dropped to one knee and waited for Buck and Pitbull to bound ahead.

Just when he stepped out of the shadows, Pitbull heard a burst of gunfire. A moment later, an explosion ripped through the air.

"What the hell?" Pitbull stared to the north where a fireball rose into the sky, lighting the ground below.

With huts between him and the edge of the village, he couldn't see where the fire was coming from.

"Damn," a voice came across the mic. "We better hope Marly wasn't headed for her plane."

"Why?" Pitbull ditched protocol and started running toward the fireball. "Why, damn it?"

"The fireball?" T-Mac paused. "Was her plane."

As if a giant fist slugged him in the gut, Pitbull stumbled and fell to his knees.

Buck raced up behind him and helped him to his feet. "She wasn't in it."

"How do you know?" Pitbull looked up at his friend. "She would have gone to her plane."

"Maybe she was caught. Maybe she's waiting for

us to rescue her." Buck dragged Pitbull toward the side of a building. "You can't give up hope now."

"That was her plane." Pitbull shook his head. "She loved that plane."

"Yeah, well, we have different problems now." Buck jerked his head in the direction from which they'd come.

Pitbull glanced toward the lights and the trucks. The people who'd been loading the crates and cages were running in their direction.

"Look out, gang. All hell's about to break loose," Pitbull said into the mic.

"Hunker down and hold your fire. No one shoots until the first shot is fired," Big Jake said.

The men running toward them were armed with rifles and machine guns.

Someone fired shots, and like a chain reaction, bullets flew.

Pitbull waited as long as he could, but when the men came within two yards of him, he opened fire. One of the advancing men fired at Pitbull, hitting the wall of the building behind him, barely missing his head.

Big Jake took the enemy out with one shot to the forehead.

When they saw their buddies dropping, the men in the rear turned around and ran in the other direction, climbing into whatever smaller, faster vehicle they could find. Moments later, the night grew silent but for the sound of engines fading into the distance.

"Perimeter check," Big Jake said.

"All clear."

"Bring it in. Go door to door," Pitbull said, his voice dull, his heart no longer into the mission. He stared at the flames leaping into the sky.

"Is that a fuel truck next to the plane?" Buck pointed at a vehicle as the tires caught fire.

"Holy crap!" Pitbull exclaimed.

At that moment, the tanker truck exploded, knocking Pitbull back on his heels. His head reverberated from the concussion, and he couldn't hear past the ringing in his ears.

"No sign of Marly in the big truck or any of the crates or cages on board," T-Mac reported in.

Pitbull could barely hear through the roar in his head.

"Buildings are empty. Everyone left. No sign of Marly," Diesel reported minutes later.

Pitbull pushed to his feet and stared at the wreckage. "Marly, baby. I'm sorry. I should have been there for you."

Buck came up behind him and laid a hand on his shoulder. He spoke slowly and clearly. "She wasn't in the plane."

"But she was here." He pulled the pink bra from his back pocket. "She was here."

"But she's not here now." Buck nodded toward the plane. "And she wasn't in the plane. You have to believe that."

"I never should have let her go back for her logbook. It could have waited." Pitbull shook his head. "I'm so sorry, Marly. I wish I had never let you out of my sight."

MARLY HAD PULLED the trigger, determined to keep the boss from getting away with all the atrocities he'd committed. She had no idea how long his operation had been in business, or how many women he'd sold into slavery. All she knew was he couldn't be allowed to continue.

She aimed the rifle at the man and shifted to the fuel truck closest to the plane.

"Tell the women to duck and hold their ears," she warned Celeste.

Celeste translated and lay down with her face to the ground, her hands over her ears. The other ladies followed suit.

"Sorry, baby," Marly said to her plane and pulled the trigger, holding it long enough to release a burst of bullets. Seconds later, the world rocked with the explosion. She was knocked backward, where she hit her head on a tree and passed out.

How long she lay in the dark, she didn't know. When she came to, she sat up. Her ears rang and her head hurt. A ball of fire rose from what was left of her plane and the fuel truck. Her heart hurt, but she couldn't regret her decision.

Men's voices sounded nearby and they were speaking English, but she couldn't make out the words. Her ears rang too loud, and she didn't have a whole lot of control of her motor movements.

When she finally pushed to her feet, another explosion ripped through the air, again knocking her to the ground. She lay still. The stars she could see through the trees blurred and faded to black.

When she surfaced again, she blinked up at tree branches and more stars. Her ears were still ringing, but her vision was beginning to clear. She moved her fingers and toes, then her legs and arms. Nothing hurt, other than the bruises she'd received from her captors. Then she remembered the nine other women she'd been trying to get to safety.

Marly sat up too fast. Her head spun, but she pushed past the dizziness, refusing to pass out again.

The women lay on the ground around her. Some sobbed quietly, while others lay with their hands over their ears as if waiting for the next explosion.

Celeste pushed to a sitting position beside her and blinked.

"Are you all right?" Marly asked.

Celeste nodded and winced. "My ears hurt and I can't hear well."

"That would be a concussion from the explosion. Hopefully, it will go away soon."

She stared out at the plane and fuel trucks. "Did you get him?"

Marly nodded. "Nobody could have lived through that explosion. You felt it from here and we're over two hundred yards away."

Celeste nodded. "Still, I want to see the body. Proof."

Marly understood. She, too, wanted proof the man died in the explosion, never to torture, sell or trade in humans and animals ever again.

Now that they were free of him, would they be able to get away from the others? She'd destroyed their means of transportation, and going back to where the others had been loading trucks would be a very bad idea.

Marly glanced at the road leading away from the village. They might have to walk. "Let's ask the others if they can walk."

Celeste and Marly went around to each of the women to make sure they were okay. Some were so distraught, they couldn't stop crying. Others sat in shock, almost catatonic. All of them seemed physically well enough to walk, though.

Marly glanced back at the village. A light still burned near the other end where the trucks had been and the animals had been loaded. The engine noise had ceased, and she couldn't make out any shouts. Then she remembered hearing voices before the last explosion. Voices speaking English. American English.

Her pulse sped up, and she pushed to her feet. "Keep them here. I want to check on something."

Celeste grabbed her wrist. "It is too dangerous."

"I'll be careful. If don't come back in five minutes, take the women and start walking. Follow the road, but don't walk on it. Stay in the shadows and move at night. Understand?"

Celeste nodded. "Please don't go."

Marly squeezed her hand. "I have to." Deep in her heart, she knew she'd heard something. Had it been a dream? Had she had a flashback to her time spent at the All Things Wild Resort? Or were there really men here who spoke American English? And if there were, who were they and what were they doing here?

Marly stood and walked toward the village, moving from tree to tree, still a little wobbly on her legs. Her hearing was coming back slowly. She could swear she heard the murmur of voices. She worked her way toward them and came to a stop when she heard one very familiar tone.

"I'm so sorry, Marly." The voice came from the shadows beneath a tree. "I wish I had never let you out of my sight."

Her heart skipped several beats and then raced, pounding so hard against her eardrums, she was afraid she would lose her hearing altogether.

"Pitbull?" she whispered. Then she was running, crashing through the trees. "Pitbull?"

"Marly?" A man materialized out of the shadows, caught her in his arms and crushed her to his chest. "Oh, Marly, I thought you were gone. I thought I'd lost you in that explosion."

"You found me," Marly said. "I can't believe you found me."

"I'd have searched to the ends of the earth. I never should have let you go back to your plane alone."

She cupped his cheek and leaned up on her toes to lightly kiss his lips, her heart so full she thought her chest might explode. "You found me."

Pitbull held her close, his lips crashing down on hers. Marly winced and jerked back.

"Did I hurt you?" Pitbull held her at arm's length.

She touched her hand to her mouth. "I have a split lip. But I don't care. Kiss me again." She pressed her mouth to his, but he refused to kiss her.

Instead, he raised a penlight and scanned her face and body. "Sweet Jesus, Marly, what did they do to you? Are you bleeding?" He shone his light over the blood stains on her flight suit. "Buck! We need a medic! Stat!"

She touched his cheek again and shook her head. "I'm okay but for a few bumps and bruises. This blood isn't mine."

"Not yours?" He let go of a long, heavy sigh.

"No, it was the guard who gave me these." She pointed to her bruised cheekbone and jaw.

"Dead, I hope?"

She nodded. "Very."

By the fierce look on Pitbull's face, the dead man was lucky the SEAL hadn't gotten to him first. He'd have made him suffer for hurting Marly.

Pitbull didn't belabor the discussion of the man's death, which suited Marly fine. She still wasn't sure how she felt about killing. Though she hadn't killed the man who'd hit her, she had been responsible for the death of his sadistic boss.

She shook off the thought and hugged Pitbull again. "How did you find me?"

Buck appeared behind Pitbull. "Actually, T-Mac found you and we all came to rescue you. Poor Pitbull was so distraught, we were surprised he didn't catch your plane with his bare hands before it left the ground. If he could have run eighty miles per hour, he might have done it."

"I saw you," she said. "And I couldn't do anything about it. They threatened to kill all of you with a grenade. I had to fly." She pressed her cheek to his. "And then the bastards pulled me out of the pilot's seat and knocked me out."

Pitbull's arms tightened around her waist. "I'm sorry you had to go through that. I'd kill them all over again if I could."

"All over again?" Marly glanced around. That's when she saw the bodies lying on the ground. "Are these the men who were working this operation?"

Pitbull nodded.

Her gaze shifted to Pitbull's. "They were trading in baby animals and human trafficking."

"Human trafficking?" Big Jake shook his head. "Death was too good for them."

She nodded in the direction of the women hiding in the woods. "Celeste, you can come out now. It's safe."

Moments later, the nine women walked out of the woods, following the sound of Marly's voice.

They held back when they saw Pitbull, Big Jake and Buck's big, burly bodies surrounding Marly.

"Don't worry, they're here to rescue us." Marly hurried over to Celeste, took her arm and walked her over to the men. "This is Celeste. She helped me get all the women out."

Celeste nodded. "Thank you for coming to help us."

Big Jake chuckled. "It appears you didn't need us, after all."

Marly raised her eyebrows and stared around at the men littering the ground. "We would be dead if you hadn't come. These men would have killed us after I took out their boss."

Pitbull frowned. "You took out their boss?"

She tipped her head toward the smoldering fire. "I sacrificed my plane rather than let him get away in it."

"You were responsible for the explosion?" Buck asked.

Marly nodded. "I couldn't let the man behind this operation get away. He would have gone on to kill more animals and kidnap more women, only to sell them to the highest bidders. I couldn't let him do that." She shook her head, staring at the smoldering heap. "I'd do it all over again."

T-Mac, Harm and Diesel joined them, each giving Marly a huge hug.

"We weren't sure we'd find you," Harm said.

T-Mac backhanded Harm in the gut. "What are you talking about? It was only a matter of time before I located her. I had no doubt in my mind we'd find our Marly." He frowned at the fire. "I'm sorry about your plane."

She shrugged and slipped her arm around Pitbull's waist. "I'm just glad you guys are okay." Marly frowned. "By the way, how'd you get here?"

Pitbull grinned. "Our unit sent helicopters."

"Oh, dear Lord. You flew in one of those death traps?" She winked. "Well, I'm glad you didn't crash."

"I'm sure the 160th will appreciate the sentiment," Big Jake said. "Speaking of which, I put in a call for extraction. They should be here in just a minute."

Pitbull pulled her close and held her tight.

Marly turned in Pitbull's arms. "But we can't leave."

"What do you mean? We're in the Democratic Republic of the Congo without permission. As far as you and anyone else are concerned, we aren't here," Pitbull said.

"But the crates." Marly grabbed Pitbull's hand and dragged him toward the light in the center of the village.

"Where are we going?" he asked.

"We have to take care of the animals."

"We can't airlift them out of the Congo," Pitbull said.

"No, but we can drive them out," Marly said. "The men loaded them into the trucks. All we have to do is drive them east back into Kenya and take them to a sanctuary where someone can care for the babies until they're old enough to be on their own."

Pitbull chuckled. "You make it sound so easy."

"What's hard about it?" Marly stared around at the men in the night, their eyes shining by the light of the moon. "They got them here by truck. We should be able to get them out the same way."

Pitbull looked over her head at Big Jake. "What do you say? Want to pull an all-nighter and get the kids to a safe place?"

"I'm game," Buck said.

Big Jake drew in a deep breath and let it out. "We're already in hot water for being in the DRC when we're supposed to be in Kenya. We should let the crew get the women home, and those of us on *vacation* can get the trucks loaded with animals and headed somewhere safe, where they won't die or be sold."

The helicopters flew in just then, landing on the road a couple hundred yards away from the dying fire. The SEAL team, minus the six who'd chosen a relaxing vacation in Kenya, escorted the women to the helicopters.

Pitbull bent to kiss Marly's lips. "You need to go with the women."

Marly shook her head. "I'm going with you."

"As much as I'd love to have you with me, I know those women need a strong lady like you to make them feel more comfortable flying off with a bunch of men. Especially after what they've been through."

Marly frowned. He was right. She hadn't gotten them this far just to abandon them. "Promise me you'll be okay if I don't go with you."

He held up a hand. "I promise." Pitbull pressed his lips to the top of her head. "You know I'd have given anything to see you go all commando and blow up your plane."

She smiled. "You have no idea how hard it was to pull that trigger."

"Oh, baby, I do. I know how much you loved that plane." He hugged her one last time and then escorted her to the waiting helicopters. "Now, don't jinx the pilot. This helicopter is perfectly safe and won't drop out of the sky. I'll see you soon."

"You bet." She climbed aboard, turned and threw him a kiss. Then she was being hustled into a harness, and the helicopter lifted off the ground.

As the chopper rose into the air, Marly focused on the man who'd changed her life and made her feel like a woman, not just a grease-jockey pilot.

Soon he became a speck and all she could see was the plume of smoke that had once been her plane.

Her heart hurt. Her plane had been like a friend. The decision to destroy it hadn't been easy. But now that it was done, what could she do with her life? The possibilities were dauntingly endless.

First, she had to get these women to safety. Sure, the SEALs could have done it without her, but the ladies had been through so much at the hands of ruthless men. Having another female around would help calm their fears in the transition.

Marly smiled. Most of them had never flown in a helicopter. In the limited light from the helicopter control panel and from the starlight, she could see the terror in their faces. As much as she wanted to be with Pitbull at that moment, she'd made the right decision to fly with the freed captives.

The big question in her mind was what would happen next between her and Pitbull?

Chapter Fifteen

Once Marly's helicopter disappeared into the night sky, Pitbull hurried to the trucks the men had been loading. The animals in the cages and crates were showing signs of extreme stress. Many of the babies had probably gone without nourishment for far too long. The best they could do for them was to get them to a rehabilitation sanctuary as soon as possible.

The men finished loading the last few crates and cages. After a final check around the village for any remaining animals or people, the men piled into the trucks and headed out, wanting to make good use of darkness to get out of the DRC and back into Kenya.

The roads were rough. Pitbull worried about the animals in the back. The men didn't have the supplies or the knowledge of each creature to stop and feed them, or he would have. Still, they were better off than being abandoned in the village to die of starvation and dehydration.

The SEALs pushed on, finally crossing into Kenya as the sun popped up from the eastern horizon.

Big Jake had contacted Talia via the satellite phone

the team had brought for them. She had arranged for the delivery of the animals to a refuge fifty miles into Kenya. They were greeted by an army of volunteers who helped unload the animals, sort them and place them into better environments.

Pitbull and his teammates stayed to help care for the baby animals until all had been fed and housed. Every one of the creatures survived the trip, some in better shape than others.

By the time they left the sanctuary, the men had been awake for over forty-eight hours. They were exhausted, hungry and in need of a full day's sleep. Still, they pushed on, driving the trucks they'd taken from the illegal compound, finally reaching the All Things Wild Resort as the sun rose on a fresh day.

Talia greeted them in front the big house in her khaki uniform, her hair perfectly combed, a frown pulling her eyebrows together. "Tell me you got some sleep along the way."

Big Jake rubbed a hand across his three-day-old beard. "No, ma'am. And I'm sure we smell like the animals we rescued."

"Go get yourselves cleaned up. I'll have food on the table in ten minutes." She paused. "Unless you'd prefer to sleep first."

As one, the men said, "Food."

She smiled. "Then food it is." Talia turned toward the house.

Before she disappeared through the door, Pitbull called out, "Any word from Marly?"

Talia shook her head. "Sorry. I've heard nothing."

Big Jake laid a hand on Pitbull's shoulder. "The 160th wasn't supposed to be in the DRC or in Kenya. I'm sure they had to fly low on the radar, literally and figuratively. Marly will contact us as soon as she is able."

"It's been more than twenty-four hours." Pitbull scrubbed a hand over his tired face. "Talia, I won't be at the breakfast table. I'd rather get sleep."

"I can have someone deliver a tray to your bungalow, if you don't feel like coming to the big house," she offered.

"No, thank you." He walked away, heading for his assigned cabin. Once inside, he closed the door and leaned his forehead against the wood paneling. As tired as he was, he couldn't stop thinking about Marly. He had to tell himself she was in good hands, free of the man who'd dared to deal in humans and animals.

She must be hurting, possibly scared. Without her plane, what did her future hold for her?

Pitbull wished he could scoop her into his arms and tell her everything would be all right.

As he walked to the bathroom, he stripped out of his dirty clothing, letting the items fall to the floor along the way. He switched on the shower and stood in the spray for almost half an hour, his body and mind so drained he could barely remember to work up a lather and scrub the dirt out of his hair and skin.

When he finished, he dried himself, wrapped the towel around his waist and walked into the bedroom.

A tray piled high with breakfast foods sat in the middle of the bed.

His stomach rumbled loudly.

"How long has it been since you've eaten?" a familiar voice asked from the adjoining sitting room.

Pitbull spun toward the sound, his heart banging hard against his ribs. "Marly."

She stood framed in the doorway, wearing a long, colorful caftan cinched at the waist, her sandy-blond hair hanging long and loose down her back.

"Miss me much?" she asked, not making a move toward him.

"You have no clue," he whispered.

She chuckled, the sound warming the air between them. "Then give me one."

He opened his arms and she walked into them. "I haven't stopped thinking about you since we left Djibouti on our way to a little vacation safari in Kenya."

She rested her cheek against his chest. "Your heart is beating so fast."

He cupped the back of her head and pressed a kiss to her forehead. "I missed you, Marly Simpson. When I thought I'd lost you, I realized just how much you've become a part of my life."

"In a very short amount of time," she added, tipping her head up to stare into his eyes. "Do you believe in love at first sight?" she asked.

He shook his head. "No. But I believe in love at last." He framed her face in his palms and bent to brush his mouth lightly over her lips. "I don't want to hurt you."

"I trust that you won't," she said.

He knew she was talking about more than the cut on her lip or the bruises on her jaw and cheeks.

"Where are you going from here, Marly? Will you get another plane and continue your flying service?"

She tilted her head to the side. "I don't think so."

"No?" His pulse beat a little faster, hope taking root in his heart.

"I haven't been back to where I was born in a very long time. Do you think they have need of pilots in my home state of Virginia?" She smiled up at him. "Not that I'm asking for strings attached or commitment, but it would be nice to try my hand at dating again. I feel as if I haven't given it enough of a chance."

He laughed and kissed the spot on her face that had the least amount of deep purple bruising. "I think you'll love it, as long as you're dating the right man."

"It all depends on whether he bucks up enough courage to ask me."

"Oh, I can guarantee he'll ask you. But in the meantime, we have a few more days of vacation left here at All Things Wild. Anything special you want to do before we leave?"

She walked her fingers up his chest and pressed one to his lips. "I can think of a few things I'd like to accomplish."

"Accomplish? That sounds like work."

"Seriously, I'd like to find out who else was involved in the human trafficking and the animal sales. The man in charge of that little operation was American. He could have had a partner stateside, facilitating the sales to the US or on to other countries."

Pitbull tucked a strand of Marly's hair back behind her ear. "I agree. We need to find out who else was involved in the trafficking ring." He circled his hands around her waist and then slid them lower to cup her bottom. "Can you think of anything else you'd like to accomplish before we leave?"

She ran her tongue across her lips and smiled. "I'd like to get better at the art of seduction." She stared up at him. "Do you know anyone willing to teach me? I'd really like to become an accomplished flirt."

"I might know a guy." He brushed his thumb over her swollen lip. Pitbull moved closer, reached down and released the towel around his waist. "Anything else you'd like to do before we leave?"

"Oh, yeah. There is something you should know." She leaned up on her toes and whispered in his ear. "I'm going commando. There's absolutely nothing but me underneath this dress."

Pitbull's hands tightened around her waist. "Marly, you're an amazing woman. You don't need lessons in flirting. You already know exactly what to say and do to capture my interest." He gathered the fabric of her dress and pulled it up and over her head, then tossed it to a chair in the corner.

"Don't you want to eat breakfast?" she asked as she slid into his arms, pressing her naked flesh to his.

"Later, babe. I have you in my arms. I don't want to waste a second."

"Oh, good. But we can eat later, can't we? I think we'll be starved by then."

"You've got it, but first, I want to hold you like there will be no tomorrow. To feel your body next to mine and to make love to you all day and all night long."

"I've never heard of anything sweeter. Maybe I'm getting the hang of this seduction thing. It seems to be working on you."

He touched a finger to the tip of her nose. "Hold that thought and don't move." Then he stepped away from her, gathered the tray of food, set it on the table in the sitting room and returned.

Marly hadn't moved. She stood as naked as he'd left her, wearing nothing but a smile.

She was long, lean and perfect in every way. He couldn't imagine any other woman he'd rather be with or have in his life.

"Are you going to stand there staring at me all night long, or make love to me?"

Pitbull laughed, swept her up into his arms and carried her to the king-size bed, where he laid her down gently.

He lay on the bed beside her and gathered her in his arms. "I don't know what will happen when we leave here or how our relationship will progress, but I know one thing."

"What's that?" Marly asked, leaning over to press her lips to his.

"I want you in my life with all the strings attached and a heaping helping of commitment. You're an amazing woman, strong, selfless and independent— everything I never knew I wanted in the woman I can see myself spending the rest of my life with."

"Wow," Marly said. "Just days ago, you were dead set against relationships. As a SEAL, you would never be around. Relationships never work, you said." She tipped her head to the side. "What made you change your mind?"

"You, baby. The person you are. The unassuming way you go about your life. Your fierce independence. If anyone can put up with the life of a SEAL, baby, it's you. You gave me hope for a future I never thought I'd have."

Marly frowned. "I don't know. I'm not anything special."

"You're wrong. You're the best thing to ever happen to me. I don't need a year of dating to come to that conclusion. I know now, you're the one for me. But if you want to date and take your time to come to the same conclusion, I'll do whatever it takes. As long as you end up in my arms, in my life and in my heart."

Marly moved closer, pressing the length of her body against the length of his. "I don't need a year to know what's already in my heart. It's you. Are we clear now? We care about each other and don't want it to end after we leave here."

He chuckled and kissed the tip of her nose. "We're clear."

"Good, because I'd like to stop talking and start loving."

"Bossy much?" he said, pulling her closer. He bent to kiss her lips, ever so softly. "Who knew a vacation could end up being a new beginning?"

"I like to think I keep an open mind. Now, shut up and make love to me."

* * * * *

TEXAS GRIT

BARB HAN

To my editor, Allison Lyons, for being a dream to work with—thank you! To my agent, Jill Marsal, for always having the right words of encouragement—thank you!

To my children, Brandon, Jacob and Tori, who inspire me to be the best version of myself every day. I'm eternally grateful. Whether we're up late carving pumpkins or cheering each other on in our daily adventures (some might say antics) I'm always grateful for our close relationships. Brandon, welcome to the 1m challenge. I'd wish you luck but since you're one of my competitors…game on, buddy! I love you all so very much!

And to John, for laughing no matter how silly we get and for jumping in with both feet for every challenge no matter how crazy. I can't imagine a better partner in crime and in life. I love you!

Chapter One

Carrie Palmer planted her shoulder against the back door of her cold-treats shop and, with a grunt, gave it a good shove. The latch could be tricky and required a certain touch. Humidity always caused the solid wood door to swell. It was August in south-central Texas, with the threat of rain hanging in the air. She twisted the key and listened for the snick of the lock.

The heat combined with a successful annual week-long festival had brought another day of fantastic sales to Carrie's Cold Treats. Aside from an annoying festival worker who seemed bent on dating her, this year's AquaPlay Festival and Cattle Run had gone off without a hitch. People were laughing again, and everyone in Cattle Barge needed the distraction. The town could use a sense of normalcy after being turned upside down for the past couple of weeks following the murder of a prominent family's patriarch, Mike Butler, a.k.a. Maverick Mike.

The man who was notorious for living large and on his own terms had made national news after being found gunned down on his beloved ranch.

Every time she thought about his son, Dade, her heart squeezed. She'd heard that he'd been discharged

from the military recently and had only been in town
a few weeks. She could only imagine what her childhood friend was going through. Not only had his father been killed in a bizarre manner that had caused a
media frenzy *and* an attempt had been made on his sister's life, but an adult child no one had known about had
been summoned to town, bringing with her a murderous ex-boyfriend. Carrie shuddered, because after her
recent breakup with Brett Strawn had blown up, he'd
made terrible threats—threats she knew in her heart he
couldn't mean. Before she would've chalked them up to
him being emotional, a temporary reaction to the disappointment of a relationship ending. Now, she worried.

With Brett, it probably was just the heat of the moment that had him saying words she knew he'd regret
when he had some time to think about them. And yet
her problem was nothing in comparison to Dade's. Her
heart went out to him as she watched his worst nightmares play out in the news, wishing she had some way
to contact him. Even at nine years old, he'd had the most
serious blue eyes beneath thick, curly, sandy-blond hair.

Theirs had been an unlikely friendship. His family was one of the most prominent in Texas, while she
had no parents, moving from group home to a distant
relative's house and then back into foster care through
the early part of her life. Funny how little kids never
noticed how much or how little money another kid's
family had. Interesting how much that changed later in
life. By the time she'd returned to the same high school
after being relocated and bounced in and out of another
home, everything had changed. Dade had grown into
his athletic frame. He'd become popular and, outside

of a few glances in her direction, she was sure he didn't even remember her name.

It was dark outside. She normally closed at dusk, but the AquaPlay Festival broke down at sunset and she'd agreed to stay open late to accommodate all the children not quite ready to wind down on a summer night. At least her business was working for her, even though it seemed like everything else in her life was standing on shaky ground. She'd hoped to find a home in returning to Cattle Barge to open her store. But she felt just as much an outsider here as she had everywhere else she'd lived since college.

The overwhelming feeling that someone was watching caught Carrie off guard. This feeling was a little too familiar since her relationship with Brett had ended a couple of weeks ago, and she often thought she could feel him watching her.

She tried to shake it off, figuring her heightened emotions had to do with the breakup, the words that had been spoken out of anger. And the dozens of apology texts that she had yet to read all the way through, let alone answer.

"Beautiful night," a male voice boomed from behind, startling her. He was close, and she hadn't heard him walk up.

"What are you doing back here, Nash?" A chill raced through her and her fingers tightened around her key ring as she pulled the key out of the lock. She whirled around and had to back up against the wooden door to put some space between her and the tall, thick-around-the-middle festival worker. He brought his hand up against the door, trapping her on one side. His long hair was soaked with sweat after breaking down and loading up the rides. He wore a stained tank top underneath a button-up denim shirt that had half the sleeves cut off. Threads frayed over thick forearms used to lifting heavy equipment.

"Festival's over. Thought you might like to spend some time together before I leave town." The smell of alcohol on his breath assaulted her as he leaned closer. She held her breath. He'd stopped by three times over the course of the weekend to ask her out. Each time she'd declined. She'd been crystal clear. There was no doubt in her mind that he hadn't somehow misinterpreted her rejections, and standing there any longer would cause her to pass out. "Or, maybe I'll find someone worth sticking around for and get a local job."

"It's late. I have to get home and let my dog out." Carrie ducked under his arm and tried to sidestep him, blowing out a breath in the process. He moved with her, blocking her, and the hairs on the back of her neck stood on end.

Nash was big. Too big. Fighting him off would be a challenge. She palmed the small can of pepper spray attached to her key ring and flicked the leather cover open using her thumb, hoping she wouldn't need to use it. As long as she was wishing, she might as well go for it and wish she was already in her car.

The back parking lot was lit by a single light in the far corner. Out of habit, she'd parked in her usual spot behind the building. Regret stabbed her that she hadn't realized how dark it would be after extending her hours. Or how vulnerable she'd be walking to her car alone after she sent her employees home early, reassuring them she could close up by herself with no problem. The festival had ended two hours ago and everything was quiet—everything but the sounds of her pounding heart rushing in her ears.

"What about a movie first?" The cinema was at the end of the strip shopping center, and as much as Carrie liked the idea of being around people right now—lots of people—she didn't want to give false encouragement to a man who gave her the creeps.

She strained to hear voices, anything that might signal life was near, but was met with silence save for the sounds of Nash's heavy alcohol-infused breaths. If she got lucky, a movie would end and people would exit the cinema. She really hoped so, because she might need the help. As it was she doubted anyone would hear if she screamed, and Nash seemed to realize it, too, as a show of yellow teeth stared back at her.

"I've been working extra hours and haven't been home since lunch. Like I said, my dog needs to go out or I'm afraid she'll have an accident." Carrie looked up and didn't like what she saw in Nash's eyes. She flicked the safety off the pepper spray. Experience had taught her that she'd get some in her eyes, too, and hers started watering just thinking about the burn. Her lungs would seize and her chest would ache. But it would give her the edge she needed to get to her car, where she could lock herself inside.

Even at night, the August temperatures in Cattle Barge were in the high nineties. Sweat beaded on Carrie's forehead, a mix of fear, adrenaline rush and sweltering heat. Experience had also taught her not to show her emotions when facing down a bully, no matter how shaky she was on the inside.

Carrie looked straight into the man's eyes, and her

heart skipped a beat at what she saw behind them. She resigned herself to a fight and fisted her free hand.

He slicked his tongue across his bottom lip and made a move to grab her.

She screamed as she brought the pepper spray toward his face.

"Everything okay here, Carrie?" The sound of Samuel's voice was a welcome reprieve, like a soaking rain in the desert on a hot day.

Nash took a step back and turned his attention to her neighbor, sizing him up. "We're just talking."

Carrie used the distraction to dart toward her savior. He was a quiet guy in his late twenties, or maybe early thirties, who'd moved in with his elderly aunt in the same cul-de-sac as Carrie last fall. She presumed he'd moved to Cattle Barge to help his aging aunt, but she wasn't sure because she'd been busy with the shop and only interacted with a few people in town on a personal level. Personal level? Carrie would laugh if anything about that or this situation was actually funny.

"I'm so glad you're here." She grabbed his arm, noticed he was shaking, and an icy chill raced down her spine. She withdrew her hand, chalking up the reaction to overwrought emotions. Nash seemed to realize immediately what she already knew. Samuel was no match. He was close to her height and had no muscle mass, but he'd distracted the worker and that was good enough for her to make an escape. Between the two of them, she had a chance of getting out of this unscathed. She wouldn't look a gift horse in the mouth.

"Walk me to my car," she said to Samuel, dodging Nash's attempt to catch her arm.

Her neighbor shot the worker a look that was probably meant to scare him.

"Keep walking," Carrie told Samuel in a low voice.

"The lady and me were trying to have a conversation," Nash said. Based on the nearness of his voice, he wasn't more than a step or two behind them.

Could they make it to her car without an altercation?

"It's okay. Just keep our heads down and feet moving." She didn't want to provoke Nash any more.

Ten more feet and she'd be home free.

A callused hand gripped her shoulder, pinching hard, and she suppressed a yelp.

Samuel spun to his left to face off with Nash.

"She's with me," Samuel squeaked out, his voice shrill. He was trying to be a hero and was clearly not cut out for the job, because she could feel him trembling next to her. His skin had gone sheet white, and beads of sweat trickled down his forehead.

Like a shark zeroing in on a vibration of fear, Nash took a threatening step toward Samuel.

"Back off, little man," Nash demanded, his rough hand clamping around Carrie's arm.

She jerked it free and brought up the pepper spray. Nash caught her arm in time to stop her from aiming at his eyes.

"Carrie, is that you?" A dark rumble of a voice boomed from the end of the alley, and all three of them froze. She recognized who it belonged to immediately. Dade Butler's voice made her heart thump a little faster, and for very different reasons than being scared. The inappropriateness of her reaction to him caught her off guard, especially after all this time.

"Dade," she said, her voice sounding as desperate as she felt.

"Everything okay here?" Dade had to be at least six foot four, with a body built for athletics. Ripples of solid muscles were apparent underneath his white T-shirt and low-slung jeans. He seemed to size up the scene accurately, based on the deep wrinkle on his forehead and the fact that he was frowning.

"Yeah, why wouldn't it be?" Nash threw his hands up in surrender. "I was just leaving."

Samuel stepped between Carrie and Dade as though sizing up a new threat.

"It's definitely better now that you're here," she said to Dade to calm some of Samuel's tension. The message? Dade was a friend. Samuel just got the muscle he needed to avoid getting his face bashed in. He should be grateful instead of tense.

Nash seemed to take the hint, backing away before heading toward the cinema with a few choice words mumbled just loud enough to hear.

"How long has it been since the last time I saw you?" Dade asked Carrie, his eyes intent on Nash.

She stepped away from Samuel and toward the sound of Dade's voice as a sensual shiver rocketed through her.

"Too long." She hadn't seen him since the news of his father broke and hadn't talked to him in years. She could never forget that voice, and even though dark circles cradled his still-too-serious crystal-blue eyes, he looked damn good. She turned to Samuel, whose body language was even tenser now. "Thank you so much for stepping in when you did. I don't know what I would've done if you hadn't shown up. I'm good from here, though, so you don't have to stick around."

The quiet neighbor didn't respond as he eyed Dade up and down. A glint of metal in his hand reflected in the light as he turned to face her. For the first time, she noticed that Samuel was hiding a knife. She appreciated that he was trying to help her and, sadly, they might've needed the weapon to fight off Nash. Between Samuel's knife and her pepper spray, they might've had a prayer. But the festival worker seemed to know better than to try to take on Dade.

"Everything all right?" Dade's brow arched as he seemed to process Samuel's resistance to leave.

Samuel still seemed to be looking at everyone as a potential threat.

"It's okay. I'm fine now. Dade's a friend of mine," Carrie said to Samuel. These were probably the most words she and Samuel had exchanged, and she was grateful he'd appeared when he did. It was probably adrenaline that had him still tense and ready to defend. He was somewhat awkward, and she figured he'd most likely dealt with his fair share of bullies in his lifetime, being on the scrawny side. The thought made her feel sorry for him. She knew what it was like to be pushed around and unable to defend herself. An angry riptide pulled at her thinking about it, about a past that had left her helpless. She dismissed thoughts that brought her back to that place where she was an innocent girl, fighting off someone who was supposed to be protecting her.

She shook off the reverie, focusing on Samuel. He nodded and seemed like he wanted to say something, but whatever it was died on his tongue. He settled on, "Good night, Carrie."

He seemed so sad, and she wanted to do something to thank him. From the way he carried himself, she doubted he'd stood up for himself or anyone else for most of his life and it had taken a lot of courage for him to do what he'd done. "Stop by the shop tomorrow for an ice cream on the house, okay?"

"Thanks." He smiled and she noticed his lip twitching—a nervous tic? Poor guy. He really was distressed, and she was even more grateful he'd tried to help. She'd send him home with a gallon of her signature ice cream blend for his aunt, too.

"'Bye, Samuel." She stepped into a friendly hug with Dade, ignoring the shivers racing through her body with contact.

"What was up with him?" Dade pulled Carrie against his chest, and she felt how truly muscled he was. His sandy-blond hair and serious blue eyes made for one seriously hot package. And those were all things former friends weren't supposed to think about each other. Notice, maybe, but not have a visceral reaction to.

"I really appreciate what you did after all these…" She diverted her gaze. In his arms, it was a little too easy to forget the awkwardness she'd felt toward him since high school. She pulled back, because thinking clearly while being barraged with his clean and spicy male scent made her pulse erratic.

Carrie was tall—not Dade tall, but tall—with midnight-black hair and tight curls that had minds of their own on humid days. She'd tamed them today with a straightening iron and had no idea why she was thinking about what her hair looked like after what had just happened. Stress caused her thoughts to bounce around, she reasoned.

"Are you shaking?" Dade asked.

"I guess so. That whole situation was stressful, but

I'm fine now," she said a little too quickly. She wasn't okay. Recent events with Brett had her off-balance, and Nash had really done a number on her insides. "Nash has been hanging around the shop and tonight he had alcohol on his breath."

Dade's hand found hers, like they were still kids and running across the playground—which was as much as the action probably meant to him. It caused her heart to beat wildly against her chest. She chalked her out-of-control reaction up to the stressful encounter with Nash; his eyes had told her everything she needed to know about his intentions.

"What was going down a few minutes ago?" With Dade next to her, she should be able to relax, and she could in some ways, because he'd just saved her from what could've turned out to be a very bad situation. One that brought a few harsh memories threatening to crash down around her and reduce her to tears.

She couldn't help but shudder when she thought about how close she'd been to history repeating itself. Well, now she was twenty-seven, not fourteen.

Dodging those heavy thoughts, she looked at Dade instead.

"That festival worker cornered me, and it got awkward. He's been asking me out all week, but I refused, so I guess he decided to take matters into his own hands before he left town." Hearing the words brought on another wave of anger.

A grunt tore from Dade's throat, but he didn't immediately speak, even though his jaw muscle ticked. "Tell me everything that happened."

"He surprised me in the parking lot when I was closing up the shop. Things got a little weird and, luckily, one of my neighbors happened to be near. Samuel must've heard my voice or something, because he showed up just in time to distract Nash. I'm so glad the festival's over so I won't have to deal with that guy again. He'll be long gone by morning."

A dark look crossed Dade's features and for a split second she thought she'd imagined it. "If I'd known, I would've been less friendly."

That was him being friendly? She'd hate to see someone on his bad side. "I'm just relieved it's over."

His eyes darkened anyway, and that jaw muscle bulged again. "Only because I showed up. What if I hadn't?"

She almost pointed out that Samuel had, too, but she knew he couldn't have held Nash off for long.

"It's my fault. I should've parked out front. Out of habit, I parked in back. I don't usually close up the store after dark." Thinking just how close the call had been caused her to shudder again.

"Don't blame yourself for being harassed by a jerk." Dade's free hand fisted. Tension radiated from him in waves. "Did he physically threaten you?"

"He had me trapped against the wall before Samuel arrived." The whole experience had tipped her off-balance, and she wasn't thinking straight. She should be angry, not scared. Too many memories haunted her, bringing her back to that defenseless fourteen-year-old girl she'd been when her foster father had abused her. Well, she was a woman now and could stand up for herself, and she sure as hell didn't need to make excuses for Nash or blame herself.

"I think it's best if I take you to the sheriff's office

to give a statement," he said with calmness to his tone and something else… Possessiveness?

She really was imagining things now.

Shock was wearing off, and the adrenaline rush was making her hands shake. "I appreciate the offer."

"I don't trust Nash." Dade's jaw clenched as he scanned the area.

He was right. She glanced around. Nash could be anywhere, hiding, biding his time in order to make another move.

DADE RAKED HIS hand through his hair. He'd seen the look in the festival worker's eyes, and he hadn't liked it. Thankfully, Carrie's neighbor had been there to serve as a distraction until Dade could get things under control. The neighbor registered as a little odd, but Dade was grateful Samuel had been there to slow Nash down. Dade and Carrie went way back, and the thought of anything happening to her sat like a hot poker in his gut.

Seeing her shell-shocked and pale was like a physical punch, and his past shame roared to the surface. He hadn't helped her in high school like he should've, but there was nothing stopping him now. Besides, she wasn't thinking straight or she would've already come up with the idea of filing a complaint. Another reason leaving her alone wasn't a good idea.

"My truck is parked this way." He motioned toward the end of the alley.

She glanced at her sedan and then at him. "I don't know, Dade. I'm tired. Part of me thinks I should just go home and try to forget this night ever happened."

"This guy could harass a woman in the next town he's in. We don't know anything about his background or if the festival vetted him out before he was hired. He could have a record and he might escalate if we don't nip this in the bud."

Carrie stayed quiet, standing in the back alley. The thought of a man forcing himself on her hit Dade in a very dark place.

Finally, she nodded and took in a sharp breath. "You're right. Let's go."

Dade ignored the fact that holding her hand felt different now. Of course it would—they weren't nine-year-olds playing tag at school. Her hand was softer and more delicate, especially in comparison to his. He spent most of his time outdoors, first in the military and now on the family ranch, where he'd always been hands-on. His showed the long hours he spent in the elements. She didn't seem to mind.

Electricity pulsed through him at the point of contact, but it couldn't be more misplaced. She needed a friend, and the last thing he needed was another complication in his life. Besides, how many times had he vowed to explain himself to Carrie if he got the chance? Years had gone by and he hadn't seen her. He'd been back for a few weeks now, and he'd come up with a million excuses for not telling her what he'd really want to say to her all those years ago when he'd been a jerk instead.

There were some wounds that ran so deep not even time could heal.

Chapter Two

All the words Dade had wanted to say to Carrie since high school died on his tongue. Too many years had passed and, his own guilt aside, she might not want to think about what had happened anymore. Besides, she'd escaped an assault tonight and he could clearly see how rattled she was. This wasn't a good time to bring up more pain.

"I completely forgot to ask what you were doing in the alley," Carrie said, stretching her legs in his truck as she fastened her seat belt.

"Trying to stay away from the media while I picked up the bronze statue my family donates to the festival." He turned the key in the ignition, and the engine hummed to life.

"Oh, right. The cattle run kicks the festival off." Her shoulders were still tense, her posture defensive.

"And is part of the closing ceremony, which is why I'm here carrying on the family tradition," he added. Being a Butler came with a price.

"I heard you left town for a few days after news of your father broke." Carrie gave him the most sincere look of compassion. "I'm sorry for your loss, Dade."

Those words spoken with such sincerity threatened

to crack the casing in his chest. Dade couldn't afford to go there, so he focused on Carrie instead. Her lime-green shorts and cream-colored halter highlighted soft-looking pale skin. Taupe ankle boots—at least that's what they'd called that same color of paint when he'd had his house redone—showed off her calf muscles, and Dade reminded himself that he shouldn't be noticing any of those things about his friend.

"The Mav and I weren't the closest, but his being gone leaves a huge hole at the ranch." Dade thanked her for her sympathy. He gripped the steering wheel and navigated his truck away from the back street and onto Main. For the first time it struck him at how odd it must seem that he called his father Mav instead of Dad or Father like everyone else. But then, nothing about being a Butler made his life normal.

"When did you get back?" She pushed a few curling tendrils of hair from her face as she crossed those long legs.

"A few days ago," he said, adding, "Seemed like I was needed here with the attempt on my older sister's life and then finding out about having a sister we never knew existed."

"I read about what's been happening with your family. Finding out you have another sister must've been a shock. And then her life was in jeopardy. Right?" she asked.

"Madelyn had an ex-boyfriend with a violent streak who tracked her down and attempted to kill her," he said. "We're damn grateful the criminals in both cases have been caught."

"Neither was connected to your father's murder?" Carrie asked.

"We thought Ella's might have been at first. Now, we know different. The Mav's killer is still at large. Every new threat against the family has more reporters descending on Cattle Barge."

"How's everyone doing?" Carrie asked.

"It's been rough."

"I can imagine." The note of compassion in her voice struck him, threatening to shed light in a dark place hidden behind layers of anger, frustration and regret.

"But we're finding a new normal. Everyone's looking out for each other." Dade needed to armor up, and the best way to do that was to redirect the conversation. "The sheriff will need a description and the name of the guy from the alley."

"That's not a problem. Unless… Actually, I don't know his last name. He introduced himself as Nash, and I never asked for his last name." Her voice was still shaky. "He gave me the creeps every time he came into the shop."

"A first name and description will go a long way toward helping the sheriff find him. If memory serves, the workers usually leave town early in the morning. Sheriff Sawmill or one of his deputies should have no problem locating this guy tonight." How many men by the name of Nash could be employed by the festival?

Carrie's cell buzzed inside her purse, and the unexpected noise caused her to jump.

"Sorry." She stuck her hand inside the bag and came up with her phone. After checking the screen, she refused to take the call.

"Does Nash have your number?" Dade doubted it, but the question had to be asked.

"I wouldn't give personal information to a stranger." Her indignant tone said he'd offended her.

"He might've gotten it from someone else or the internet," he offered by way of explanation.

"The phone call was my ex-boyfriend," she stated with the kind of emphasis on the *ex* that said there was a story there.

Dade hadn't thought to ask if there was someone special in her life. It made sense there would be, with her looks. A burst of light zapped his chest at the thought that she was single.

"We broke up recently, and he didn't take it well." Her cheeks flushed, and he wondered if he was making her feel uncomfortable talking about her relationships. He tried not to think about his, although the wounds were still fresh.

"How bad was it?" he asked.

"He said things I know he didn't mean. He just needs time to cool off." She shrugged it off, like it didn't bother her, but he could tell by her tone that it did.

"That's nothing to take lightly." Considering one of his siblings had just been targeted by a murderous ex-boyfriend, Dade figured he owed Carrie a warning. "What happened?"

"Brett said a few things he didn't mean. He was hurt and it came out as anger," she defended. "He's most likely trying to apologize. Things got a little heated."

"It's none of my business, but I wasn't kidding. Take his threats seriously." He pulled into the parking lot of the sheriff's office and found a good spot. There was a flurry of activity. A news reporter spotted them and made a beeline toward his truck. Damn. He hadn't anticipated this, but he should've. Seeing Carrie again threw him off-balance. "We could drive around the block a few times until the swarm calms down."

"It'll be fine." Her voice sounded anything but.

Flashes started going off through the truck windows, blinding Dade.

Carrie's arm came up to shield her eyes.

"I'd understand if you didn't want to be seen with me right now," he offered.

She touched his hand, and the contact sent electricity rocketing through him, searching for an outlet. "This is awful."

"Yep," he agreed. "They're camped out everywhere. I take a breath and it's on the news with some shrink or expert analyzing it."

"I've seen some of the coverage. No one should have to go through this." Carrie took in the kind of breath meant to fortify someone. Dade should know. It was a little too familiar. He'd done the same countless times since this whole ordeal began.

From the outside, their family probably did look perfect. No one knew the real truth. And it was too late to change the past.

"I'm ready whenever you are," she stated with a squeeze.

"Keep your face down and feet moving. I'll meet you around the back of the truck." He shoved his door open, pushing back the swarm, and then hopped out. Making his way to the back of the truck proved a challenge with all the cameras in his face, but he took his own advice. The brim of his Stetson blocked out some of the shocking blasts of lights that had the effect of fireworks being lit inches from his face.

A sense of calm settled over him when he looked

up and saw Carrie moving toward him. Something felt very right in that moment. He chalked it up to nostalgia. Losing his father had him wishing he could go back. Change the past. He couldn't. So, it wouldn't do any good to make useless wishes.

Dade ignored the stirring in his chest that tried to convince him being around her again was a good idea.

"Take my arm." He held it out, and she took it. More of those frustrating zings of electricity coursed through him. *Way to keep the hormones in check around a beautiful woman, Butler.*

Reporters tried to follow him and Carrie inside the lobby, but a deputy quickly reacted, forcing them outside.

In the next minute, he and Carrie were being ushered into a hallway. He recognized the building all too well. He'd been there countless times since his father's murder. Always with the same result—no solid leads. A conference room had been converted into a makeshift command center where volunteers took shifts answering phones, jotting down leads. At least a dozen intake spots were set up around the long mahogany conference table. The room sounded like a Jerry Lewis telethon with the constantly ringing phones, hushed voices and volunteers with their heads hunkered down, speaking quietly into receivers.

The sheriff's office was large, simple. There was a huge desk, also mahogany, with an executive chair and two flags on poles standing sentinel on either side. A picture of the governor was centered in between the poles. Two smaller-scale leather chairs nestled near the desk. A sofa and table with a bronze statue of a bull with rider sitting astride it—commissioned by Dade's father—sat to one side of the room. Dade had been surprised to see the statue in the sheriff's office. But then, Mike Butler always had a few cards up his sleeve, and he'd been a complicated man.

Dade's oldest sibling, his sister Ella, kept talking about how she felt like their father was still watching over the family. She'd gotten closure from a note their father had given her days before his death. Dade was happy for his sister—finality and peace were two very good things—but his relationship with the old man couldn't have been more different. And he'd known the minute his father snatched a toy away from him at age seven and told him to quit wasting time and get to work that his father didn't look at him in the same light.

Expectations for Mike Butler's sons took on a whole new level. Dade and his twin brother, Dalton, had endured, not enjoyed, childhood. Both had been forced to grow up fast. And neither could really wrap his mind around the fact that the big presence that was their father was gone. A pang of regret hit Dade. He wished he could go back and have the conversation he'd needed to have with his father. Now it was too late.

"I wish I had news for you," the sheriff started as he took his seat in his executive swivel.

More useless wishes, Dade thought.

"I'm not here to talk about my family's case." Dade tried to mentally shake himself out of his reverie. Chewing on the past wouldn't make it taste better. Reality was bitter. His father was gone and their relationship was beyond repair. Case closed.

Dade focused on the sheriff, noticing the wear and tear on his features as his office continued to be inundated with phone calls, questions and leads about the

Mav's murder. Deep lines bracketed the sheriff's mouth, and worry grooves carved his forehead.

"Would either of you like a cup of coffee before we get started?" Sheriff Sawmill asked, gripping his own mug of still-steaming brew. There was a packet of Zantac on top of his desk. "Janis would be happy to get it for you while we talk."

"No, thanks," Carrie said.

"I'll get a cup on my way out," Dade stated, not wanting to waste time.

"What brings you to my office?" Sheriff Sawmill took a sip and set the mug down. He picked up the packet and tore the corner. He dumped the small pill onto his palm and then popped it into his mouth, chasing it with water from a bottle on his desk.

"When I was closing my store earlier, I was cornered by one of the festival workers in the alley." Carrie crossed her legs and rocked her foot back and forth. Dade remembered her nervous tic from high school.

"Did he touch you or hurt you in any way?" The sheriff's gaze scanned Carrie as though looking for any signs of struggle.

"Not exactly." The admission seemed to make her uncomfortable, considering the way she started fidgeting.

"Threaten you?" Sheriff Sawmill leaned forward, making more tears in the corner of the empty Zantac packet.

"He backed me up against the wall but was interrupted be—"

The sheriff's desk phone rang. He glanced at the screen. "Excuse me for a minute while I take this."

Carrie nodded.

Dade could see where this was going, and regret stabbed him for dragging her here in the first place. The sheriff, his staff and the volunteers were overwhelmed. The festival worker hadn't exactly threatened Carrie—*intimidated* was a better word. Her neighbor had interceded, and then Dade had arrived on the scene. The worker had left without so much as making a threat for anyone else to hear. As frustrating and scary as this whole situation was for her, nothing illegal had happened.

The sheriff ended the call and shot them an apologetic look. "It's been a little hectic around here. Please, continue."

"I was backed up against the wall, so I got ready to use my pepper spray when Samuel Jenkins showed up and interrupted Nash," she said.

"I know the Jenkins boy," Sawmill said with a nod of acknowledgment. It didn't matter how old a man was in Cattle Barge. He would always be known by his family association. *The Jenkins boy. The Butler boy.* No matter how much Dade tried to distance himself in order to be his own man, he'd always be Maverick Mike's boy. "And Nash is…?"

"The festival worker," she clarified.

The phone rang again, and the sheriff let out a sharp sigh as he pinched the bridge of his nose. "Hold on for one second."

Dade could see this was going nowhere. He stood and Sheriff Sawmill immediately put his caller on hold.

"I'm sorry about the interruptions," Sawmill began. "We get several dozen calls a day from citizens who think someone might be following them or their crazy uncle is hatching a plan to murder them and some of those complainants have access to my direct line considering most of us have lived in this town all of our lives. We all go way back." His eyes flashed at Dade. "The town's been in a tizzy for weeks and everyone's on alert."

"We understand. We'll give a statement to one of the deputies out front." Dade waved off the sheriff.

"My office will do everything in its power to ensure the safety of its citizens." It was the line the sheriff had most likely given to every small-time complainant since his world had blown up.

When Dade really thought about their case, he couldn't argue. No real crime had been committed, and that tied the sheriff's hands. Normally, Sawmill would go talk to the offender and that was deterrent enough, but his plate was full and the festival was on its way out of town in the morning. Problem solved for Carrie.

"We'll check the festival's schedule and reach out to local law enforcement and ask to be made aware of any similar complaints."

"Thank you," Dade said as Carrie stood, seeming to catch on immediately to the underlying current. Anyone could see that the sheriff's office was being inundated, so a case like Carrie's would be swept under the rug. Not for lack of concern, but because resources were too thin and solving a high-profile murder would take precedence.

"Everyone holding up okay at the ranch?" Sawmill asked.

Dade nodded as he put his hand on the small of Carrie's back.

"Anything you can do is appreciated, Sheriff," he said, leading her toward the same hallway they'd traversed moments before with the knowledge it wouldn't be much.

THE SHERIFF'S OFFICE boomed with activity even at this late hour. Carrie was tired. She wanted to go home, wash off the day and cuddle her dog, Coco. Giving her statement to the deputy hadn't taken long, but it was getting late.

"He can't help, can he?" Carrie released her words on a sigh. This seemed like a good time to be grateful Nash would be long gone in the morning and her life would return to normal as soon as the situation with Brett calmed down.

"Doesn't appear so." Dade seemed as frustrated as she felt.

Bright lights assaulted her the second she stepped out of the air-conditioning and into the August heat. There was so much flash and camera lighting that it seemed like the sun had come out.

The swarm followed them to Dade's truck, and a couple of cars tailed them even when they got on the road, snapping pictures. It was a dangerous situation. She could certainly see why Dade had taken the alley in order to stay under the radar.

"I'm sorry the sheriff's office wasn't more help," he said. "I should've realized what the place would be like."

"There's been a crime wave in town following your dad's..." She couldn't bring herself to say the word *murder*.

"Seems most of it has been targeted toward my family." There was an undercurrent of anger in Dade's voice.

"Have you even had a chance to process any of this?" Carrie wished there was something she could say or do. "Here you're helping me when you have so much on your plate already."

"Good to think about something besides my own problems for a change." He put on his turn signal and changed lanes. "Did you eat dinner? We could stop off."

"I wish I could." She started to apologize but he stopped her. "I have a dog that needs to go out. Her name's Coco and she's a Sharp Eagle, which is a cross between a shar-pei and a beagle. She has the beauty of a shar-pei and the sweet temperament of a beagle." Carrie realized about halfway through her monologue that she was talking too fast. Being alone in a truck with Dade shouldn't make her feel anxious, so she chalked her heightened feelings up to the crazy end of the day and not the electricity pinging through her body being this near him. "I'm talking too much."

"Where am I taking you?" Dade half grinned, one side of his mouth curling in a smile that had been cute on a boy and was sexy as hell on a grown man.

Carrie felt her cheeks burn.

"Back to my car is fine. That way I'll be able to get to work in the morning without calling in any favors." She had no idea who she'd call. Carrie had been too busy with the sweet shop to make friends. At least, that's the excuse she gave when she sat at home Friday nights after work instead of meeting pals for dinner. Her social calendar wasn't exactly full, and she still felt like that gawky teenager she'd been. The truth was that ever since she'd returned to Cattle Barge in high school after being shifted to a group home in Kilburn City, she'd felt like an outsider. But then, no other place had felt like home, either. As silly as it sounded, even to her, the last time she'd felt like she belonged somewhere was primary school in Cattle Barge. Coming back had been an attempt to recover the feeling. So far, she'd supplied the town with the best ice cream she could create—at least that was something.

Thinking about the past, about *her* past, had a way of creating instant tension in her body. A headache threatened, so she pinched the bridge of her nose.

"The ice cream shop seems to be doing well. It's all anyone can talk about." The hint of pride in Dade's voice caused ripples of hope—maybe a sense of belonging?—to bubble inside her chest.

"It's definitely been keeping me on my toes, and I'm grateful people seem to like it." The store made her feel part of the community, even if a counter stood between her and the rest of the world.

"I hear your employees like working for you," he continued, more of that pride in his voice.

"One of my business professors taught me to hire for attitude. He said everything else can be learned." She'd completed her associate degree at the community college in Kilgore while waitressing nights. Studying and working was about all she'd had time for in her early twenties. She couldn't deny her focus was paying off now.

"Sounds like the guy knew what he was talking about," Dade said.

"What about you?" Carrie wanted to know what had happened to Dade after high school when she'd moved away to go to college.

"I joined the service after graduation. Served my country and came home to the ranch to work the land," he said, pulling into the alley. "Not sure how long I'll stick around once the dust settles, though."

Before she could ask what that meant, a strong sense

of foreboding settled on her shoulders, like a heavy blanket. But it was probably nothing, right?

Until she caught a glimpse of red on the driver's side door of her car. A single rose.

Strange. It hadn't been there earlier.

Chapter Three

"Getting a flower should be a good thing," Carrie said to Dade, who pulled alongside her sedan and parked. She shoved aside the notion that he might be planning to move away. She had no real right to ask about his personal life. "But this just feels creepy."

"I'll check it out." He hopped out of the cab.

She didn't budge. There was something safe about being with Dade, despite the media scrutiny and everything going on with her pulse. Too bad the secure feeling wouldn't last. And she needed to get home to Coco anyway.

Dade came around to her side and opened the door. "Whoever left this didn't identify himself."

He snapped a pic and said he was texting it to the sheriff.

"It's probably from Brett." He'd given her a single rose early on in their relationship.

"Either way, the sheriff needs to know," Dade quickly said.

In Brett's last voice mail—the one he'd left after he calmed down and started thinking rationally again— he'd said that he'd do pretty much anything to win her back. Was he trying to remind her of happier times? She frowned. There was no chance she was going out with him again. Her favorite pair of jogging shorts was at his place—or at least she thought so, because she couldn't find them in her house even though she could've sworn she'd worn them last weekend. Maybe she hadn't looked hard enough. In all the stress and confusion of the past couple of weeks, she was starting to lose her mind. Another reason she wished Brett could accept the breakup and move on. Being the cause of someone else's pain wasn't exactly a good feeling.

"Does this guy have a hard time understanding when a relationship is over?" An emotion—jealousy?—passed behind Dade's serious blues.

Carrie was most likely imagining it, seeing what she wanted instead of what was really there. Compassion. And sympathy? Damn. She didn't want his pity.

"Like I said, the breakup didn't go over well." With a sharp intake of air, Carrie exited the truck.

"You'll be okay?" More of that concern was present in Dade's voice.

"Yeah, fine. Thank you for taking me to the sheriff and especially for wandering down the alley when you did. I'm sorry the media has you banished to the shadows, but I can't imagine what might've happened if you hadn't been there." An involuntary shiver rocked her. She thought about Dade reporting the rose to the sheriff. It wasn't a crime to do something that many would consider a nice gesture from an ex who was most likely saying he was sorry. But after hearing about Dade's sister, she could see why he'd be overly cautious.

"Do me a favor. Park in front of the building tomorrow." Dade took a step back, like he needed more space in between them. Not exactly a reassuring move.

"No question there," she responded, dodging eye contact. As it was, electricity hummed through her body being this close to Dade. If only she'd felt this way about Brett, things would've turned out differently. Brett wasn't Dade. The two couldn't be more different. Dade was serious and could be intense, but there was something comfortable and magnetic about being with him. Brett rode a motorcycle and had an edge to his personality, and that had been the initial draw. He was so completely different than her, than anyone she'd dated in the past. Maybe a little bit dangerous, too. Looking back, he was more show than substance, which was one of many reasons she'd walked away before the relationship became too serious.

Brett liked to consider himself a thrill seeker, thus the motorcycle and the biker attitude. Real danger was deploying halfway across the world to face a foreign enemy in order to protect an ideal—freedom—not riding around in a leather jacket looking for a fistfight.

"Do you want me to take care of this?" Dade nodded toward the flower dangling from his hand at his side.

"Would you mind? I don't want to deal with it right now." She made a huge mistake in glancing up. Sensual shivers skittered across her exposed skin. She could admit to being embarrassed that she'd been blind enough to get into a bad relationship. She could blame her lapse in judgment on a million things, not the least of which would be working long hours to get her business off the ground. But the truth was that she'd been lonely. Brett was good-looking and charming when he needed to be—especially in the beginning. He'd seemed so proud of her at first, but then it had turned into something else, something possessive. She'd lost interest, and he wasn't taking it so well. "I must seem like a complete idiot for not seeing this coming."

"In my experience, people don't always show their true colors until you really get to know them. That takes time," he said after a thoughtful pause, and she figured there was a bigger story behind those words. "You have good judgment, Carrie. You always were smarter than the rest of us. Everyone makes mistakes now and then. Don't be too hard on yourself."

His reassuring words calmed her. She shouldn't allow them to. She knew better than to let herself depend on anyone else. Carrie had learned early in life that all people let her down eventually, from addict parents she'd never met to a system that put her in the hands of an abuser to a distant aunt who'd claimed Carrie and then dumped her back in the system when it became inconvenient to keep her.

Where'd that come from?

This night and the reunion were taking a toll, and she needed to get her emotions in check.

"Stop by the shop sometime," she said. "Dessert is on the house."

Dade cracked a smile. "Guess there are perks to knowing the owner."

"The first treat is for old times' sake. You're on your own from there," she quipped, thinking how nice it was not to have to work at conversation for a change. It had always been like that with Dade. Easy. Light. Fun. *When we were young*, she corrected. High school had been another matter altogether.

Things changed. And so did people.

The serious blue eyes Dade had possessed as a child were even more intense now. As easy as conversation had been between them all those years ago, neither had spoken about their demons—demons that grew and changed people over time. Demons that could make a man sign up to travel halfway around the world to fight a monster he couldn't see.

The two chatted easily for another fifteen minutes, catching up on more of each other's lives in the past few years.

"It's good seeing you again, Dade," she said, finally looking up and realizing what a mistake that was. Because he was looking, too. And the way he was looking made her body ache in a way it hadn't in far too long.

"You, too, Carrie."

Neither made a move to leave right away. Another mistake. They were racking up. Because she'd learned early on that feelings could trick her. All she was experiencing was a bout of nostalgia. She'd taken psychology as an elective to help sort out her own emotions. Dade represented the past—a time before life became confusing and people who were supposed to take care of her had hurt her. A time before the group home leader had snapped and taken out his frustrations on her and a handful of other kids. A time before she'd been placed in a foster home with a real monster and had a social worker who seemed content to look the other way in order to check a box on a file—*placed*.

"I better get home to Coco."

"The Sharp Eagle?" The corner of his mouth lifted in a grin that tugged at her heart.

She laughed despite all the memories churning through her mind.

"Yep." She returned the smile. "Like I said, stop by some time."

Neither seemed ready to leave, but it was time, so she made the first move, digging her keys out of her purse. She palmed the pepper spray.

"Keep that ready to go just in case." Dade's eyes went straight to the palm-sized black canister in the leather casing as he stepped aside to allow passage.

"I will." She took the first step toward her vehicle, grateful the rose had been removed from the driver's-side door handle. Brett's timing couldn't be worse. But then, timing wasn't his only issue.

"Hold on to it even when you walk the dog. Madelyn had a restraining order against her ex, and it didn't stop him from coming after her." His warning sent a cold chill down her back. He was right. She'd read about the whole ordeal in the news and, even though she thought she knew Brett, Dade's half sister must've felt the same about her boyfriend.

Dade fished a card out of his wallet and handed it to her. "The sheriff's office might be too busy to handle this properly, but if this guy shows up again or your ex doesn't take the hint and you need a hand, give me a call. My personal cell's on there."

"Thank you." She dropped his card in her purse. Nash should be gone by morning. She hoped Brett would leave things alone. Experience had taught her that he didn't give up so easily. But she could handle him. Right?

As DADE WATCHED Carrie drive away, regret filled his chest. Since that was as productive as drinking well water next to a nuclear facility, he started the engine of his truck and navigated out of the alley.

Dade spent the half-hour ride home lost in his

thoughts, one of which hadn't dawned on him until later. Being close to Carrie might bring unwanted media attention to her and dredge up her past. People talked. He'd never been truly sure what had happened to her in the years she was away from Cattle Barge, but she'd returned a different person. The chatty and sweet girl from their youth had seemed...he didn't know...lost?

Adding to his sharp mood was the simple fact that his own life was a mess. First, there'd been an unexpected breakup with his girlfriend, followed by the Mav's murder and everything that had happened to the family since. Going back to the ranch didn't hold a hell of a lot of appeal lately, but he had nowhere else to be and was needed at home. He was restless, though. Working the land was the only activity that had ever given him a sense of peace. The Mav had been right about one thing—hard work made for clear focus right up until Dade came in from the range. Honestly, focus had been hard to come by lately, but he figured he could get it back if he kept moving forward. Was it the fact that someone had murdered his father right under their noses in such a violent fashion and on the land they all loved so much that kept him on edge?

Going to bed would be useless. Sleep was as close as Helsinki to Houston. He made a beeline for the kitchen after parking in his usual spot. The light was on, and six weeks ago that might've seemed odd. Nothing surprised him now.

"Did you just pull in?" Ella seemed happy for the first time, but then Dade's older sister had gotten the closure she needed from the past. She'd also met a man she truly seemed in love with, and while Dade was happy for his sister, seeing her in that state of bliss reminded him just how far away he was from it. He wouldn't begrudge her, though. She deserved every bit of it.

"Got sidetracked on my way to pick up the bronze." Dade realized that he'd never made it over to the mayor's office.

"I figured as much after Mayor Bentley called. Dalton volunteered to go instead." She sat at the long wooden table behind a bowl of ice cream. "Everything okay?"

"Yeah." He'd thank his twin brother when he saw him in the morning. Days on the ranch began at 4:00 a.m., so that wouldn't be long. Dade went for the coffeepot, figuring a caffeine boost would help him think clearly. After seeing Carrie again, his mind was going to a place he knew better than to let it: an inappropriate attraction that had him remembering the lines of her heart-shaped face framed by inky-black hair, her creamy skin, smooth aside from that little scar to the left side of her full lips. When she smiled, she had one dimple on her left cheek, and part of him wanted to see that again.

"We're out of beans in the kitchen." Ella nodded toward the pantry.

"Since when is this house out of anything?" There'd been someone around to stock the pantry and make sure meals were cooked and the kids put to bed for as long as Dade could remember. None of the good people providing those tasks had been his parents.

"I'm sure there's more somewhere. May's been overworked, and I thought she should take it easy. I asked her to take a couple of days for herself."

Dade almost laughed out loud. May, take a break? She wasn't the lounging type. "How'd that go over?"

Ella looked at him. "It'll be worse if she realizes we wanted something and had to do without."

"Why would we do that? I'll check dry storage to see if we have a can of coffee hiding in there. She'll never know. Besides, we're all grown. We can do for ourselves." She would take it to heart. Feel like she'd let them down in some way. It was just coffee, but May wouldn't see it that way. May had always done everything for them when they were kids. May was a saint.

"Where were you tonight?" Ella had taken to prying in everyone's business since their father's murder and the subsequent crimes against the family.

"There was a disturbance in town and I got distracted." He searched for pain relievers to stem the dull headache focused in the center of his forehead.

"What happened? Are you okay?" There was so much worry in her voice now. The reason was understandable, but Dade could take care of himself.

"Nothing that involved me directly. I helped a friend," he conceded, taking a seat across from Ella.

"You're sure about that?" Fear widened her eyes.

"Certain. Carrie Palmer had a run-in with a festival worker. I took her to file a complaint." The world would know tomorrow anyway. There was no sense in hiding it.

Ella glanced at her bowl of ice cream and started to speak.

"Have you heard from Cadence?" He changed the subject, not yet ready to discuss Carrie with his sister. Hell, he wasn't sure what he was feeling toward her other than a strong urge to protect her.

"She's still down with the flu and, honestly, with everything going on around here, it's probably best she's out of town until the hysteria dies down." Ella pushed around the ball of ice cream in her bowl.

"What she did to Madelyn was inexcusable—"

Ella was already nodding in agreement. Leaving a threatening message to try to force Madelyn out of town was a low blow. "Our baby sister messed up. I'm just grateful Madelyn has found it in her heart to forgive Cadence. Their relationship still has a long way to go but they're making progress, talking almost every day."

"I'm guessing their reconciliation has a lot to do with you," Dade pointed out.

"With everything this family has been through we need each other now more than ever." Ella's heart was always big and her judgment sound.

"There's no rush for me but Ed can't read Dad's will until we're all present. He also said the date's been set," Dade informed. Ed Staples was the family's lawyer and longtime friend of their father. Some people might say that Ed was Maverick Mike's only true confidant.

"Ed told me, too." Ella rolled the spoon through her ice cream.

He eyed the label. It came from Carrie's Cold Treats.

"Ed said there was some kind of stipulation." Dade didn't care a hill of beans about what he stood to inherit. The only reason he cared about the will was because there might be a revelation in it that could blow open the investigation and bring their father's killer to justice. It sat hard on his chest that his father had been murdered on the ranch, that someone had had access and had wanted to prove they could do whatever they wanted at Maverick Mike's home. What did that say about security? About Dade and his brother? Early on, folks had speculated that Andrea Caldwell, the Mav's girlfriend, had shot him in his sleep. Dade hadn't taken the rumor seriously. Andrea was a sweet person. She might not be able to take care of herself but she wouldn't hurt a fly. It wasn't her nature.

"Wish I knew what he was talking about," Ella admitted. "Do you?"

"Guess we'll learn together." Dade filled a water glass and drained it. "When does Holden get here?"

"A couple of days," she said, her eyes getting a little spark in them when she referred to her fiancé. "He's closing out his accounts in Virginia so he can move here. I wanted to go with him, but he thought I'd feel better if I stayed on the ranch while everything's been so crazy."

"He's probably right," Dade agreed.

Ella stood, moved to the sink and rinsed out her bowl before placing it in the dishwasher. "Guess my eyes were bigger than my stomach."

"I'll see you in the morning," Dade said. By the time he returned to the kitchen with a can of ground coffee, Ella had gone to bed. It was late. A shower and the idea of sleep won out over making coffee.

After climbing in bed, Dade drew the covers up. His mind drifted to the last gift from his father, a fishing rod. Not just any fishing rod, but the one he'd wanted as a kid. There'd been a note, too. One that Dade had balled up and tossed into a drawer without reading. He'd been filled with anger and figured one small gesture couldn't wipe away the abuse Dade had suffered at his father's hands. Now he'd never have another chance to make things right with the old man. To add insult to injury, the note had gone missing.

The sheriff was no closer to making an arrest now than he'd been a week ago. There were too many leads and too many distractions between the media and others who'd descended on Cattle Barge. Claims of paternity or debts owed from Maverick Mike were through the roof. Only one paternity claim had panned out so far, and Madelyn Kensington had arrived at the ranch seeming even less thrilled with the news than the Butlers had been.

Rather than chew on those unproductive nuggets, Dade flipped onto his back. He'd been in bed long enough for his eyes to adjust to the dark, so he stared up at the ceiling, at the texture he'd heard his sisters describe as orange peel. The pattern stretched from wall to wall.

Out of nowhere, Dade felt hemmed in. He used to love having his own wing in the main house, but now it felt like a cage.

Tonight must be the night for fruitless thoughts, because his mind turned to Carrie and how good it had been to see her again. He told himself it was her safety that had him wanting to check on her in the morning when he had work to do.

What time did her sweet shop open? He picked up his phone on the nightstand and glanced at the time. One o'clock in the morning. Work started in three hours. He thumbed the internet icon and then entered the name of her shop.

She opened at eleven o'clock, which meant she probably arrived by seven or eight to prep for the day.

The festival worker should be long gone by then.

Shouldn't he? It was probably the brush with death two of his sisters had had recently that had Dade's mind twisting over his thoughts, concerned about Carrie.

Because what if Nash had left that rose? What did that say about the man's intentions?

Chapter Four

"Coco, come here, girl." Carrie glanced around the backyard of her one-story bungalow, looking for her dog. Normally, she liked living in a suburb on the edge of the small town with its cul-de-sacs and third-of-an-acre lots. Tonight, she looked out into the blackness with apprehension. Was it always this dark outside on a weeknight? All the homes on her street were blacked out, and no one seemed to see the need to waste electricity by leaving a porch light on.

This had never bothered her before, but Nash had caught her off guard, setting her nerves even more on edge after dealing with Brett. Where was her dog?

Carrie stepped onto the back porch and called for Coco again. Her dog had run around the side of the house, which wasn't unusual, but Carrie didn't like it tonight. Out of habit, she'd dropped her keys next to the front door, along with her pepper spray. All kinds of worrisome thoughts plagued her. Technically, the festival wouldn't pack up and leave until morning. Could Nash have figured out where she lived? He might've followed her home one evening. No. She would've known. She would've noticed an unfamiliar car or truck.

"Coco," she repeated, louder this time. And then

she listened for the sounds of the dog tags clanking together—the proof of rabies vaccination always jingled when she moved. All she could hear were cicadas and crickets, which sounded haunting tonight. Keep thinking along those lines and she'd really psych herself out. Okay, it was too late for that. *It'll be fine, Carrie.*

Glancing into the shadows, a prickly sensation that someone was watching overtook her. This time she studied the dark corners of her yard. The glow from the back porch lit up barely more than her deck. Again, she asked herself if Nash could've followed her home. No way. She and Dade had talked for a long time after the encounter and they'd gone to the sheriff's office. Her nerves were fried, and what she really needed was a cool shower, a good meal and sleep. It was time to put this awful day to rest and wake with a clean slate tomorrow.

The sound of a truck engine hummed from down the street. As the noise moved toward her, she whistled for her dog and made kissing noises. Those usually did the trick. Not tonight.

Carrie took a couple of steps back, placing her hand on the doorknob leading into the kitchen. As soon as Coco darted onto the deck, Carrie would be ready to usher her baby inside and quickly lock the door behind them. Why did her dog always exert her independence at the worst possible times?

Gravel crunched underneath tires as her neighbor's truck engine roared and then died. The bungalow next door had been rented six months ago by a single guy who seemed intent on keeping to himself. After several fruitless attempts to stop by and introduce herself, Carrie wondered if he wanted to be on friendly terms at all. Tonight probably wasn't the best time for a conversation and since he'd made no effort so far, she figured he might be a jerk anyway. He kept odd hours, even to her, and she hadn't seen him outside since he moved in. He was gone for days at a time with no indication of where he'd been. Lights in his house were on at odd times. Carrie had noticed them when Coco was sick and needed to go outside during the night. He never had company—or at least he didn't while she'd been home. She could admit that wasn't often since she'd opened the sweet shop last year.

"Your trash keeps blowing into my yard," an irritated male voice snapped. That was a nice introduction. He must've seen her in the porch light. She sure as heck couldn't see him, and the thought sent an icy chill racing up her arms.

"Sorry. It's the raccoons. I work long hours at—"

The truck's door slammed a little too loudly, causing her to jump. *Take it easy, buddy.*

"Lock it up." His voice was almost a growl.

If he was going to be this much of a jerk, she saw no point in introducing herself or trying to make nice, so she didn't respond at all.

A few seconds later, she saw a light flip on inside his house. Guess he'd made his neighborly intentions clear. She blew out a breath. This had been one redletter day for sure.

Coco's tags jingled, and relief washed over Carrie as her little dog bolted into view, barking. Instead of hopping onto the deck, Coco diverted right and ran in a circle as fast as she could, disappearing into the shadows only to dart back inside the light. Her barks intensified with each sighting. Her reaction came a little too late to have an impact on Jerk Face. Coco was a sweetheart, but her neighbor didn't have to know that, and she could sound menacing when she really wanted to. She looked more like a shar-pei than a beagle, which made her a little more threatening.

Even though Carrie was starving, she stood on the porch a few more minutes, almost daring her neighbor to come out and say something again about the noise. Her dog had been inside since lunch. She needed a little freedom, and Carrie was finding her bravado again after the encounter with Jerk Face. She didn't have enough audacity to walk out front and check the mail, she thought, realizing she'd forgotten to do that on the drive in. It could wait. No way was she walking out the front door in the dark and to the middle of the cul-de-sac, where all the mailboxes were clumped together to make it easier on the mail carrier.

There were four houses to each cul-de-sac in this neighborhood and hers sat directly across from the Hardin place. Marla Hardin was Samuel's aging aunt and he lived there with her.

Humidity filled the air, and the promise of a rare August rain hung low and heavy. Shiny white stars cut through the pitch-black canopy overhead.

Coco finally conceded her playtime was over and hopped onto the deck. Her tongue hung out one side of her mouth as she panted. She had the snout of a shar-pei—it wasn't exactly created to thrive in the heat.

"Are you ready, sweet girl?" Carrie bent down and scratched her dog behind the ears. The eerie feeling of being watched crept over her, so she made kissing noises at Coco before scooting inside. She closed and locked the door behind them. Her purse hung off a chair in the eat-in kitchen, and she noticed crumbs on the floor underneath it. She'd mopped the floor before work, which meant that Coco must've dug into the garbage again.

She scooped them up. Odd. They had a distinct smell…like the ham-flavored training treats Carrie had stopped buying when the vet had said Coco was tipping the scale. Carrie thought she'd thrown them all out, but she must've forgotten a bag in her pantry. She glanced around, the eerie feeling returning. She thought about the pepper spray attached to her key ring on the credenza by the front door and decided to sleep with it next to the bed. The incident with Nash had really thrown her off-balance—that must be why she felt on pins and needles in her own home.

Coco followed on Carrie's heels as she double-checked all the doors to make sure they were locked. She took a quick shower, ate a bowl of cereal and then climbed into bed. She'd always considered Cattle Barge a safe place to live in general, and especially after the horrors she'd endured when she was taken away. She'd never really thought about being a single woman living on her own and working long hours at the treat shop until now.

Between Brett, Nash and her unfriendly, keep-to-himself Jerk Face neighbor, she figured it wouldn't hurt to look into having a security system installed. Coco provided some insurance against a surprise predator. She usually barked at strangers. But after Coco's lackluster performance with the neighbor, Carrie decided her backup needed backup. Even so, with her dog curled up at the foot of the bed, warming her legs, Carrie felt a little safer. Unless someone tossed a piece of meat onto the floor, Carrie thought with an almost smile.

The next morning, she woke to the sound of Coco growling. Her dog was at the doorway to the bedroom, starting down the hallway. Carrie grabbed the small canister of pepper spray off the nightstand and threw the covers off.

Coco wasted no time darting toward the noise. Carrie couldn't hear much of anything over the barking, but all she could think was *so Jerk Face neighbor gets a free pass but the UPS guy is suspect?*

It was the UPS guy, right?

She followed her dog to the front door, checking out the window for the brown van. To be fair, this was the same reaction Coco had to the postal worker and the guy who'd tried to deliver flowers once. Amazon delivered to her door, but she didn't remember ordering anything online. Then again, she'd been busy, working extra hours since the festival, and sometimes she entered her home address when she meant to use the sweet shop's.

Speaking of which, Nash should be packed up and out of town this morning. That was a relief. Too bad he couldn't take Brett with him, she thought with another almost smile.

Coco was doing her mix of bark-howling, which had been so cute when she was a three-month-old pup. Not so much at a year.

There was no way Carrie was opening the door until she could confirm who was out there. She stroked her dog's head, thinking Coco must've heard a squirrel. Wouldn't be the first time this had happened. "It's okay, girl."

After double-checking and being perfectly satisfied nothing was going on, Carrie opened the door. A stuffed animal lay at her feet. She picked up the black-and-white orca whale. *Brett.*

She scanned the front yard. There were kids riding bikes around the cul-de-sac, and that was about it.

"Okay, puppy. Way to keep me safe from the neighborhood children. Let's get back inside." Brett was the only one who knew whales were her favorite. She checked her phone and found several texts from him. They'd be more apologies. More of him being frustrated that she wasn't returning his calls. She'd deal with those and with him later. Now, she needed coffee.

Carrie walked by the trash can in the kitchen and tossed the awkward gift on top. *Take a hint, buddy.*

An hour later, she parked under a tree in the lot of the strip shopping center. The rain never came last night, so the air was still thick with humidity. She noticed the festival trucks were still there. Everything was packed up and looked ready to go across the street in the lot of Ventnor's Park. *Not another day of Nash*, she thought with a groan. Going to the sheriff last night seemed like an even better idea this morning. A complaint was on record. If Nash irritated her, she had every intention of telling him she'd reported him.

The icy chill returned—it was becoming a little too familiar.

Focusing on her morning routine at the store kept her distracted. Carrie liked to be the first one in the shop. She could prepare the bank deposit and relock it inside the safe before anyone showed up for work. That way she could deal with money so her employees wouldn't even have to know where it was kept. Protecting her employees was always at the top of her priority list.

Harper Stoddard was the first to arrive. The nineteen-year-old's cell was in her hand, and as soon as she looked up at Carrie, her brown eyes widened. "Everything okay?"

"Peachy. We need to cover a few things when Eric shows, but I'd rather wait until the both of you are here before we talk about last night."

Harper walked over to Carrie and embraced her. "I'm just glad you're all right."

How did she know something had happened? Then it dawned on Carrie that being seen with Dade Butler would be news. Social media seemed to keep people constantly in the know. "Me, too. We'll put some controls in place to make sure you and Eric don't run into any problems."

"I'm not worried about us. You always make sure we're covered. I'm concerned about you." Harper had a point. Carrie always made sure her employees left together, while she locked up alone most nights.

"I'll be more careful." Harper's thoughtfulness touched Carrie deeply.

Eric, her assistant manager, arrived, breaking into the emotional moment. Harper excused herself.

"Everything all right with you this morning, boss?" he asked as Harper opened the freezer to bring out tubs of ice cream to stock the front bins.

Carrie acknowledged Eric's frown. He must've heard the news as well, judging by the concern written in his intense expression.

She deflected the sudden burst of emotion springing tears to her eyes by saying, "That was nothing. Coco kept me up barking last night."

But her employees' genuine concern touched her in a deep place.

"That stinks." Harper flashed her eyes at Carrie. "Puppies can be so much work."

"What time did you get in this morning?" Eric asked, motioning toward the fresh rack of waffle cones.

"Early." Carrie followed Harper into the fridge, picking up a heavy container of Vanilla Bean-illa, a Carrie's Cold Treats favorite. She'd set up several trays of baked goods in the front counter and signed on to the cash register. She needed to figure out the best way to discuss last night with her employees.

"In early after staying late last night?" Eric moved beside Carrie. "Let me help with that."

"I got it."

Overseeing every detail of Carrie's Cold Treats had been her passion—the shop was her passion. And a little voice reminded her that she didn't have much else, considering she lived in a rented house. Coco was a bright spot, but her pup was a little short on conversation.

Fresh from a breakup, dating was out of the question at the moment. Maybe she needed to step out of her comfort zone and share her pet project a little more. The last thing she wanted was for her employees to feel like she didn't trust them. Eric was a nice guy, a strong assistant manager who was working to put himself through the local satellite campus of the University of Texas.

"I could be better about sharing some of the load, and I have complete trust in both of you to do a good job." She handed over the tray as a knock sounded at the back door. Fear caused her to freeze, because for a split second she thought it might be Nash returning to finish what had been interrupted last night. The thought was irrational, and yet it had her pulse pounding anyway. The festival trucks had not pulled away yet as she'd hoped they would've done by now.

"I got this," Eric said.

She wouldn't argue. She deposited the freezing-cold tub into the front bin and walked toward her office, figuring it was most likely a delivery.

Teddy Ginger, her milk delivery driver, waltzed in and stopped at her office door with one of those cheesy used-car-salesman smiles. He was a little taller than her and lanky. Teddy had a ruddy complexion and beady blue eyes. He was midthirties and on the thin side. "How's business?" Teddy was always good for a smile and a joke.

"Good. Thanks for asking. I have your check right here." She held up the offering, standing on the opposite side of the glass desk.

Teddy reached out for it. "Thank you much."

"Cooler's open, so feel free to load up," she said, softening her expression.

"I'll be out of your way in a jiff," Teddy replied. He made quick work of delivering his product.

"Have a good weekend, Teddy."

"Same to you." Teddy waved as he wheeled out his dolly.

"I see we already have a customer waiting for us to open." Harper motioned toward the front of the store. Plexiglas made up half of her office wall. She'd had it constructed that way so that she could be in her office while keeping an eye on business in case one of her employees needed help at the counter.

Carrie glanced at the clock. Five minutes until opening. She looked at the front window. *Samuel?* "I know him. He's not really a customer. He's most likely checking on me after what happened last night."

"And what was that exactly?" Eric whirled around to face Carrie as she walked up.

"I thought you already knew," she said.

"We'd like to hear it directly from you. I mean, you can't always trust what people say." Harper motioned toward the phone she kept in her apron pocket.

Carrie needed to explain the situation without scaring them.

"I had a weird run-in last night with a festival worker in the alley." Carrie regretted her shaky tone. She didn't really want to go into the details but realized her employees had a right to know, for safety's sake.

"What happened?" Harper asked.

"It was probably nothing, but I filed a report with the sheriff as a precaution. From now on make sure you park in front of the building." Carrie's attempt to lighten her tone didn't have the intended effect. Instead she sounded even more strained. She cleared her throat. "To be on the safe side."

"Was it the guy who kept coming in here loitering?" Eric's gaze intensified.

Carrie nodded.

"I knew I should've stayed late and walked you out." Eric had enough on his plate between summer school and work without worrying about her.

"It's fine. There were people around, and I got lucky that Samuel and an old friend of mine happened to be walking through the alley. I had all the backup I needed." She appreciated the thought, though, and the concern. "But I don't want either of you closing the shop on your own. From now on, we double-team everything." It might cost a little more to have two employees stay until closing, but the money was worth it to guarantee their safety. Besides, business had been good. The shop had gotten into the black sooner than she'd expected. Having something she created take off so well brought an enormous sense of accomplishment and security to Carrie. She would do whatever was necessary in order to protect what she'd created from scratch. "Buddy system from here on out."

She walked toward the door. She unlocked it and turned the open sign over. "And, I'll probably start bringing Coco in with me again if I get in a position to close by myself."

"We'll make sure that doesn't happen but we like having Coco around." Eric seemed to accept that answer.

Samuel looked pasty and nervous, like he was still shaken from the encounter with Nash last night. Carrie turned to Harper before opening the door and motioned toward the register. "Might as well open up and get business flowing. It'll be hard to top this week's sales, though."

She smiled at Samuel while scanning the parking lot looking for signs of Nash. Across the street she could clearly see the line of festival trucks parked there. That sensation of being watched had returned, and a creepy-crawly feeling sent chilly tingles up her spine. Too bad the caravan was still across the street. Not one truck had moved.

"Come on in, Samuel. I owe you an ice cream."

DADE HAD BEEN working for seven hours by the time Carrie opened her sweet shop. He'd been distracted today. He blamed lack of sleep, but the truth was that he kept thinking about running into Carrie again after so many years. And he wanted to see to it that she was all right after last night. She'd been on his mind since he'd returned to Cattle Barge and had learned that she'd opened a shop downtown.

"Remind me later that I have to get an emergency delivery of hay for the horses when we head inside. We won't last another day with the feed we have on hand," Dade's twin brother, Dalton, said.

"I'll pick it up in town." A visit to the feed store would be as good excuse as any to pop into town. He could drop in to collect that cold treat from Carrie while he was at it.

His twin brother shot him a look.

"It's on my way," Dade hedged, needing a minute to come up with a plausible excuse. He and Dalton had always been close, and his brother could read him a little too easily.

"Why do you need to go into town again?" Dalton's brow arched.

"The Olsen widow has something for May. Figured I'd save her a trip if she hasn't picked it up yet. Ella thinks May's been working too hard since the funeral." Dade had no plans to share that he really wanted to check on Carrie.

Dalton's brow hiked up, but he didn't say anything.

"Since when do you care why I need to run into town?" Dade deflected.

His brother shrugged. "Guess we're all acting a little different since the Mav's…"

Dalton didn't finish his sentence—didn't need to. The air at the ranch had been thick with tension ever since their father's murder. Neither of them ever discussed the man, the past.

Dade didn't want to make small talk when he could be in the shower cleaning up before heading into town. He turned his horse, Flame, toward the barn. He'd been named as a nod to his fiery chestnut coat. "I better head out before May overdoes it again and wears herself out."

"Nice of you to think of her." Dalton's eyebrow was raised, but to his credit he left it alone. "See you at supper?"

"Maybe." Being around the family, carrying on traditions held little appeal for Dade since retiring from the military to take his position on the ranch. He loved the land and his brother and sisters, but being home was complicated and his feelings were all over the map since the murder. "How about fishing on Sunday instead?"

"Deal." Dalton seemed satisfied. His brother's concern came from a good place, and Dade appreciated the sentiment. He really wasn't trying to be a jerk. He needed space. And besides, he couldn't talk about what he didn't completely understand himself—his relationship with the Mav.

In half an hour, he was showered and on the road into town, grateful to be putting the ranch in the rearview. There was still plenty to do when he got back. Modern ranching involved patience, laptops and near-constant logging of herds. At least the recent herd of calves had sold well at auction this summer. Focusing on work had provided a good distraction in the past couple of days. But Dade didn't want to think about ranch business now. His thoughts kept bouncing back to Carrie.

By the time he made it to her shop, there was a line out the door. There was nothing like August sunshine to make folks want ice cream. He could see that the festival caravan was still parked in the lot across the street. As much as he didn't like it, there wasn't much he could do about Nash being around. The man would disappear soon enough.

Dade squinted against the sun as he strolled through the parking lot, telling himself all he was doing was checking on a friend. He considered it good news that she hadn't used the number he'd given her last night, but a tinge of regret pierced him anyway, because he liked seeing her again more than he wanted to admit.

Carrie was a strong, capable woman, and he figured there wasn't much she needed from him or anyone else. But she'd seemed rattled, and he wanted to see for himself that she was okay today first thing after she opened.

Since there was a line and she would be busy, he planned to stick his head inside the door and leave it at that.

There was a commotion going on inside the shop and...*shouting*?

Dade bolted toward the noise. His hands fisted at his sides. Carrie's voice raised above the sounds.

He listened carefully.

A shrill cry pierced his ears.

Chapter Five

"I already said I didn't leave a flower on your car, and you still haven't explained what you were doing with another dude last night." Brett's shouting caused a stir inside Carrie's shop. People scattered and mothers hid their children behind them. A couple of mothers raced toward the door, children in tow.

"I don't believe you, Brett." His iron grip on her arm had caused her to cry out in pain once already. She jerked her arm free. "You're hurting me."

The line at the counter took a couple of steps back.

"Everything's under control, folks. Mrs. Banner, bring Elsa over here. Harper will take care of both of you." Other than embarrassing Carrie, which he was, Brett was also frightening customers and her employees. And that was aggravating. Carrie had worked too hard to build her shop into the success it was becoming for one person to trample all over her sacrifices.

"Keep your voice down," she warned Brett. Carrie moved to the opposite side of the shop, far away from where Harper was handling a scared-looking Mrs. Banner.

"You need to listen," he continued, stalking around the side of the counter.

"We can talk in my office." Carrie turned, but Brett clasped her arm again. Eric, who had been watching the exchange, made a step toward them.

"It's okay," she said to Eric, peeling Brett's fingers off her. "He's not going to do anything he'll regret."

With that, she shot a warning look toward Brett.

"If you'd return my calls, it wouldn't be like this," Brett accused. Did he really believe any of this was her fault?

Wow. That was a choice.

"Keep it up and I'll call the sheriff," she muttered under her breath before turning her attention back to Eric. She motioned toward the customer who was waiting for him to retrieve her waffle cone. "Take care of Mrs. Whittle. I can handle this situation."

"How hard is it to answer when I call?" Brett demanded. Harper's shoulders tensed when Brett slammed his fist against the wall. "Or are you seeing someone else?"

Carrie needed to get him out of the shop and away from her customers.

"Let's talk about this outside." Carrie pushed past him as the door opened and the bell jingled. She glanced up. *Dade?*

Embarrassment flamed her cheeks, thinking he was about to come face-to-face with one of her biggest mistakes. She told herself that she'd have that reaction no matter who walked through the door, but a little piece of her brain protested the lie. Her bad choice being paraded in front of the one person she really wanted to impress was the worst feeling and shrank her other accomplishments to zero.

The shop hadn't been open twenty minutes and it felt like all hell was breaking loose.

"What are you doing here, Dade?" She tried to sound calm, but her heart raced inside her chest. Brett caught up to her, anger radiating from his five-foot-ten-inch frame, so she didn't wait for Dade's response. Instead, she turned to Harper. "Can you take care of my friend? He did a huge favor for me last night and I promised him dessert on the house."

"Who's this guy?" Brett gripped her elbow possessively, his fingers digging in harder this time.

She took in a fortifying breath, not wanting to cause an even bigger scene in her place of business or in front of her friend. "Not now."

"When, Carrie? You don't talk to me anymore. You're not returning my texts or calls." Brett clamped harder. "You start accusing me of leaving stuff on your car and then this guy shows up."

"Then maybe you should take a hint and leave her alone," Dade ground out. A muscle in his jaw ticked, and his blue eyes glared a warning at Brett. She couldn't help but wince as she sidestepped Brett's grasp, praying Dade would let this go.

Brett had no idea what he was getting himself into.

"Thank you, Dade," Carrie said, trying to keep the peace in front of her customers. There were already too many side glances coming her way. "The Vanilla Bean-illa is amazing on the waffle cone dipped in chocolate. I highly recommend it."

"Sounds like the breakfast of champions, but I'll wait until the line dies down." Dade motioned toward the door.

"Things are a little hectic right now. Give me a minute. I'd like to thank you for last night."

Well, that really set Brett off. He started to say something, but seemed to think better of it when Dade's lips thinned and anger pulsed from him.

"I'll be back after I speak to my friend," she said with a glance toward Brett.

"Do you need help talking?" Dade asked, his gaze firing warning shots at her ex.

Carrie couldn't hold back a smirk. "I got this."

Brett seemed to shrink in Dade's presence, and she couldn't help but enjoy seeing him cower a little bit. He'd been a bully so far and deserved to be backed down. She would've preferred that he listened to her, but this worked, too.

"Let me know if that changes." He winked, and she should ignore all the butterflies fluttering in her stomach. Dade was being kind by stopping by. It meant nothing more to him, and she needed to keep her own emotions in check. Besides, his life was in chaos right now. It was most likely easier to think about helping someone else. He probably just needed a break from the media and being on the ranch. And speaking of complications, she made a note to herself to remember to drop off a gallon of Samuel's aunt's favorite ice cream on the way home from work. She hadn't seen the woman around lately and meant to ask Samuel if everything was okay. He was a quiet person to begin with, and his aunt did all the talking on the few occasions she'd stopped by the shop. Carrie hadn't seen Ms. Hardin in a while. Days? A week? Carrie wasn't sure.

"Will do." She led Brett outside, away from the gawking line of people and toward the trees. The August heat came at her from all angles—the sun above, the pavement below and even the breeze was hot. Typical August in Texas. It might take a while, but the weather would eventually change. *Like everything*, she thought as she spun around to face Brett. Heat radiated off him, too, in the form of anger and impatience…and possessiveness. He didn't own her and she didn't owe him an explanation for being with Dade last night.

Could her association with any crime, victim or not, impact her business? She wanted to say the idea was crazy. Reality was writing a different story. Panic gripped her. She could not lose the one good thing in her life.

"I already told you that I needed time away from *this*." She jerked her arm free from Brett's grasp. "And what you're doing right now isn't helping your case."

"What you really mean is *us*," he ground out, and she could see that he was working himself up.

"Okay. Yes. I don't want to be together right now." She wasn't used to fighting for her own needs. The last foster home had trained that out of her. "Why don't you give me a chance to miss us?"

His anger softened to frustration, and she thought she might be making progress until his gaze narrowed and his hands fisted.

"You're not giving us a chance." The fire was back in his eyes.

The movie theater at the end of the strip mall was letting out, and a line of people spilled into the parking lot. This was probably not the best time to tell Brett he had no chance, especially with the way he'd been behaving since the breakup. He needed a couple of weeks to cool down and then they could have the conversation that had been brewing inside her for weeks.

"I don't want to hurt you. But give me a chance to think about what I want. You already know how many hours I work—"

"I backed off before and look where that got me." He'd been more and more demanding that she spend time with him in those last few weeks, and she'd pushed back at every step.

"You have to stop texting me every five minutes and leaving gifts at my house…" Before she could finish her sentence, he threw his hands into the air and walked a tight circle.

"Then what? What is it, Carrie? Because I don't have to think about whether or not I want to spend time with you." Anger radiated off him as he smacked his fisted hand against his other palm.

Nothing good could come of such heightened emotion. She hoped she could ease him down. The idea of causing another person pain didn't sit well, yet he wasn't giving her another out. She'd been through enough hurt in one lifetime and hated the idea of causing that horrible feeling in someone else.

Carrie took in a slow deep breath, trying to keep her emotions in check. On the one hand, false hope was bad. On the other, everyone was staring at them, and this whole scenario was escalating. She was losing patience and Brett was on the verge of just losing it completely.

Brett hadn't been this interested in her when they'd been together, and she figured half of his fixation on her now had to do with her rejection. If he'd been the one to do it, he wouldn't think twice. Being on the receiving end didn't feel nice, and that's why he wanted this to work out so badly.

"What if you decide to move on while we're on a break?" He brought his hand up to touch her, but she stepped out of reach.

"You don't want to be in a relationship with someone who isn't into it," she said defensively. "You deserve better than that, Brett."

"Maybe you don't know what you want," he shot back.

"The rose. The stuffed animal. Showing up here unannounced, making a scene at my place of business. It's too much, Brett. Surely you can see that." She paused, because he was already shooting daggers at her with his glare.

"I already said that I didn't give you the whale. You didn't say anything about a rose before." This must've struck his macho core, based on his expression and how he puffed out his chest. "Someone's trying to win you over. I bet it's that jerk you were photographed with last night."

If he hadn't given her those gifts, then who had? Nash? An icy chill raced through her. *Win her over* weren't exactly the words she'd use to describe what Nash wanted from her. But Brett trying to force her to stay in a relationship she didn't want wasn't much better.

"It's not like that. Dade's an old friend," she defended. Brett had to be giving her those gifts. If not, someone was trying to mess with her…

And speak of the devil, Nash walked out of the movie theater. He must've seen her, too, because he started making a beeline toward them. Tension caused her to tighten her grip on her cell phone. The thought of

Nash and Brett being together was about as appealing as pouring gasoline onto a raging wildfire.

"I just bet he is." Brett moved within inches of her face with a glare that would've melted an iceberg. It wasn't going to work on her and he needed to be made aware of that fact. Back down from a bully and she might as well roll up the tent and leave town, because experience had taught her that once a bully knew he'd gotten to her, it was all over.

"I need to get back to work, Brett. The line is getting longer and my employees need my help." She could feel the heat of Nash's stare on her and prayed she could get away before those two clashed—cold air moving in on a heat wave. "Think about what I said and give me a little breathing room."

Brett's gaze locked on to Nash.

"Do you know him?" Too late for wishful thinking. This day seemed determined to get a whole lot worse.

"Not really." Carrie looked right in time to see Nash making progress toward her and Brett. She needed to think, to come up with something fast before those two massive storm systems collided. "I gotta go. If you can't understand my point of view, there isn't much else I can say anyway."

"We break up and you turn into some kind of sleaze?" The anger and disgust in Brett's voice sent fire shooting through her.

"How can you say something like that and wonder why I don't want to be with you anymore, Brett?" The words fired out, rapid and angry. It was one thing to cause a scene at her place of business, but to insult her to that degree caused a wildfire to rage inside her. She was barely keeping it together after last night anyway, and her nerves were about to snap.

Brett's hands fisted at his sides, and for a second she thought he might rear back and hit her. She backed up a couple of steps until her hands felt the tree. Out here, alone, she couldn't stop him from belting her. She felt around for something she could use as a weapon, just in case. There'd been a huge rock at the base of the tree. Maybe she could drop down and pick it up before he made a move.

Brett's gaze cut right and left sharply before fixating on something behind her.

She expected an argument, or more insults. Instead, Brett muttered something low under his breath before punching the tree. She ducked and her hand flew up to stop him, but he connected with the trunk anyway.

Gasps sounded from behind her and she assumed they came from her customers. *Great.* If she had to file a restraining order to keep him away, she would. She'd do whatever it took to force him to keep his distance after this exchange.

Thankfully, he'd missed connecting with her face. She glanced at the line, flustered, and a part of her needed to stick up for herself for all those times she hadn't when she was little and being bullied by a foster sibling or parent.

"This isn't over, bitch," Brett shouted as he stalked off.

That last insult was fingernails on a chalkboard to Carrie.

"No, it isn't. You better stay away from me and my shop. Or I'll see to it that you do." She picked up the rock at her feet and tossed it at his back, regretting her actions the instant she released it.

The rock made contact. Brett spun around with a look on his face that sent an icy chill down her spine. Nash was closing in, and suddenly the air became thicker. Her chest squeezed. And then both men stopped, looking past her. A second later each turned tail in different directions and took off. Why was Nash still in town? Why was the carnival still sitting there packed up but not gone?

The minute she turned toward the sweet shop, she knew what had gotten into both men. *Dade.* He was stalking toward them. He was big—the military had filled him out—but it was the expression on his face that had to have been what had gotten to the men. Pure steel with a severe look that said *back off.*

Carrie's heart fluttered as she took a couple of steps in Dade's direction. She had no doubt that he could handle either Brett or Nash—or both at the same time, to be honest. His muscles rippled underneath his white T-shirt, and neither man would cause him to break a sweat. She appreciated the unfamiliar feeling of someone having her back for a change. For most of Carrie's life she'd been alone when bullies threatened, left to her own resources, and it was nice to have backup for once.

Don't get used to it, a little voice in the back of her head warned.

The roar of Brett's motorcycle engine cut angry lines through the now-stale afternoon air. He spun his back tire, spewing gravel at cars in the parking lot. A mother covered her child's eyes before stalking out of the line. A couple more followed. *Great.* All she could do was helplessly watch as her customers, her business, dissipated before her eyes.

"Looks like you've had one heck of a morning,"

Dade said, and when his gaze reached hers, a thousand butterflies released in her stomach. She had the sensation of falling with nothing to catch her and no care in the world.

That was not her life. Reality set in. Carrie had had to work for everything. Her life had been about struggle and stress. She'd believed that coming back to Cattle Barge and creating a successful business would make her feel something…like she belonged somewhere. This episode reminded her that there would always be someone there waiting to take away everything she'd worked for. That no matter how fast she ran toward the light, darkness would stalk her.

"I wouldn't argue that." She glanced at him and then focused on the line of customers that had dwindled, resigned to the fact that she'd never really belong anywhere. "I apologize for the disturbance. All of your treats are on the house today."

Creating a success out of her life meant more to her than anything, especially after the start she'd had in life. A very deep part of her needed to prove that she could be successful in her hometown. If she couldn't be happy in Cattle Barge—the one place she'd felt was home—she couldn't be happy anywhere.

"Have to say, this is the best ice cream I've ever had." Hearing Dade say that started to ease the tension causing the spot in her left shoulder to send stabbing pain radiating down her back.

She glanced from the line back to him, wishing she'd crawled under that rock instead of chunking it at Brett. "I better get to work. Thanks again for last night and today."

Carrie wanted to be seen as an equal in this community by everyone, especially Dade. Not someone who needed constant protection. The thought fired her up again.

An older woman whispered something about the past repeating itself as she gave Carrie major side-eye before leaving the line.

And Carrie wondered if her past would always haunt her. If she'd always be that loveless orphan being passed around from home to home with no one to really love her.

"Who was that guy and what was he doing here?" Dade asked.

"He's my ex." Embarrassment heated her cheeks.

"Wish you'd hit him in the head with that rock instead of the back," Dade said with a smile that didn't reach his eyes. He pushed off the glass. "See you around."

Tears brimmed but there was no way she was going to let her customers see her break down. She turned away from Dade.

"Hey, Carrie," he said, and his voice was warmth pouring over her cold body.

She stopped. "Yeah."

"Be careful."

Chapter Six

A pounding noise shocked Carrie awake. Coco went berserk. Carrie shot to her feet and glanced around before shaking her head and struggling to get her bearings. The TV was on. She must've fallen asleep on the couch. Another five raps of fist on wood fired off behind her, shocking her fully awake.

She glanced down to make sure she was decent. Yoga pants and a T-shirt were respectable enough to answer the door. Right?

"It's okay, Coco," she soothed. This was no way to be jarred out of sleep. It felt like she was walking in slow motion, and she couldn't quite get her body to respond in the ways she wanted it to. She hoped everything was okay at the shop. Before her breakup with Brett, everything had been going well. *Too well*, a little voice reminded. Life had never been that smooth for Carrie for long. Memories of finally thinking she'd landed in the perfect foster home when, in fact, she'd moved into hell assaulted her. The anger. The beatings. The suffocating feeling of being trapped with no means of escape.

Another round of rapid-fire knocks jarred her out of her reverie. She shoved the memory deep down and hurried to the door, tripping over a lump on the floor. She glanced down to see the orca shredded, white stuffing all over the carpet. Coco had gotten into the trash again. It was Carrie's fault for not taking it out before bed last night.

"Hold on. I'm coming." She stepped over the strewn pieces. Those needed to go to the outside trash. Coco had had a field day with the animal.

She wondered if Jerk Face neighbor had decided to stop by. Beating down her door to let her know that her trash had blown into his yard again seemed like something he'd do.

She glanced out the window as another round of banging practically split her head in two.

Sheriff Sawmill?

Carrie opened the door as her stomach sank. This couldn't possibly be good.

"What's going on, Sheriff?" she said as she opened the door and stepped aside to allow passage.

"Sorry to disturb you so late, ma'am." He tipped his hat with a look of apology. And exhaustion. The man looked beyond tired.

She glanced at the clock that read half past five a.m.

"Everything all right?" She held on to Coco's collar to keep the dog from jumping up on him.

He took two steps inside the door and stopped. "We need to talk and I'd like to do it in my office."

His words set off all kinds of warning bells. Her first thought was of her employees. "Did something happen to Eric or Harper?"

"No, ma'am."

"Did Nash do something?" She couldn't help but wonder if he'd harassed someone else.

"Not that I'm aware of," he responded.

"Is this about someone I know?" she asked, realizing the answer was pretty obvious.

He bowed his head. "I'm afraid so."

"If it's not my employees then who?"

"We'd be more comfortable having this conversation in my office." The sheriff's feet were in an athletic stance and his hands were clasped in front of him.

More warning sirens blared. Carrie noticed that Coco was trying to position herself in between her and the sheriff, growling.

"It's okay, girl." Carrie bent down to scratch Coco between the ears. "Whatever's going on I want to help. I just need a few minutes to let my dog out and get my purse."

Carrie coaxed Coco to the back door. She spun around to ask a question and almost walked into the sheriff.

"Sorry, ma'am. I have to keep you in my sight."

"What on earth do you mean by that? What's this about?"

"We'll have a chance to go over everything at my office."

"Do I need a lawyer?" Her mind started spinning with possibilities. She thought about the card Dade had given her with his cell number on it. He'd be up and already working.

"Not if you don't mind answering a few questions," he stated.

Carrie let her dog out while she stood in the door frame where Sheriff Sawmill could watch her. An uneasy feeling pounded her. Why would he need to keep her in sight?

"Sheriff, can I ask another question?"

"Yes, ma'am." There he went with that *ma'am* again. He was treating her formally, which gave her even more pause.

"Can I refuse to go with you?" She most likely knew the answer to the question before she asked, and yet she needed to hear him say the words anyway.

"I wouldn't advise it," Sheriff Sawmill said with a curious look.

"Do I get to know why you want to talk to me in your office before we leave my residence?" Her balled fist was on her hip, and her mind raced.

The sheriff bent his head down as though out of respect for something... What?

And then he released a breath and looked at her. "Brett Strawn was found dead in his home a few hours ago."

"Are you sure?" Air whooshed from her lungs and tears welled in her eyes. The sheriff must be mistaken. His information had to be wrong. "What happened?"

"That's what we're trying to figure out."

IT WAS PITCH-BLACK on the way to the sheriff's office. Carrie's mind raced, unable to accept the news that someone she'd cared about was gone. Brett might not have been the man Carrie was in love with, and he'd been hard to deal with since the breakup, but she didn't wish him harm.

A swarm of media people circled the sheriff's vehicle as he parked in his reserved spot. She put her arm up to shield her face from the cameras as she wove her way through the crowd and inside the door.

Bright lights made it feel like daytime inside the

building. Janis's desk was empty, as Carrie suspected it would be this time of morning. The wall clock read nearly six in the morning. The sun wouldn't be up for another hour or more.

A deputy met them in the hallway, and the sheriff turned to Carrie. "I'll let Deputy Kirkus take it from here."

Sawmill stepped aside to allow passage. She stood there, momentarily stunned, because the sheriff's office was to the right, but Kirkus was motioning for her to walk past it. She followed him down the hall toward a room at the end of the hallway, the farthest from an exit. Suddenly, she was glad that she'd thought of picking up Dade's business card and sliding it inside her purse before she left her house. She had a feeling that she was going to need a friend and a good lawyer.

A dark thought struck. Did the sheriff think she was somehow involved with Brett's death? The idea that she could have information was beyond anything she could imagine. Surely, this was protocol in an investigation and didn't mean what she feared.

Sheriff Sawmill might not be in the small rectangular room with them, but she would bet that he was listening. There wasn't room for much more than a table and a few chairs. Sawmill, no doubt, stood behind the two-way mirror on the long wall facing her. Any hope that she was being looked at as a witness died with the knowledge eyes watched her from the other side of that mirror. She was a suspect, as impossible as that sounded, and she wanted to scream that there was no way she would hurt anyone. Instinct told her to keep quiet instead.

"Where were you between the hours of midnight and

2:00 a.m.?" Deputy Kirkus asked, bringing any thought she'd had that this might be a misunderstanding crashing down around her.

"I was asleep on my couch." She watched his gaze travel over her, assessing her. Her mind zipped through possibilities, as she was still trying to wrap her thoughts around the fact that Brett was gone. It couldn't be true, could it? She'd seen him earlier in the afternoon. Disbelief descended on her. There had to be an easy explanation for all this. Or there'd been a misunderstanding. "Are you sure it was him?"

The deputy nodded.

"So, you're positive that there's no chance there's been some mistake and he's okay?" She thought about the phone in her purse as she leaned back against the strap. She cupped her face in her hands. This couldn't be happening. Brett couldn't be…gone. Tears streamed, and she bit back a sob as reality slammed into her like hitting a tree at a hundred miles an hour.

"No, ma'am. I'm afraid not." Deputy Kirkus's voice was laced with respect in the way people spoke when they were talking about a deceased person, and that just splintered her heart even more.

"What happened to him? How was he killed?" He was young and healthy.

"We'll get to that in a minute," Kirkus said. "Were the two of you in a relationship?"

"Yes. Well. Not anymore, but we were." She didn't see what their status had to do with his death. She wanted to ask what Kirkus was doing in there with her when there was a killer on the loose, but instinct told her not to. The deputy had the same look of disbelief she'd seen when she'd told her case worker that the doughnut shop owner, Mr. Berger, had been trying to touch her in places that made her uncomfortable. The eyes always gave away how a person felt about what they were being told, and even a skilled investigator like Deputy Kirkus was no match for Carrie's experience at reading people. Being able to interpret the slightest shift in body language had helped her survive Mimi the drunk, a woman who could be nice until she opened a bottle of whiskey.

And that made dating Brett even more of a lapse in judgment. Even so, she didn't want to think badly of him after hearing the news that was rocking her world.

"When did the relationship end?" Kirkus continued.

"A couple of weeks ago. Two weeks and two days to be exact," she recalled.

"Who initiated it?" Kirkus's questions were invasive and awkward coming from a near stranger. Carrie didn't like the feeling of being interrogated even though she had nothing to hide.

"I did," she admitted. "Why?"

"How did he take the news you wanted to see other people?" Kirkus asked.

"That's not what I said," she defended.

Kirkus sat straighter in his chair. "What was the reason for the split?"

Carrie shrugged. "I wasn't having a good time with him anymore."

Kirkus barked a laugh.

"That's not what I mean. He became too possessive. We weren't right for each other." She glared at the unsympathetic deputy.

"You believe he left a flower on your car the other night," Kirkus continued.

"Yes. But what does that have to do—"

"A part of you wanted him out of the way."

"He showed up at my business ranting and making a scene. He grabbed my arm so hard…" She showed him the bruises.

"Mr. Strawn was an inconvenience to you, wasn't he?"

"What are you accusing me of?" Carrie pushed to standing.

"I'm just looking for the truth." Kirkus folded his arms and leaned back in his chair.

"Will you please tell me what happened to Brett?" Carrie couldn't bring herself to say the other words— words like *killed* and *murdered*. "I can't help if you don't give me anything to go on."

"Mr. Strawn was electrocuted." A physical shiver rocked Deputy Kirkus.

Her mind snapped to a job site, but how on earth would that happen between the hours of—what had he said?—midnight and 2:00 a.m.? "I guess I don't understand. You said he was at home?"

She was still trying to absorb the information.

"Yes, ma'am," Kirkus said with a small head shake.

Shock shot through her. A picture was starting to emerge. Brett had been electrocuted in his own home.

"How do you know he was…that *it* happened on purpose?" Where was Tyson, his pit bull?

"I don't know too many people who would toss a hair dryer into the shower while they're still in it." His words were heavy and too straightforward. She figured some of that was from lack of sleep, given the dark cradles underneath his dull gray eyes. For someone in his midforties, Kirkus's hair was a little too gray for his age, his physical demeanor a little too fatigued-looking.

"Wait. It happened in his bathroom?" Now her mind really was racing. Again, her thoughts jumped to some kind of freak accident.

"When was the last time you had contact with Mr. Strawn?" Kirkus leaned forward and rested his elbows on the table. He motioned for her to sit so she did.

"Yesterday morning. There were witnesses. He showed up to my shop angry and threatened me," she said.

"You didn't call him or text?"

"I didn't. And I didn't answer any of his attempts to reach me, either. It's why he said he came to the shop in the first place." She stared at Kirkus. Did he believe her? "Feel free to pull my cell phone records and check."

"We will." Kirkus softened his approach a little when he said, "This is a murder investigation, ma'am. I'm not trying to offend you. What can you tell me about Mr. Strawn's other relationships? Was he seeing anyone else?"

"Not that I know of," she said.

"What about fights? Had he been in an argument with anybody other than you lately?"

"I'd been avoiding him, so I couldn't tell you." She crossed her legs and rocked her foot back and forth.

"Did he owe money to anyone?" Kirkus's gaze intensified on her.

"Brett owed money to a contractor." She snapped her fingers. "His name was Jimmy something. Oh, what was his last name? I remember him saying something about that before we broke up. He'd seemed unsettled and a little scared, which I distinctly remember because he usually put on a tough guy routine in front of me."

Carrie glanced at the deputy. He sat there, shoulders forward and clasped hands resting on the table.

"Maybe you should write this down," she urged.

He pulled a small recording device from his shirt pocket and set it down in front of her. "Please, continue."

She flashed her eyes at him. "Brett owed Jimmy-what's-his-name money."

"And Jimmy is what kind of contractor?" the deputy asked.

"He does tile," she said.

"Is there anyone you can think of who might want him out of the picture or benefit if he was gone?" Kirkus asked, still studying her.

"I stayed out of his work affairs and we really hadn't dated long enough for me to know everything about him." She scanned her memory. "That being said I can't think of anyone off the top of my head."

"Mr. Strawn had a dog." The door opened behind her and the deputy nodded toward whoever stood in the doorway.

"Of course he did. Tyson." It had taken Carrie weeks before she would go to Brett's house after he'd explained that he'd trained the dog to protect his equipment on job sites. Once she got to know Tyson, she loved him and got on Brett for being too hard on him when he did something Brett didn't like. In fact, his cruel side had been one of the many reasons she'd decided to walk away from the relationship in the first place. "Oh, no. What happened? Is Tyson okay?"

"The dog's fine." The sheriff walked in and stood

beside her. "In fact, he was so calm that he let the killer walk right past him to get to the bathroom where the victim was showering."

Carrie sat there, dumbfounded, for a long moment. Reality crashed down around her like a carefully constructed building tumbling down in an earthquake. The handwriting on the wall said she'd been rousted awake in the middle of the night because she was the primary suspect.

Anger burst through her. Cooperating so they could find Brett's killer was one thing. Being accused of *being* Brett's killer was another story altogether.

"Am I under arrest, Sheriff?" she asked.

"No, ma'am."

"Suspicion?" she pressed.

"How well did you know that dog?" The sheriff took out a Zantac packet and opened it. He popped a pill in his mouth and dry swallowed.

"I'd been to Brett's house dozens of times. I knew Tyson." The sheriff might not realize it, but this interview was about to be over.

"Well enough to walk right past him when his master was home?" The sheriff returned the half-empty packet to his pocket.

"Yes." Carrie reached inside her purse.

"I'll be back in minute." The sheriff walked out the door, leaving it open and giving her the feeling that she was no longer a trapped animal. She was, though. The deputy followed Sawmill into the hallway, where the two men spoke in hushed tones.

While she waited for the sheriff to return, she located Dade's card and pressed it flat to her palm. With her cell phone in the other hand, she started to punch in the number, unsure of what she'd say except that maybe she needed his help and a recommendation for a good attorney.

"I'd hold off on making that call if I were you." Deputy Kirkus's voice startled her.

She gasped. "Why?"

"We're just having a conversation," Deputy Kirkus said, but his tone had changed.

"I'd like to make a phone call. Is there a law against it?" she asked, turning to face him so she could get a good read on his body language. She didn't like the accusation in his tone, but looking at him only made it worse. His frame blanketed the door. He was tall and thick around the midsection. Too much sitting in a cruiser, she thought.

"No, ma'am." There he went with that *ma'am* business again.

"Well, if I'm not doing anything wrong, I'd like a little privacy, if you don't mind," she said, needing to see if he would leave her alone.

"Is there anyone who can verify where you've been tonight?" Deputy Kirkus asked.

Carrie blew out a breath. "I'd like to make that phone call now."

"Are you sure you want to do this?" Kirkus's brow arched, and the worry lines bracketing his mouth intensified.

"Make a call? Yes." Carrie tightened her grip on the card, rubbing her thumb along the embossed letters.

The deputy leaned against the doorjamb and folded his arms. "Forgive me for bringing up the past, but you were moved around in the system quite a bit as a child, weren't you?"

Where'd that come from? "I'm not sure what my childhood has to do with my life today and especially with Brett."

"It's just that you ended up with the Berger family, if memory serves," he continued. He needed to get to the point.

Carrie crossed her legs and rocked her foot back and forth. "I still don't see—" It dawned on her where he was going with this. "I can assure you that I'm perfectly stable."

"It's not healthy for a kid to get passed around so much, is it?" he continued, and fire lit in her chest.

"What are you trying to say, Deputy Kirkus?" She locked on to his gaze. "That I'm unstable? That I'm crazy because I didn't have the best childhood? I'm not the only one who ever had problems while growing up."

"I've seen the photos," he said, and he was getting a little too close for comfort.

"And?"

"Mr. Strawn had a reputation for putting his hands on women." He bowed his head, and she couldn't really tell if he was being respectful of the dead or sorry for the accusation sitting in the air between them.

"If I understand this correctly, you're accusing me of getting rid of him because he hurt me," she clarified.

"Abuse does things to people, especially kids. Maybe you'd had enough and this guy caused you to make a mistake," he stated.

"The only thing I'm fed up with is being accused of something I didn't do." She stood and shouldered her purse.

Kirkus's hands went up in the surrender position. "Hold on there. No one's accusing you of anything."

"Except having a bad childhood, right?" She tapped her toe against the tile as anger built inside her. It didn't matter what she said or did. She'd never break free from people judging her, not here or anywhere else. "I'm upset now. Are you afraid I'm going to do something stupid?"

He shook his head.

"So it seems that I can be angry and still behave like a normal person." She took a deep breath meant to calm herself. "The reason Brett and I broke up is because I saw a side to him that I didn't like. In case you're wondering, he never put a hand on me."

"The dots aren't hard to connect," Kirkus countered with an apologetic look. "A jury might feel the same way."

The thought of living the nightmares of her past all over again, and especially for public consumption, caused her to shiver. "I doubt a jury would convict anyone who'd been at home with her dog while someone she once cared about was murdered."

"Says you," he stated. "You say that you were home with your dog. Unfortunately, your pet can't corroborate your story."

"Whatever happened to being innocent until proven guilty?" she countered, reminding herself to breathe. The walls felt like they were closing in around her and she needed to get outside for some fresh air.

"Like I said, I'm just thinking like a jury," he claimed.

A noise tore from Carrie's throat. "Let's hope juries have more common sense than that, Deputy."

"I'll get the sheriff." He turned toward the hall but didn't leave the door frame.

Carrie started to pace.

"Ma'am, I'm afraid I have to ask you to sit down." There was nothing friendly about his expression or posture now.

Carrie prayed the card in her hand would give her strength. "Why's that, Deputy? Am I not free to go anymore?"

"It's in your best interest to cooperate," he stated with a frown.

"I asked this before and I'm asking it again. Am I under arrest?" All he'd told her so far was that her ex-boyfriend had been electrocuted—the thought still ripped her heart out—and the person responsible had walked right past his dog to do it. She wasn't the only person in the world who knew Tyson, and Brett would have a long line of people he'd upset at one time or another. The guy didn't always use tact when trying to get a point across.

"No, ma'am. And I'd like to keep it that way." He leaned against the doorjamb again.

"So would I. And since I haven't done anything wrong, I don't expect any change in that statement." She stalked toward him. "So if you'll excuse me, I just learned that someone I once cared about is dead. I'd like to go home and cry before taking a shower and finding someone to open my shop this morning, because I have a feeling this is going to be one heck of an awful day."

The deputy didn't move.

"Excuse me," she said, looking him square in the eye. His were a dull, watery gray outlined by red. Too many late nights. Too much coffee. Too much sitting. His judgment was horribly off, and she'd blame those three things for him standing there, blocking the door, and not the fact that he really might think she'd killed Brett.

Chapter Seven

"Deputy, I'd like to go home," Carrie stated boldly, realizing that she didn't have any leverage in this situation. She didn't even have a ride. It didn't matter. The walls were closing in, and she could scarcely believe the accusation hanging in the air. Asking to walk through the door would tell her exactly where she stood. *At least for the moment*, a little voice reminded her, because even if they allowed her to leave, that didn't mean it was over. Brett would still be *gone*—she fought against the onslaught of emotion threatening to crack her in two—and she could be hauled back in at any time.

"The sheriff picked you up?" Kirkus craned his neck, looking behind him before acknowledging Carrie's request and stepping aside.

"Yes," she conceded.

"If you can be patient a few more minutes, someone will give you—"

Carrie's hand was already up and waving off the deputy. It was far too late for talking, and she had no plans to stick around the sheriff's office a minute longer than she absolutely had to. She recognized the stall tactic for what it was. "I can manage on my own."

She stalked past Kirkus without a sideways glance.

She'd walk home if she had to. Dade would be up but possibly out of cell range and she wanted to get out of there now. There had to be an app for a car service. She hadn't needed one until now and didn't have the first clue what to do to find the app. The App Store? Could she call for a car this early? She had no idea how it worked, but that wouldn't stop her.

If not an app, then what? Or who? One of her employees would pick her up in a heartbeat, but how would she explain being in the sheriff's office following Brett's murder?

A little voice in the back of her mind said, *Dade*. She rubbed her thumb against the embossed letters one more time. She hated the thought of disturbing him. But hold on. Living on the ranch, wouldn't he already be awake and working?

She stalked outside into the balmy air. More rain threatened, another rarity for August in Texas, but shocking truths were lining up tonight. Media people descended on her. She turned tail toward the lobby as tears threatened to overwhelm her. She made a beeline for the women's restroom and cleared the door before the first sob tore from her throat.

A stall opened, and an overwrought Ms. Strawn stepped out. Her eyes were puffy and red as she zeroed in on Carrie.

"What did you do to my boy?" Ms. Strawn came at her with balled fists.

"I would never hurt him," Carrie defended herself, and a flash of guilt assaulted her because she already had just not in the same way.

Carrie caught the woman's arms as she thrust them toward her. The older woman was surprisingly strong for someone in her late fifties who was on disability. Carrie guessed it was grief causing her to act out, to wrongly accuse. She couldn't possibly believe that Carrie would hurt another human being. Could she?

"I'm so sorry about what happened," Carrie offered, releasing the woman's hands.

Brett's mother exhaled, her tall, willowy frame shrinking like air out of a balloon.

Ms. Strawn drew back to smack Carrie, who side-stepped the flat palm coming toward her.

"You ought to be in jail for what you did to my boy," Ms. Strawn seethed. "I knew you'd cause something like this. Bad stuff clings to you and hurts everyone around except you."

Carrie backed against the sink and gripped the porcelain. Words could be so much more damaging than physical blows.

Ms. Strawn stepped forward, pointing her index finger at Carrie's face. "Mark my words. You won't get away with this."

"I didn't do anything." Why was she defending herself to a woman who didn't care about finding out the truth?

"I know all about you and what you said happened. I told my son to steer clear of you from the get-go. You're a liar and a murderer," Ms. Strawn accused. "And now my boy is paying the ultimate price."

"I wouldn't hurt Brett." Carrie stepped out of reach of the shaky finger being pointed at her.

"You did. And now my boy's..." Ms. Strawn shrank back, unable to finish. She covered her mouth with her hand, and tears streamed down her sallow cheeks.

The door opened and Brett's sister, Brenda, caught

sight of what was going on. She darted to her mother's side.

"Let's go, Mama," Brenda said, shooting a nasty look at Carrie. "She's already done enough. Leave it alone and let the sheriff do his job."

The woman collapsed against her sturdy daughter.

"She'll pay for what she's done," Ms. Strawn cried out.

"I know she will," Brenda soothed, glancing back to shoot another dagger at Carrie with her eyes.

Carrie stood there, stunned and motionless for a few minutes. It took several more before her hands stopped shaking enough to make the call to Dade. She could only pray he was in cell phone range. He picked up on the second ring.

At the sound of his voice, a sob burst through. She could barely gather her thoughts before blurting out, "I'm so sorry to bother you but I didn't know who else to call and so much has happened I don't even know where to start."

"Slow down, Carrie. Where are you?" His warm rumble of a voice washed over her, bringing a sense of calm that she knew better than to allow. It wouldn't last. Good things never did in her life.

"I'm at the sheriff's office," she stated as calmly as she could manage before another sob retched from her throat.

"What happened?" By the tone of his voice, it occurred to her that he thought Nash had pulled another stunt. It was reassuring that his first thought was she was hurt or in danger rather than her being a suspect in a murder investigation.

"It's Brett," she said, unable to speak the horrible

truth without tears streaming down her cheeks. "Something's happened. He's...*gone*."

"I'll be right there," he said. The line was dead before she could say another word.

Just thinking about it made her stomach churn and threaten to revolt. She moved to the sink and splashed water on her face before locating a rubber band in her handbag and pulling her hair back into a ponytail and off her face.

Brett was gone. The two of them had been in a bad argument. And now she was a suspect in his murder.

It seemed the fear that had haunted her entire life was real.

The storm cloud that had followed Carrie had returned, and it might just swallow her whole this time.

"DADE," CARRIE SAID the moment he walked through the doors of the police station. She charged toward him and buried her face in his chest as he wrapped his arms around her.

He could see that she'd been crying even though she tried to cover it. He could feel her trembling in his arms even though she tried to appear brave. And he could sense her fear even though her chin rose in defiance as she met his gaze.

"The sheriff just showed up at my house and brought me here for questioning," she stated, so much torment in her voice. "They think I'm involved in Brett's murder."

"That's crazy," he defended as shock and anger fired through him. This was not the best time to have a sit-down with the sheriff about how off base the man was, but Dade had no plans to gloss over this. Sawmill couldn't possibly believe Carrie was guilty of murdering her ex-boyfriend. And if he did, Dade had something to say to the man to straighten him out. He and Sawmill hadn't said a bad word between them, but that was about to change if he didn't leave Carrie alone.

"I didn't have anyone else to call," she said.

"You did the right thing," he reassured, thinking that he needed to get her the hell out of there. More anger fired through his veins at the thought she'd be questioned for her ex's murder under the circumstances. Dade might not've been in touch with Carrie for a long time, but he still knew her well enough to know she was one of the kindest people. She didn't deserve to be treated like this, especially with her background. She'd been through hell and back, and he hadn't been there to protect her.

Where did that come from?

He'd analyze that later. Right now, the problem he faced was getting her out of the sheriff's office without drawing more unwanted media attention.

Dade tucked her under his arm. The forecast called for rain, and it was starting to sprinkle outside. That got him thinking as he walked into the temporary command post that had been set up to take leads on his father's murder. "Does anyone have an umbrella?"

A volunteer motioned toward a coatrack while recording details from a phone call.

"I'd owe you one if you'd let me borrow this." Dade picked up a small red offering and held it up.

The volunteer was on a call, but she glanced up anyway. Her gaze fixed on Carrie for a split second before connecting with Dade's. She covered the receiver and said, "Go ahead and use it. I'll make do."

Dade mouthed a thank-you before fishing a wad of cash out of his pocket. He peeled off a few twenties and set them on the table in front of the older woman. Her eyes brightened and she smiled before quickly returning to the call in progress.

"Let's take you home," he said to Carrie as he opened the umbrella before exiting through the front door. He could hide her face from the media attention for now. But they'd been seen together the other night, and that probably wasn't good for Carrie. Being seen with him could have the media digging into her painful past.

After depositing her on the passenger side of his truck, Dade took the driver's seat. "I'm sorry about all those reporters."

"Thank you for picking me up," she said, and he hated how small and vulnerable she sounded. This was not the Carrie he was used to, but he understood why she'd be coming from that place and his protective instincts flared.

"We'll figure this out. We have Ed, who will arrange a defense for you should this go to court. He's the best and he'll make sure the truth comes to light," he said, liking the fact that he was thinking up a game plan to help her with a murder defense even less. "Let's get him on the phone right now."

Dade used hands-free Bluetooth technology to call the family lawyer.

Ed picked up on the first ring. "What's going on?"

The lawyer skipped perfunctory greetings. No one would call him at this hour with good news.

"I have Carrie Palmer in the truck with me. You're on speaker," Dade supplied.

"Okay. What's going on with Miss Palmer?" He sounded surprisingly awake now. The family lawyer's ability to snap to strategic thinking on little to no sleep had always amazed Dade.

"Her ex, Brett—" He glanced at Carrie.

"Strawn," she supplied with an overwhelmed quality to her voice.

"Brett Strawn was murdered earlier this evening," Dade finished.

"Okay," Ed said, and Dade could almost hear the dots connecting while he offered sincere-sounding condolences.

"How long ago did the relationship end?" Ed asked.

"It's been a couple of weeks," she said after thanking him.

"Forgive the question, but was the breakup amicable?" His voice was a study in calm.

"Not really," she admitted.

"When investigators dig into this case, and I'm assuming the sheriff already picked you up for questioning, what kinds of communications between the two of you will they find?" he asked.

"What do you mean? Like emails? Texts?" She sounded disoriented and a little confused. No doubt still in shock.

"Exactly like that," he encouraged.

"Mostly texts and unreturned phone calls," she said.

"I take it you were the one who ended the relationship," Ed stated.

"Yes."

"Did he ask for another chance?"

"Almost constantly." This time she sounded deflated

and guilty. Both understandable emotions, given the circumstances.

"And this caused discord between you," Ed concluded.

"Yes. It did. A great deal, actually." More of that defeated tone came across.

"Were you considering taking him back?" Ed probed.

Dade didn't want to acknowledge how eager he was to hear the answer to that question. Certainly not to her and especially not to himself.

"Not one bit," she said with assuredness.

"I know this is going to sound harsh given the situation, but had he become a nuisance?" Ed was forging ahead.

"Yes. He came to my business to try to convince me to take him back and didn't like it when I said I needed time to think," she admitted.

"How'd that go?" Ed's voice raised an octave.

Dade remembered the fight she and her ex had had in the parking lot and the crowd of people who'd witnessed the exchange. At the time, he'd been proud of Carrie for standing up for herself, but he would've handled the situation differently if he'd known this was where it would end up.

"About as badly as it could've. He shouted, which frightened my customers. A few left. He yelled at me." She stopped.

"Did he try to lay a hand on you?" Ed asked, his tone even.

"Yes. We exchanged heated words in the parking lot, and he reared his hand back to strike me. I backed up against a tree, saw a rock and chucked it at him as he walked away," she admitted. "I was angry, but I would never…"

A couple of beats passed before anyone spoke again.

"Did the sheriff give you any idea of what happened to Mr. Strawn?" Ed asked.

"He was electrocuted in the shower," she said, again with the same small voice.

Ed apologized again.

Carrie released a sob, and her hand came up to cover her mouth.

"Why do you think the sheriff came to her first?" Dade asked, realizing she needed a minute before she'd be able to continue. Her emotions were understandably raw.

"It's routine. I'm sure someone witnessed their fight, and it's customary in a murder investigation to look to those closest to the victim." Ed paused. "In this case, it sounds like the sheriff brought her in so he could get a feel for her emotions. See if she had a good alibi and he could rule her out."

"I was at home, alone with my dog," she supplied.

"Can anyone corroborate your story?" Ed asked.

"No." Carrie went dead silent.

Carrie exhaled, sounding like she was barely keeping hold of her emotions.

"What's the next move?" Dade asked.

"Just stay low until I speak to the sheriff to see what evidence he might have that could put Carrie at the scene," he said.

"His mother was there. I ran into her in the bathroom. She accused me…" Carrie's voice trailed off as though remembering the exchange was too hard. Or hurtful.

"I take it she doesn't like you." Ed's sympathy was a welcome reprieve.

"Not a bit," Carrie supplied.

"Is there anything else the sheriff mentioned that I should know?" Ed asked after a thoughtful pause.

"He mentioned something about Tyson." Carrie sat a little straighter in the seat. "Tyson is Brett's dog. The killer walked right past him and dropped a hair dryer in the shower."

"So, the assumption they're making is that the victim knew his killer." Ed's tone shifted. "That makes even more sense why the sheriff wanted to talk to you first."

"Tyson would never let a stranger walk into the house without a fight. He'd been trained to guard construction sites and Brett didn't let a lot of people around his dog," she supplied.

"Did Mr. Strawn bring a lot of people to his home?" Ed asked.

"He kept a lot of tools there. So, no. He didn't trust people not to steal and that's why he got Tyson in the first place. To guard his equipment." Carrie glanced at Dade, and that one look sent electric currents rocketing through him. He chalked them up to his need to protect her on overdrive.

"Was his business going well?" Ed perked up at the last piece of information.

"He always seemed to have plenty of work, but he supported his mother and sister, so that didn't leave him as much to live on. The neighborhood where he lives is a little sketchy. He also recruited workers from around the neighborhood when he needed more hands." She wiped away tears before giving the family lawyer a few names of Brett's associates, saying she'd given the same ones to the deputy earlier.

"Any chance you were present during the fight, Dade?" Ed's tone changed.

"Yes."

Chapter Eight

"I'm sorry," Dade said to Carrie after ending the call with Ed.

"We fought in front of everyone yesterday. That has to be why they'd think I did something like this to someone I once cared about." She twisted her hands together in her lap. The lost look had returned.

Those words, this situation were abrupt warnings to keep his distance. His last girlfriend had been tangled up in a messy situation with her ex, and Dade had sworn off any involvement with another woman in the same predicament. If he and Carrie hadn't been so close at one time, he would have connected her with Ed or a great defense lawyer and then walked away.

Experience had taught him these situations were messy. In the case of his ex, Naomi, she'd never been able to get over the loss of her high school sweetheart, who had died on the football practice field senior year. When her relationship with Dade became serious enough for him to consider a trip to the jeweler, she'd sprang it on him that she could never truly love anyone other than her ex. The only problem was that she'd kept Dade in the dark and the relationship going until he caught her with another guy. She'd blamed her overwrought emotions for the affair. Dade had licked a few wounds over the whole ordeal at the time. Now, he was mostly glad he'd dodged that bullet and hadn't married someone who couldn't let go of the past.

"Who can you call to open the shop today?" He needed to remember how it felt to have his heart trampled on and keep his distance, especially as he was trying to get a handle on his emotions following the Mav's death.

"Once news gets out that the sheriff thinks I'm a murderer, no one's going to bring their kids into my shop for ice cream." There was a defeated quality to her tone.

He hoped the town of Cattle Barge was more supportive than that and yet he'd witnessed the people giving her dirty looks and leaving her business because her ex was causing a scene. She was probably right. Once details of her past emerged—something she'd never spoken about to him and he'd never felt right digging into on his own—then all the history-repeating-itself accusations would fly. Dade needed to think of a way to spare her now, because he'd let her down before and he couldn't live with himself if he did it twice. Her friendship was worth more than that to him.

"Everything'll be fine. You'll see." The words were hollow no matter how much he wanted them to be true.

Her lack of response said she knew it, too.

"I'd like to stay with you for a while." He pulled up in front of her house and cut off the engine.

"Are you sure? I know you need to get back to the ranch." Carrie opened the passenger door. Her voice was even, and he couldn't read her.

"Dalton can cover for me," he reassured her.

At the door, Carrie's hands shook as she tried to position the key properly, clueing him into her emotions. He covered her hand with his and she stiffened like she was preparing for something before she handed him the key. She didn't immediately move away from his touch, and he could see that she needed comfort—the kind of comfort he knew better than to give while she was this vulnerable. He unlocked the door, opened it for her and hesitated before following her inside.

Damn slippery slope he was about to walk onto. His life was already in chaos and hers had been turned upside down. Neither one of them was in a position to think clearly. The attraction that had been sizzling between them was a distraction they couldn't afford.

Dade flexed and released his fingers. They still vibrated with tension from touching her. It was so far beyond a bad idea to go inside her home that Dade almost thought better of it. Almost. Because before he could overanalyze the situation, the sweetest little dog came barreling past his legs.

"Coco," Carrie shouted a little too late. The critter had already bolted outside and off the porch. A frustrated Carrie called for her dog.

Dade put two fingers to his lips, slicked his tongue across them and whistled.

The little firecracker immediately cut right twice and was on her way back toward the door at full speed. Carrie stepped aside in time for the excited pup to fly inside. Dade stepped in after the dog and closed the door behind him.

Carrie looked at him, stunned. "How on earth did you do that?"

He smiled. "It was nothing."

"That's the first time she's ever..." Her eyes started welling up again.

"It's because I'm not familiar. She most likely came back to protect you," he said.

"That usually means hackles raised and rapid-fire barks," Carrie argued.

The dog returned to Dade, alternating between sniffing his boots and barking up at him excitedly. Her entire backside wagged like crazy. He bent down and scratched her behind the ears. "See, it's the foreign smells."

"I doubt it." Carrie looked down at her with a frown.

"Being brought up on a ranch helps when it comes to animals," Dade said by way of explanation.

Carrie stared down at her dog for a long moment. "Guess so."

"I'll put on a pot of coffee." She bit back a yawn. It was easy to tell that she was trying to cover her exhaustion with a half-hearted smile. It was a lot like trying to put a Band-Aid on a geyser.

"I can do that if you point me to the kitchen," he offered.

"Great. It's over there." She motioned left. "I'll let Coco out the back. If she'll still come to me."

Carrie called her dog as she walked toward the door. Coco followed Dade into the kitchen.

"What did you do? Rub fresh meat on your boots?" Carrie stood there, hands out, exacerbated.

"Coco and I are going to get to know each other in the kitchen while you find someone to cover at the sweet shop." Dade leaned against the counter and folded his arms. "No arguments."

"How about another plan? I'll freshen up and then we'll see where I stand," she countered.

"As I remember from playing tag on the playground, you were always good at getting your way. Even when you were tagged out, you'd figure out a way to negotiate your way back into the game."

"Then you know there's no point fighting me on this," she said with a smile that was a lot more genuine this time. The dimple on her left cheek emerged, and an overwhelming urge to kiss it shot through Dade. He needed to keep his hormones in check. Yes, Carrie was a beautiful woman, and in the midst of all their problems—and combined they were doozies—he wanted nothing less than to get lost in her, with her. But since that idea was about as smart as sweetening his coffee with cyanide, he forced himself to focus on something productive—making coffee.

While he could hear water running in the bathroom down the hall, he texted Dalton.

You've been gone a lot lately, everything okay? Dalton texted back.

Need a change of pace, Dade responded.

That all?

Dade thought for a long, hard minute, and then texted, A break from the ranch, too.

You need anything? came Dalton's response.

Not me. Helping a friend.

You need an assist? Dalton responded.

How many times had they used that term on the

playground as kids during a basketball game? Their relationship was one of the few good things that had carried over from childhood. The two of them were solid
through thick and thin.

Thanks for not asking who it is.

Figure you'll say when you're ready, Dalton responded.

A thought struck. Was he dodging his own problems
in order to help Carrie? He wouldn't deny how much
easier it was to focus on someone else's rather than face
his own. Besides, his couldn't be fixed. The Mav was
gone. There was no going back and erasing the harsh
words Dade had said to him. He'd regretted them instantly. Before he could find the right words to apologize, there'd been that fishing pole, the note, and then
the Mav had been killed. All those unspoken words left
to sour and fester.

His cell buzzed in his hand, jerking his thoughts to
the present.

Take the time you need, bro.

Dade reassured his brother that he intended to pull
his weight around the ranch and would explain everything later. He didn't want to talk about Carrie or analyze his deep-seated need to protect her.

Pictures of the two of them were most likely on every
local news outlet by now and his family would be able
to put two and two together as to whom he'd been helping. Ella already knew, but she'd keep his confidence.
Everyone else would be aware soon enough if they

weren't already. No matter how much everyone tried to avoid the news lately, it seemed unavoidable. Dalton wouldn't ask unnecessary questions. Ella might, but only because she was concerned about keeping everyone safe. Dade would have to address the situation with his family and let them know what was going on soon. Not today, though.

When he really thought about the way the sheriff was investigating his father's murder in contrast to Carrie's situation, he was surprised Sawmill hadn't hauled him in for questioning. He and Dalton had suffered plenty of abuse over the years at the hands of the Mav. They both lived at the ranch and had had complicated relationships with the man. Wouldn't that make them suspects?

Why had Sawmill jumped to Carrie so quickly? Considering he'd brought her in for questioning in the early morning hours, the sheriff couldn't have had a chance to talk to witnesses, could he? Unless he had someone who'd walked in and placed Carrie at the murder scene. Dade made a few mental notes of questions he had for Ed after the lawyer spoke to the sheriff.

Dade had taken the first sip of black coffee by the time Carrie reemerged. He tried not to focus on how thin the material of her T-shirt was as her full breasts lifted with every breath she took.

Coco was happily curled up next to his boots as he poured a cup for Carrie.

"Thank you." She took the offering, and he ignored the frisson of heat where their fingers grazed. "I reached Harper. She'll open the shop for me."

The heat between them would only get him in more trouble, and his emotions were already getting away from him. Carrie offered a peek of light and that made her even more dangerous, which was why he needed to resist the urge to reach out and her and pull her in his arms, taking in her fresh-from-the-shower flowery scent.

And he could do that even though his fingers flexed, acting as if with a mind of their own.

He could control this attraction that was trying to get away from him, like he'd handled every tough situation he faced, with focus and determination.

Or so he tried to convince himself.

CARRIE TOOK A sip of the freshly brewed coffee and then set the cup on the counter. Seeing the insides ripped out of the once-stuffed whale sitting on top of the dryer almost kicked off a fresh wave of tears. Brett had denied being the one to give it to her, but he was the only reasonable option. No one else knew her well enough to know orcas were her favorites.

After letting Coco go outside, Carrie pointed to the stuffed animal. "I'd like to get that thing out of here."

"You didn't mention this before." Dade picked up the orca and examined it.

"My first thought after Brett was Nash, but it can't be him, can it? I mean, he's gone. The festival packed up and left already, didn't it?" she asked.

Dade pulled out his smartphone and opened the internet application. He entered AquaPlay Festival. "They're in Nacogdoches, opening tonight."

"That's not far." Her face paled. "But at least he's not here."

"Ed has a meeting set up in a couple of hours to probe the sheriff and find out what law enforcement is doing to find the person responsible for Brett's death."

He realized he was getting his fingerprints all over potential evidence. He set the stuffed animal down and took a step back.

"What's wrong?" Carrie had always been perceptive.

"Other than destroying any chance they could get DNA from the orca?" Damn. He blew out a frustrated breath. And then another when he saw the look of horror on her face.

"I didn't even think about that." She muttered the same curse he was thinking and it was a lot stronger than *damn*. "After Coco chewing on it and me handling it, the only things they'll find are dog DNA and teeth marks."

"I don't know how easy it would've been to pull prints off fabric anyway. I'll let Ed know what's going on here. He'll be able to tell us what to do." Dade fired off a text. He didn't like the feeling of being helpless. "Is there something significant about this being a whale? Does it mean something important to you?"

She'd never told a soul the reason, just that she loved them.

A hot tear stung as it rolled down her cheek.

"When I was little, maybe seven or eight—" she shrugged "—I can't remember exactly how old I was, only that I lived with this sweet old woman. She was the kind of grandmother everyone wished they had. Her name was Mildred and her husband's name was Bronson. They were the kindest people I think I've ever met, aside from you and your brother and sisters."

Dade seemed taken back by the comparison. "Us? Kind? Nah. We could be better people."

She doubted it. His oldest sister worked tirelessly to make Cattle Barge a better place to live for everyone. She was involved in more charities than Carrie could count and had been targeted for murder because of her work in trying to build an additional animal shelter. Dade and Dalton were probably two of the best men she'd ever met. *And especially Dade*, a little voice pointed out.

"Bronson retired and wanted to spend their last few years together traveling the world. Mildred—Grandma Millie to us—refused, because she wanted to see her foster work through. They'd taken in me and another girl, Sandy, who was a teenager. Then Bronson got some bad health news. I don't remember what happened exactly. But he got sick, and Grandma Millie almost wore herself out taking care of him. We pitched in as much as we could, but now I realize how much of a burden we must've been to her."

"She sounds like an amazing woman," Dade said, and his words were a blanket of comfort around her.

"I know he was taking a lot of medicine for a while. He was bedridden. And then he got up and walked out the back door. He sat in the backyard for an hour. Every day after, he improved until he got close to where his health was before." A surprising spring of tears leaked from her eyes. She wiped them away with an apology.

"Don't be sorry for crying."

"She hugged us and told us how much she loved us but that she'd almost lost her Bronson. She wanted to spend as much time as she could with him. We all crumbled onto the floor in a puddle of tears. I'm not sure that I even knew what I was crying about. I just didn't like seeing her sad. I had no understanding of how much my life was about to change or that she meant we weren't going to be part of the picture anymore." Carrie paused to wipe away a few stray tears.

"I'm sure that was a hard decision for her to make." Dade's gaze pierced her. There was so much compassion embedded deep behind the fortress he'd constructed.

"Before she allowed our case workers to take us, she wanted to spend one last weekend together. Looking back, they didn't have much money, so it must've cost a fortune for them to take us to the whale park in San Antonio. They'd bought a small RV, and we stayed in a nearby park. I just remember how hot it was outside, and then suddenly I didn't care because I was watching this massive animal do all these amazing tricks. It was the most awe-inspiring thing I'd ever seen."

"She sounds like an amazing woman," Dade offered with such sincerity Carrie nearly released all the pent-up emotion bottled up inside her.

The couple didn't have much and had planned to travel the country on a shoestring budget. Losing Grandma Millie had left a hole in Carrie's heart that threated to swallow her. The next group home wasn't so kind, and the others...

Carrie didn't want to go there, so she gripped the stuffed animal and walked outside to the trash. Her neighbor's king-cab truck was gone, and she wondered where he went. He'd disappear for days on end, some-times weeks. She opened the lid to the plastic container and dropped the orca inside. More unexpected tears sprang from her eyes, but she immediately wiped them away.

Dade stood in her kitchen, sipping his coffee. Emotions roared through Carrie. Instead of analyzing them, she walked straight toward Dade, pushed up on her tip-

toes and kissed him. He stiffened for a split second before wrapping his arms around her waist. She threaded
her fingers through his hair, and he deepened the kiss.

His big frame corded again, and she almost thought
she'd done something she was about to regret. And then
his hands, rough but gentle, cupped her cheeks and he
tilted her face to gain better access to her mouth. His
full lips covered hers, and she leaned into his hard body.
He was strong and brave and everything she wasn't at
the moment. His kiss was so tender, and yet so hungry,
it robbed her of breath.

She brought her hands up to his muscled chest and
flattened her palms against him. She smoothed her fingers over the ridges of his pecs as he pressed his lips
harder against hers. Her breath hitched when she looked
up at him and saw so much hunger there, hunger that
matched her own.

Dade seemed to come to his senses first, pulling back
just enough that if he spoke his lips would still brush
against hers. She could feel his breath on her and taste
him, a mix of peppermint and coffee.

He'd done the right thing. The kiss was supposed
to slap her back to reality, stop her from overthinking.
But the heat that had been missing in every other kiss
for her entire life had her mind churning even more.

And the attraction that she knew better than to allow
took deeper root.

DADE HAD WANTED to kiss Carrie from the moment he'd
seen her again in the alley behind her shop. After hearing more about what had happened to her years ago…
all he wanted to do was protect her. She'd lost so many
people. Others had abused her. He'd tried to avoid lis-

tening to talk about the neglect she'd suffered after becoming a ward of the state. She'd needed him when she'd returned to Cattle Barge. He could see it in her eyes, even if she couldn't admit it to him or herself. And what had he done?

He'd been a typical teenager too caught up in his own issues to do what he should've done then…step up and protect her.

Since then, his mind always circled back to that one time with her before she'd disappeared. They'd been in seventh grade, and he'd asked if she wanted to study together. He'd taken her to a popular hangout spot, the Barn. The two of them had been laughing and talking easily, and he'd liked the way he felt around her.

Until his friends had shown up. One of his jock buddies, Todd, had stopped by.

"What are you doing here with her? Shaylee tried to call your house earlier and invite you out with us tonight," Todd had said.

"Nothing," Dade had said defensively. Then he'd motioned toward the stack of unopened books on the table. "Trying to make sure I pass Harris's English class."

Todd had made some arrogant crack that Dade had laughed at before walking away.

Dade would never forget the look in Carrie's eyes.

"I gotta go. Study. So I can pass and get out, away from the jerks in this town," she'd said, pushing past him. Now he realized she'd been too strong to cry in front of him.

She'd gotten away from him so fast that by the time he discerned just how much of a jerk he'd been and figured out a way to apologize, she was long gone. She'd been in such a hurry that she'd forgotten her books on the table. He'd tried to return them but she refused to see him after that day, so he'd stopped trying. He'd let her down in the worst way and still felt residual guilt because it wasn't long after that a relative had claimed her. Then, she'd been abandoned and transferred to another home...*the* other home with the Bergers.

She'd disappeared not long after. And he'd never had a chance to explain what he was struggling to understand for himself as a teen—his feelings.

He'd never experienced that kind of intensity with anyone before. He'd been too young and dumb to know what to do with it. His lack of maturity had caused him to handle the whole situation wrong, and before he could make things right she'd been shuffled around again. She returned the summer before senior year and she'd grown into those long limbs. In fact, she was even more beautiful than she'd been before, and everyone seemed to notice, except her.

Dade wasn't making excuses for himself. Everyone thought life as a Butler was easy because his family had money. He had just as many hardships as the next guy. The Mav had worried all his money would make his sons soft. He'd come down hard on Dade and his brother, saying he was making men out of them.

Dade, in turn, had signed up for the military the day he could enlist. Basic might've been hard for some, but not Dade. In more ways than one, it had been his salvation. He'd let go of the anger—or so he'd thought, until the Mav had tried to make amends. But he never really trusted anyone again except his brother and sisters. He'd constructed walls that made it difficult for anything or anyone to penetrate. The Butler kids had been forced to band together to survive their childhood with Maverick Mike.

Dade knew one thing was certain. Thinking about the past never made it better, and it sure as hell didn't change anything. Dade judged people by their present actions. He looked at Carrie, who was studying him curiously. Intelligent, beautiful Carrie.

"Say something," she said, and he could tell that, for once, she was having trouble reading him.

He stood there, looking into her beautiful eyes. He fisted his hands to keep himself from reaching out to touch her silky skin.

And then a little voice in the back of his head reminded him how much he'd regret not doing just that. Touching her. Kissing her. *Oh, hell.*

Throwing common sense out the window, he stalked toward her, took her in his arms and kissed her again.

She responded, tunneling her fingers into his hair and moving her sweet lips against his. All arguments imploded, and the world righted itself for just that one moment when she was in his arms.

This time she pulled away first. Dade sure as hell couldn't have done it.

She blinked up at him, and he couldn't read her. "Your job in the military train you to run toward danger?"

"Yes. What does that have to do with you?"

"I'll hurt you, Dade. I won't mean to, but I will." She stepped away and turned her back to him.

Whatever craziness was going on in her life didn't matter this time. "You need to know that I have no plans to walk away from you until I've seen this through."

She rubbed her arms as though a chill had run up them, but it was hot outside.

"Will you let me?" he asked.

There was no hesitation when she nodded.

He spun her around, hauled her against his chest and kissed her again.

And there was so much power in that one kiss he knew he had to figure out a way to help her without touching her again.

Chapter Nine

Carrie woke after a couple hours of sleep. Glancing at the clock beside her bed, she realized it was almost one o'clock in the afternoon. Panic gripped her that she'd somehow forgotten to open the store and then she remembered making the call to Harper earlier. Images of everything she'd worked so hard to build tumbling down the drain smacked her in the face. It was a sobering thought and one she didn't want to give much energy to.

Her movement woke Coco, who was curled up at the foot of the bed. She hopped down and Carrie immediately missed her warmth.

There was a note propped up on the nightstand from Dade. She picked up the folded paper and turned the edges over with her fingers, thinking about the couple of kisses they'd shared before they'd come to their senses and put a little distance between them. He'd insisted on staying to make sure she was okay.

"Call when you wake up," the note read. She didn't make calls before coffee if she could avoid it.

Thoughts of last night at the sheriff's office and of Brett's murder stalked her, sitting like a heavy lump in her chest that made breathing almost impossible. At least Nash was gone.

She pushed up on her arms, still in disbelief any of this could be happening.

Maybe coffee could somehow wake her up from the nightmare of learning that someone she once cared about was gone. *Brett.* Her heart felt like it might burst out of her chest. He was so young, and she couldn't even imagine how much pain he'd felt in those final few moments of his life.

Carrie threw her legs over the side of the bed and walked into the adjacent bathroom to splash cold water on her face and brush her teeth.

Her ringtone belted out from down the hall as she rinsed. Her heart stuttered, because her immediate thought had been that it was most likely Brett calling. But he wouldn't be contacting her ever again. Carrie's legs went rubbery, and she had to grip the wall with both hands to steady herself.

Don't look up. Don't look down. Keep forging ahead and life will catch up. Mrs. Sanders's words wound through Carrie's thoughts. She must've just turned sixteen years old when she'd lived in her group home. The kind woman had been diagnosed with a rare bone cancer and had had to shut down her operation.

Carrie's heart lurched. The short time she'd lived with Mrs. Sanders had given her a chance to begin the healing process after that last brutal attack. The thought that Mrs. Sanders might be watching over Brett now offered some small measure of relief. Mrs. Sanders had a way of bringing hope to the hopeless. Brett might've turned out to be a jerk but Carrie didn't wish him dead.

Fighting against the onslaught of emotion building,

threatening, Carrie got to her phone as the call rolled to voice mail. She didn't recognize the number, which was probably just as well. She wasn't in the mood to speak to anyone anyway. Although based on the number of messages on her phone, quite a few people were trying to reach her. All from numbers she didn't recognize as she thumbed through the log.

There were dozens of unread messages from Brett, waiting. His last attempt to reach her had been less than an hour before his death. She still couldn't grasp the thought that Brett was gone. Even though she knew it was true on some level, her mind wanted to argue against the fact. Somehow offer proof that this was all some kind of awful dream and she'd wake any minute to find that he was very much alive.

She glanced at the spot on the counter where the stuffed orca had been, grateful it was gone. A text from Dade said that Ed had stopped by this morning with a deputy to pick it up even though there might not be any evidence on it. Dade had shown them where it was outside in the trash.

Coco stood at the back door, whimpering.

"Okay, sweet girl. I'll let you out." Coffee could wait another minute. And then she'd call Dade. Carrie unlocked and opened the back door.

Coco hopped out but then spun around. Something on the ground had caught her attention. Carrie gasped, and her pulse skyrocketed. Hold on. It was probably nothing more than a cricket. She leaned forward and looked down, catching a glimpse of red. A single rose.

Carrie's heart pounded painfully against her ribs. She shooed Coco away from the wilted flower and bent over to pick it up. Then she remembered the fingerprints and froze. Could Brett have left it? No, that was impossible.

Someone was messing with her. Anger ripped through her, and her skin flamed.

Coco bolted toward her, causing Carrie to jump. She was on edge and needed to calm down. No, what she needed was a gallon of caffeine so she could think more clearly. She stared at the flower like it might come to life and attack her. There was no way she was picking it up.

After her dog darted inside, she locked the door and stalked over to her phone. A mix of anger and frustration and helplessness—which made her even angrier— fueled her steps. The minute she gripped her cell, it rang. She jumped, dropped it and took a step back. Okay, now she was letting every little thing get to her.

Glancing at the screen as she picked it up, she saw that the call was coming from an unknown source. Anger pulsed through her as she answered. Whoever was on the other end was about to get an earful. Before she could speak, a male voice cut her off.

"Ms. Palmer?" the masculine voice asked. She didn't recognize it.

"Yes." Impatience rolled off her in waves.

"My name is Darion Jones and I'm with *NewsNow!* on the cable channel—"

She ended the call before he could finish. How had the media gotten hold of her private cell phone number?

News of Brett's murder had to be out by now. She would think that the sheriff would want to keep an ongoing investigation as quiet as possible. Her employees would never give out her personal information to a stranger, especially not with everything going on. The only person who was capable of doing such a thing was

Brett's mother—he'd given his mother her number for emergencies, if she couldn't reach Brett first.

Carrie needed to have a conversation with Dade's lawyer. Speaking of whom, she needed to call Dade. But a conversation before caffeine was a bad idea, and she also needed to figure out what to do with that rose.

The first sip of coffee couldn't make a dent in how exhausted she felt. She put a few ice cubes in a glass. They crackled as she poured the brown liquid over them. Iced coffee was quicker, and she drained the glass a minute later before pouring a second cup, warm this time. She had a feeling that she'd need all the extra energy she could get today.

Equipped with a little more of her mental faculties, she called Dade. He answered on the first ring.

"Everything okay?" was his first question.

"What time did you leave my house?" She intentionally dodged his question. Things couldn't be less okay.

"Around nine o'clock," he said. "Why?"

"You didn't happen to see anything suspicious at the back door, did you?" She got straight to the point. She and Dade had always been able to talk to each other. Well, up until things had changed between them in high school.

"No. I let Coco out before I left and there wasn't anything at the back door. Why? What did you find?" His concern was outlined in his rich, dark voice—a voice that wrapped around her and promised everything would be okay. But everything would not be all right. A man was dead. She was suspected of murder. And someone had decided this would be a good time to mess with her. Nash? Or someone else? Was there someone from her past who had come back to torment her?

"What is it, Carrie?" There was so much concern in his tone. His voice was the calm in a raging storm, but she knew better than to allow the comfort. Nothing was okay. Nothing would be right again. This was Carrie's life, history repeating itself. Any time she found something good to hold on to, it would slip out of her grip.

"What if it was his mom? Or sister? Maybe he told them about it." She gasped, thinking out loud.

"Tell me what you're talking about, Carrie. What did you find on your doorstep?" His strong male voice demanded an answer.

"The rose." The words coming out of her mouth sounded impossible even to her when she heard them spoken aloud.

"You didn't touch it, did you?" he asked.

"No. But Coco started clawing at it," she informed.

"Stay where you are. I'm on my way."

"Okay." The two exchanged goodbyes.

Carrie double-checked the back door, making sure it was locked before pacing in the kitchen. She needed something to do, something to occupy her thoughts. She glanced into the laundry room and remembered the load of laundry that needed to be put away. First, she checked in with work. Her mind was too scattered to go over numbers or the details of orders but she got a high-level update from Harper. Her employee mentioned that reporters were showing up, asking questions.

A few minutes later, a few deep breaths, and her nerves were beginning to settle with the busywork. All she had to do was wait until Dade got there, she thought as she pulled out the last item from the laundry basket, a pair of jogging shorts.

But hold on a minute. Where was the sundress she'd

worn a few days ago? She might be going crazy—and that was a very real possibility lately—but she could've sworn she'd washed it with her jogging shorts.

She got up and bolted toward the closet to check. Not there. How about the clothes hamper? Her next stop was the master bathroom. The hamper had clothes from the last two days in it and nothing else.

Carrie wasn't going crazy. The dress was missing.

DADE HADN'T MADE it halfway to Carrie's house when his cell ringtone cut through the air. He answered it hands-free.

"Someone's been in my house," she said breathlessly, and he could hear the panic in her voice.

"When? Now?" A shot of panic gripped him. He wasn't close enough to get to her if an intruder was in the house.

"No. The other day," she supplied, and the tightness in his chest loosened up a notch. He was far from comfortable, but at least there was no immediate threat. But someone had been there this morning if they'd left the flower. He would've seen it when he let Coco out otherwise.

"How do you know?" Dade needed to be certain she wasn't in danger. And he sure as hell would handle things differently moving forward. The first of which would be to add security to her residence.

"One of my dresses is missing. My favorite jogging suit disappeared, too, but I thought Brett had it and now I'm not so sure." She paused a beat. "Oh, no. There were crumbs on the floor the other day. Dog treats that Coco used to love, but I stopped buying them because the vet said she was putting on weight too fast. I thought she found a leftover bag, but I was sure I'd tossed them all out."

"Stay right where you are. I'll call Ed."

"I don't want to be here and I have to go into the sweet shop. My employees need to see that I'm okay. And—" Carrie was a little breathless.

"Slow down. Tell me what you need me to do."

"There's nothing you can do, Dade. You can't fix this. Not with Brett's murderer still on the loose and some unknown person messing with me. My world is suddenly spinning out of control."

"We'll find out who killed Brett and we'll put a stop to whoever is bothering you," he reassured her, but she was dangerously close to a complete meltdown.

"I keep thinking about that *thing* on my back porch and I don't want to be inside my house right now. Bad luck is like a boomerang and keeps coming back." Based on her quick bursts of air in between words he figured she was pacing.

"I'll see to it the deputy takes it in as evidence. I can assure you it won't return." He'd ask if there was any way he was going to convince her to stay put, but he didn't much care for investing time in lost causes. Especially when he already knew the answer. She was as stubborn as she was beautiful.

"I'll take Coco to work with me. She has a bed in my office from the early days before I could afford employees and I literally spent every waking moment at work." She was offering assurances to him that she'd be okay. Her mind was already made up, and there was precious little he could do to change it.

Carrie having her dog with her at all times did make him feel a little more comfortable. Still, he'd been on edge since hearing about Brett's murder. Since another rose had showed up, he worried about something else, too—her safety while at home. "I'll meet you at the shop."

Dade ended the call and banked a U-turn at the first intersection. The sweet shop was actually closer than her house, so he beat her there and parked in the empty lot across the street. He needed to make a couple of calls while he made sure she arrived intact. And then he'd take care of her house.

There was chaos across the street at her sweet shop. Slipping past the clump of media crews to get inside without drawing more unwanted attention would be next to impossible. At least the festival workers were gone. That should bring Carrie a small sense of relief that she wouldn't have to deal with Nash on top of everything else. Which also, most likely, meant that he wasn't responsible for the flower. Her ex was instantly ruled out, but someone connected to him, like his mother, was a real possibility. Especially after the outburst at the sheriff's office that had upset Carrie.

Dade cut off the engine and grabbed his cell. His first contact was Ed.

"I just got out of a meeting with the sheriff," Ed started right in.

"Where does Carrie stand?" Her status as a witness or suspect heavily influenced their next couple of moves.

"He's looking at her as a witness, but that could change," Staples supplied. "Samuel Jenkins corroborated the story about Nash from the other night. It's giving her more credibility."

"I also think I can help out with that." He told Ed about the flower and the missing clothes.

"The sheriff needs to know immediately." Ed said he'd call Dade back after updating Sawmill. It didn't take more than a couple of minutes for Dade's cell to ring and the two of them to pick up the conversation where they'd left off.

"What did Sawmill think?" Dade asked.

"He found it interesting and assured me that he'll do everything he can to find the responsible party," Ed said. "We need to take measures to ensure her safety while the investigation continues."

"You think the person leaving her gifts and Brett's murderer are the one and the same?" Dade was already on that trail.

"It's suspicious. I hope I impressed the sheriff with that thinking," Ed supplied.

Now that there was a murder involved, her case should rise on Sawmill's priority list. "Did he say what evidence he has that she could possibly be involved in Brett's murder?"

"Right now, he has a statement from the deceased's mother indicating that Carrie had threatened her son if he didn't leave her alone," Ed said. "There are others who have come forward to witness the argument from yesterday and the fact that she attacked him with a rock."

Dade released a disgusted grunt.

"I know what you're going to say, and I also know that's not what happened. I'm telling you what people think they saw." Ed's sympathy came through the line. At least Ed didn't believe the lies. His confidence in Carrie would go a long way toward building a strong defense. There was nothing like truth and righteous belief to make a man go to the ends of the earth to find proof of innocence.

"Even if Carrie threatened her ex, and I doubt that she did, I don't believe Brett would've taken them seriously. Not with the way I witnessed the man treat her in front of her shop. The guy was trying to bully her back into a relationship with him." Dade white-knuckled the steering wheel with his free hand. *Unbelievable.*

"The sheriff requested a statement from you."

"I figured that was coming." Dade was more than happy to provide his side of the story, especially if it could help Carrie.

"Witnesses put you at the scene of their falling-out, and some believe that the two of you are in a relationship." Ed's voice changed and Dade immediately sensed the reason.

"I didn't hurt the man, no matter how much I dislike the kind of men who think it's fine and dandy to put a hand on a woman. I'd be willing to take a lie detector test if that'll clear my name and keep the sheriff from chasing down crazy theories." Dade knew all about how lost the sheriff's office could get during an investigation—they weren't any closer to finding out who'd murdered the Mav.

"That shouldn't be necessary, and I didn't suspect you in the least. I need to ask Carrie if she'll relinquish phone records to the sheriff," Ed said.

"She has nothing to hide, so I doubt that'll be a problem." Dade was confident on that point.

"I didn't think so."

"Can't the sheriff subpoena her records, though?"

Dade figured either way the sheriff would get what he wanted.

"This would be a lot faster, and her cooperation will go a long way toward keeping her where we want her, which is on the witness list. Plus, if she volunteers the information, the sheriff will see her as aiding his investigation. It'll win points."

"She'll be here in a few minutes. Tell me what you need her to do." Dade didn't figure there'd be any pushback from Carrie. She wanted Brett's murder solved.

Dade listened as Ed rattled off a couple of items to add to today's to-do list. At the top was giving the sheriff access to her cell phone records and her house. Dade took notes before asking, "Did the sheriff mention anything about the complaint she filed the other night against the guy who threatened her in the alley?"

"He mentioned a festival worker known as Nash, who his office is tracking down," Ed said.

How hard could it be to find a man who worked with a festival that publicized its schedule? "I can probably tell him where to look with a quick online search."

"You might find the festival, but you won't find him. He can't be located," Ed stated.

"I saw him yesterday late morning in the parking lot of Carrie's shop," Dade supplied.

"Then that makes you the last person to see him." There was dread in Ed's voice.

"What about the people who witnessed the argument yesterday? Surely they saw him, too." Dade didn't like the sound of those words.

"They weren't looking for him, so even if they saw him they most likely wouldn't remember." Ed had a point.

"What you're telling me is the man could be anywhere." Dade raked his hand through his hair, trying to tame the curls. Nash might've left that flower at her doorstep after all.

"According to his employer, he's most likely sleeping off a hangover on someone's couch. Or at least that was the excuse he gave when he didn't show up for work last month for three consecutive days," Ed supplied.

"If he has a drinking problem, why would they hire him to work around kids?" Dade asked.

"Apparently he's in recovery, but he seems to be having trouble keeping it together since losing his brother," Ed said. "His boss told him three strikes and he's out. This is the third."

"Which means he won't be showing up at work asking for another chance," Dade said.

"I asked the same question. His employer says he'll be back. Said he has no other family and the news about his brother hit him hard. His boss said he's a decent person when he's sober," Ed supplied.

Dade wasn't so sure about that. But then, Carrie had said the man had had alcohol on his breath when he'd threatened her. Dade released the white-knuckle grip he had on the steering wheel. "What happened to his brother?"

"Overdose," Ed supplied. "He'd been an addict for most of his life."

"I'm sorry."

Dade maintained a moment of silence.

"There's no history of crimes against women with Nash," Ed supplied.

With this investigation, Dade hated the thought that

rumors would abound, possibly dredging up painful memories for her.

"Is there anything in Carrie's past I need to know about?" Ed asked.

"She had it tough growing up, being tossed around from foster family to group home," Dade shared. "There was abuse, in some cases severe."

"I'm sorry to hear that." Ed paused for a couple of beats. "I'm even sorrier that I have to ask if she's been involved in illegal activity."

"You wouldn't be good at your job if you weren't thorough," he conceded. His protective instincts always flared when it came to Carrie. Speaking of whom, he saw her car slow down and then pass right by the parking lot. "I don't know everything she's endured, but she has amazing internal strength to have gotten where she is today after the start in life she had."

Dade's phone buzzed in his hand, indicating another call was coming through.

"It's Carrie. I'll have to call you back," he said to Ed.

"Let me know when the sheriff can access her house and make sure no one goes inside until evidence is collected," Ed reminded him before ending the call.

"Where are you?" Carrie asked as soon as Dade answered.

"I'm in the lot across the street from your shop." He caught sight of a trio making a beeline straight toward him—reporters? They might've recognized his truck. "But I'm about to be on the move. Can your business at the shop wait until later?"

A long sigh came through the line. "Doesn't seem like I have much of a choice."

"Meet me at Grover's," he said.

"The auto repair shop on Beekman Avenue?" she asked.

"That's the one. And Carrie—" he started.

"What is it, Dade?"

He didn't want to tell her, but she needed to know. "Nash hasn't reported to work—"

She gasped.

"No one knows where he is, so be on the lookout in case you get to Grover's before I do."

Chapter Ten

Carrie drove slowly to Grover's, scanning the area at every stoplight, looking for Nash. The thought of him being out there, somewhere, didn't do good things to her pulse, and for a split second she questioned whether he could have something to do with Brett's murder.

Logic said it was impossible because Nash had no idea who Brett was other than seeing her talk to him in the parking lot yesterday. Unless there was a connection she didn't know about.

Nash had been far more intimidated by Dade and so would most likely try to erase him in order to get to Carrie. Right? But nothing made sense anymore and she couldn't rule anything out.

After being brought up to date on Dade's conversation with Ed, Carrie surmised that Nash was a transient festival worker who was losing his battle with alcoholism. He had no history of rape or assault, although Carrie feared he might've been well on his way to his first that night in the alley. And, there was no way Tyson knew who Nash was. *Tyson.* What would happen to him now that Brett was gone? He was too aggressive with other dogs for her to feel safe leaving him alone with

Coco, or Carrie would volunteer to take him in herself. But then, Ms. Strawn would surely want her son's dog.

She circled the block until she saw Dade's truck pull into the parking lot, not wanting to take any chances of being alone even though she had her dog. Based on Coco's performance with the neighbor and seeing how easily she'd warmed up to Dade—although Carrie couldn't fault her dog there—she didn't want to tempt fate. She parked next to him and locked her doors. Coco eagerly followed Carrie into Dade's truck.

"We'll keep a low profile until the buzz settles down at your shop," he said. "With all the media surrounding the case, I filled my family in on the way over. They'd like to offer help in any way they can. I've arranged for extra security to control who has access to your property and keep an eye on your home. Media might blitz the place as soon as someone figures out your house is being treated like a crime scene."

"Right. I hadn't even thought of reporters." She appreciated Dade's thoughtfulness even more. Emotions tugged at Carrie's heart, emotions like acceptance and warmth. Experience had taught her they'd be ripped away before she could get used to them.

She buckled into her seat and thanked him with as much sincerity as she could without breaking the emotional dam protecting her heart.

"Ed thinks it would be best if you turned your phone over to the sheriff." She was trying to absorb everything. Dade was covering a lot of bases for her, and life was moving at such a high rate of speed that she needed to kick into high gear to keep up.

"Okay." She paused to process what he was saying. "Sawmill wants my statement, too, so we should swing by together. I doubt it'll take long," he said. "Ed informed me that Samuel went in for questioning and basically said the same things we did about Nash the other night, which bought us some credibility."

"I keep going over and over everything in my head, and I can't figure out who could've gotten past Tyson," she finally said, taking a sip of the coffee Dade had offered. Carrie absently stroked Coco, who was curled up on the front seat between her and Dade.

"A dog bred and trained to protect is usually good at his job," Dade agreed.

Carrie searched her brain for the missing piece, the link that would click everything together and paint the picture. "None of this makes sense."

"I know." His voice was calm and held none of the panic hers did. She wanted to get lost in that feeling, if only for an hour or two.

"It just keeps following me," she said quietly.

"What does?" Dade kept his gaze on the stretch of road in front of them. He was so good at moving forward despite everything going on around him.

"A dark cloud."

"There's no such thing." His reaction was so fast, so instinctual that she almost believed him.

"I'll lose my business. Everything I've worked for." She hated the defeat in her voice, but it hurt to say those words.

"It won't come to that." Easy for Dade to say. Everything in Carrie's life had been fleeting. This would be no different. And there was no way a man like Dade could understand where she was coming from. The Butler kids had always been close. It was common knowledge that if one was in trouble, the others rallied around to help, no questions asked. Carrie had no idea what it would feel like to have so many people around ready to catch her if she fell. The concept was foreign to someone used to being alone and looking out for herself. And it wasn't self-pity causing these thoughts. It was truth. And her strength had always been in looking at what she had to deal with honestly and then figuring out a way to survive.

Dade must've sensed her thinking because he added, "I won't let your business fail because of this." His words were so quiet she almost didn't hear them. There was a promise there that even Dade couldn't deliver on. He couldn't take away the darkness that followed her. Not even Dade Butler could bring Brett back to life, stop the person who was messing with her or keep her business afloat.

A FEW QUIET days could hardly erase the shock of Brett's murder. National broadcasts had picked up Brett's story, reporting on a wave of crime in small-town Texas, and his mother and sister had already given several tearful interviews, some of which Carrie was certain they'd received payment for. At least Ed had warned them about going on air and accusing Carrie of murder. He'd been quick to point out that he'd file a lawsuit if that was the case.

Ms. Strawn had lost her only son and Carrie could only imagine how horrible that must be for any mother, especially one who depended on him for pretty much everything. She could forgive his mother for her outburst and the interviews. Carrie refocused on stirring the ice cream, grateful that she was at work and had something to distract her. She had had to close the front of the shop because of reporters and curiosity seekers, but there were enough standing out-of-town delivery orders to keep her head above water. At least that part of her business was still going strong. How long would it take for news to spread and other businesses to distance themselves from her?

The media camped out every day but seemed to have no idea that she was coming in during the middle of the night to work, and she wanted to keep it that way. Any time her mind drifted to what people must think of she wanted to give up. Why was it so important that the people of Cattle Barge accepted her?

Because she loved this town, a little voice reminded her. Because this was the only place that had ever felt like home, the voice continued. And, the voice repeated, if she couldn't fit in here, then where?

Hand mixing the ice cream, having something to focus on besides all the craziness going on around her, was keeping her sane. The trick was to stir the mixture every three hours for thirty minutes as it froze.

Carrie had slept very little her first six months of business before she could afford to hire help. Having a successful business had made her feel proud of herself for the first time. She couldn't let that be taken from her, even though all she really wanted to do was crawl into bed and stay there. Having security control access to her home brought a sense of relief on one front. On another it made her feel like she was in prison.

Coco had been quiet for the last twenty minutes, and Carrie had left the door to her office open so she could hear her dog in case she needed something. An animal wasn't allowed in the food prep area due to health regulations. She had a bed in the office and another spot out front where she liked to curl up when the store was closed.

Carrie's new throwaway phone buzzed as she put the last of the ice cream away. She'd given her old phone to the sheriff for analysis and, even though she was innocent of doing anything wrong, it didn't feel that way. Giving up her phone also brought a strange sense of relief. Was it all those unreturned messages from Brett that had had her on edge and feeling guilty? Dade was calling exactly when he said he would, at quarter to four in the morning.

"How'd it go tonight?" he asked.

"Better. I think I have everything under control again, but I need to be back early tomorrow night to keep things rolling," she replied, not wanting to admit how much hearing his voice calmed the raging winds stalking her.

"Ever think about taking a night off?" he asked.

She almost blurted out, *To do what?* She hadn't had much of a social life since moving to Cattle Barge. Brett had been her "get back on the horse" attempt, and look how that had turned out. Besides, she didn't want to be seen in public. She could only imagine the rumors swirling around town about her. She had to have round-the-clock security at home to keep everyone at bay. "I might not have a choice if I can't open my shop any time soon."

"I'm out back," he said.

She thanked him and ended the call, coaxing Coco out of bed and toward the back door. On second thought, she doubled back to make sure the front was locked, too. Recent events had her unwilling to take any chances.

The door was locked, so she put Coco on her leash

and headed out. Her gaze immediately flew to the twin headlights peering at her from the alley. Her eyes hurt looking at them, which Dade must've realized, because he immediately turned them off.

Carrie saw stars. She blinked a few times before throwing her shoulder into the door and locking it.

With no front-end sales, she would be on shaky ground very soon. She hoped everything would blow over and get back to normal before the business she loved, that she'd built from nothing, completely tanked. The shop was all she had. Admitting that made her life seem truly empty as a sense of defeat overwhelmed her.

Don't go there. Don't think like that. Everything will be fine.

But fine wasn't a given in Carrie's life. And darkness stalked her like cancer cells waiting for the right trigger. She glanced at the alley with a prickly feeling running down her spine. It was the sensation of being watched.

Anger roared through her as she fisted her hand tighter around Coco's leash. Because the feeling was just a feeling. There was no one out there watching her. And that feeling didn't get to win today. It was probably just her frustration clouding her emotions, but the revelation felt good.

"Did you speak to Ed today?" she asked Dade as Coco settled into her comfortable spot between them.

"There's nothing new to report," Dade supplied. He'd given his statement days ago, and a deputy had collected evidence from her house.

"I'm guessing that Nash still hasn't turned up yet." There'd been no sign of him in Cattle Barge as far as she could tell. If he had been the one to…cause harm to Brett…wouldn't he be smart enough to get out of town?

Dade shook his head.

"What about the stuffed animal or the rose? Did they find any prints on either?" Carrie was getting short on patience as the sheriff worked through the details of her case at what felt like a snail's pace.

"Forensics is still working on it. That, or the sheriff's office isn't releasing the information to us." He navigated onto the main road, his headlights leading the way.

"Or anyone else. It'd be all over the news if they had." Carrie had been avoiding coverage as much as she could. She'd bought a temporary phone at a convenience store that couldn't be traced. News of the complaint she'd filed against Nash got out, and it seemed everyone in town was looking for him.

There was even more reason for him to hide now. And the sheriff might never find him, considering they already knew that he didn't have a cell phone—which was unimaginable to her in this day and age—and he seemed to have gone off the grid completely.

Dade kept her posted when the occasional friend of Nash's made news by giving an exclusive interview talking about how close the two had been and how this or that person had tried to help Nash battle his demons. The trail from him leaving the festival had gone cold almost immediately. It seemed that no one knew where he was and he could keep on hiding indefinitely. At least her cell phone records along with witnesses had cast suspicion about Brett's murder away from her.

"Ed mentioned that Nash's employer had said the reason his foreman had decided to stay around Cattle Barge was to give them time to find him before they headed onto the next city," Dade said.

"And then they eventually had to leave in order to be in Nacogdoches?" she asked.

Dade nodded.

"I keep thinking that Nash has something to do with all this, Dade. I do. But he couldn't have known about the stuffed whale." She paused a beat. "What are the chances that Nash even knew Brett?"

"There's no way to be sure," Dade said.

"What if Nash decided to stick around and asked Brett for work?" Her mind was spinning with possibilities.

"He could've been looking to settle down somewhere," Dade agreed.

"Brett had a temper. It wouldn't have taken much to set him off, and especially if Nash was crazy enough to mention something about me," she continued, feeling a little momentum gathering. "He said something in the alley about thinking about sticking around town. At the time, I just thought he was saying whatever came to his mind. I was so disgusted by him that all I could focus on was getting away. But now, what if?"

What if.

"Think Brett would've invited him over to his house?" Dade asked.

"Anything's possible, I guess." She shrugged because that's where she hit a wall. "Tyson wouldn't have let him by that night after only one meeting. He would've stopped him. Tyson was trained to go after anything suspicious, and the neighbors didn't report any barking."

"A stranger, even if Tyson had met him once before, would never get past him without a fight," Dade said. "And if that's the case, there would've been evidence of a struggle. Ed said the person opened up the front door and would've walked right past the dog."

"We're right back where we started." She released a heavy sigh.

Dade pulled up next to her house and parked before following her inside.

"Not exactly. Nash could still be around," he said. "We didn't consider that possibility."

The thought scared her more than anything else, but he had a point.

"He could've met people and decided to stick around to party," Dade said. "There are a few hotspots around the area for people so inclined."

"The old Hiller land." She'd never gone to it when she was in high school, but she'd heard there was always alcohol flowing. The property sat between two ranches, and neither family laid claim to it. It was mostly pasture with a few trees. She'd heard of bonfires and parties. "You used to go there with…what was her name? Shaylee?"

Dade didn't seem thrilled that she'd brought up a girl he'd dated. She started to apologize but couldn't figure why she'd be doing so. Surely he wasn't embarrassed by having gone out with one of the most popular girls at their school, if not *the* most popular.

His jaw muscle ticked, and it looked like it was taking great restraint not to say the first thing that came to his mind.

Coco barked at the back door, interrupting the moment of tense silence.

Chapter Eleven

"You ever think about having a security system installed in your home?" Dade needed to change the subject. He didn't like talking about his past with Carrie, especially not after the way he'd treated her back then. He couldn't go back and change things that had happened. Moving forward, he could help her out with more security. Whatever Coco had barked at was gone by the time they checked.

"I called the other day when everything started getting…weird, for lack of a better term. Every company I talked to said they were backed up. I couldn't get an appointment until next month." It made sense that everyone would be in a panic after the crime wave in Cattle Barge.

"That's not good enough." Dade called Terrell Landry, head of security at the ranch, and made arrangements. He turned to Carrie after ending the call. "Someone will be here tomorrow evening to install a system."

"What's it like to be able to snap your fingers and get anything you want?" There was a hint of admiration in her tone, but Dade didn't like the implication. Because she was saying that being a Butler made his life a walk in the park compared to everyone else's, and the truth couldn't be further. Her comment shouldn't grate on him like it did.

"I'm trying to help, if you hadn't noticed," he countered with a little more ire than he'd planned.

Her hands came up. "I'm sorry. I didn't mean to offend you. I've just fought tooth and nail my whole life for what I have, and it's all about to disappear. Everything comes so easy for you."

"You think it's easy being the son of Maverick Mike Butler?" He pushed off the counter.

"It isn't?" The look of surprise on her face shouldn't send fire shooting through his veins.

Dade bit his tongue rather than say something he'd regret.

"Stop. Don't tell me that I'm wrong. I always thought having money would make everything so much easier. If it doesn't, I'm not sure I want to know that just yet, considering I've spent my entire adult life trying to get a little of it." She held her ground. "With all the news surrounding me and my shop, I'm afraid everything I've been working toward will crumble into tiny pieces."

How the hell was Dade supposed to stay mad at that? Dade still hadn't figured out what his next move was going to be. Stay on the land he loved once the will was read? Or, get far away from all memories of Maverick Mike?

"Whatever happens can be put back together," he said.

"Easy for you to say." Disbelief darkened her eyes. When he really looked in them, there was something else sparkling, too. It looked a hell of a lot like desire, and that was another unproductive road.

"You think all I need for life to click into place is a last name?" He scoffed.

"I remember you in high school, Dade. You always had a group of people surrounding you, vying for your attention," she countered. "It wasn't like that for me."

Although he'd argue to the death that she had no idea what she was talking about when she hinted that life as a Butler was easy, she didn't need to hear that right now. She'd had a few really bad days strung together. Her shoulders were tense, her posture aggressive, and even though this was better than the look of defeat he'd seen in her eyes one too many times, he still wanted to ease her pain. There were dark circles from lack of sleep cradling her eyes. He took a step toward her.

Her pulse hammered, and he wasn't sure if it was from anger, frustration or desire. He ran his thumb across the base of her neck where he could feel her heart beat. "What happened to you after you left Cattle Barge?"

"Nothing." She looked up at him with defiance in her eyes. Talking could be overrated when it came to digging into emotional holes. Exactly the reason Dade preferred to keep his mouth shut. But he wanted to hear it from her instead of hearing it from the grapevine.

"Then why didn't we talk anymore when you came back?" he pressed as a mix of shock and horror flitted across her expression.

"Not you, too," she said.

"I'm your friend, Carrie. We used to tell each other everything," he shot back.

"I did talk." She glared at him.

"Not to me, you didn't." He stared deeper into her eyes, searching for something…desire? Permission?

"You weren't exactly lining up to have a conversation with me, either."

"I won't deny that. I wanted to talk to you, but I never got the vibe it was okay," he admitted.

"We were teenagers with hormones raging through our bodies. You were Mr. Popular Jock. I was an office aide because it was just too sad to work in the library. We didn't have anything in common once we started growing up." There was a hint of sadness in her voice but, again, it was better than defeat.

"I think we spent half our childhood on the tire swing. You remember that one on the playground? It seemed so huge then. Saw it the other day and it looked different," he said, trying to break down a little of those stone walls.

"We grew up, Dade." All the warmth was gone from her expression now. "Our perspectives changed."

Damn if that wasn't true, even if chemistry pinged between them. Pure electricity and heat pulsed from her neck to his hand. He could tell she felt it by the way she stiffened for a split second every time they stood too close or their skin grazed. Don't get him started about the kisses they'd shared. He'd thought about those almost nonstop. So much fire. So much promise.

So much trouble.

She seemed intent on keeping him at arm's length, and after his last relationship, he had no plans to get involved with someone who wasn't into it. No matter how much his heart wanted to argue and say Carrie was exactly into it.

Carrie looked him right in the eye and said, "We should talk about something productive, like who might've killed Brett."

Her words had the effect of a slap across the cheek, jarring him back to reality. Dade dropped his hand. "I'll make coffee."

"Dade." Her sweet voice made him want to turn around. He missed the easy way she'd made him laugh.

"Yeah." He didn't turn around to face her. Instead, he paused at the doorway.

"I'm sorry. This whole ordeal has me turned upside down, and I'm not sure if I'm coming or going anymore," she said. "That was really rude and you don't deserve to be treated like that, no matter how much stress I'm under."

"No need to apologize." He made quick work of the machine and produced two cups of coffee while she moved to the couch.

"This should help," he said.

She took the one being offered and thanked him. She was sitting on the sofa, her left leg curled underneath her bottom, and hugging a throw pillow. "My mind just keeps going in circles. Who would want Brett gone?"

"Who would benefit from his death?" He took a sip, remembering how it had tasted on her lips. *Great one, Dade. Way to leave it alone.*

"I keep asking myself the same question."

His cell phone buzzed. He checked the screen. "It's Ed."

"Sheriff Sawmill is requesting that Ms. Palmer voluntarily appear at the station to speak with him," Ed said.

"Why's that?" Dade had no plans to walk Carrie into a trap.

"He has a few questions. That's all he would disclose." Ed's voice was even.

"Does he plan to arrest her?" Dade asked.

"I asked the same question. He said no."

"What are her options?" Dade wanted to make sure he understood the situation correctly so that he could accurately relay the information to Carrie.

"She can refuse." Ed's voice was still even, and that was usually a good sign.

"But you wouldn't advise it," Dade said.

"Sheriff Sawmill gave me the impression he had news to share," Ed supplied.

Dade would stop short of trusting Sawmill, but he had complete faith in his attorney. "I'll take her in. Will you be there?"

Ed hesitated. "There's been a security violation at the ranch and Ella has asked me to stay here."

"What does that mean?" Dade dug his heels in and looked out the window. "What kind of violation?"

"It's under control now but a gentleman sprinted across the lawn and was then subdued by Terrell." Ed's words were reassuring. He had been the Mav's best friend and would want to make sure the family was safe. "Since the sheriff seems to view Ms. Palmer as a witness instead of a suspect, it's safe to say she's above suspicion for now. Will you escort her and let Terrell, Dalton and me take care of things here?"

"What happens on the ranch is my business." Guilt for neglecting his duties at home was a sucker punch to Dade's gut. None of his family would tell him that's what he'd been doing. He'd been working odd hours to keep up his part of family business. But Dade's guilt wouldn't allow the cop-out. He could be doing more.

"Understood." Ed's voice was calm.

The problem was that being home made Dade think about his relationship with the Mav.

THE SHERIFF TOOK his usual spot across the expansive desk after ushering Carrie and Dade into his office. The ride over had been quiet, and Carrie wondered what was going on in Dade's mind. She could tell based on his expression that he was still stewing over the situation at the ranch. Ed had reassured him that everything was fine—no one had been hurt when a mentally challenged middle-aged man sprinted across the lawn with a knife in his hand. But right now her attention was on the sheriff.

"I sent the stuffed animal and the flower to the forensics lab. Mr. Staples apprised me of the situation, and I assure you that we're doing everything we can to find out who's targeting you," Sawmill began. His hands were folded on top of his desk. It sounded like his standard line, but at least Carrie didn't feel like a suspect anymore.

"Could someone want it to look like I murdered Brett?" she asked. "To throw your office off the trail?"

The sheriff paused thoughtfully. "That's an angle we're taking under consideration."

"But you don't think it's plausible," Dade interjected.

"Of course this is just my personal opinion—"

"Backed by twenty-five years of investigative experience," Dade added.

Sawmill nodded with a look of appreciation for the compliment.

"The person who committed this crime didn't come at it straightforward. Whoever it was wanted to avoid a personal confrontation, which is why he or she—" he glanced at Carrie with an apologetic look "—surprised the victim in the shower."

"Which means this person isn't strong enough to take Brett on," Dade said. "So, you're possibly looking at someone small in stature."

"That's the thinking. The initial reason Ms. Palmer fell under suspicion was because of her familiarity with the dog and her general size. Female perpetrators often don't attack a someone directly because of their weight and strength disadvantage."

Carrie was beginning to see a picture emerge. There were three women in Brett's life—her, his mother and his sister. None of them would do any harm to him, but at least she understood why she'd been questioned.

"The first thing we look for is motive," Sawmill supplied. His demeanor was softer this time, more cooperative.

"An argument in front of my store could hurt my business, and I've worked hard to be a success," she admitted.

Again, Sawmill nodded. "But those types of crimes usually occur in the heat of the moment, which didn't exactly add up, considering the victim in this case was murdered hours later."

"And one public disagreement wouldn't likely be enough to ruin what I have going," she added with a nod toward the sheriff.

"Right. So, we interviewed a few witnesses who stated that you were the one to end the relationship and that the victim didn't take it well." Another apologetic look in her direction, and she assumed it was for the invasion to her privacy.

"That's true. But what does that have to do with anything?" For the sake of finding Brett's actual killer, she could look past the intrusion, no matter how icky it felt to realize her life felt on display.

"In those cases, the person murdered is generally the one who broke off the relationship," Sawmill supplied.

Carrie didn't follow. "Why's that?"

"The jilted person can't stand the thought of the person he or she loves being with another man or woman, whichever being the case." Sheriff Sawmill leaned forward. "That's usually when things turn sour."

"Brett didn't want to break up. That was causing a lot of friction between us," she supplied. But Sawmill would already know that based on the texts.

"I apologize for the question, but what happened? What was the reason you ended the relationship?" Sawmill asked.

"Honestly, the whole thing was a huge mistake on my part to begin with, and it didn't take long to realize. I'd been working too many hours at the ice cream shop and it was paying off professionally. Personally, not as much. My life had become nothing but work, and I decided to put myself back out there. Brett seemed nice enough in the beginning. I guess I liked the fact that he rode a motorcycle. It made him seem dangerous in a way. Reckless. He would come into the store and must've asked me out a dozen times before I finally agreed. Guess I knew all along that nothing would ever come of us." Admitting this in front of Dade made her uncomfortable, but she would do what it took to help the sheriff get on track to find the person who'd killed Brett.

"Was there an event that was the final straw? I'm curious as to what made you finally decide your relationship was over," the sheriff said.

Dade was studying the tile floor intently, and she couldn't get a feel for his reaction to what he was hearing. It seemed odd to be talking about her past relationship with him sitting next to her, but there was no reason it should. It wasn't like she and Dade were in a relationship. He was helping her sort out the mess that had become her life. He was being a good friend. And even though chemistry pinged between them, they both seemed to know acting on it would be a mistake. She would hurt him or vice versa.

"The writing was on the wall from the first date. We were too different. I mean, I thought we'd have something in common because we both grew up in tough circumstances," she said thoughtfully. "But I guess our reactions to that upbringing were totally off-kilter. He used his as an excuse to drink too much, to be a little too rude to people who were just trying to be nice. It was pretty obvious that we didn't look at the world in the same way."

"How long did the two of you go out?" The sheriff's gaze darted back and forth between Carrie and Dade.

"Longer than we should've. At first, it was nice to have someone to catch a movie with or eat dinner. We'd grab a drink after work. That lasted a few weeks before he surprised me by taking me to his family get-together. He said he wanted to go to the lake but he didn't tell me his mother and sister would be there. I freaked out and said I was sick and that I needed to leave. Then I started making excuses about having too much work. I let it drag out longer than I should've because I didn't want to hurt him. He was so into the relationship that I wanted to let him down softly." And she had a little guilt for letting the so-called relationship go on because she was tired of spending Friday nights alone.

"But he didn't agree." Sawmill picked up the Zantac packet but then tossed it down again, seeming to think better of taking one.

"No. He became even more convinced we should be together. Said he wanted to show me that we were meant to be and that I should give him a chance." Carrie crossed her legs and bounced her foot back and forth.

"And did you see things his way?"

"I told him that I needed a break in order to distract him and give him enough space to think clearly. My plan didn't work. He started trying to win me back. He texted almost constantly, which you've already seen, and left gifts at my business. He'd drive by to see if my car was in the parking lot when I said I was at work." Admitting how bad the relationship had become made her even more nervous about how it had ended. "I didn't mind parking in the back so he wouldn't know when I was there."

"And that's where Nash Gilpin found you the night you came in to file the complaint against him," the sheriff supplied.

Reality dawned. "I've considered that before, but the two of them couldn't have known each other, could they?"

"It's a connection we have to consider." The sheriff pinched the bridge of his nose, looking like he needed to stem a headache. He picked up the Zantac packet and ripped it open. "Which brings me back to the stuffed animal."

Reality hit with a hard smack. She felt like she might not be able to breathe if the sheriff was confirming her fear that Brett had been killed because of her. She couldn't help but think the dark cloud was extending to those she touched.

"Your ex keeps showing up, trying to win you back at the same time someone else is vying for your attention." The sheriff popped a Zantac in his mouth and took a swallow from the water bottle on his desk. "Nash had motive if he believed it was possible you'd get back together with Brett. Was Nash ever in your shop at the same time as Brett?"

"I'm not sure. I never really paid attention. Business was good before…all this started happening. The days would fly by." Carrie thought long and hard. How many times had Nash been in? Every day for two weeks. What times? He'd pop in throughout the day when he was on a break. "It's a definite possibility. In fact, I'm pretty sure he was there at least once at the same time as Brett, and it was a couple of days before the murder."

Dade turned to the sheriff. "Have you gotten any closer to locating Nash?"

Sawmill shook his head. "His employer gave us a couple of names of his next of kin, who we're currently trying to track down now. They're distant relatives so we're not hopeful. He doesn't exactly come from a stable family background, and it's most likely that he quit his job and moved on. The two events aren't necessarily related. The waterslide operator said Nash had been talking about making enough money to relocate to Florida. And that very well might be where he is. Until we locate him and have a conversation, he's at the top of our suspect list."

"From what you know about him already, does he fit the profile of a stalker?" Carrie asked.

"A guy who moves from town to town. Doesn't have many friends to speak of. It's possible. If this crime is romantically linked, a love-obsessed stalker is someone who would develop a fixation on a person he has no real personal relationship with. He would display some form of delusional behavior. Most of them suffer from a mental disorder."

Carrie's foot was making double time. "The guy did seem out of touch with reality, but I don't know about being delusional." She was no expert, but something had seemed off about him during the few times she'd interacted with him. She'd blamed it on alcohol but it could be more.

"One of his coworkers said he spent a lot of time alone, babbling about nothing in particular. Most of the people we spoke to knew about his drinking problem," the sheriff stated.

"What did his employer have to say about it?" Dade asked.

"The festival said they don't have funds to dig too deeply into every worker's background, because it's not uncommon to employ people who hop from job to job. He might have given them a fake Social Security number. Judge Watson subpoenaed the parent company's records first thing this morning. Funtimes Inc. has been ordered to give my office access to their files."

"And how did they respond?" Dade asked.

"We hope to know more in a few days when files arrive," the sheriff responded truthfully. "These things take time."

"Have you spoken to Samuel recently?" she asked. The sheriff nodded.

"Is he okay?" She paused a beat. "He seemed really

upset the night Nash cornered me. And then the next morning he stopped by the shop but Brett showed and I haven't seen Samuel since. Or Mrs. Hardin for that matter. Of course, I've been preoccupied so they could walk right past me and I might not realize it."

"He stopped by yesterday to find out if there were any leads in the case," the sheriff said.

Carrie leaned forward, unsure if she really wanted the answer to the question burning in the back of her mind about the investigation into Nash.

Did she have time to give?

Chapter Twelve

"What else can you tell us about a love-obsessed stalker?" Carrie wanted to know what she was up against.

"One of the key points to think about with a love-obsessed stalker is that he believes he can make the object of his affection love him, and that's where we believe the courtship is coming in with the stuffed animal and flowers." Sawmill flashed his eyes at Carrie. "Did Nash say anything to you that could give the impression he was obsessed?"

"He said I'd learn to love him a couple of times when he stopped by the shop." Carrie felt the blood rushing in her ears.

"This type of person would be desperate to develop a positive relationship with you," he added.

"I'm not so sure about that. He didn't seem to care if I wanted him around or not. In fact, he didn't seem to mind forcing himself on me."

Sawmill jotted down a couple of notes on the file in front of him. "He would most likely have built an entire fantasy life of relationships with people he hardly knew."

"How far does this fantasy life go?" Carrie felt nauseous at the thought someone like that could be stalking her. All those times it had felt like eyes were watching her brought a chill to her spine.

"To the extent that he'd begin trying to act out his fictional plots in the real world," Sawmill supplied.

"Sounds like a crazy person," she shot back, rubbing the chill from her arms.

"A person like this is usually calculating. Deranged, yes. Crazy, no. The latter tends to be apprehended before any real crime has been committed based on a smaller offense," he supplied. "If we're dealing with what we think, in his mind, it's your fault that he has to do what he does."

"Is that because in his twisted mind I'm somehow responsible for his feelings toward me?" More chills assaulted her as the sheriff nodded.

"Which also tells me that he believes I'm asking for the attention in some way." Carrie swallowed the bile burning the back of her throat. "How far would this scenario be carried out? Say, for example, would this person kill his intended for her affection?"

"It's within reason," Sawmill said, and she could see that this wasn't any easier for him. He still hadn't solved the first high profile murder case on his desk, and crime had been multiplying in his county ever since. His reputation was on the line, and people were antsy. Her frustration at being treated like a suspect earlier dissolved a little bit more. All she could think about was bringing Brett's killer to justice and helping the sheriff catch the person who was obsessed with her.

"And at any point none of this seems wrong to the person?"

"Again, the person transfers that to the object of

their obsession." Right. The sheriff had said that a few moments ago. "And what if Nash isn't responsible for Brett's death?" she asked. "Surely he can't be the only suspect. Did you check the couple of names I gave your deputy the other night?"

Sawmill said he had. "My deputies are dotting every i and crossing every t, interviewing everyone who might be connected. So far, we've gotten nothing on any of those leads. In the process, we've uncovered a few names to add to the list during our investigation, and we're hoping that you might be able to help us out by telling us if you've heard of any of these people."

Thinking about Brett had her also thinking about his dog, Tyson. Her heart fisted.

"Before we get into it, can I ask what's going to happen to Tyson?" she asked before the sheriff could continue. He must be scared now that his master was gone.

"Ms. Strawn didn't want him, so he's at the animal shelter." The sheriff shook his head.

"I'll take him," Dade said before Carrie could offer.

"From what I can see, he's not a very well-adjusted animal." Sawmill looked at Dade apologetically.

"Doesn't matter. We'll find a job for him on the ranch and train him. He'll be right as rain in no time." Carrie shouldn't allow her heart to swell at the gesture.

"I wish I could take him, but he's aggressive with other dogs and I have Coco," she offered.

"You can visit him any time you want, and within a couple of months Coco will be able to, as well." Dade's confidence in his ability to work with the animal was sexy, and Carrie's stomach gave a little flip. But then, he did own a ranch, or would when his father's will was read and had grown up around every kind of animal imaginable.

She smiled at Dade. A simple gesture, but it felt so right to be looking at him and smiling, even in the midst of all the craziness. It was probably just residual feelings from their childhoods, from a time when life was no more complicated than chasing each other around the playground in a game of tag. Just like it had felt right to kiss him, a little voice said, but she shut that down immediately. First of all, the thought couldn't be more inappropriate under the circumstances. And secondly…well…secondly didn't matter. The thought was inappropriate. Period.

"Sheriff, you said that you usually look at people close to the victim. Is there any chance his mother or sister could've been involved?" Although she couldn't imagine they would be. At this point she was throwing anything at the wall to see if it would stick.

"We're checking out his financials to see if there've been any recent changes," the sheriff said.

"And the names I supplied?" she asked again, reminding herself that thinking about Dade was as productive as trying to milk a chicken.

"Each had an alibi," he answered.

"What about his business?" Dade asked. "Any hint that there might've been trouble from there?"

"He'd been busy leading up to his murder. A pair of men who used to work for him have come forward to make a claim against his estate," the sheriff supplied.

"What right do they have?" Carrie couldn't help but come off as indignant at the thought of essentially grave robbers creeping out from all angles.

"They say they weren't paid for work they performed," the sheriff said.

"I might know who they are if you give me names," she offered.

"Ever hear Mr. Strawn talk about a man named Carl Buckley?" Sawmill asked.

Carrie searched her memory. She really wanted to help find the killer. But she came up empty. "He must've worked for Brett before we dated." Hearing the word *dated* seemed odd to her now. They'd barely been in a relationship to begin with and now she was trying to help find Brett's killer. It was surreal, but life had taught her to expect the worst and she should've known better than to get too comfortable. Everything had been going a little too well before all this started and she blamed herself for getting involved with Brett in the first place. That sounded horrible now that he was gone, but it was true. She should never have agreed to go against her better judgment and date him. And he could be dead because of their relationship if someone had killed him because of an obsession with her.

The sheriff picked up the packet of Zantac and stuffed it in his shirt pocket. "Buckley's pretty well known around town for his drinking. He doesn't have a reliable track record of showing up to work at previous jobs."

"If he was late too often or showed up drunk on the job, Brett would've fired him right then and there. He wouldn't have put his men or livelihood at risk." Carrie shook her head. "His strict policy might've made the guy angry if he felt justified."

"There's another gentleman by the name of Dave Lancaster," Sawmill stated.

"I know who he is." She didn't have to dig deep into her memories for that one. His carelessness had made him unpopular on job sites. "He was an OSHA nightmare fully realized. I remember Brett said he was careless. He'd drop tools from scaffolding and not shout a heads-up for anyone who might be walking below. Brett didn't like to use him. I can't remember how many times Brett said Dave was going to kill someone if he couldn't toe the line."

"How did others on the job site react to his behavior?" Sawmill asked.

"They didn't like Dave at all. Some of the guys threatened to quit if Brett didn't get things under control." She rocked her foot back and forth, figuring the sheriff was no closer to figuring this out than she was.

"Were there any threats made to Brett?" Sawmill quirked a brow, and she could almost see the wheels turning in his head. At the very least, this information seemed to change things for him—hopefully it would get him closer to finding out who had killed Brett. Yes, Nash was a possibility, but he was feeling more like a long shot to Carrie. What would his real motive be?

"Nothing that he shared with me." *Oh. Wait. Hold on.* "Hector was hurt by one of Dave's actions. He left some tool lying around on the ground that Hector stepped on—maybe a nail gun?—and whatever it was shot a nail right through his foot. Hector made all kinds of threats in the heat of the moment, but Brett didn't take it too seriously. He said Hector would cool down and come around."

"And he fired Dave after that?" Sawmill's brow shot up.

"He must've. I don't know for certain. Things had

already started to unravel between us, and I was trying to get him to give me space when he was going through all of that," she admitted.

"Did you ever meet Hector Reglan?" Sawmill asked.

"Not face-to-face, no. But I felt like I knew him, because Brett talked about how Hector's wife would make homemade tamales for the guys on Fridays if they'd had a good week." Carrie had wanted to love someone enough to want to cook for his coworkers. "They have two kids."

"And his wife never brought them to your shop?" Sawmill seemed to catch onto this last bit of information.

"Not once. I think money was tight and she didn't want the kids to get used to spending money on things they could make at home." She paused. "I offered to treat them, but Brett said Hector would be too proud to accept, so I left it alone."

"I'll talk to Hector and his wife. See where they were on the night of the murder." Sawmill took down a few notes. "What about his neighbors? Was he close to any of them?"

"If you're asking if he knew them well enough for one of them to walk right past Tyson, then no," she stated. "Brett was having trouble with one of his neighbors."

The sheriff perked up.

"They were having fights over messes he was leaving in the front yard. His work truck was old and he parked it out front. She called and had it towed a few times. I never met her and she might've been justified in her complaints, but I forgot to mention her before."

"Which side?" Sawmill asked.

"She's to the right. I don't know her name." She gave a helpless shrug. Based on his line of questioning, she was becoming more certain that he was digging around for possibilities.

"What about ex-girlfriends?" Sawmill continued. "He talk about any bad blood there?"

"Regina Kastle—with a *K*—kept texting him long after the breakup," she supplied.

"Did he say what she wanted?" Sawmill asked.

"Money, mostly. She had a baby, and I think he was helping her out financially while they dated." She shook her head. "I didn't know anything about this until close to the end of our relationship. In fact, she was another in a long list of reasons Brett and I weren't a good match from the beginning. He kept too many secrets."

"Was the baby his?" the sheriff asked.

"I don't think so," she said. "They started dating when her little girl was already six months old."

"And he didn't tell you any of this right away?" Sawmill asked.

"Are you married?"

Sawmill nodded.

"Really? How long?" she asked.

He quirked a brow but played along. "Twenty-two years."

"Congratulations," she offered. "That's a long time."

He was quick to nod.

"You remember much about those early days of dating? When everything was new?" she asked.

"Most of it. Sure," Sawmill admitted.

"Did Mrs. Sawmill tell you everything about every guy she'd dated during those first few dates?" Carrie asked.

Sawmill's hands were already up in surrender. "No, she did not. In fact, she'd dated one of my best friends the year before and I didn't know about it until right before our wedding, when she confessed. Said holding in the secret was making her sick and that she'd understand if I didn't want to go through with the wedding."

"So I'm guessing you already know the answer to your question," she said.

"Yes, ma'am. I believe that I do." Sawmill repositioned in his seat. "I've seen the line out the door of your shop."

"Not anymore. All the media attention I've been getting is going to run me out of business," she stated with a little more heat than she'd intended.

"I'm sorry to hear that." The sheriff seemed sincere. "My wife can't get enough of your Vanilla Bean-illa."

"Most people love that one." She smiled, but it didn't reach her eyes. "I'd be happy to have a batch ready if you want to stop by after work."

"I'm curious," he continued without answering, "how do you get the flavors just right? I mean, I've eaten a lot of ice cream in my day." He patted his stomach, which admittedly was a little big. "I'm normally a home-style vanilla guy, but the vanilla in yours makes my old one seem…" He paused. "I don't know, lacking in some way."

"Practice, Sheriff Sawmill. That's how I perfected the recipe. I spent a few weeks on that recipe alone and I had to have the vanilla shipped in." She was proud of the care she took in developing each recipe.

"Then you understand what it means to be thorough. I have to ask questions. Even the ones I know the answers to in advance. I ask anyway because it's my job and every once in a while—not often, mind you, maybe a handful of times in twenty-five years—someone surprises me with a different answer and a case is solved out of what feels like thin air." He clasped his hands together and placed them on top of the desk.

Dade stood. "If there's nothing else Carrie can help you with, I'd like to take her home."

"I'll take you up on the ice cream sometime," he said to Carrie.

"Anytime, Sheriff. Don't be shy."

And somehow she had a feeling he was going to take her up on that offer.

Chapter Thirteen

"Can you drop me off at work in a few hours?" Carrie asked Dade as she let Coco in the back door of her
home. It was almost dark, and she didn't want to risk
leaving her car anywhere near the shop for the reporters to see it. "I'll take her in with me."

"There are a few things I need to take care of at the
ranch," Dade supplied. "Will you be okay if I don't stick
around after I drop you?"

"Of course." The thought of Nash running around
loose somewhere didn't do great things to Carrie's stress
levels. Focusing on work would take her mind off everything going on, and especially all the confusing feelings she had toward Dade.

A truck engine roared next door, and gravel spewed
underneath tires on the drive.

"Guess my neighbor's finally home," she said. "He
made a big deal out of my trash blowing into his yard.
Cursed me out the other day."

"What's his name?" Dade asked. The look on his
face said he wasn't thrilled.

"I'm not sure." She shrugged. "I tried to go over a
couple of times when I saw his truck was parked out
front. I know he was there, but he didn't answer the

door. And then I was letting Coco out the other night and he came home yelling across the yard for me to keep my trash on my side. I tried to explain that it was probably raccoons, but he didn't want to hear any of it."

"When did he move in?" Dade asked.

"Around six months ago, I think. He's almost never home, though." Carrie couldn't contain the frustration in her voice.

"Maybe I should have a talk with him," Dade said, his tone indicating he'd be doing most of the talking.

"Don't worry about it. He's a jerk," she said. "He's not worth the energy."

Speaking of neighbors, the mail carrier had mistakenly put a piece of Samuel's aunt's mail in Carrie's box. She hadn't seen either of them lately, but then, she'd been consumed with her own problems. She remembered making a note to drop off ice cream the other day. Another thing that had fallen off her radar.

Her life felt like it was slipping through her fingers lately. And there was no way to catch hold and take back control, no matter how much she tried.

The deep ridges in Dade's forehead said he was determined to defend her. She already had bad relations with her neighbor, and she didn't want to make things worse.

"Promise me you'll leave it alone." She looked into Dade's eyes and almost faltered when he studied her. "I already have more going on than I can handle."

And then his stone features softened. "What happened?"

"I already told you," she said.

"I don't mean with him." He gestured toward next door. It dawned on her what he was talking about. She lifted her shoulder as casually as she could. "It was a long time ago. Doesn't matter now."

Dade took a tentative step toward her. "It does to me."

If she opened up that dam, there'd be no way to handle the flooding. Part of her wanted to let go, to finally talk to someone about it, but she couldn't. It was too hard. Tears burned the backs of her eyes. Just thinking about it brought a heavy cloak around her shoulders.

"Carrie." The softness in his voice, the compassion made it hard to breathe.

She needed to do something to change the subject before her ribs cracked and her chest exploded.

"I need a shower."

By the time Dade picked Carrie up from the shop the next day, exhaustion had set it. The thought of losing the business she'd worked so hard for sat heavy in her chest. The stabbing pain in her left shoulder blade had intensified.

After greeting Dade, she coaxed Coco onto the seat, where the Sharp Eagle perched in the center.

Dade's expression was intense. Deep grooves were carved in his forehead, and worry lines underlined his serious blue eyes. His jaw clenched as he turned the steering wheel, guiding them out of the alley.

"Everything okay?"

"There's a lot going on with my family, a lot of media," he said. "I'm sorry they've picked up on me helping you."

"Don't be, because I'm not. I'm grateful for everything you've been doing for me, Dade."

She liked that the muscle in his jaw released some of its tension when he half smiled.

"You're welcome," he said. She liked making him feel better, even if she wasn't ready to tell him everything.

"I keep mulling over the possibilities of who could have killed Brett," he said.

"Same with me," she admitted, leaning her head against the seat and rubbing her temples. "I still can't fathom anyone wanting him gone, and especially not because of me. Look, I know he wasn't always the nicest guy and I realized my mistake in dating him. But no one deserves this."

"I'd like to speak to Nash," Dade said.

"Me, too. I just wish he'd turn up somewhere. I feel like he holds the key to what we're looking for, and it's beyond frustrating that no one can locate him." She gripped her cell. There were no messages on it. Not like her last phone. This one was quiet, and it was a strange feeling. "I've been thinking about what's next for me. Sales are dwindling, and it's only a matter of time before I have no customers left."

"People are skittish right now. The town's been through a lot recently. It'll settle down, and you'll be able to open your doors again when people forget," Dade reassured. "And they will."

"Have you forgotten about my past?" Carrie scoffed. What if they didn't forget? She had to think about an exit strategy. She had a little money saved. Maybe she could move to Austin and start a new business. It would only be a matter of time before she'd run out of money at this location. Eric and Harper were still on Carrie's payroll, coming in overnight to help with mail orders. She'd managed to get her dairy and dry goods vendors to send deliveries earlier in the morning. Her staff had assured her they'd work whatever hours she could give and she felt responsible for their jobs. She'd take a pay cut if she had to in order to keep them employed. There were the reporters outside her house—a place that felt even less like home now. Which reminded her, she needed to let Samuel know what was going on. He must be wondering why she suddenly had security at her house.

"I can probably guess what you're thinking right now." Dade broke through the thoughts spiraling her to a pit of hopeless.

"Then tell me, because I feel like I'm all over the place." She blew out a frustrated breath.

"What city are you considering?" he asked as he waved to Adam, the security guard working the overnight shift. Dade had made a point of having photos of each guard sent to him as an extra precaution.

Dade pulled into her driveway.

Her neighbor's truck was parked on the pad next to his house.

"I wasn't—"

Dade shot her a look.

"Austin," she relented. "How'd you know?"

"We've been friends a very long time." He put a lot of emphasis on the word *friends*. Was that because he didn't want her to confuse his kindness for something else? The few kisses they'd shared held a lot more heat than a friendly gesture. But she figured that he was reminding himself as much as her that the two of them trying to be anything but friends was worse than a bad idea.

She didn't figure this was the time to remind him that they'd been childhood pals and nothing more. They'd gone their separate ways in high school and certainly didn't run in the same circles then or now. Seeing him in the alley the other night was the most they'd talked since they were kids. So how did he think he knew her?

He might've made a lucky guess, but Dade had no idea what was really running through her mind or he would've hightailed it in the other direction a long time ago.

Carrie got out of the truck. "Come on, Coco."

Stubbornly, Coco went out the driver's side at Dade's heels.

"She probably smells Flash on me," he said by way of explanation.

"Who's that?" Carrie unlocked the front door, ignoring her frustration that even her dog liked Dade more than she liked her owner.

Dade followed Carrie, and her heart gave a little flip because her emotions were so mixed up, so confused that they had her wanting to reach for comfort in his arms.

"I changed Tyson's name," he supplied. "We're giving him a fresh start with his life, and he needed a new name to go with it."

"That's a great idea. I like the name." She wished the messes in her life could be untangled so easily. "How'd he respond to the change?"

"He adapted right away."

"What made you give him the name Flash?" She was curious as to his thinking.

"That's all it takes to change." Dade snapped his fingers. "And Split Second was too long."

She laughed despite the heavy feelings weighing her down.

Change? She wished she knew that trick, because her past had always haunted her. She felt like a slave to a life she'd worked so damn hard to get away from.

Dade took a step toward her, and she backed up a few steps until her back touched the door. He looked so far into her eyes that she felt like he could see right through to her toes. "Don't go away again, Carrie," he said and his voice was low and gravelly. Sexy.

With those intense blue eyes staring into hers, she'd be willing to promise just about anything. Except that she'd stick around.

"If I lose my business, there'll be nothing left for me here." Her voice shook with uncertainty.

"You won't." He was so confident even as hurt flashed in his eyes.

She wished she shared his opinion, that she could believe it was true from deep down and not somewhere on the surface where it could be pulled under. *She* could be pulled under.

His gaze dropped to her lips, and her throat went dry.

"Do you plan to kiss me or stand there and stare at me all night?" she asked with as much bravado as she could, which was saying a lot. With his strong male presence toe to toe with her, she could feel masculinity pulse from him, and it made her legs weaken. Afraid they might not be able to carry her weight, she braced herself against the wall behind her and tugged his face down to meet hers.

He took in a deep breath a half second before their lips crashed together. Hunger rolled off him in tangible waves. Electricity hummed through her as the kiss deepened.

With his mouth moving against hers, she got lost... lost in his touch as his hands cupped her face...lost in his clean masculine scent. He was all outdoors and male and strength.

Before she could debate her actions, her hands went to the hem of his T-shirt. He helped her by shrugging out of it, and then she unbuttoned her blouse. Her shirt joined his on the floor next to them as he cupped her breasts in his hands. They swelled and pressed against the lace of her bra. Her nipples beaded as his thumbs rolled over them and a low raspy breath poured from his mouth.

She undid her bra, needing to feel skin against skin. Hunger burned through her as his strong hands grazed her skin. His touch was light at first, causing need to swell inside her, overtaking every rational thought that this might be a bad idea.

"You're beautiful, Carrie. You've always been beautiful," he said in that low, gravelly voice that sent sensual ripples skittering across her skin.

All that did was fan the flames burning inside her.

Need overtook logic again when her hands flew to his zipper. She helped him shed his jeans and boxers, and there was just enough light in the room to show the ripples of his abs, the patch of dark hair trailing south from his belly button.

Carrie was out of her shorts and lacy underwear in two seconds flat and he groaned other words of appreciation for her body. She doubted that she was beautiful in reality, but he made her feel like she was. She should be embarrassed, standing there naked and exposed in front of Dade, but it felt as natural as the sun shining.

She realized that she'd wanted this, to be with him, for longer than she cared to let herself remember or admit.

Her arms wound around his neck as he lifted her off her feet easily. Their lips found each other's as he made his way to the bedroom. She could feel his thick length pulsing against her skin. Her stomach gave a little flip, and she pressed her lips to his even harder. She needed this—him.

In the next second she was on the bed and his strong body was on top of her, pressing her into the mattress.

She reached for the nightstand next to her bed and felt around for a condom. She held it up to him and he ripped it open before she helped him roll it onto his silky length. She stretched her fingers around his erection, and he made another guttural groan of pleasure.

"Carrie." More sensual skitters flitted across her skin when he said her name. She could get used to the sound on his lips. She loved the way he tasted, minty and like he'd just had a cup of coffee. And he probably had.

This should feel strange, but it didn't. Being with Dade seemed like the most natural thing. She brought her hands up to his neck and tunneled her fingers into his hair as he dipped his tip inside her. A battlefield of sensation lit as he teased himself deeper and deeper toward her core.

It didn't take long for him to bring her to the edge of ecstasy as he threaded her nipples between his thumb and forefinger. His tongue inside her mouth built to a fever pitch.

Carrie matched him, stride for stride, as need climbed to impossible heights. And just before she let go and flew off the cliff with him, free-falling toward the earth at a dizzying pace, she thought she heard Dade whisper, "I love you."

Chapter Fourteen

Dade stirred, instinctively reaching for Carrie. All he felt was cold sheets next to him. He untangled himself and checked the clock on the nightstand. Three thirty a.m. He pushed off the bed and glanced around. Light from down the hall made it easy enough to locate his boxers, which had been folded and placed on top of a neat pile on the chair next to the door. His boots were tucked underneath.

He threw on his boxers and jeans and headed out to find her.

"Hey," she said as he emerged from the hall. She sat on a chair near the front window with her legs tucked underneath her sweet round bottom. Her hand was at her face, and it looked like she was chewing on her nail.

"What's wrong?" He strode across the room and bent down to kiss her.

"Nothing." She turned her head in time for him to catch her cheek instead of her lips. Whoa. What the hell did that mean? She'd put on the brakes awfully quick.

"Seriously, what's going on?" He needed something from her, some kind of sign to know what had happened between them was okay. A few hours ago had changed everything. He'd hoped she felt the same.

She smiled up at him, but it didn't reach her eyes. She grabbed his forearm. "I'm sorry. I don't mean to be distracted. I've just been thinking."

There was an empty coffee mug next to her, indicating she'd been awake for a while. Had she gone to sleep at all after they'd made love? He'd been out pretty quick after what he'd thought was the best sex of both of their lives. Now, he felt a little insecure. He almost laughed out loud at the thought. Dade Butler had never had an insecure moment when it came to his love life in the past.

This must have something to do with his relationship with his father. Recently, the Mav had been making an effort and Dade had shot his father down, confused over the timing. Hell, why now? After all these years, why had his father suddenly wanted to have a different relationship? It had all been pretty clear-cut before. The Mav did his own thing and his children did theirs. The only common thread was that everyone deeply cared about the ranch, the land and—at least in the case of his kids—each other.

Not being able to find out why the Mav had had a change of heart now that he was gone was eating away at Dade's resolve. He could admit that—and it was most likely why Carrie's rejection stung so much.

"I need coffee. Want some?" he asked as he turned toward the kitchen.

"I've had enough," she said.

He returned a couple of minutes later with a new perspective following a little bit of a caffeine boost. He took a seat on the couch across the room from Carrie. She looked exhausted, and a moment of guilt hit that he'd kept her awake when she should've been sleeping. It was probably his pride turning her rejection over and over again in his head. That and the fact that Dade hadn't been rejected much in his life. Wounded pride had him feeling like this was a bigger deal than it was. Sure, they'd had great sex. His body got going again just thinking about how silky her skin felt against his hands. *Way to keep things light, Butler.*

"What's keeping you from sleep?" He sure as hell hoped she wasn't about to say the fact that he was in her bed.

Coco hopped up on the couch next to him and settled down.

"A few thoughts keep rolling around in my head, and I can't seem to let them go," she said.

He waited as she gathered her thoughts, taking a sip of coffee to get his own mental engines revved up.

"Do you remember the profile the sheriff gave of the kind of person who could be watching me?" she asked.

"Sawmill said something about a loner. He would most likely suffer from a mental disorder," he supplied.

"I was so sure that it was Brett leaving those 'gifts' on my car and here at home. I know that summer dress was here." In going through all the possible suspects, she could cross one name off the list, and that was her ex. It was obvious to Dade that she couldn't even begin to process the guilt that had her convinced his death was somehow her fault. "And then I started looking at everyone differently. Could it have been someone I knew? Eric or Teddy the delivery guy?"

"Eric definitely doesn't fit the profile. Sawmill said he had a girlfriend who vouched for him. He has no criminal history and hangs out with quite a few friends on the weekends. He plays on a recreational volleyball team and volunteers to coach in his church league," Dade reminded her.

"I know. The profile of a stalker is quite the opposite. The person the sheriff is looking for probably has a mental disorder, which could be difficult to detect if the person was good at hiding it. He most likely spends most of his time alone and doesn't have friends. The sheriff also said that he suffers from delusional thought patterns and behaviors, and that brings me to Nash." She crossed her legs and started rocking her foot.

"We don't know as much about him. The fact that he doesn't have roots anywhere doesn't necessarily make him a stalker. But then, his lifestyle of moving around and not really making any friends could put him in that category," Dade continued. "And we don't even know where he is."

"He could be anywhere," she said with a visible shudder.

"Including Canada by now for all we know."

"True." She stared out the front window. "Or right here under our noses."

"He hasn't been seen in town," he reassured her.

"Another good point. But what if it's not him? So far, he's the only person I keep coming back to. But what if it's someone else? I mean, he's a drunk. Does that fit the profile? He was sloppy, too. And that gets me thinking that it might not be him. The sheriff is still digging around for suspects. I'm starting to wonder who else it could be." She looked out the window toward her neighbor's house with that blank, defeated expression that Dade had come to hate. "I have no idea who my neighbor is, and I've never once seen someone visit. From all that I can tell, he's a loner and he could have a disorder.

He keeps odd hours, and who knows what he's really doing when he's gone for days on end. He snapped at me when I tried to speak to him the other day. Maybe us being nice to each other is not in the fantasy world he created if it's him."

Dade moved to the window. He didn't want to acknowledge the sting of rejection he felt that intensified the closer he was to her. "There's a light on at his house. Maybe it's time he and I get to know each other a little better."

She reached out and touched his arm. More of those frustrating frissons of heat zinged through him, and especially at the thought she didn't feel the same. The sexual chemistry was obvious, but he wanted more than one night.

"Be careful," she warned.

CARRIE SAT IN the chair, looking out the front window. Making love to Dade had thrown her completely off balance. Her world had tilted on its axis.

To make matters worse, she'd thought he'd said he loved her. Everything inside her wanted to believe those three words, to believe that the fantasy could come true and that she and Dade could have a future together.

But then she remembered everyone she'd lost and she would lose him, too. Loving Dade would mean opening herself up to unimaginable pain if he walked away. And that was the problem. She couldn't allow herself to open that vein again. Not even with Dade.

When this whole ordeal was over, and it would be at some point, she would have to be okay with leaving Cattle Barge. It hadn't turned out to be the welcoming home she'd been searching for when she'd opened the shop last year.

Maybe she would never feel like she was home anywhere. A little voice in the back of her mind said she was home when she was with Dade. She wouldn't argue against it because she'd be wasting her time.

But she didn't have to give in to the feeling, either.

Whatever it took, Carrie had to protect herself even if it meant shutting out the one man she could see herself loving for the rest of her life.

Chapter Fifteen

Dade gave the door a couple of taps. The light inside the bungalow-style house turned off. *Come on. Don't be a jerk.*

Dade intended to have a conversation with the man. He needed to feel him out and get a read on the guy.

A few more taps, harder this time, and there was no sign of movement. Obviously, the guy was home. Dade's blood pressure spiked as he turned away, resigned to speak to the man another time.

The door swung open fast and an intense-looking man a few inches shorter than Dade stepped forward in a threatening manner. Well, it would be threatening to someone smaller and weaker than Dade. The second his eyes sized up Dade, the guy's posture instantly changed.

"Hey, sorry. I thought you were someone else," he said with his hands up, palms out toward Dade in the surrender position.

"Do you mean like your next-door neighbor?" Dade kept his feet positioned in an athletic stance.

"Not her in particular, but women in general," he snapped.

Didn't that boil Dade's blood pressure? The guy might not be intimidating to Dade, but he would be to someone smaller than him. And this creep might be trying to scare Carrie.

"And what exactly do you have against women?" Dade fisted and released his hands at his sides.

"How long do you have to hear about it?" The joke fell flat. He stuck out his hand, a peace offering. "I'm Kyle, by the way."

"Dade Butler." He took the outstretched hand after a pause and realized Kyle's hand was shaky. Did he have something to hide? Or was he afraid of Dade?

"Sorry about before." Kyle looked to be a few years older than Dade, but not by much. "My mind's been in a bad place since the divorce."

The last word tipped Dade into a new direction. Being divorced could make Kyle angry toward women. Although Sawmill had said stalkers were usually single. To be fair, this guy was single now, but loners didn't usually get married in the first place. Although, there were always exceptions. Dade remembered that a notorious serial killer from Kansas had been married with kids.

"Come in." Kyle motioned.

Going inside would give Dade a chance to check out the place. See if there was anything suspicious.

Dade thanked him as he stepped inside. Kyle closed the door.

"You want a beer or something? I don't sleep well anymore and having a beer calms my mind." Kyle's living room consisted of a couch and a flat screen that had been mounted to the wall. There was a Blu-ray player on the floor. A sound bar had been placed on top of a book. Other than that, there were kids' toys spilling out of an opened chest with a cartoon print on it.

"No, thanks. I'm waking up, not winding down," he replied.

"Mind if I have one?" Kyle asked.

"Nope." Dade followed him into the kitchen. There wasn't much to the decor, but the place had all the necessities and was neat enough.

"Butler," Kyle repeated, popping open the top of a can of brew. "I've heard that name before."

"My family owns a pretty big cattle ranch around here," Dade offered, not wanting to go into the details of the Mav's murder—and most likely the real reason Kyle had heard the name—with a stranger. Dade could admit that his emotions were heightened with everything that had been going on in his family.

Kyle nodded.

"What's your problem with Carrie?" Dade asked outright.

"Who?" Kyle looked genuinely surprised.

Dade motioned toward her house. "Your neighbor."

"Oh." Recognition dawned. He shot another apologetic look. "I guess I've been a jerk to her. To just about everyone since the divorce."

"That what brought you to Cattle Barge?" Dade asked. Anyone new in town was suspect to him after everything that had happened, was still happening. And that wasn't exactly fair.

"It was as far away as I could get from my ex and her family in Austin without putting too much distance between me and my son," he admitted. He sounded angry when he mentioned his ex. Dade could feel ripples of annoyance pulsing from Kyle, and his thinned lips gave away his attitude toward his ex. Toward women?

"Bad divorce?" he asked casually.

"That's putting it lightly." Kyle located his phone and pulled up a pic of a smiling kid with a round face who looked like a younger version of the man standing next to Dade. "But my son is nothing like his mother. He's seven."

The guy's posture changed when he spoke about his child. His face lit up, and the worry lines etched in his forehead eased. "She's taking me to court again, trying to get full custody."

That kind of anger toward one woman could translate to others, right?

"That's a tough break." Dade had seen firsthand the damage when a relationship went sour. If that's all there was to this, Kyle would be in the clear.

"I lost my job because of her father. He owned part of the company I worked at. Had me fired when I refused to give up my son." There was so much venom in the guy's expression now. This seemed to go a little deeper than a father's love for his child—there was a bigger story behind this kind of hatred. But it did offer a plausible explanation as to why the guy would want to close out the rest of the world. The thing Dade couldn't reconcile was, wouldn't the guy want revenge on his ex?

"Cute kid," Dade said.

"He's my world," Kyle admitted, and there was so much love and admiration in his voice that Dade believed it. "But she almost cost me that, too, planting ideas in his head about me."

"I can see why you'd need a minute to reboot," Dade stated. He couldn't help but think about his own situation with his father. Had the Mav ever loved his kids as much?

"I don't always know the right things to say or do,

but I'd do anything for that kid." Kyle drained the beer and crunched the can in his fist. "I came here for a fresh start, but that witch won't leave me alone. She already has everything—our house, our dog, our son for most of the time. And that's not enough for Daddy's spoiled princess. She wants me to disappear. I should never have married up. I was out of my league and had no idea what the fallout would be when she didn't get her way."

"Sorry to hear it. That's rough on you and has to be hard on the kid, too. It's obvious you love him." Dade couldn't believe he was about to say that making mistakes seemed par for the course for a parent. And yet a nagging voice said it was true.

"Liam's the best kid. He doesn't deserve any of this, and especially not the way I yelled at him a few weeks ago. The pressure of everything has been getting to me. He dropped a glass of milk by accident and I went off," Kyle said, and there was so much torment in his eyes.

A former father-in-law with money who was used to giving everything to his little princess wouldn't take any of this well. Dade had enough experience with powerful men to realize how much they were used to getting their way and how determined they could be to bend another's will.

A court battle and a woman hell-bent on waging war could make anyone a little crazy, and especially with a child involved. Could it make Kyle want to lash out at all women?

"Do you live next door?" Kyle asked. "I haven't seen you around, but then I'm not here much."

"Carrie's a good friend of mine. We've known each other since we were little kids."

Kyle's eyes narrowed. "Always starts out that way,

before they get your heart, and then you're not the man either one of you thought you were when they trample all over you."

Kyle had suffered a bad breakup, was deep into a fight for his child. But that brought up a good point. Would he risk losing the kid?

"What are you doing for work?" Dade asked, wondering if that had anything to do with his coming and going at odd hours.

"Anything I can." He shook his head. "Mostly construction jobs here and there around Texas." That could explain why the guy kept an odd schedule. "The crazy thing is that the judge wants me to show consistent income, and I need that in order to pay child support. But my ex's father is doing everything he can to keep me blacklisted from working as an accountant, where I could make a decent living."

"Tough situation," Dade agreed.

"They haven't heard the last of me." Kyle banged his fist on the counter. "I won't give up on being in my son's life. He's not happy with me right now, and I messed that up. I should've been calmer and handled the whole situation better."

Dade had to admit that he felt a certain tug toward believing the guy based on his passion for his kid. All parents should be so dedicated. But he was trying to keep his personal feelings out of it and look at the situation objectively, for Carrie's sake.

"Sorry about your situation," Dade said, watching for his reaction.

"I'll figure it out," Kyle said.

"Next door. She's been through a lot and deserves a break."

Kyle's posture tensed. "Guess I've been too caught up in my own mess to think much about anyone else. You could say that I've been a class-A jerk to pretty much everyone around me."

"A bad relationship can do that." Dade was satisfied that Kyle wasn't a threat. He made a move toward the front door.

"Thanks for stopping by. I haven't really talked to anyone in months," Kyle admitted. "Guess I've been holed up here, licking a few wounds."

Dade understood constructing walls. He was starting to see the cost of them, too. Those same walls keeping him safe would shut everyone else out. Construct them high enough and he'd never be able to see over them.

"Easy to see why," Dade stated.

"I don't want to be *that* guy who everyone sees coming and crosses the road to avoid. I figured it would be better if I just kept to myself completely." Worry lines creased Kyle's forehead and bracketed his mouth. "I used to be pretty social before all this—" he glanced around "—before my life was held up in court and waiting for visitation while trying to pull together enough scratch to make my child support payments and keep a roof over my own head. Once this nightmare is over, I should get out more. I had no idea how difficult it would be to move to a new city and go back and forth to see my son."

"It can't be easy," Dade agreed, figuring Kyle was spilling his guts because he hadn't had anyone to talk to in a long time. He'd isolated himself and Dade was even more grateful for the love and support of his brother and sisters. They kept him from going too far and vice versa.

"You wouldn't believe how much my soon-to-be ex

freaked out when I took Liam fishing. She said that I violated my visitation and called me a flight risk. Me. I'm a guy who grew up in Austin and only left to move to San Antonio to be closer to her family after college." That deep well of anger surfaced every time he spoke about his ex. "She got a court order for supervised visitation, complaining that I took him out of town without permission. It's been too easy to stay under the radar, and especially with everything that's been going on. I should've gotten the hell out of that relationship when my future in-laws started telling us when and where we'd go on vacation." He flashed his eyes at Dade. "I'm not exactly the roll-over-on-command type, and my marriage was affected. Eventually, it cracked, then broke, but I got a great kid out of it."

"Sounds worth it to me." For the first time, Dade thought about having a family of his own. The notion of having his own child hit him.

"Yeah, I guess I've had one focus for the past few months," he admitted. "But, hey, is everything okay next door?"

"She's had a rough go lately," Dade stated. "Have you seen anyone hanging around, looking in her windows?"

"Now I really feel like a jerk for the other night." Kyle rubbed the day-old scruff on his chin. "I ripped into her for her trash getting into my yard. I owe her an apology for that."

"She mentioned it." Dade shot a warning look and Kyle acknowledged.

"No, I haven't seen anyone around, but then, I'm probably not the right guy to ask. I've been keeping my head down and sticking to my own business," Kyle admitted.

"Someone's been leaving her unwelcome gifts, like a rose on her back porch and a stuffed animal out front." Dade specifically mentioned the items to see if the guy flinched. One little twitch could give away if a person was lying. Kyle's body language didn't change, which gave Dade the impression the guy didn't know anything as Dade had already suspected.

"This person make threats or is he just leaving her stuff?" Kyle's brow shot up.

Fair question. "Someone's keeping tabs on her."

"That's pretty creepy, if you ask me." Kyle's posture tensed. The horrified look on his face gave Dade the impression this was all news to him.

"She's not liking the attention, but the guy won't show his face, so she has no idea who he is," Dade continued. "Her ex had been harassing her and something happened to him."

"Like what?" Kyle seemed genuinely shocked when it dawned on him. "He was murdered?"

Dade nodded.

"Damn." He rubbed that scruff again. "I had no idea any of this was going on. I feel like an even bigger jerk. Guess it's time to pick my head up and out of the sand and be a better man."

Kyle said all the right words. Dade could admit it, and some of them even hit him in an unexpected place and got him thinking about his own actions with his father.

"What can I do to help?" Kyle asked.

"Let me know if you see anything suspicious going on at her place." With everything going on he figured Carrie would be safer at the ranch. If he could talk her into it, and that was a big if.

The two exchanged cell information.

Getting her to agree to stay with him at his place was going to be his second order of business for the day. "She might not be around much, so I'd appreciate a second pair of eyes on her place."

"Yeah, man, whatever I can do. When I'm home I'll make sure no one's hanging around or bothering her," he said.

Loud barks cut through the air. The owner was unmistakable as another round fired off. Coco.

Dade glanced from Kyle to the back door.

"Go out this way. It's faster," Kyle said. "I'll come with you."

Dade was already gunning toward the door. "Call the sheriff."

Chapter Sixteen

Dade's heart threatened to explode at the thought of something happening to Carrie. Dammit. He shouldn't have left her alone.

Coco barked wildly, so he bolted toward the sound.

"Sheriff's up to speed. Said he's caught up in something else, but a deputy will swing by as soon as he can. Said it might be a while," Kyle said from behind him.

"Does he know the guy he's been looking for might be right here?" Dade bit out as he reached her house.

"He didn't say."

The back door was locked, and Coco was going wild inside. Dade took off his shirt, wrapped it around his fist and punched out the glass so he could unlock it. If someone was in there he hadn't come through the back, so he wasn't worried about trampling on evidence.

Inside, Coco darted toward him, whining helplessly. The dog running to him was bad, because she wouldn't leave a stranger in the house. Dade's heart pounded his ribs, and the thought of never seeing Carrie again smacked into him like a rogue punch.

Sure, he had feelings for her...intense feelings. But this was a whole new ballpark, and he realized he wanted forever. He'd messed everything up in high school and let her go without clueing her in. He wouldn't do the same thing twice. Dade would find her and tell her exactly what was going on in his mind, his heart. She could reject him and that would be okay. Well, not fine, but he'd learn to live with it. Not trying would cause regret enough to fill a lifetime. And Dade couldn't live with that.

"I'll look out front. You good with checking the house?" Dade asked.

"Yes. Go."

Dade bolted to the front door as he heard the distant sound of tires peeling out. And gunfire. Damn. He pulled his cell as he redirected toward his truck.

Kyle must've heard, too, because he flew out the front door. "There's no one here."

"You sure about that?" Dade asked.

"I'll double-check." Kyle immediately disappeared into the house.

Dade called security.

A bad feeling settled over him when Timothy Andover, the guard working this shift, didn't pick up. Dade climbed into his truck and started the engine. He flew down toward Timothy's post. *Come on. Come on.*

He tapped the steering wheel with his thumb as he gunned it.

Timothy's van was parked at the street entrance. His was the only vehicle. Dade roared up beside it and cursed when he saw the door open with the young guard splayed out on the floorboard, blood all over him.

Dade jumped out of the truck and immediately started administering CPR. Timothy was unconscious and he wasn't breathing. The hole in his chest was pumping blood. Dade cursed again in between rounds. The shooter must've used a silencer.

Dade fumbled for his cell and called 911. After relaying the information, he called Kyle.

His new friend made it in a couple of minutes.

"I gotta go," Dade said. "Ambulance is on its way. Out here that could mean twenty minutes. Will you stay with him?" Dade started to explain why, but Kyle was already shooing him away.

"Call me when you find her," Kyle instructed. "Let me know she's okay."

"Will do. Keep an eye on Coco for me. Make sure she doesn't get out." Dade's cell rang, and he fished it out of his back pocket after wiping blood on his jeans. He needed to go, but the other vehicle was long gone by now and he had no idea where to look.

"Sheriff Sawmill," he said, hoping for some good news.

"I've been apprised of the situation. An ambulance is on its way to your location," Sawmill said.

"Carrie was taken by the person who shot Timothy," Dade said.

"I've issued a BOLO, be on the lookout, for the person who took her," Sawmill said.

"Wait a minute, are you saying you know who it is?"

"Samuel Jenkins's aunt, Marla, has been found dead in a broken down RV on a remote corner of the Billings property on the outskirts of town."

"Murdered?" Dade asked.

"The cause of death is pending autopsy," Sawmill said.

"What condition did they find her body in?" Dade pressed. The name finally clicked. Samuel was the man from the alley on the first night Dade had seen Carrie again.

Sawmill didn't respond.

"Sheriff, you owe it to me to give me some answers. It might mean the difference between life and death for someone I care about very much." There were no ends to which Dade wouldn't go to find Carrie.

"There are no signs of trauma," Sawmill said. "But she was wearing the warm-up suit that Ms. Palmer described as hers."

Damn. Damn. Damn.

"Ms. Hardin wasn't the only deceased person found in the RV," Sawmill continued. "A white male believed to be in his early forties was found as well. The cause of death is believed to be a gunshot wound, and according to the coroner, the victim has been dead for at least four days, maybe more. He fits the description of Nash Gilpin. Indications are that he was murdered elsewhere and brought here postmortem. I'm on-site, and there are pictures of Carrie taken in her shop and in her home pinned on the walls. The filling from a stuffed animal similar to the orca found on Carrie's property is pinned to the wall."

"Did Samuel kill Brett?" Anger roared through Dade for not figuring it out sooner, for not being able to protect Carrie. He remembered that Samuel had been in the shop the morning after the alley assault. He could watch her from his aunt's house across the cul-de-sac. He would have access to the house even with security roaming around.

"We found tranquilizers onsite and dosage information on giving it to a dog the size of Tyson and a person roughly Carrie's weight. There's chloroform, too," Sawmill supplied.

Dade issued a sharp breath. "Carrie wouldn't have thought anything about him knocking on the door. She might've thought he was scared or needed something."

"A half-used roll of gauze with a fake blood vial from one of those party supply stores is here. He might've given her the impression he'd hurt herself," Sawmill said. "We couldn't pick up DNA from the stuffed orca but I'd bet money this filling will match."

"Any idea where he would take her?" Dade asked.

"That's the question," Sawmill said in an uncharacteristic break of character. Dade could hear frustration in the man's voice. He'd let another murderer slip through his fingers. Maverick Mike's killer was still on the loose. The high-profile case brought a whirlwind of unwanted attention to Cattle Barge.

Samuel wouldn't hurt Carrie. Not right away. But if she fought too hard—and she would—he could end up hurting her in the struggle.

Voices sounded in the background.

"I'm being summoned and I need to go," Sawmill said. "Dade." A beat passed. "I'm really sorry."

"I know, Sheriff. If I think of anything that can aid the investigation, I won't hesitate to call," he said.

"Call my cell directly," the sheriff offered before severing the connection.

Dade relayed the information to Kyle as the ambulance roared onto the street.

"I can take care of this," Kyle said. "And then I'll make sure her dog's okay."

Dade thanked Kyle and then walked over to his truck, searching his mind for anything that might give him a clue. Samuel definitely wouldn't take her back to his aunt's place. That's the first place anyone would look.

Before long the sheriff would send a deputy to process the place as a crime scene and maybe evidence would be found, but Carrie's life depended on Dade fitting the pieces together now.

The roses. The stuffed animal. The summer dress. What did those things have in common?

And then it occurred to Dade. Samuel would take her on a date.

He knew exactly where.

Chapter Seventeen

The old fairground was a twenty-minute drive from
Carrie's house and far away from downtown Cattle
Barge. The place on the outskirts of town had been shut
down for the past ten years or so but had been bustling
once a year for almost a month at a time when Dade
was a kid. As soon as he confirmed his suspicion, he'd
inform Sawmill. The sheriff's current location was on
the opposite end of the county.

Dade had never driven so fast. Questions pierced the
quiet. Could he get there in enough time? Was she hurt?

She wouldn't go with Samuel willingly, and he had
to know authorities were closing in. Did he realize that
he had nothing to lose? Because that would mean life
or death for Carrie.

Samuel was bound to figure out a few things on his
own—like that he'd be the most wanted man in the
county if they put two and two together. Maybe he realized someone had come across his aunt's RV and figured he had to act. The thought didn't do good things
to Dade's blood pressure.

He parked alongside the railroad and kept a low profile as he ran into the dilapidated grounds. He wasted
no time jogging the perimeter and came upon a silver

sedan in the second lot. He texted the license plate to the sheriff. There was blood on the passenger seat.

The sun would rise soon, bathing the area in light. Dade positioned himself to come in from the west. Where on the grounds would Samuel take her? Dade's first thought was the Ferris wheel, which was the highlight of any fair. But it was also high up and would expose them too much. It would require too much power to get working and it would take a large generator for that. Dade doubted Samuel would go to those lengths. Maybe something smaller in scale. Maybe he'd had a favorite ride as a kid. Thinking back, there was the tilt-o-wheel, and it seemed like most kids loved any spinning-type ride.

What was the name of the other ride that had been so popular with everyone? It had been even more popular than the wheel ride. Dade remembered. It was called the round-a-bout. It had a bench-like seat with a metal bar that came down to secure riders. Hormone-fueled teenage boys took dates on it so their bodies would be smashed together when the ride spun in a circle.

Where was it located in on the grounds? And then he remembered that, too. Dead center. It was one of the big draws, and its central location practically ensured that no one would pop in and out—there was too much temptation along the way to entice people to spend more. To the opposite side was the midway. Across from that was the trail to the less popular rides and fun houses. Pretty much all roads led to the tilt-o-wheel.

Dade moved quietly through the high weeds covering the once vibrant scene, remembering there'd been a time when this place had thrived. Happy kids had skipped along the streets now vacant save for the overgrowth that came up to Dade's belt. Rust covered rides, and even though the property had been cordoned off and marked as no trespassing, it was easy to access. Dade had the financial means to do something about that once this was all over. He needed this place to be something other than a beat-up old ruin where the love of his life… Was he admitting what his heart already knew? Carrie was the love of his life?

A resounding yes echoed in his ears. The noise had come from a place deep inside him, and although he was the only one who could hear it, that didn't mean it wasn't loud. Carrie was the person he'd thought of when he was overseas. She'd been the one he wanted to talk to, to laugh with. And as corny as it sounded, he'd wanted to see her belly full with his baby after he put a ring on her finger. She seemed intent on fighting the chemistry between them, but he had to give it another shot. Would she walk away so easily if she knew how deep his feelings ran for her? If she knew that he wasn't going anywhere?

He scanned the empty grounds, trying to convince himself that this was no different than any other assignment. Except it was. This was personal.

He'd been an idiot. The first time he'd had a chance to tell Carrie how he felt, he'd been a jerk instead capitalizing on the chance, and he'd blown it big-time. But now? He was just being a good old-fashioned idiot. He of all people should know that it was impossible to go back and change the past. But letting it control his present and his future? That was about as smart as a piece of driftwood.

The good news was that he was never too old to learn, and he couldn't even go there mentally about the possibility of bad news when it came to Carrie. He needed to have another chance with her. And if she'd take him, he needed to make it right.

Dade checked his position against the sun as his cell buzzed in his pocket. He pulled it out and checked the screen. Kyle had called the sheriff and wanted to help find Carrie. Dade relayed his location and then he did what he'd done on countless missions…located his target.

The sight of Carrie caused his heart to stutter. Seeing her there, propped up on the broken-down carousel in that summer dress, sent his thoughts spinning. Her motionless body slumped over the safety bar sent rage thrashing through his body.

He drew on every bit of willpower he had to stop himself from charging over and taking her off that ridiculous ride. He needed to locate Samuel. The man had to be around there somewhere. Getting Carrie out of there and to safety was the only thing important to Dade.

Samuel had a gun. Dade had no doubt the desperate guy would shoot if he felt cornered. Given that he had no idea what other weapons Samuel had, charging in like a bull was an even worse idea, despite every muscle in his body fighting to do just that.

After changing his vantage point a couple of times in order to gather as much intel as possible, Dade surmised that Samuel had to be inside the control booth of the spinning ride, and he had to be working on something. If this was part of the fantasy he'd built up in his mind, he might be trying to get the ride working. Dade needed time to ensure Kyle made it to the fairgrounds. Going in alone would be a last resort, because if anything happened to Dade without backup, Samuel could kill Carrie.

His own family would be there in a heartbeat, but the ranch was too far and Dade needed support now. He could only pray that Carrie was still breathing. He quashed the unproductive thought. Samuel would want her alive so he could carry out his date fantasy.

Dade's cell buzzed again, indicating that Kyle was on-site. Dade directed his newfound friend to his location, advising him to keep a low profile.

After giving Kyle a minute to get up to speed with the situation, Dade said, "We need a distraction, something to draw him out."

"Okay, let's see. I can…" Kyle paused to think, but Dade was already shaking his head.

"It has to be me. I won't put you at risk." Dade's hand came up as Kyle started to argue. Dade's mind was made up. The guy who went in first had the best chance of being killed on any mission, and this risk, this mission, was Dade's. All he cared about was Carrie getting out safely.

Besides, Kyle had a kid, and Dade wouldn't be responsible for a son losing his father. "The way you came down on your son. Do you think he'll forgive you?" Dade asked.

"He already has." Kyle studied Dade carefully. "The trick is forgiving myself."

Those words, that truth, hit Dade like a stray bullet. He would chew on that later.

"Did you hear from the sheriff?" Dade asked.

"He's still on-site at the crime scene. It'll take him a while to get out here, but he said he'll come in without lights or sirens," Kyle said. "He wants you to wait for further instructions."

"She could die. Every minute I wait could cost her life." Having backup—the more, the better—was good. But Carrie could be killed, and then what would've been the point? Dade had to move. Now. "I'm going in from the other side. I'll get him as far away from her as I can."

"As soon as you do, I'll move fast," Kyle reassured.

Dade patted him on the shoulder. "I appreciate your help. I owe you."

"No, you don't. Feels good to be part of something again." Kyle waved him off.

Dade could appreciate the sentiment. He stayed low as he moved away from his newfound friend. The point adjacent to the ride near the midway would lead Samuel in the opposite direction, away from Kyle and Carrie.

He'd need a distraction, though. What?

Dade preferred to face his enemy head-on. In this case, a blitzkrieg attack would be more efficient. It would be a mistake to think Dade could get to Carrie without Samuel knowing. Wherever he was, he'd be watching his prize.

The sound of an old engine cranking up billowed through the morning air. Lights came on.

Dade crouched low, the weapon from his trunk extended in front of locked arms as he backed away from the noise. Until he got a good look at Samuel and a vantage point to take him out…damn. His training had kicked in, telling him to take out the enemy. But he was stateside now, and the sheriff's words echoed. Samuel could have a mental disability. Some of the wind knocked out of Dade's sail remembering those words.

He wouldn't shoot a mentally handicapped person, any more than he could shoot a woman or child.

So he would find a way to subdue Samuel instead if at all possible.

Pat Benatar's "Love Is a Battlefield" blasted through the speakers, echoing eerily as the car Carrie was belted into made its first rotation around the carousel. Her slumped body sent Dade's pulse racing, so he took in a couple of bursts of air and then slowly exhaled. He needed complete control of his emotions, and normally he could separate them from a mission. But this was Carrie, and he'd never forgive himself if he could've saved her and didn't.

Dade figured Samuel was at the ride's controls, so he maneuvered around the weeds to get a look. He stood there grinning, clapping like a child. The ride started spinning faster. Dade couldn't make out what Samuel was saying over the song's chorus. Sawmill had said that the fixated person played out a fantasy. Having a date at a fair included playing games.

Dade moved to the midway, which was located directly behind him. Since Samuel seemed to have been planning this "date" for a long time he would most likely have figured out how to power a game or two so that he could get the full experience. The fact that Coco had barked and yet Carrie hadn't made a noise led Dade to the conclusion that Samuel had used something—that same drug he'd used on Tyson?—to make her pliant. He must've put the dress on her while she was out cold.

Dade scanned the area, looking for something to serve as a distraction. What could he use? What would be important to Samuel?

Samuel's idea of a perfect date seemed to include the

High Striker, more commonly known as the swing-the-mallet game. Dade figured it might be rigged so that Samuel could show Carrie how strong he really was. He must've seen the few times Dade had shown up as being emasculated. Damn. If Dade could only go back and change the past. There were so many things he'd do differently.

Dade needed to let it go, forgive himself like Kyle had said and concentrate on being the man he wanted to be now. He surveyed the area, careful to trace Samuel's steps in the weeds. If anything was out of place or sent up a warning signal, Samuel would be tipped off that someone had figured him out. Since Carrie's life hung in the balance, Dade had no plans to let that happen.

If he could make Samuel believe the game had been turned on by accident somehow...

He fiddled around with it and...bingo. The lights were set on a timer. Samuel's elaborate plans would play to Dade's advantage. If the lights turned on too early, Samuel might believe he'd messed up the timer. Okay. Good. Dade could work with that. Next, he scanned the area for a good hiding spot. There was a basketball hoop next to one of those dart-throwing games. Dade could hide in between them, and when Samuel bent over to reset the timer, he'd strike.

Adrenaline coursed through him. He needed a minute to get his nerves under control. He'd never once balked on a mission. But then, he'd never been on an assignment this personal before. Taking in a fortifying breath, he decided to use the tension to make sure he didn't mess up. Adrenaline brought a clear focus as long as it was controlled.

He reset the time to light up in two minutes and then

took his position. He fired off a text to Kyle letting him know what was about to go down.

Kyle immediately responded with a text telling Dade he was ready.

Two minutes passed. The lights blared. Dade held his breath, waiting for a sign it was go time.

The music stopped. The ride stilled. And it was now or never.

He took his position, careful not to leave tracks through the underbrush.

He'd like to be closer to the game and, to be honest, he wanted a better position to make sure Kyle made it safely to Carrie.

Seconds dripped by until a minute had passed with nothing. And then two. By the third minute and with no sign of Samuel, Dade's patience wore thin. He was risking Kyle's and Carrie's lives, and the weight of it sat heavy on him.

Maybe he should move to get a better look. But then, doing so could expose him if Samuel was kneeling somewhere close, watching. Dade already knew the guy liked to hide and watch.

Dade checked his phone again, waiting for a text from Kyle that Samuel was on the move. No text came.

He took in a sharp breath, needing to come up with a different plan. And then his phone vibrated. The screen said Samuel was on his way. He was glancing around, suspicious, according to Kyle.

As soon as Samuel came into view, Dade would fire off the text that told Kyle to move in. He waited.

Nothing.

Samuel's caution sent warning bells flaring.

Dade knew he would win on strength alone, but he

had no idea what tricks Samuel had up his sleeve. He just needed the guy to show up so that Kyle could get to Carrie.

And then he heard the sound of movement in the tall weeds. Could be an animal. His cell was already in his hand and the text ready to go. All he needed was to see Samuel and then hit Send using his thumb.

Samuel appeared. Dade thumbed the button on the flat screen of his phone as Samuel began inspecting the game.

Dade stayed low as a confirmation text arrived. Kyle was on the move. There'd be no more contact until Carrie was off the ride and safely inside Kyle's truck, unless she wasn't breathing, in which case Kyle would text immediately.

Even from a distance of twenty feet, Dade could see Samuel's rifle.

Patience won missions. Normally, Dade had an abundance. This was different, and his hands trembled from the adrenaline spike. He clenched and released his fingers…waiting. Controlling his breathing.

Seeing Samuel didn't help. Another shot of adrenaline coursed through Dade as he watched Samuel follow the power cord, no doubt looking for the timer. He was aware of his surroundings, watching for anything unusual. A hunting rifle rested on his forearm, but that was better than a handgun. It would buy Dade an extra second or two, which could mean the difference between life and death.

Samuel turned his back. The moment to strike presented itself. Dade flew from in between the games, launching himself toward Samuel with a primal grunt.

He made contact with the back of his knees, and Samuel's head flew backward.

The two landed with Samuel on top, but Dade quickly disarmed the man and tossed the rifle as far away as possible. It landed with a click and a thud. Using his powerful thighs, he put Samuel in a scissor-like lock. Dade spun, reversing their position and was shocked by the smile on Samuel's face.

"If I can't have her, no one will." Those dead eyes would haunt Dade forever—especially if Samuel killed Carrie.

Dade drew back his fist and knocked Samuel out with one punch. He immediately located his cell and called Kyle.

"Stop. Whatever you're doing. Stop. He rigged the ride to kill her," Dade got out through heavy breaths.

Kyle shouted the curse word that Dade was thinking.

"Don't go near her," Dade said.

"Too late. I'm already on the platform."

Chapter Eighteen

"Samuel Jenkins is tied up with an electrical cord where those lights are," Dade told Sheriff Sawmill when he arrived half an hour later. "He was unconscious when I left him. Either way, he's not going anywhere."

Sawmill instructed one of his deputies to check it out.

"What are we working with here?" Sawmill nodded toward the ride.

"Dade?" Carrie's voice was weak and her head bobbed as though she'd had too much to drink, but this was the first sign of life. Hope ballooned in Dade's chest.

"Can you be still for me?" Dade asked her. If she so much as moved, the whole place could explode for all they knew.

The bomb robot was scanning the area, and it was slow going.

Carrie didn't respond. Her head lowered to her arms that were positioned across the bar.

"There are a bunch of wires underneath the ride. I have no idea what kind of device. I emptied Samuel's pockets in case he woke and found the cell I already handed over." Sawmill had called a bomb squad to be flown in from the city. He'd called in a few favors for the speed, and Dade figured the sheriff needed a win on this one as badly as he did.

A man covered from head to toe with protective gear urged them to step back.

"I have no plans to get in your way, but I'm not leaving." Dade folded his arms, standing his ground on the perimeter.

The officer started to protest, but the sheriff stepped up on Dade's behalf.

Time was the enemy and the bomb guy needed to get to work as far as Dade was concerned, not worry about him in case there was shrapnel.

"Killing his aunt most likely triggered this," Sawmill said. "We won't know for certain until we complete our investigation."

"If Samuel is familiar with sedatives, that could explain how he got past Brett's dog," Dade said, and the sheriff was already nodding.

All Dade needed was for Carrie to come out of this alive. It was time to pick up the pieces and move forward in all areas of his life. He'd forgive his father, himself. He'd build the life he wanted moving forward, a life with Carrie.

"I can't stay here this close in case..." Sawmill's voice trailed off. "My men are looking to me as an example and they'll insist on joining me if I don't move back."

"Understood."

Carrie's head bobbed again, and Dade's heart clenched.

"Don't move. We're going to get you off that ride in a minute. Keep still," he warned and was grateful she listened. Kyle was like a statue on the platform, a few feet away from Carrie.

The sheriff moved behind the barrier that had been set up as the bomb team agent worked a joystick controlling the robot.

Tension was thick.

After what felt like an eternity, the bomb guy declared the area clear.

In the background, Dade heard the bomb tech tell the sheriff that the setup was a hoax, most likely a deterrent. There was no bomb, just a tangle of wires meant to buy time if Samuel's fantasy had been interrupted.

Dade sprinted toward Carrie. Kyle was already working the bar holding her inside the bench seat. EMTs were a second behind as Dade reached her.

Her head bobbed up, and her gaze locked on to Dade.

"I love you, Dade," she said as she held out her arms. Tears streamed down her face as she seemed to gain more awareness of what was going on around her. Samuel must've drugged her to buy her cooperation.

"You're safe now," Dade said and he didn't care who was around when he said, "I love you, too."

DADE PACED THE hallway in the hospital, waiting for word that he could see Carrie. He'd stalked past a dozen reporters three hours ago, and the place was humming with activity. Extra security had been called in to protect patients.

A nurse wearing a name tag that said Bonnie stepped out of Carrie's room after what had felt like an eternity. "She's awake and asking to see you," she said.

"Thank you, Bonnie." He'd put on a clean shirt and had washed off the blood from earlier. Thoughts of

Timothy's death weighed on him. Dade had already put a fund in motion for Timothy's wife to ensure she never had to worry about money again. It wouldn't bring Timothy back or replace him, but it was the least Dade could do. He'd also spoken to Kyle about coming to work at the ranch. The family welcomed honest people looking to earn a living.

Dade took a few steps inside Carrie's room. His heart stopped at seeing her there, hooked up to machines.

The minute her eyes opened, he moved to her side.

She patted the bed for him to sit but he shook his head.

Instead, he got down on one knee right then and there. He took her hand in his.

"Carrie, you were my first friend. I didn't do right by you in high school—"

She started to protest, but he said, "Hear me out."

She nodded as a tear rolled down her cheek. He hoped that was a good thing, because he couldn't read her this time.

"I should've been the friend you were to me. Loyal. Caring. Kind."

Her smile brought light inside the dark recesses of a chest that he thought would always be hollow, empty.

"I have to live with my mistake for the rest of my life. The only way I'll survive is if you're by my side. I've never felt this way about another human being. You're home to me, Carrie. *You're* my home." He paused long enough to look into her beautiful eyes. "Will you do me the tremendous honor of sharing your life with me as my partner, my wife?"

"I love you, Dade, and I'm in love with you. I've had a crush on you since second grade, but—"

His heart free-fell as he waited for her to finish.

She repositioned on the bed, sitting up to really look at him.

"You don't have to do this," she said. "I'll be okay. I'll pick up the pieces of my business."

"I'm not doing this to save you. This is the most selfish thing I'll ever do. I want you to be my wife, Carrie. To be mine for as long as I have breath left in me. Nothing here is the same without you. You're the only thing that's real to me. The only person I need."

A knock at the door interrupted them.

"Come in," Carrie said with a glance toward Dade.

Bonnie walked in carrying a large bouquet of flowers.

"What is this?" Carrie asked with a note of caution in her voice.

"There's plenty more where this came from," Bonnie said with a shrug. "Read the card."

Carrie opened the small envelope and read aloud, "'Our thoughts are with you. Can't wait for your shop to reopen when you feel better. Signed, the Houston family.'"

"Looks like you have a lot of people in the community who care about you," Bonnie said as hospital volunteers moved in one after the other, filling the room with beautiful flowers.

Carrie wiped away a stray tear and then smiled. It was easy to see that she was blown over from the kind gestures.

"I guess news is out." Dade couldn't contain his smile. "My family sends their love. They want to visit as soon as you're up for company. You're a celebrity in this town. You might as well get used to the attention."

"You're the only reason Cattle Barge has ever felt like home to me, Dade. So, yes. If you're still asking, I will marry you. I'll be your partner in this life and your best friend."

Those were the only words that mattered to Dade. He kissed her.

A sense of peace he'd never known traveled through him as their lips pressed together. The past no longer mattered. He could forgive his mistakes. He'd found the love of his life, and part of him had known it all along.

With Carrie, he'd found a real home.

* * * * *

COMING SOON!

We really hope you enjoyed reading this book. If you're looking for more romance, be sure to head to the shops when new books are available on

Thursday
14th June

To see which titles are coming soon, please visit
millsandboon.co.uk

LET'S TALK
Romance

For exclusive extracts, competitions
and special offers, find us online:

f facebook.com/millsandboon

⊙ @millsandboonuk

𝕏 @millsandboon

Or get in touch on 0844 844 1351*

For all the latest titles coming soon, visit
millsandboon.co.uk/nextmonth